It Always Rains on Wednesday
by R. Douglas Hackeny

ISBN 978-1-64663-410-1

Published by

3705 Shore Drive
Virginia Beach, VA 23455
800-435-4811
www.koehlerbooks.com

Dedicated to all who teach children and youth with visual impairments.

It Always Rains on Wednesday

book one: genesis

R. DOUGLAS HACKNEY

VIRGINIA BEACH
CAPE CHARLES

CHARACTERS

TEACHERS/ADULTS

Monte Alonzo Scott: vocational rehabilitation counselor

Clare Elizabeth Augsburg: teacher, daily living skills (DLS)

Benjamin Alexander Booker: guidance counselor and teacher

Thelma Thompson: secretary to the Academy superintendent

Dr. Bristow Mullens: Academy superintendent

Charles "Charlie" Talbert: history and government teacher, wife Nancy

Ramona Simpson: Blind Department secretary

Brad Fletcher: principal of Blind Department

Dr. Rudolph Bartlett: math teacher

Elizabeth Blanchard: music teacher

Anne Walden: art teacher

Clarence Gladstone: English teacher

Cathy Henson: librarian

Claude Goodwell: PE teacher and coach

Richard Weisner: boyfriend of Clare

Dr. Reginald Davenport: Academy psychologist

Arthur James Brooks: history and Latin teacher and best friend of Monte

Stanley and Dolores Hartman: next-door neighbors to Monte in trailer park

Vernon Southwood: friend of Monte and Arthur, lieutenant with Richmond police

T. Allen Bridgemeyer, III: father of Theodore Bridgemeyer, IV, high school student

Atkins Turnage: employment specialist

George and Ralph Dunsmore: brothers to Jimmy

STUDENTS

Arnold Schnellich: elementary

Gerald Sampson: high school

Amy Sullivan: high school

Milton Souderton: high school

Linwood Boyer: high school

Betty Davidson: junior high

Alec Beasley: high school

Withrow Mulligan: junior high

Jellyroll Jackson: high school

Rosanna Worthington: high school

Eric Rockwell: high school

Caroline Lehman: high school

Tim Sommers: high school

Leon Blackwell: high school

Jimmy Dunsmore: high school

Annabelle Sharada LilyMae Johnson: elementary

Ronald and Oliver: high school

Joshua Blandenburg: high school

Talmage Grobanheimer: high school

Millard Crumbley: elementary

Norton Zimmerman: high school

Erskine Nesbitt: elementary

Dillon Grabowski: high school

PLACE NAMES

Talerton: small valley town, location of the Academy

Rivanleigh: home of Monte, east of Blue Ridge Mountains

Stonebridge: town north of Talerton, home of Richard Weisner

Wolvercote: small town at western foot of Blue Ridge, home of Clare

CHAPTER ONE

"JUST GO OVER THERE and see what they want from us!" Marlon Danforth bristled, his words rattling around the small office, disdainfully impatient. Had he thrown a handful of sharp rocks, the effect would have been much the same. "You're the fourth and damn well better be the last!" the man hissed.

Monte Scott, standing rigidly in front of his supervisor's desk, was unsure if the warning carried expectation of future guilt or merely ongoing frustration. "The school's in your territory anyway," Danforth said more reasonably, "less than an hour from your office, or will be when the Interstate's completed. Be there the first Wednesday in September, and for God's sake, keep a low profile and don't stir things up!"

The sultry July day invited trickles of sweat to course down Monte's spine with an almost pleasant tickling sensation. Stale, sour odors pervaded the room, steeping his nostrils with subtle whiffs of curdled milk or some disremembered fish garnished with cheap cologne. Seated before him was an ostensibly unhappy man approaching middle age—anorexic face waxen and pasty, long, narrow neck affixed atop delicately rounded shoulders, suspiciously dark hair glossy and slicked to a domed skull. Given as he was to unaccountable bursts of anger, strength emanated from his harshly intimidating manner and voice.

Intrusive and challenging, his blazing eyes demanded silent acquiesce with nothing more than a glance. Even in the oppressive heat, Monte felt certain the man would not permit the slightest token of sweat to taint his person; he controlled surroundings and, when possible, manipulated everyone in his sphere.

An imploding envelope gathered about Monte's body, as though the office walls were compressing the space to a narrow, claustrophobic chamber. He longed to move, wave arms or shuffle feet, shout or sing—anything to define some concrete reality within this captivity of time. Coiled in readiness, the supervisor's stare dissuaded him to stone stillness.

"Benjamin Booker's the guy you need to contact," Danforth said, dropping attention to an open folder lying before him. "As you no doubt know, he doesn't care for our agency, or our counselors, it seems. He rejected all three of the men we sent this past school year, three of our best."

Monte did know, had heard stories of the brief lifespan each had weathered at the Academy, able individuals by reputation, with more tenure and experience than himself—"thrown to the wolves without a rudder," one of the men had complained illogically. With no official job description for the new position, Monte judged the flimsy, arcane agreements between agency and institution hardly more than another bureaucratic enigma destined to fail.

As if pleading before a jury, Danforth pointed out tightly, "It's only one day a week, Scott, and all you have to do is show up, be a . . . a presence." On reflection, he added, "You'll have a few more clients added to your caseload, but that won't amount to much. Some reports and forms, listening to students' questions and complaints. Nothing of consequence."

• • •

September came all too quickly, first Wednesday heavily circled like a mark of doom on Monte's office calendar. Anchored atop a broad prominence fringing the classically Victorian streets of Wilson

Plat in the Shenandoah Valley town of Talerton, the State Academy for the Deaf and the Blind vested secure distinction without excess of resplendence. Gathered about a properly majestic Main Hall, red brick and limestone buildings were grouped with no obvious pattern or rank, utility of function the sole justifying interpretation. Yet the effect was neither cold nor indifferently institutional—rather, more appealingly mystifying and intangibly gracious.

With complicated directions from Thelma Thompson, secretary to the superintendent, he made his way from Main Hall on a roofed and elevated walkway over a large asphalt courtyard to a deserted and dim Perkins Hall, eventually finding a door labeled *Blind Department Office*, behind which slow, steady clicking could be heard. Hesitating only a second, he entered a bright, moderately sized room. Behind a long glass counter, hunched and focused at a large wooden desk, a young woman sat methodically typing. Waiting politely while she carried on unperturbed for several lengthy minutes, Monte dared to mildly clear his throat and ventured pleasantly, "Good morning." Unmoved, she continued to hunt and peck, by all appearances oblivious to his presence.

Placing hands flat on the countertop and leaning forward, he once more gently loosened his voice in greeting and smiled patiently. As if resigned to intrusion, the typist stonily lifted her head, demurring actual eye contact, and without discernible emotion or visibly moving any part of her mouth garbled, "May I help you?" Twinged with sudden sympathy, Monte could now see both her jaws were decidedly swollen, lending the absurd image of a drowsy chipmunk.

"Sorry to bother you," he intoned, "but I'm supposed to meet with Mr. Booker this morning. Uh, Monte Scott . . . with the Bureau of Services for the Visually Impaired?"

Swiveling torturously in her chair, which screeched sharply, she stared at the typewriter with puzzled impotence before initiating a slow, haphazard rummage through stacks of papers piled on her desk. Watching with hopeful interest, Monte observed a full-figured, pale young woman, probably no more than twenty, her short, fizzy hair the color of weak tea. More cheerful, she might have been healthily attractive despite the robust nose and small, distant eyes further minimized behind gaudily pink, horn-rimmed glasses.

"Mr. Booker's expecting me, I think," Monte offered encouragingly. "I just need to know where to find him."

After lazily shuffling folders and notes about her desk, she collapsed back in her chair, grimacing as though exhausted, hands folded lifelessly in her lap. "I'm going to need to call somebody," she moaned. Stretching painfully for her phone and resting one finger on the dial, she retreated almost at once and mumbled, "But it's too early, so you'd better sit down."

Two heavy oak chairs loitered against the wall, and Monte sat without further comment. The counter separating him from the secretary was actually a display case cluttered with memorabilia: trophies, medals, ribbons, and pennants crowded on two shelves, most deteriorated, tarnished, and frayed of former sheen and glory. Bending forward to peer through smudged glass, he scanned inscriptions: *State Wrestling Championship, 1936*; *Track and Field Third Place Finalist, 1955*; *Valley Invitational, Gold Medal, Shot and Discus, 1919*; *Athlete of the Year, John Raymond, 1941*; and so on for perhaps two dozen or more; the oldest a silver plate dated 1877; most recent, a brass plaque dated 1968.

As he studied the items, a man of perhaps forty, well dressed in greyish seersucker suit, tripped in from the hallway, stopping short when he caught sight of the young visitor. Stepping toward him and extending a hand, he said heartily, "Good morning! I'm Brad Fletcher, principal."

Monte stood, receiving a firm grip from the thickset man with polished manner—doubtless accustomed to greeting visitors. He said, "Good morning. Monte Scott, with—"

"Oh, yes!" Fletcher burst out as though chagrined. "I know who you are, of course. Marlon called and said you'd be coming today. Of course, of course. Our rehabilitation representative! Didn't expect you quite this early. Hope you haven't been waiting long." Continuing to pump Monte's hand, he smiled broadly.

"No, sir. I just arrived a few minutes ago."

"Well, it's so nice to have one of you with us again. Have you met Ramona?" Releasing Monte's hand, he lifted an arm in the secretary's direction as if inviting her to rise and take a bow. She remained fixed to her chair, staring noncommittally at the silent typewriter, lips resolutely squeezed together.

"Ramona's our departmental secretary," Fletcher rushed on. "Been with us now, er, what, Ramona? Two years?" She neither moved nor spoke. "I've been principal now for almost ten years, Mr. Scott, which is hard to believe," he continued rigorously, rolling his eyes. "You know how time flies when you're having fun, they say!" He chuckled and hesitated briefly, searching his visitor's face in the event an additional comment on the passage of time might be forthcoming.

Receiving only silence, he went on, "Well—*ahem*—I know you'll be wanting to get on with things, and I don't want to, er, hold you up with small talk." He chuckled again. "We'll try to find time to get together very, very soon. I'd like to hear your plans and some of your thoughts and ideas." Winking and grinning, he moved toward his office door, then turned and said, "If you need anything, please don't hesitate to ask. Just talk with Ramona. And good luck."

Talking with Ramona, Monte considered, seemed an unlikely and remote possibility, even with best of luck. *And the man's comments about getting on with things. Thoughts, plans, and ideas?* Monte wagered Fletcher never expected to see him again after this morning—after meeting Mr. Booker and inevitably being banished from the premises as were the three previous counselor candidates.

As Fletcher vanished into his office, Ramona picked up the phone and mumbled a few words. Hanging up, she glanced obliquely in Monte's direction and groaned wearily, "Someone should be here shortly."

Thanking her, he returned to the hard oak chair and perused the display case once again as Ramona continued with her imperturbable, desultory typing.

Within ten minutes a very small boy, maybe seven or eight, slipped quickly through the office door, sliding to a halt in front of the counter.

Even stretching to full height on tiptoes, the lad was too short to see over the top, and, hunkered down, Ramona was buried too low to notice he had come in. Rocking his head side to side and executing a rotating dance routine with tiny, shuffling feet, he waited without speaking—hoping, nonetheless, for recognition. After an impasse of several unproductive minutes, Monte pondered the wisdom of interceding in some way, deciding to wait and observe how the situation played out.

After a minute or two of fidgeting back and forth in front of the counter, the boy discovered an unfamiliar figure close beside him, seated and watching. Drawing nearer the strange sighting, he blinked curiously through thick-lensed, black-framed glasses, gawking, huge eyes raptly attentive. Monte grinned and said hello, but the youngster turned away, disappointedly disinterested, and moved back to the counter.

Next, the lad bent over slightly to peep through the display case, jamming his nose against the glass and cupping hands around his face only to find his view hindered by trophies. Ramona continued to tap away steadily, still unaware of her newest visitor. After a few additional grunting dance movements, growing progressively agitated, the boy made a small, tight fist and knocked on the counter front. The whole case rattled and shimmied precariously. Partially aroused, Ramona called out with surprisingly decisive volume, "Come in, please! The door's unlocked."

Straightening quickly and effecting an exemplary standing leap, the boy's head bobbed for a split second above the countertop as he yelled, "I'mmmm . . ."—then, landing and vaulting once more with another rather impressive leap, higher than the first—". . . innnnn!" After which he was hidden once more from Ramona's view. With evident exertion, accompanied by a laboriously extended exhalation, she lifted from the relative comfort of her chair and in two or three protracted steps tilted over the counter to stare down at the top of a small human head covered in confusions of reddish curls.

"Is that you, Arnold?" she heaved sternly, panting. "Why didn't you say something? How long have you been messing around down there?"

Not intimidated, Arnold gawped up at Ramona and retorted with some firmness, "I was *told* to be quiet whenever I came in the office again. Mr. Fletcher told me that several times, and so did you, and so, I was quiet."

"You weren't quiet when you banged on the cabinet," Ramona said, voice rising slightly with no noticeable effect on unshakeable rationale of the lad. "And that's not what we meant, Arnold, and you know it. We meant 'don't interrupt' and 'don't sing and shout' like you usually do." Rapidly tiring, she rested her upper body across the countertop. "Anyway, now you're here, I have a job for you." Her mouth and jaw movements, at least momentarily, were loosening, though larger parts of her person projected futile contests with fatigue. Invisible in his chair, Monte felt like an intruder of sorts to the proceedings.

"What is it, Miss Simpson?" Arnold's interest suddenly piqued. "I have to be in Dr. Bartlett's math class in ten minutes, and if I'm late again, I'm in big, big trouble, you know."

"This won't take long, and it's on the way to your class anyway," she drawled. "That man needs to be shown how to get to Mr. Booker's room." At this point Ramona and Arnold pivoted heads in unison and stared at Monte skeptically. He stood with a feeble smile.

"Gee, wah-wah!" Arnold blurted, looking him up and down. "He's big! What's your name?"

Before Monte could answer, Ramona interjected, "This is Mr. . . . Mr. . . ." and then blankly, ". . . uhhhh . . ."

"Mr. Uhhh?!" Arnold jeered facetiously before she could recover. "Is that some kind of foreign name?" Shaking his head to and fro and giggling, he reignited a jittery dance on his toes.

"Stop trying to be funny, Arnold," Ramona said with a strong hint of warning, "and rude. His name is Mr. Scott. Okay? Now get going."

Thanking Ramona for her assistance, Monte followed Arnold into the hallway, which in the intervening span since his arrival had become a virtual sea of students streaming in both directions, many bearing armloads of books, papers, cumbersome braillers, and long white canes. The morning desolation of a tenebrous corridor was gone, filled now with the hums and rhythms of blurred movement and youth. Anxiety, which had moderated minutely while in the office, returned to scorch the pit of Monte's stomach.

Before him were living, breathing beings, newly acquired encumbrance existing in undeniable reality. He felt as an alien plunging into uncharted land, his inadequacies crashing down with the weight of an avalanche. Theoretical, nomenclative agency agreements casually prescribed on paper no longer mattered, were moot; these flesh-and-blood individuals bore names, personalities, dreams, questions, and emotions, fearfully untouchable, strange and foreboding, inhabiting a world unknown. And he had come unprepared and deficient to confront their expectations and demands, a false prophet unworthy to proscribe truth or do justice—a hollow mannequin, useless and flimsy as a cardboard cutout.

Much that had gone unseen earlier was now in better view: polished oak flooring and thickly varnished chair rail, pale-green plaster walls and dull-white ceilings from which hung sparingly placed globed light fixtures shedding meager illumination. Arnold trailed along close to the wall in an aimless manner, dragging fingers on the chair rail and occasionally stopping to inspect some presumed imperfection or defect. Monte wondered at his obvious lack of books or other materials, and was about to ask when Arnold suddenly halted, turned, and, peering up, shouted, "What's your first name? And do you have a middle name? And what kind of name is Scott?"

Before Monte could answer, the piercing shrill of a hall bell sounded above their heads, Arnold ranting on as though unbothered. "And don't worry. I won't call you those names. I'd get in trouble if I did that. I'll always call you Mr. Scott, at least when other people are around or if you really insist, because you're a grown-up and a teacher or something and it wouldn't be proper unless you said it was okay or until I'm much older, say twenty-one or eighteen."

Instead of revealing information the boy wanted, Monte said, "Tell me your names, Arnold."

Though in the wash of traffic, Arnold straightened as if preparing to recite a lesson, and blurted in a single breath, "My full name on my birth certificate is Matthew Arnold Schnellich, but I go by Arnold because I hate the name Matthew even though my parents love it and call me that when they're mad or when we have company or family reunions. But when I'm old enough, I'm going to change my name to Arnold *Sebastian* Schnellich because I think that sounds just about right for my type of personality and's really quite cool, don't you think? And by then I'll have a mustache and probably a car or a motorcycle."

Monte marveled that one so small could have such lung capacity. "Thanks, Arnold. Now tell me about your, uh, lateness to math class."

"Oh, yes!" he confessed gleefully, demonstrating no remorse. "See, I'm just a late person, my mom says, and my dad won't even talk about it. I'm usually late for most things. Coach Goodwell says I'll probably be late for my own funeral, whatever that means."

"How do you manage that? Being late all the time?" Monte asked over the commotion, dodging canes and braillers as they plodded farther down the hall.

"It's easy," Arnold said airily over a thin shoulder. "Just comes natural to my nature. But I'm thinking about trying to do even better." Monte wondered if he meant doing better at being on time or better at being late, but did not ask.

The hallway narrowed into a kind of vestibule and logjammed the mob into a funnel of ear-splitting, shoulder-to-shoulder humanity. Swept along, dodging and twisting, they made landfall of sorts into an adjacent building even older than its neighbor. A tarnished bronze plaque read, *Cameron Hall, 1908*. The assemblage continued no less turbulent, students of all description charging like superheated molecules, energetic and determined, occasionally bumping braille writers with cymbalic clangs or falling prey to a potentially disastrous cane entanglement. And yet, Monte noted, all suggested an overall systematic structure, a controlled, informal traffic pattern, each person homing in on his or her destination.

Arnold weaved through the throng undeterred, a skilled veteran. Monte followed close behind, mostly sidewise, arms aloft. Braking suddenly at an intersection of hallways, Arnold announced loudly, pointing, "That's it! That door over there. See ya later, Mr. S!" Executing a hard starboard turn before any reply was given, the little elf scurried around a corner and absconded without a trace.

The designated door was closed, and tapping elicited no response. Peeping inside revealed a fairly large classroom with three tall windows overlooking the courtyard, allowing dazzling flourishes of unbridled morning sunlight to spill over four rows of empty student desks like polished copper, unhindered by shades or blinds. Cautiously, he took one step inside. Diagonally across the room was a second door.

Wending trepidatiously around desks, he stood at the portal and listened. Indistinct low murmurings of conversation filtered through. Waiting a few moments, perfectly still, taking in an eclipsed view of a large brick structure across the courtyard through a window to his right, Monte opted to gently knock. Strains of voice ceased and curtly dispensed words asked, "Who is it?"

Speaking into a door panel, Monte said, "I'm sorry to interrupt. It's Monte Scott. I just wanted—"

"Who?" the voice boomed.

"Monte Scott, sir, from the—"

"Wait a minute!" After extended silence, the man growled, "I'm very busy right now, Mr., er . . ."

"Scott," Monte offered helpfully.

"Scott. Yes. Well, I'm very busy right now, Scott, and will be for most of the day. Come back at three thirty and I should be free." The directive was delivered with decisive finality.

"Yes, sir. I will. Three thirty. Thank you." Shockingly disappointed at blatant dismissal, Monte wandered out to a now deserted hallway to ponder a course of action. A wall clock in Mr. Booker's classroom had read 8:30, seven hours until his appointment. *Is this an oblique banishment,* Monte wondered, *expulsion without cursory hearing or observation? But why then tell me to come back?* Spinning toward an exit door leading to the bridge, he nearly collided head-on with a man hustling in the opposite direction, avoiding a crash only by the quick reflexes of both.

"Whoa!" the man gasped loudly with relief, lifting large hands to Monte's shoulders. "Sorry, friend! We almost had a wreck there, didn't we?"

"It was close!" Monte grinned sheepishly, composure shaken.

"I'm Charles Talbert," the man said, voice strong and genial. "And who might you be, young fellow?"

With a broad, square face and bright, squinting eyes, the man's solid stance manifested brazen exuberance, as though prepared at any moment to burst into peals of laughter. He may have been fifty, yet retained a shameless corpus of youth, shambles of dark, wavy hair lightly salted at the temples abetting an impression of overall ruggedness.

"Well," Monte began, still flustered, "I'm Monte Scott, rehabilitation counselor with the Bureau of Services for the Visually Impaired, visiting the school today, and—"

"Wonderful!" Talbert barked with gusto, gripping and shaking Monte's upper arms. "Come down to my room . . . if you have time! We're into something that might be of interest."

In a classroom similar to Booker's at the far end of the hall, thirty or so students in desks were arranged in a U shape, open end enclosing two small tables placed side by side several feet apart in the center, two students at each, facing still another table about eight feet in front of them where a young man sat as though presiding. Lightly animated conversation and laughter faded noticeably as Talbert and Monte came in.

"Okay, class, are we ready?" the teacher trilled energetically. "We have a guest today, so make him welcome." Slapping a hand on Monte's shoulder, he said to the group, "This is Mr. Scott, Monte Scott, counselor with BSVI."

Smiling awkwardly, the young man bobbed his head to the class, quickly realizing most might not see either gesture. Recovering, he said, "It's very nice of you to, uh, let me visit today. And . . . thanks." Curiosity hinting at wariness reflected in the faces. *An outsider in their midst,* he thought. *Another unknown, transient invader.*

Finding an empty desk, Monte sat down uneasily. Talbert stationed himself at the front and announced, "Today we begin the trial. I'll intervene if needed, but this exercise is basically yours, so remember what we've been studying and go for it."

The young man at the front table—the judge's bench, Monte gathered—banged a small gavel to start proceedings. Strikingly handsome and broad shouldered, complexion the hue of a walnut shell, he was realistically adorned in black robe and spoke with confident authority. "We're here today for the trial of Mr. Albert Dressler, accused of the theft of one cherry pie from the dining hall kitchen of the Academy for the Blind on or about the first day of September this year. I am Judge Gerald Sampson presiding. We are pleased to have Miss Amy Sullivan and Mr. Milton Souderton for the prosecution, and Mr. Linwood Boyer for the defense. Would Mr. Dressler please stand?"

A tall, thin boy, pallid with short orange hair, obligingly stood at the defense table, smirking with amusement, small eyes roaming about the room. His attorney seated beside him belatedly rose, doing his best to promote dignity tempered with solicitous deference. Judge Sampson, in a clear, strong baritone, asked the defendant, "How do you plead, Mr. Dressler? Guilty or not guilty?"

Dressler's attorney leaned into his client and mumbled a few words in his ear. Smugly, the defendant lifted his head to the front and declared, "Not guilty, Judge. I mean, Your Honor." Soft sprinkles of laughter coursed around the room.

"All right, you may be seated," the bench directed, and Dressler and Boyer sat down quickly. "Is the prosecution ready?" The judge nodded toward the second table where two attorneys sat waiting. Scooting back her chair, the girl stood to face the front, unconvincingly self-assured.

Monte stared with fascination, for he had never seen anyone quite like her before—a very pale, delicate human figure, the smooth skin of her face, slender neck, and arms, and her long, flowing hair whiter than Asian marble. Petite and fastidiously lovely, tiny hands loosely poised at her sides, she could have been a heavenly apparition but for the earnest, bright-coral eyes fixed upon the judge as she voiced in hushed, wavered tones, "We are, Your Honor." Hesitating for but a second, cheeks flushing, she waited as co-counsel handed over a sheet of paper, which she took and held close to her face, sweeping a small alabastrine nose back and forth across the page.

"Then you may proceed," the judge directed, leaning back in his chair and sliding the gavel closer.

Several members of the jury spread along one wall squirmed in their desks with anticipation, ready to hear evidence. Drawn with increasing interest to the judicial demonstration, Monte eagerly hunched forward, as did Talbert.

The prosecuting attorney moseyed over with the sheet of paper held to her chest and stood before the jury to present an opening statement. Clearly outlining circumstances of the alleged thievery, giving time, date, place, and object of the incident, she then moved on to list what they, the state, intended to prove and by what means. The case in general was quite simple: Dressler was alleged to have accessed a rear door of the school dining hall kitchen on the afternoon in question and, with stealth for which he was well known and admired, made off with one double-crust sour cherry pie and pie plate, still hot from the oven. The stolen good, she affirmed, was then taken to a dorm room and devoured by Albert and several friends.

Consulting her paper, the prosecutor averred that the state had numerous witnesses she intended to call who would verify the allegations and prove without doubt the defendant's guilt. Standing stiffly, a tiny but commanding presence, she stared at each juror with the ambient nobility of a finely sculptured statue. Judge Sampson, anxious to move proceedings along, cleared his throat, and she retreated to her table and sat down.

Judge Sampson gestured to the defense table and said tediously, "Mr. Boyer?"

He popped up, knocking his chair over backward, rousing a wave of mirth from surrounding desks. Several decibels too loudly, he announced, "The defense, uh, reserves its opening statement until after the trial." Snickers and giggles erupted around the room once more. "Excuse me, Your Honor," Boyer muttered rapidly, "I meant after the, uh, after our turn comes . . . sir." Sustained laughter brought an extended banging of the gavel from the bench. The defense attorney melted into his chair, head bowed, a beaten man for the moment.

"Okay, Amy—I mean, Miss Sullivan, you may call your first witness," the judge instructed. Unexpectedly, the boy beside her at the prosecution table jumped up holding a clipboard. Though donning sport coat, white shirt, and tie, his overall impression was slovenly—due in part, Monte noted, to long, stringy blond hair tied in a tight ponytail. More annoyingly, he rocked slightly side to side as though dancing to phantom music or struggling to maintain balance on the deck of a heaving ship. Clearing his throat and checking notes on the clipboard with fingertips, he was addressed by Judge Sampson. "Will you be questioning your first witness, Mr. Souderton, rather than Miss Sullivan?"

"Yes, Your Honor, and may I approach the bench?" the boy inquired like a seasoned barrister. Obtaining permission, he took a few careful steps toward the front table. "Your Honor, our first witness is the roommate of Mr. Dressler, and his good friend, so we'd like to have him declared a hostile witness." The request was granted, as Talbert beamed.

Attorney Souderton called a large, good-looking lad named David Stein. At that point, it became apparent no chair had been provided beside the judge's bench for witnesses, and one was quickly procured by a juror and put in place. Stein at first refused to answer even the most benign questions; however, being warned with threats of contempt by the judge, he gave in and supplied key evidence for the prosecution, howbeit not without continued duress and prodding from Souderton and the bench.

After prolonged periods of alleged memory lapses, Stein's testimony indicated Dressler had shown up in their dorm room on the afternoon in question with a cherry pie, upset because he claimed to detest anything containing cherries. He was, therefore, more than generous in sharing portions with several friends. Asked where he obtained said pie, Dressler told Stein it had come in the mail as a gift from his aunt. No one, not even Stein or Dressler's other friends, believed him and thought the story laughable. Monte noted with amusement that Souderton failed to ask how the aunt could possibly have managed to keep a pie hot during a two-day trip through the mail.

On cross-examination, Boyer asked Stein if he had actually seen Dressler procure the cherry pie. At first stymied by the word *procure*, thinking the definition possibly meant "to bake," the witness requested clarification and requestioning, then answered in the negative. When asked if Albert did in fact have an aunt who often sent goodies and gifts to the school, Stein said he thought so, though was not sure. Amy objected and was sustained by Gerald, and the answer was stricken. Satisfied for the moment, Boyer sat down.

The next prosecution witness, a chubby boy whom Souderton referred to as Snookie Belcher, was called and wriggled squeamishly in the witness chair, never once raising his eyes from a thorough analysis of his shoes during the entire examination. Under skillful and persistent questioning by the prosecutor, he admitted that Dressler had been seen by a group of boys, of whom Snookie was part, on said day in the vicinity of the dining hall, carrying an object and walking very fast toward the boys' dorm. Two other boys who were part of the group were also called and testified similarly.

Boyer, with more confidence and brashness than previously exhibited, questioned each of the boys at length. "How far away from the dining hall were you, Mr. Belcher, when you claim to have seen my client?" he asked, drawing out the word *claim* as far as he could without actually setting it to music. Snookie timidly estimated a distance of "fifty yards or maybe about a hundred and fifty feet," which Boyer leaped on immediately, shouting at the witness, "Which is it, Mr. Belcher!? Which!?"

Blubbering and nearly in tears, Snookie gasped, "I don't know! Really, I don't!" Boyer turned triumphantly to the jury and stated with a broad smile of satisfaction that calculating distances was not a forte in which Belcher showed much promise or experience. His satisfying moment of reverie was short-lived, however, when Judge Sampson broke in, commenting from the bench that both estimates amounted to the exact same thing.

Taken aback for only a few seconds, Boyer charged ahead and went for the ultimate jugular, speaking distinctly and directly into Belcher's ear. "And what, if I may ask a personal question, sir, is your visual acuity?"

Amy bounced up straightaway and said with as much volume as she was capable, "Your Honor, I object to this uncalled-for incursion into Mr. Belcher's private—"

Judge Sampson, not hesitating, waved his hand and said blandly, "Overruled, Miss Sullivan. Witness is directed to answer the question." Across the room, Monte noted a pleased Mr. Talbert keeping watchful eyes and ears on proceedings.

Belcher's answer, revealed with great reluctance, admitted vision only in one eye, recently measured at 20/400 at best. The other two boys in the group, when questioned, admitted that between them they had "one good eye" with acuity of no more than 20/200 in bright light. For the sake of jury and record, Boyer patiently explained what those numbers meant clinically and in practical fact, concluding they represented very poor vision indeed.

Mr. Talbert stood at this point, just as the hall bell reverberated with finesse of a locomotive charging down the hallway, and roared, "All right! Our time's up for today. We'll continue tomorrow. Thank you all for your great work!" The room vacated in short order amid whoops, arm punching, and backslapping. Talbert walked over to Monte with a broad grin.

"That went well, I think. What's your take?"

Without hesitation, he concurred, "Very nicely done, I'd say!" Talbert then shared how the class had worked for most of two weeks preparing for the mock trial, making up storylines, and studying proper procedures, responsibilities of various participants, and their function in an actual trial. During one period, a local attorney had spoken to the class and answered questions.

As they drifted into the hall, Talbert suggested they go for a coffee, his next period designated "prep and conference," neither of which was scheduled. Monte agreed, having had little nourishment of any kind that morning. Joining forces, they made their way across the bridge to a place Talbert labeled the canteen, chatting and chuckling as they went.

• • •

Proving to be no more than a shallow alcove, the canteen hid under a stairway descending from the bridge to the courtyard, carved at ground level into a large Greek Revival brick building behind Main Hall designated as the chapel. Coffee was served politely but tediously by an elderly man in apron and stocking cap standing behind a makeshift wooden counter. Over Monte's objections, Talbert paid, and with no seating provided, they strayed a short distance into the courtyard to bask in a now more elevated morning sun.

Insisting Monte call him Charlie, Talbert launched into a sermonizing soliloquy on the relative merits of available java on campus, knowledge he deemed essential for survival. Emoting animation and grotesque expressions, he demonized what passed for coffee in the teachers' lounge.

"Too weak, stale, and bitter, and never hot enough," he evaluated distastefully, convoking all corners of his face into a scowl. "Dining hall's better." He brightened minimally. "But Mrs. Fitzgerald, the manager, discourages teachers and staff coming over to kill time and get in her way."

Overcome then as if by a sweeping burst of euphoria, he confided that the very best place to obtain a caffeine gift worthy of the gods was to be found by descent into the Baldwin Hall basement and Daily Living Skills kitchen. Charlie appeared caught up at that point in some dreamy, poetical swoon, describing not only certain subtle tastes and aromas but also a comforting ambience of surroundings—particularly, he emphasized, the warm pleasantness of the DLS instructor. "She's a peach," he gushed. "And very attractive and well spoken."

For most of Talbert's break, devouring two cups of coffee each, they handily conversed, touching broadly on subjects mainly related to history and current operations of the school. On return to Cameron Hall, Monte alluded to his 3:30 meeting with Booker, prompting Charlie to suggest that he might want to visit a few other classes, for which he enumerated precise names and locations. Given that he had over another five hours free, Monte thought the idea an excellent opportunity.

CHAPTER TWO

HIS NEXT STOP WAS close and opportune, directly across the hall from Booker's classroom. Dr. Rudolph Bartlett, white haired and rotund, was a man of about sixty, math instructor at the Academy for over thirty years. A dozen high school students worked at their desks while Monte was told about a program including not only basic arithmetic, but also algebra, trigonometry, geometry, and Advanced Placement subjects such as calculus and plane and analytical geometry. The school, Dr. Bartlett said, had three full-time math teachers and one part-time specialist assisting with kindergarten through second grade.

Between breaks, when Dr. Bartlett attended questions from pupils, Monte was shown items foreign to previous training or experience: braille slide rules, Cranmer abaci, tactile models of various shapes, such as cylinders, cones, pyramids, square and rectangular blocks, spheres—images often difficult for the blind to comprehend, the instructor said. In addition, he mentioned a close working relationship with the school's physics instructor, Dr. Cecilia Van Buren, who happened, he said with a smile, to be his youngest daughter.

Explaining aspects of teaching visually impaired children and young people foreign to Monte, Dr. Bartlett enumerated vastly different challenges and methods in working with congenitally blind as opposed to adventitiously blind, or those totally blind and those with limited but partial sight. He elaborated on etiology as he described medical conditions affecting sight and, in some cases, learning ability in areas like math, such as retrolental fibroplasia, or RLF. Explaining Nemeth Code, he demonstrated a braille system of symbols used in math and science invented by a blind professor of mathematics only twenty years before and still being revised.

An hour Monte expected to be lifelessly dull had come alive with excitement and avid respect. Whether from years of service or passion held for his subject, Dr. Bartlett's dedication of mission was obvious and complete. His work at the school, as for so many teachers, had defined his life.

A piercing blare of the bell shook Cameron Hall as Monte worked his way outside and trekked across the courtyard and down a gentle grade behind the chapel in the general direction of the gymnasium Dr. Bartlett had suggested he might want to visit. Here he was surprised and delighted to come upon Gerald Sampson, the judge from Talbert's class, moving rapidly a few paces ahead. Monte called out, "Mr. Sampson! Gerald!"

He had heard Monte's voice but once, yet recognized him immediately. "Mr. Scott, hello!"

"Sorry to bother you," Monte said, "I just—"

"Hey, no bother. I'm heading down for PE in the gym."

"Mind if I tag along?" Monte said, catching up. "I'd like to see the gym and maybe meet your teacher." And so, together, blind leading the sighted, they moved down the slope. The gymnasium was relatively new, light cordovan brick with long, rectangular windows pressed up under wide eaves of a low-slope roof. Monte noted Gerald used his cane sparingly, confidently familiar with the route. Their brief chat during the walk and his performance in the mock trial left a definitively positive impression. Gerald, Monte concluded, was a young man with great promise.

An hour later, trudging back up the hill toward Perkins Hall and the Blind Department office, Monte bathed in the abundance of fresh air and sunshine, shelving for the moment apprehensions of Mr. Booker.

Dense with cloying scents of disinfectant, alcohol, and human sweat, the gym had been predictable, though the coach hardly so. Claude Goodwell looked the part, his visitor conceded at first glance: thickly built with intimidating muscular demeanor, sharply hewn jaw sternly set, sandy flattop and ruddy complexion, all belying, Scott soon discovered, humane tenderness of heart and attitude of servanthood. Their conversation in hindsight had uncovered an unabashed dogma of convictions and principles, exposing a man deeply committed to his calling, his words resonating still in the raw ears and mind of this mystified fledgling.

They sat together on a wooden bench, watching while twenty boys divided up for calisthenics.

"Warming up for a few workout routines before we get started," the coach had explained. Mellow, his voice was measured and almost warm. "We've been working on basic physical fitness since school started. So many of these kids—*most* probably—are completely out of shape. They get little or no exercise, or don't do much of anything when they're home during summer months." Both men gazed across the broad, glossy floor at a ragged string of students engaged in jumping jacks and sit-ups, a tall, olive-skinned youth counting cadence loudly.

"Are there specifics, Mr. Goodwell," Monte asked, "certain regimens specifically for the visually impaired?"

Monte felt his insides go suddenly tight as the man's eyes settled blandly on his startled, naïve face. "The last bloke who called me that is still recovering. Made him run a hundred laps." A salvo of laughter quickly redeemed the moment, and Monte blushed with relief. "Seriously," the teacher said, "please call me Coach, or Claude. And to your question, the simple answer is, in most cases *no*. With a few, we have to be aware of retinal detachments or limiting medical conditions or recent surgeries. What we attempt to do is develop a program that fits needs and abilities, geared to each person. You can't expect a grossly overweight kid to do fifty push-ups, or twenty pull-ups, but"—and here Goodwell extended his hands, palms facing each other a few inches apart—"we measure progress in small increments, believing in each child's potential. And," he emphasized more strongly, speaking concisely, "helping each kid believe in himself or herself. For some, three or four push-ups or one pull-up is success, maybe great success. And we can build and keep building on that success."

Engrossed with his train of thought, Monte attended the man's words carefully, aware from his own background the worth of such philosophy. Pausing briefly, Goodwell leaned closer, speaking softly. "The biggest hurdle to overcome, most of the time, Monte, is a kind of self-imposed, or society-imposed, or sadly parent-imposed defeatist attitude which shows up simply as laziness, or an 'I don't care attitude' used as excuse to never try or to give up at the slightness difficulty.

"And it's really not their fault. For many, it's a safe place to be, to sit and be pampered with no expectations. You have to understand that so many of these kids have been told since the time they were born that they were *handicapped*, limited and disabled, which to them means they can't do anything like sighted kids do, so-called *normal* kids. And what a tragic, terrible waste of human life that is!"

He paused again, staring at the visitor with calm determination, heartfelt supplication that this one, maybe *this* one, would comprehend the deeper thrust of his words. Gauging his thoughts, he went on, outwardly casual, voice low: "People think my job's to teach physical education, what I get paid for, and I suppose it is. But . . . on a much larger scale, much deeper, I believe our foundation mission, what we as educators have been commissioned to do, is far greater and far more comprehensive."

Drawing a breath and lowering his eyes, his tone became reverential. "Because if what we're doing here, Scott, can help these kids discover self-worth, get over that . . . that fear of life, fear of failure, fear of being different and of little value, that demoralizing attitude of always being second rate and dependent, then maybe we've done more than build muscles and stamina; maybe we've instilled, or at least stimulated, some confidence and belief in their minds and spirits. If only an iota. Not every kid can do everything, but, dammit—pardon—every kid can do something."

He breathed deeply, perhaps embarrassed at the vulnerability of frankness and possible misinterpretation, then mumbled, "Sorry, I didn't mean to preach." Raising his head, regaining a slight smile, he said, "But for some reason, I don't know why, you struck me as, well, someone who might empathize with our goals."

Whether worthy of such trust, Monte was distinctly moved by the man's observations and risk in sharing so much of himself, remarkably with one likely to be expelled to whence he came in a matter of hours. Still, the compliment ranked as one of the nicest he had ever received.

A vague yet expanding image was building slowly within his mind as he trudged up the long grade to Perkins Hall, forming piece by piece the peculiar character of an institution drearily and glacially known as *The Academy*. Name alone intimated the worst aspects of Gothic novels: dark and creepy castles, mansions, and dungeons; strange, stalking characters entombed by sinister plots, victims of doom, despair, and revenge. Readily admitting that the small sampling of students, teachers, and staff introduced during his few hours on campus gave little license for firm conclusions, Monte yet could not deny inner stirrings difficult to explain, confirming on every dimension an elemental, embraceable worth of the arena wherein he now found himself—impetuous veneration germinating on behalf of a place which, only a sunrise before, he had ignorantly considered to be little more than a convenient state-sponsored asylum segregating sightless, pitiable, invalid children from the mainstream, seeing world with custodial dispassion. Scales were falling from his eyes, one by one, revealing painfully that he, and not they, had been blind.

• • •

The Blind Department office door was closed and locked. *Lunchtime*, Monte realized; one cold slice of stale pizza at six that morning was but a distant memory. Resting his back against the wall, visions of food faded as an intrusive and persistent knell reverberated from far down the shadowy hallway, tolling eerily in the emptiness.

Twisting round for the source, he observed a small, waggish body tacking very slowly in his direction, the metal-pail pendulum hanging from a thin arm synchronously metered to the pace of his steps and clanging sharply against the tile wall. With his head crooked sideways, sauntering with no apparent purpose, he looked very much like a sleepwalker. "Arnold?" Monte wondered aloud.

Supposition was confirmed in short order. When the boy was several paces away, he halted to raise his head and peer into the dimness. Investigation was rewarded as he moved cautiously closer, face breaking into a stunned grin. "Mr. S! What a bamalooza shocker! I didn't think I'd ever see you again."

"Well, I'm surprised to see you too. Aren't you supposed to be at lunch?" Monte inquired.

Lowering his voice, Arnold spoke confidingly. "I had to eat early today so I could work off some demerits. You know, washing blackboards and stuff."

"For being tardy?" Monte asked.

"Well, that . . . and other things," the lad muttered vaguely.

Monte knelt down to Arnold's level and asked, "How many do you have? Demerits?"

Pausing to calculate, the boy admitted, "As of yesterday, twenty-seven."

"Maybe sometime we could talk about that, Arnold. Being late . . . and other things, I mean."

Elated, Arnold gushed, "That would be A-okay, Monte!"

Taken aback, Monte said, "Wait a second. I never told you . . . How did you know my first name?"

"Gee whizzer, Mr. S, everybody in the whole school knows your name by now! You were formally introduced," Arnold burst out gleefully. "In Mr. Talbert's room, remember! Everybody knows now. Geez!" Huge eyes surveyed Monte as if he must be the densest person on the planet.

After several minutes Arnold meandered off and disappeared through a door at the end of the corridor, Monte realizing only then that he had not asked about the bucket, or how someone barely four feet tall managed to clean blackboards. Thirty minutes later Ramona trundled into view and opened the office. Asking about phone messages, he was informed there were none. Pouting theatrical sympathy, she attempted clichéd humor, giggling, "Nobody loves you, I'm afraid."

• • •

Afternoon was spent in the basement of Perkins Hall—first the library, followed by the music room. The librarian, a petite, affable woman of perhaps fifty with a cherub smile, gave Monte a zealous tour of facilities. Despite only a few small windows, the area was cheerfully well lighted. Cathy Henson had been at the school for twenty years and was largely responsible for most of the current organization. Items carefully cataloged in print and braille included regular print, large-print, and braille books, books on records and tape, magazines, newspapers, a section with tactile maps and globes, film strips, and a collection of eight and sixteen-millimeter films. Of particular interest to Monte was the largest world globe he had ever seen. Resting in a metal frame, the giant sphere was almost four feet in diameter with raised, textured areas outlining continents and mountainous regions, thin grooves marking major rivers, and smooth, glass-like expanses for seas and oceans.

With help from community donations and volunteer workers, Henson had established reading centers within the limited space—tables, chairs, special lighting, boxes of word games, and braille playing cards. Almost daily she conducted story times for kindergarten or elementary groups, at other times arranging for guests to give talks, often on topics suggested by students. Without sounding boastful or virtuous, she mentioned teaching herself to read and write braille visually, a great help in working with braille readers, both staff and students.

Various tools she had found important and helpful, in addition to the ubiquitous Perkins Brailler, were an assortment of handheld braille embossers for making labels and tags. She also mentioned, giving brief history and function, the American Printing House for the Blind in Louisville, Kentucky, with whom she worked closely and whose services she used regularly.

"I think it was Faulkner who said, 'Read, read, read. Read everything'!" Mrs. Henson said as Monte was leaving. "That's what I tell students. My goal is to the make the library a welcoming place they enjoy and where they can learn."

When he found the music room at the opposite end of the long basement hallway, Monte noted a wall clock showed 2:30, time passing much swifter than he had anticipated. The classroom door stood ajar, and from within musical grandeur poured forth in multilayered syntax of tonal qualities, chords, and rhythms. *Something from Brahms*, he thought, dredging memory from a college music-appreciation class. Sliding quietly through the doorway to stand in quiet observance, he studied a young man tripping fingers with finesse across a baby grand piano keyboard, eloquently as a swan gliding on the placid surface of a pond. Beside him, a dark-haired woman, tall and graceful, stood intently watching and listening, smiling with tempered satisfaction as the beautiful music rose and fell, charged and retreated, in run after run. "You're just about there, Joshua," she commented encouragingly when he finished, placing a hand on his shoulder. "That was marvelous."

The boy displayed no satisfaction and, instead, in a fit of pique summoned a jarringly dissonant chord from the instrument and seethed, jaws clenched, "Give me another week! One more week, and I'll have it!"

As he stood, Monte saw the young man's height almost equaled his own. Blessed with large hands and long, skeletal fingers, he was reed thin and displayed a manner almost severe, moderated only by a tentative, appealing vulnerability of adolescence.

As the student made to leave, Monte's presence was discovered. "Sorry to disturb your class," he ventured shyly. "The door was open and—"

"No, no, that's all right," the teacher assured happily. "You're quite welcome. I believe you're Mr. Scott, aren't you? We heard you were visiting today and might come by. I'm Elizabeth Blanchard." Charmingly attractive, rosy complexioned, and heartily youthful, she was, Monte guessed, no more than thirty. Turning, she said brightly, "And this is Joshua Blandenburg, one of my prized students."

"Nice to meet you, Joshua," Monte said. "The music was beautiful. Brahms?"

"Chopin actually." The boy grinned. "But thanks. Still a little rough."

After he left, an enlightening encounter followed—most of an hour spent discussing music programs at the Academy, combined with a constant stream of students coming in to pick up books, leave or collect instruments, and ask questions of previous assignments or practice schedules. Elizabeth gave no sign of bother or rush, her amiable bearing and words always affirming and supporting. She had been at the school for three years, having a master of music degree with specialization in music performance, the cello her chosen instrument.

"Classical music is what I'd call my foundation," she laughed, "but you'd just as likely find me at a bluegrass festival or rock concert as you would a symphony hall."

Monte asked about Joshua.

"He's one of my best. Both parents are musicians. His talent, perseverance, and dedication are beyond belief. Totally blind, he's never had vision, does anything and everything with mind and fingers; listens to a piece of music one time, then sits down and plays it. I've never seen or heard anything like it."

Monte discovered Elizabeth had organized choral groups embracing every grade. Fall and spring concerts, as well as Christmas programs, had become annual events. This year, she said, crossing her fingers, she hoped to present a musical. Sharing these accomplishments with a sense of exuberant pride in her students and the Academy, she negated any particular achievements of her own.

With Chopin floating pleasurably in his head, Monte hurried down the bleak hallway, mindful the appointed time to meet Mr. Booker was fast approaching. Halfway along, he found the stairwell descended earlier and pushed through the heavy fire door. He skipped energetically up the steps to an intermediate landing and executed a smooth one-eighty turn, hand pivoting atop a metal railing post cap, and almost fell headlong over a small body curled up sobbing.

Reflexively, he spouted, "Whoa!" in shock at seeing a tightly huddled mound at his feet, appearing to be a girl of maybe twelve or thirteen. Raising her head only enough to peer at the strange intruder, she presented but for a fleeting second a picture of despair—swollen red eyes, narrow, quivering shoulders, and gulping gasps of breath.

Head lowered once more into a nest of protective arms, she managed to wheeze so low and indistinct he could barely understand, "I'm . . . sorry." Not knowing if she meant for tears or obstructing the stairway, Monte dismissed interpretation as irrelevant. Leaning over and gazing upon a tangle of sandy-brown hair, he whispered, "It's all right. Don't be sorry."

Easing to a seat a little below the tiny bundle of distress and misery gathered awkwardly on a step, he assessed this unexpected complication, unsure of what to do or say. No immediate concern of danger or injury seemed present, no need for medical attention he could see.

With a sliver of daring, she peeped up again like a frightened turtle from the confines of a shell, but said nothing. Murky, instinctual certainty had already bound him as if to an obligatory billet, dictating that under no circumstance would he desert her. Compunction to verbalize some tangible warmth of presence urged him to whisper again, somewhat hoarsely, "Would it be all right with you if I just sit here for a bit and rest?" Smiling, he added lightly, "Running up stairways always tires me out."

No movement or sound returned either his question or statement, other than a heavy sigh buried mournfully within folds of arms and body.

And thus they remained for perhaps three, four, or five silent, lengthy minutes, passage of time moot, pressing down like the weight of a heavy cloak, endured clumsily without some bridge to breach the gulf of emptiness between them. And yet he knew enough of quiet repose to grant it more helpful, more strengthening and bonding in ways voice often was not. As he watched and waited tensely, discarding all thoughts beyond their narrow sphere, her sobbing moderately abated and breaths came deeper and more regular.

With head rising scarcely above her arms to peer once more, she blinked with puzzled scrutiny, unfocused and anguished, appraising the obscure wraith perched disquietingly on the step below. Streams of tears had imprinted little dewy pathways down her cheeks, and as Monte vigilantly followed, one salty drop welled on the tip of her nose, hanging there as if deciding, then fell away. She risked lowering her defenses to scan his face, drawing deep and snuffling breaths, then rasped, "Who are you?"

Monte grasped this small glimmer of hope with elation. One very tiny section of invisible wall splintered—a crack, perhaps, to wriggle through. "I'm Monte. Monte Scott." The tightness of his voice surprised him, left him concerned that his obvious unease would somehow put her off, create a fracture. "Kind of a funny name, isn't it? But I've gotten used to it," he said more airily, realizing immediately he may have said too much, projecting phony affinity. *Must not jeopardize,* a guttural warning cautioned, *any possibility of helping this young girl.*

Restlessly mute, they sat several grinding minutes more, she in tightly fortified prostration, and he calculating what, if anything, to do or say next. Causation of despondency, whether serious or trivial, was unknown; but for the present, Monte conceded willingness to extend whatever measures of succor seemed helpful and chance feeling the fool later. He harbored no fear of garnering a reputation for overreaction or for laxity. His focus on her predicament could be explained on strength of empirical evidence before him and that alone.

She uncoiled slightly as if revealing a measure of budding trust. "Would you . . . do you want to know my name?" she quavered.

More splinters and cracks? *But go slowly,* Monte warned ambition. "Yes, I'd very much like to know your name. Names are important."

Withdrawing slightly, studying him, she spoke as though reciting a treasured axiom: "Grandmother always told me—tells me—not to talk to strangers."

His brain shouted, *Think!* Years of counseling classes, hours of role-playing, all those many textbook cases, training films, and lectures. *Yes,* he recalled, *but did they ever construct anything like this? A sobbing eighty-pound body of agitation with no name crouched in a deserted stairwell?*

"She's right," he spontaneously agreed, knowing a grandmother's proverbial wisdom could never be categorically disputed or denied—the best he could glean from academia on short notice. Advancing prudently, modulating his voice more fluidly, he said, "Knowing the person you're talking with, especially when young like you are, is beneficial, a good rule to follow, I'd agree." For a fumbling second he started to say more, anything encouraging or conciliatory, before wisely choosing to retire to reticence.

At this point he was reluctant to tell her he was a counselor for fear such knowledge might place a wall of professional distance between them, imperial threat of perceived imbalance. Taking what he considered another peripheral risk, banking on some wavering resolution in her defenses, he said, in more introductorily informative way, "I'm visiting your school today, for the very first time. And I might be coming to work here."

She weighed the pronouncement for a few moments, eyes lowered, fragile and wary. When he offered nothing more, she asked timidly, "Are you . . . a teacher?"

"No, not exactly," he said, conversationally coy, smiling modestly. "I'm kind of like a person who helps out teachers sometimes. When they have particular questions or problems."

Pondering these banal facts for a moment or two, staring hard toward his clasped hands, she vacillated, he thought, caught between morose withdrawal and plucky confidence. When remarkably she uncoiled to lean more comfortably against the wall, he heartened.

"Oh," she said softly, as though disappointed, yet resigned to implications of his explanation for now.

Cautiously emboldened, hazarding still another parlous move, Monte ventured, "Sometimes talking with someone can be helpful, like when we're in trouble, or if something's bothering us or making us angry or sad, or frightened. If there's anyone you'd like to talk with or see, or anybody you'd like to call, maybe I could help—you know, perhaps a teacher or houseparent or nurse?"

She picked at a loose thread on her tartan plaid skirt, sighing shallowly, nose stuffy. Resting her head back and raising wet eyes to scrutinize the ceiling, she pressed rose-pink lips tightly together, by appearance negotiating whether to stay or leave, speak or remain mute, trust or withdraw. Moments passed, and then with what seemed a gamble of bravery, she murmured, closing her eyes, "My name's . . . Betty. Betty Davidson."

Somewhere inside him a tight knot uncoiled, a lessening of pressure, allowing a whisper and soft smile. "Well, Betty Davidson, it's very nice to meet you. And I'm sorry you're feeling so awful."

With a door between them marginally open, she suddenly lapsed into a sullen shell, wringing her hands and turning her face to the wall as if seeking sanctuary. Waves of pity rose up and he railed against them. Averting his eyes, he scanned the surroundings—concrete and brick a stark, institutional green, stair rail a prison of molded steel painted a thick, sickly brown, one rectangular window high above framing a cheerless grey sky, useless light bulb burning dully on the ceiling.

Surely someone would soon come and find them, offer solace, assume charge and make everything right. Weakness consumed him for lack of governance, blind paralysis without direction and order. He knew failure well, yet not quite on the minor order of this, a child weeping. Still, how was he to assume, to conclude anything? Why did sense scream of vital significance to this encounter? Strength of muscle and wit were rendered useless, no one to conquer or checkmate. A disembodied phantom foe loomed, cavorting triumphant. All that remained to offer were hollow human sounds, ephemeral strains of pittance and worthless promise.

Unbidden, his soul railed softly: "I'm here, Betty. I'm here with you."

Perhaps sensing fragments of genuine honesty too heavy, too dubious for absorption, her eyes again welled up with tears, voice wavering, reaching for control and sobbing, "I don't . . . don't belong here. Not now, not today. I need— I want to be away, far away from this terrible place. To be home. To be with, only with . . . Oh, God. I hate—despise the world. Everything. If only I could go, I'd—"

Shielding hands rushed to her forehead as though by simple touch and will pain could be repressed. Tiny crystal beads dampened her cheeks like driblets of impotence and anger as she fought desperately with hurt beyond conciliation.

He watched, helplessly ignorant, craving only in this moment to reach out and wrap arms around and hold her, prevented by engrained warnings of impropriety, knowing he must not. She had stepped, he feared, into an evil abyss and place of deepest emotion, unleashing a phalanx of demons lurking somewhere in her psyche, driven to destroy, created to maim and punish. Regretfully or thankfully, he knew the experience intimately, had dwelt there with fearful foreboding, fought battles still with blooded hands of remorseful exhaustion, never immutably victorious, ever but speciously free.

He held out a limp handkerchief and she took it charily with trembling fingers dainty as an infant's, pressing the fabric to eyes imbrued crimson, body withdrawn to exhaustion. Depredating assaults had toiled without pity, eroding mind and spirit. He feared her small steps of trust had possibly unleashed repressions of unspeakable grievance. Waiting without breath, he sat very still, praying his mere presence might impart a trivial ray of hope.

Silence assumes many faces, many characteristics, even distinct personality. Some have deemed it golden, others as a signal of wisdom and virtue, a blossoming gift of necessity for knowledge and understanding, an answer to fools. They had begun within a silence of untouchable grief, moved to fear and distrust, stepping then to wary caution and explorations of derision and blame, and now, he prayed, some island of bravery and quietude.

Of one thing he was sure, though temptation was pressing: he could not and would not demean her with vapid clichés or false assurances that all would be brighter on a nebulous tomorrow—that turmoil was but a passing phase of unhappiness to be cast aside as a soiled garment. Of her apparent hurt he was now certain, though he knew nothing of the reasons; and yet he believed he felt the depth and breadth. As never before, he coveted power of healing, to reach out and say, "All is well. Go in peace." Far too shamed and lost in valleys of doubt and bitterness, he had not the impertinence to ask for such gifts, even now.

And so, for perhaps ten minutes or more, ten minutes passing as an hour, they congregated, resigned to possibilities of defeat and failure, both hers and his own.

Then, by some unaccountable miracle of human spirit, or perhaps blessed divine hand, in staggering, unsure measures, he was proved wrong. As a phoenix rising from ashes renewed, crumbs of awakening hope gave sustenance, like the breaking of a bodily fever and whiff of emerging recovery.

As if fully aware of him for the first time, she stared in dreamy confusion and murmured, "I think . . . I think I've been in a very dark and distant place, Mr. . . . Mr. Monte. A very dark and lonely and scary place." Her gaze appealed for any wrinkle of comprehension as she implored, reaching a hand to his, "Do you know . . . ? Can you know . . . ?"

Nothing on earth or in heaven could ever separate him from this moment, so bound were they together—no possibility of denying the onerous truth within his being. Because she would know if he held back, and she would know if he lied. And her life and his were too precious for either. Perhaps he would never discern the mystery of what was happening on these steps, and whether he did or not was probably of no lasting import. Miracles always rise above comprehension, belief above suspicion, as does truth and beauty and holiness above supposition. Betty had been given, in some inscrutable form, renewal, rebirth, a rarity of gift broader than either could grasp, some sacred vision beyond reach of mortal minds. And now, without awareness of the giving, she had laid the treasure before his feet.

"Yes, Betty," Monte whispered, a single tear falling from each eye, "I do know. And it's an awful and terrible place to be."

• • •

He was late getting to Mr. Booker's room—almost three quarters of an hour late.

Walking with Betty to the girls' dormitory after leaving Perkins Hall, a cursory discussion ongoing about her life at the Academy, classes, and various interests, he lastly asked about her home and family. Intimations of discomfort rapidly crowded contentment from the softness of her features.

Conceding she lived with her grandmother and had no siblings, her next statement was confusing. Wistfully tentative, voice barely above a whisper, she spoke confessionally, as of some concealed transgression or neglect. "Today is . . . today is . . ." The words stuttered like a chain of mellow hiccups, her face turning away as though shamed. They stood now at the entry to Baldwin Hall, facing each other uneasily. Monte asked nothing, contemplating the bowed head before him.

Some gravitative interest touched him as she went on, thoughts emerging raggedly, "When you found me this afternoon, the reason I could talk with you was because at first . . . I believed you were like, like a sign, maybe like a gift—kind of an angel of . . . of comfort and salvation, just when all was . . . lost and dark. And then, you were so much like him. Like, really him, speaking to me the way he used to when I was sad or afraid . . . or lonely."

"Who, Betty?" he murmured.

"My brother, Mr. Scott. My brother, David," she sighed.

Mildly bemused, he spoke judiciously. "But . . . you said you had no . . ."

Though she lifted her head and stared at him with eyes still puffed and red, his image was not what she saw, her focus somewhere far beyond, somewhere distantly past and secretly sweet, and yet a place of fearful suffering and dread. When she lowered her eyes, a cloak of funereal grief masked her face cruelly, and he knew surely she would cry again, but she did not. Some immutable inner strength, perhaps some privileged sovereign peace on which she called and seized in moments of intimate and cloistered need, rose up to embrace and lighten the weight upon her soul.

She smiled a fragile, joyless smile and said, "I don't . . . anymore." Her head fell and a tight catch of occlusion prevented more. Monte stood quietly while her small chest expanded with deep intakes of breath, her gloomy gaze on the sidewalk beneath them. Then softly she said, "He—David—died in Viet Nam a year ago. A year ago today. My wonderful, beautiful brother."

A line from some forgotten reading came without bidding: "Everyone has reasons"—words easing his fear for her. *So often we observe and judge,* Monte considered, *fooled by a certainty of veneer, assured we have unearthed truth, not knowing we see only armor shielding brittle inner beings in hiding, coping with ravages of the world and mortality.* She had her reasons on this day—for tears, for grief, for anguish of irreplaceable loss.

As they said goodbyes, she surprised him with an impulsive warm and sisterly hug about his waist, promising to talk again soon. He watched until she slipped through the dormitory door, then turned and galloped for Cameron Hall, bursting into Booker's classroom five minutes later.

CHAPTER THREE

THE INNER OFFICE DOOR was again ominously closed. With ripples of queasy tightness, Monte knocked gently.

"Who is it?" thundered a voice within, flustered with impatience.

"It's, uh, Monte Scott, Mr. Booker. Sorry I'm a little late. I—" Blundering, he attempted a feeble apology and was deflected cleanly.

"You're not a little late, Mr. Scott. You're forty-seven minutes late." A shuffling of papers and a drawer slamming followed like an exclamation point. "There's a proverb you would do well to familiarize yourself with that says, 'When you make people wait, it only gives them more time to count your faults.' Now, please have a seat while I finish what I'm doing."

"Yes, sir," Monte mumbled, chastised, forehead beaded with sweat resting against the cool wood, smothering sighs of dashed hopes.

Slogging dejectedly to a desk, he planted himself to wait. Several minutes passed and he heard a phone ring in the inner office, followed by Booker's muffled voice speaking in brief, staccato bursts between longer periods of silence. Ten minutes later he came out. During the whole of the day, fearsome images of the man had been conjured: Genghis Khan, Ivan the Terrible, Blackbeard, Eric the Red, Stalin, Attila the Hun. Almost disappointingly, Monte discovered, the man was none of these.

The inner office was claustrophobically gloomy, floor space taken entirely by a swivel chair behind a small desk faced by an armless heavy oak chair, metal filing cabinet squeezed into one corner. Afternoon sunlight partially shadowed by the chapel and Main Hall across the courtyard forced luminance through one narrow, dusty window, mounting a weak golden square on a faded wall behind Mr. Booker's head. Far above, a grimy light fixture might have offered meager help, but remained unlit. The twelve-foot ceiling, rather than lending spatial relief, amplified a cramped, close feeling, prompting sensations of being at the bottom of an elevator shaft or silo. With Booker squeezed behind the desk, Monte was directed to the chair, knees jammed uncomfortably tight.

Benjamin Booker was compact and trim with short cinnamon hair invaded by smatterings of covert grey at the temples; Monte placed his age in a range of late thirties or early forties. A softer set of mouth and jaw may have rendered more genteel presence, smoothing an otherwise intolerant, flinty air. His scrupulously erect posture conveyed staunchness of a military academy plebe or drill sergeant, imperialist and energetic. Watching breathlessly while Booker puckered his lips as if foraging for suitable words to begin the inquisition, a mass of tethered turmoil harrowed Monte's mind, steeling nerves for expected humiliation.

Yet when the man spoke, it was with unexpected insouciance. "Well, Mr. Scott, sounds like you've had a busy day."

Dredging for cheerful confidence, nothing effusively lavish nor blandly flat, Monte heard a rather level voice answer, "Yes, sir. Busy, but enjoyable. And very informative."

"That's good. I'm glad to hear it," Booker pronounced neutrally, "even though you've had time to see only a small part of what goes on here. As you may know . . ." He cleared his throat, fist pressed to his mouth, then continued, "We've had a few of your cohorts visit in the past, who I, er, found necessary to reject for one reason or another. No need to go into that right now. Just suffice it to say that we, and particularly me, are very selective about who comes into our school and has contact with, and works with, our kids. Not everyone's cut out for the task, whether they realize it or not. And some don't have genuine interest and dedication. So, I believe it's better to find out sooner rather than later."

The set of Booker's face, Monte felt, was sufficiently kind, if confrontational. Calculating with a certain amount of resigned expectation, tingling sensations crawling icily up his spine, he waited for the hammer to fall.

Booker concluded trenchantly with, "I'm sure you would agree, Mr. Scott."

Clues to destination became clouded. Monte now feared a clever setup in preparation to boot him out as the others had been, only more cordially. Slowly, Monte said, "Yes, sir. I understand . . . and agree."

Fishing into a coat pocket, Booker pulled out a pack of cigarettes and tapped it sideways on the edge of his hand to extract a single smoke, placing the cylinder expertly between his lips for lighting with a wooden match. Inhaling deeply, he expelled a stream of smoke into a swirling cloud that hovered around his head.

"So, what do you think about our school, Mr. Scott? Now that you've had a chance to meet a few people and see a little of our program?"

Why ask, Monte thought, *given my imminent departure?* Still, the game had to be politely and formally played out. Sensing fawning platitudes would be unwelcome, guessing the sober man confronting him immune to flattery, Monte leaned forward and began by a risk of truth, having nothing to lose.

"Let me answer, if you don't mind, Mr. Booker, with some background." After a deep breath, he continued slowly. "When my supervisor, Mr. Danforth, told me I'd been chosen as agency representative for the Academy, I was, well, shocked at first, and then, on reflection, not sure I wanted the assignment . . . or felt worthy of being here. I didn't think, and still don't think, I was prepared or trained or experienced enough. And so, the more I thought about it and wrestled with the idea, the more I questioned why, of all the more senior counselors, he chose me."

Pausing to select his words carefully, Monte went on, "The truth is, and I hope you won't be offended, I didn't want to come today. Anxiety sickened me and I nearly threw up—thought seriously of turning the car around and going back home."

Booker's lips curled to a slight smile, but he said nothing.

"But," Monte added more confidently, "something happened during these few hours I've been here, something that I can't explain. Maybe you can help me understand. It was such a good day, from the very first, until the very—until even now." Booker grinned as Monte stopped to breathe deeply, sighing unintentionally. "The Academy isn't at all what I expected. The students and teachers . . . It's a very special place. I really don't know what else I can to tell you, sir."

With an abrupt tilt forward, Booker confessed brusquely, "Well, Mr. Scott, first off, just to set the record straight, Danforth didn't choose you."

"What?" Monte questioned, raising his head higher and sitting straighter, confused.

Arms spread on the desktop, Booker said calmly, "Look, you've been working up and down this valley and on both sides of it for, what, about a year or more? A lot of your clients are people I know, or have known, some ex-students of this school. People talk and word gets around."

Monte ventured, "I'm . . . I'm not quite following, sir."

"I talked to Danforth," Booker interrupted, "and others too, including the commissioner, and decided I wanted to meet you for myself. Not for a normal interview—much too staged and trite, particularly after the experiences we'd had with those other counselors from BSVI. I wanted you to come here and . . . and be on your own for a day. We'd see you and you'd see us, and then we'd both have a better idea if your being at the Academy was right or not."

Monte's mind scrabbled to assimilate all Booker was saying. Befuddled, he asked, "So this whole day has been a kind of trial, to evaluate me?"

Booker shook his head and said, "Well, yes and no. For you to evaluate us as well. Charlie—Mr. Talbert—agreed to get things rolling, and then you were more or less on your own." Settling back and smiling thoughtfully, he mused, "He was very much taken with you, by the way. Said you listened while he talked for a half hour about coffee and never yawned once."

Monte smiled, recalling Talbert's detailed discourses. However, still unclear on several points, Monte said, "I think I understand most of what you're saying, but—"

Breaking in, Booker said, "Sorry. Just let me clarify one more thing, Scott." His words, modulating to almost a murmur, came reflectively gentle. "After dismissing you this morning, we of course didn't know what you might do. After Talbert's and Dr. Bartlett's classes, you did the rest as we'd hoped and prepared for."

Clearing his throat, his voice took on a paternal, fragile tone. "All but one . . . unaccountable incident; your meeting with Betty Davidson wasn't planned, couldn't have been planned. Obviously no one knew that was going to happen." He lowered his head for a moment, then said, "That phone call a few minutes ago, before you came in, was from her houseparent. She saw you and Betty together in front of the girls' dorm. Betty's been very close to Mrs. Hindgardner and told her the whole story about what happened in the stairwell."

Monte drew a deep breath and, remembering Betty's words, seeing her face, murmured, "She said . . . I reminded her of her brother."

Booker nodded and observed mildly, "Well, I think you may have acquired a little sister today, Scott."

For the next hour they conversed nonstop, covering topics of the Academy, the agency, education of the blind and visually impaired, staff and curricula at the school, problems and rewards of a residential facility, until Booker declared necessity to leave, mumbling curtly he had to meet his wife and go to a "damned church supper." They stood and shook hands across the desk with an unspoken and undefined bond of mutual respect.

"You could easily have stormed off this morning, Scott," Booker observed frankly. "After I rudely sent you away. No one would have blamed you." Booker foundered, searching for some definitive closure, replying to Monte's silence by asking quietly, "Will you come back next Wednesday?"

Without hesitation, the young man answered, "I'd like to, very much."

Booker smiled oddly, as though recalling some humorous event. "You know something, Scott? Maybe I shouldn't tell you this, but I will anyway. Your supervisor, Marlon Danforth, highly recommended each of the other counselors he sent here, gave them glowing references, but, funny thing, he doesn't like you very much. And that, from the very beginning, was a huge point in your favor."

Restlessly, thinking the knowledge might be important, Monte queried, "I know the other counselors who were rejected, Mr. Booker, and based on what I know, they're very good at their jobs. What went wrong? What made a difference?"

Booker's head dropped as if a fitting answer escaped him, and then, with an expression akin to heartfelt affection, said so low the words were almost lost, "Because you stayed, and most of all . . . because you cared."

• • •

Outside, the clear brightness of morning had transfigured to a drab, grey evening, sky heavy with low-hanging, worrying clouds, murky in distressed fullness, primed to gift the earth with cool, primordial showers. Shunning quiescence, strata cowered in suspended vacillations of turbulent constraint until the burdensome, swelling plenitude could be borne no longer, vaporous portals now unbounded to flourish an abundance of heavenly mists upon the land.

Monte had not yet reached the highway when droplets began to scatter in dissonant clusters across the windshield, gathering strength to a full-flowing downpour so blinding even wipers flapping frantically like giant metronomes could not cope, and he was forced to pull to the side of the road to wait out the storm.

Torrents drummed steadily on the car roof, offering a sense of isolated security. With head back, he closed his eyes. Feelings experienced this day subsumed him now: quiet inner calm, assurance of direction and place, dawning comprehension of purpose and calling. Not so much an ordination to gird up and conquer nebulous obstacles, or tilt at windmills, but rather an invitation to be a conduit of possibilities and beginnings, of genesis—to be used and be useful. Told he had shown a gift of caring, he debated the pronouncement once more with wonderment, remembering all that had happened in the past hours. Perhaps Booker saw promise Monte found too vague to purport and specify. Perhaps he did care. Maybe the puzzle was simple as that.

Questions and unknowns remained, would always remain—the essence and challenge of life. Moreover, darkness still lurked, too close at times, encircling and threatening, eclipsing dreams and hope. Yet on this singular day, bathed by warm morning sun, baptized by cool, regenerative rain of the evening, the power of something, of someone beyond himself, beyond all mankind and creation, had risen, ready to lift and place lost, seeking souls back upon their feet, restored and reborn to wholeness.

The deluge abated, and he drove east out of Talerton, sustaining sun bravely breaking through dwindling clouds in the western sky, beaming shafts of golden splendor across the broad, green valley, little Bug chugging up the Blue Ridge, pointing its nose toward a waiting loneliness of Rivanleigh, and home.

• • •

After being at the Academy on Wednesday, Monte spent the next three chilly, rainy days crisscrossing the valley, visiting clients in homes, hospitals, places of work, or schools. Soon after beginning his job, the critical importance of including visits to social service and health departments, optometrists, and ophthalmologists quickly became apparent, they being major sources of information and referrals. The discovery that many professionals had never heard of the Bureau of Services for the Visually Impaired was always surprising and demoralizing.

Most difficult and easiest to neglect was exploring potential employment options with his clients. Employers, he often found, were sympathetic, yet reluctant. The keys generally came down to tenaciousness and relationship building, approaches based and modified ofttimes simply on gut feeling and confronted personalities. His self-imposed goal was to find at least one viable work situation each week, which seemed simple but was not. With an area spread over eight large counties and numerous small towns, economy chiefly agricultural and population low, job placement could be challenging and disappointing, though victories did occur, making his efforts encouragingly brighter and worthwhile.

Dearth of experience, Monte came to believe, was the nemesis of success in any endeavor—that, coupled with a sour, defeatist attitude.

Self-examination revealed a neophyte with a graduate degree in counseling, ranking in practicality rather worthless, or at least feeling so. He lacked mastery of any subject within his chosen field, functioned daily without poised savoir faire, and wandered place to place impoverished of coveted insight, abilities and skills seasoned veterans exhibited effortlessly and naturally with wisdom, tact, and competence. Over twelve months on the job, and most days he felt like a spectator plucked from a theater audience and thrust on stage of a Shakespearean play, knowing no lines or movements, or indeed hardly anything about plot or role.

Haunting misgivings of usefulness grew particularly sharp after his day at the Academy, replayed in agitated and perplexing visions measured against his many self-enumerated shortcomings. Driving up and down the valley through grey, late-summer rain, he recalled teachers and staff routinely proficient in fulfilling their roles, as though endowed with intrinsic adeptness in their areas of expertise, like skaters gliding gracefully across a surface of ice with confident finesse and no discernible effort.

Objectively, he knew these feelings were not representative of reality. No one begins life accomplished—a finished, complete product. Cups are filled drop by drop; growth comes one imperceptible iota at a time. Mozart one day in Salzburg took pen in hand for the first time and inked notes on a staff; Chopin placed virgin fingers on silent ivory keys, and Da Vinci grasped a brush with artless, untried hand before a bare and waiting canvas. Each began a life journey someplace at some time as a novice.

Nebulous predictions of future achievement or failure, Monte posited, were largely conditioned by cumulative past example and influence, particularly in younger, formative years; self-images, reinforced positively or negatively, programmed winners or losers. Nevertheless, he looked upon survivors of fate with unapologetic envy and reverence—those unhaunted, untethered souls hindered not by slings and arrows of outrageous fortune.

Questions of self-worth daily navigated through the young man's head like ships on a foggy sea, lost for the moment, yet still afloat. And thus, driving in solitary introspection between visits, Monte diverted ephemera with streams of masochistic musings. There are no easy answers to difficult questions, he had been told by elders. Mortals always desire sound-bite solutions, no matter a puzzle's complexity.

Truthfully, there are no easy answers to any question, Monte concluded, *given possible degrees and depths of response. Based on this elementary premise, one therefore infers there are no simple questions.* A single inquiry would always lead to a multitude, like the tiny piece of dangling thread one dares pull in unthinking innocence, only to unravel an entire seam—one straight path proceeding to a labyrinth. Once, Monte had read that the definition of true peace was having all one's questions answered, and of paradise, having no questions at all.

• • •

Wednesday morning dawned, and though apprehensive, Monte enjoyed a sanguine lightness of outlook. Feeling what he considered healthy fear and wariness of Mr. Booker, he accepted their relationship remained in the watchful, disquieting arena of appraisal, a circling dance of sizing up, weighing underlying strengths and weaknesses. The trip from Rivanleigh, uneventful but for heavy fog on the mountains, transpired in a blink. Along the broad, rolling valley floor, thin wisps of mist gathered in glens and dales concealed with resignation from the encroaching sun nearly clear of the Blue Ridge crest and now raging in conflagrant reflection in every east-facing window of Talerton.

The inner office door to Booker's dusky sanctuary stood open, the man sitting immobile, cloaked in drifting, greyish brumes, relishing a finale of deep draws on the stubby remnant of a Camel. He crushed the butt, small as a child's fingertip, in a glass ashtray as Monte entered, then fanned the air ceremoniously with both hands as though to erase any lingering evidence of smoky fumes and restore the pinched atmosphere to imaginary purity. On the desktop, a sizable stack of unopened mail rested aside other papers, which Booker began to investigate with sensitive-fingertip precision. Simultaneously, he turned his head and smiled in greeting.

"Good morning. You made it, and very early too." Booker was clearly an avid and accurate timekeeper as well as multitasker.

"Good morning, sir," Monte replied, dropping a tattered canvas briefcase to the floor beside the well-worn oak chair.

No sooner had he sat than a boy of middle school age, skinny as a post with dark, curly hair, materialized in the doorway, blurting with urgency, "Mr. Booker, Mr. Booker! Jason has an emergency with his pants!" The exclamation portended an intriguing tale, particularly as Monte observed Booker's smile vanish and shoulders droop.

Groaning as if clearing his windpipe, Booker said a bit harshly, "What?"

"He thinks it's centipedes," the boy enthused. "You know, those things with a million legs!"

"I know what a centipede is, Carson. What the devil does that have to do with Jason's pants?"

The boy wavered, somewhat distracted, leaning further into the room and realizing a second person was present. Resolution regalvanized, he blundered on with insistent energy, "Well . . . they're in his pants!"

Sagging like a punctured tire, Booker sank deeper in his chair and began with little zeal to question Carson's announcement: Had anyone seen centipedes? No, the boy said, not actually *seen.* Had Jason talked to the houseparent? Yes, the boy thought so. What made him think centipede infestation? Jason's legs felt creepy tingly and itched awful after he put his pants on. Why centipedes and not ants or rash or something else? Carson was adamant on this point; there was no doubt it was centipedes! Did he even know what a centipede was? For sure!

Volume increasing several decibels, he spewed, "We learned about centipedes in biology class yesterday and saw live ones in a jar. We watched 'em and they were icky!"

Light began to dawn.

With more patience than felt, Booker said, "Tell Jason to go up to the infirmary and see the nurse. Tell him to have her check his pants . . . and his shirt . . . and his underwear. Okay?"

Fired up, given a clearly authorized mission, Carson rose on tiptoes and saluted. "Yes, sir! I will, right now, Mr. Booker, sir!" Rapidly retreating through the classroom, he could clearly be heard galloping down the corridor toward Perkins Hall, shouting with desperation for Jason.

Booker repositioned his body in the chair and flexed his shoulders, mildly annoyed, and said with control, "Houseparents are supposed to deal with situations like that, yet every day . . . Oh well, what were we talking about?"

Taking the question rhetorically, Monte refrained from answering, as Booker said perkily, "Oh, right, yes, I know!" Hitching up tight to the desk, he then froze in a flash of reflection and said, "But wait. Let's get rid of this pile of stuff first." Without warning, Booker shoved an entire accumulation of miscellaneous correspondence forward. Reflexively forming a dam with chest and arms, Monte prevented the flood of letters and envelopes from cascading over the edge of the desk, only a few stray pieces escaping to flutter to the floor.

Hesitantly, he broached a question before beginning to sort through the material. Staring up to the ceiling light hanging flaccidly high above, covered with decades of dust and grime, Monte asked delicately, "Would it be all right . . . or do you mind if I, uh, turn on the light?" Their one narrow window, grubby as the overhead globe and filmed with a variegation of smudges and soot, allowed only paltry and inadequate passage for the sun's brilliance covering the courtyard outside.

"The light? Oh, sure," Booker laughed. "I never think to turn the damn thing on. Sorry." Flipping the switch added but a disappointing one or two candle power to the gloom; yet Monte was grateful for even that.

During the next thirty minutes they opened and read aloud letters, memos, assorted announcements, advertisements, and invitations. With many, Monte was halted immediately by Booker's curt "Toss it!" A few he wanted read twice while pondering content.

Light tapping on the doorframe broke momentum and boredom. Most might have unerringly described the visitor as a "natural beauty," for she was indeed one of the prettiest women Monte had ever seen outside a magazine or movie. Warm, smiling mouth dripping with moist sensuality conjured fear his eyelids might melt from pure primeval desire and ooze like butter down his cheeks. Skin, smooth and tanned to a deep olive, was perfectly complemented by huge brown eyes, auburn hair styled in a flip bob, and long, dark lashes. Outlined in the office doorway, sunlit classroom as rewarding backdrop, every curve and nuanced contour of her figure was etched in sharp proportion and singularity. When she spoke, he heard handbells chiming harmoniously in some great cathedral, soothing and magical as pixie dust.

"Mr. Booker, it's Anne Walden," she said in hushed, deferential tones. "Sorry to bother you."

Booker ignited in a way verging on sexual misconduct, dribbling throaty gurgling sounds. "No bother. No bother at all. Come in. Come right in."

Gliding into the room daintily as a ballet dancer, she bestowed Monte with a look so sweet his pancreas threatened to cramp. "Please, don't let me interrupt," she cooed like a dove. "I know you all are very, very busy. But I had just one quick concern, if I may."

As if exhibiting onset of uncontrollable sycophantic spasms, Booker expeditiously made to rise from his chair, jamming both knees and thighs with a resounding clatter against the underside of his center desk drawer. "Yes, of course," he babbled, ignoring the mishap to assume a troublingly unbalanced crouch, face blushing darkly.

"Well, it's about Withrow Mulligan," she declared, endearingly vexed, cocking her head curiously and staring rather wide-eyed at Booker. "I'd, er, appreciate your talking with him sometime about decorum in class, especially interrupting and making inappropriate comments. I've tried many times, but . . . He's a nice boy, most days, yet he's . . . Are you all right, Mr. Booker?"

Partially entrapped between desk and chair, managing only a truncated stance and leaning over sharply sidewise, Booker braced one fully extended arm against the wall and finished her sentence with rapid gasps: ". . . pest and a nuisance! And yes, I'm fine. Just a little . . ." Cheeks now frustratingly red, he appeared to be preparing to gain leverage and undertake a chancy standing vault across the desk. Monte found it hard to watch and retreated to the corner filing cabinet, cowering beside it, head lowered and breathing suspended.

"Well, yes, that's it," Anne agreed mildly, clearing her throat, obviously ill at ease.

"I'll try . . . to . . . umph . . . see himmmm today, Anne," Booker huffed and squirmed as one might flounder in a vat of molasses. "Or . . . or just haaveee him—drat—come innnn anytime." Poise and dignity failing miserably, his legs twisted tightly under him in the form of a pretzel.

"Thank you so much, Benjamin," she said nervously, taking on an askant glare of concern. Turning to leave, her eyes fell upon Monte concealed in dimness. "You must be Monte Scott, rehabilitation counselor we've heard about. Welcome to our school." Lilting, velvety words floated to his ear as though carried by the warm summer breezes of her melodious vibrato. Pursuit of concealment was foiled, undone by large oval eyes sparkling despite the shadows.

Recovering a façade of maturity and sense of proportion, Monte managed to squeak, "Thank you very much."

With naturally easy pleasantness, she continued, "I'm the art teacher here at the Academy, so I hope you'll stop by my room and see what we're doing."

Booker, remaining ensnared, drooled, "Oh, I'm sure he will, Anne, probably before the day's over."

Her departure was elegant as her arrival, and normalcy descended—only, however, for a few minutes. Booker had barely untangled himself and opened his mouth to ask a question when, unannounced and with no forewarning, a sturdy boy of high school age trooped into the narrow confines with the force of a bulldozer, calling out Mr. Booker's name and plowing into Monte reseated in his chair. Momentarily stunned to encounter such solid resistance, the surprise visitor nonetheless quickly insinuated himself into the narrow space between Monte and the desk. Being embarrassingly pinned, Monte found his nose in the alarming position of being pressed closely into the young man's buttocks. With only inches to scoot backward, barely managing escape, he fled once more to a protective niche beside the filing cabinet.

Withrow Mulligan was not overly tall, but husky, a dynamo in constant motion, a bowling ball banking off any available solid surface, shattering the porous and weak. A mop of sandy-blond hair circled his head, shielding prominent ears and gaping eyes from full disclosure. Carelessly dressed in baggy pants much too short and a white dress shirt streaked with yellow stains, his shoes were scruffy enough to convince of being dragged recently behind a car of newlyweds. Plopping down in the vacated chair without invitation, Mulligan launched into a strident round of proclamations.

"Weeellllll, Mr. Booker, sir, here I am! Knew you wanted to see me! Miss Walden told me herself, she did—said you said I should come as soon as I could. She doesn't know I came yet! But you can tell her later! Did you know she's the best art teacher in the world, and I think—"

Indignant and flustered, Booker boomed in vain attempt to regain control, "Look here, Withrow—"

Undaunted, barreling ahead relentlessly, possessed by his own docket, the youth caterwauled, "Wowwww-weeee! Hear that echo when you talk?" Craning his face to the ceiling, he shouted, "Hear that, Mr. Booker? Whoop! Whoop! This must be a veeeery small room, maybe the smallest room in the wooooorld, I bet!" Drawing a quick breath, he went on more rationally before Booker could regroup, "What did you want to talk to me about? Oh, I bet I know. Or I could probably guess. Miss Walden thinks, and so does my mom . . ." His ranting combined nicely with a sort of bouncing lurch of head and arms, twisting his body in tight gyrations as if fighting off a swarm of bees.

Booker, acting against any established rules of counseling of which Monte was aware, stood abruptly to lean over the desk—successfully this time—and thundered even louder than Mulligan, "Withrow, SHUT UP!!"

As though slapped, the stunned lad took on a look of wounded shock, entirety of presence morphing from chaotic to calm in the span of a blink. Remarkably, he rested back as if sedated, focusing on Mr. Booker with a kind of composed yet astounded admiration. Recovering composure, hands flat on the desktop, Booker adjudged Withrow with pastoral serenity, voice low and hushed.

"Withrow, when you come to my office, you stand outside and knock. You do not come in until you're invited. Do you understand?"

Withrow lowered his chin several notches, docilely repentant, and bobbed his head up and down, whispering, "Yes, sir."

"Now," Booker went on, sitting down, "you need to make an appointment to see me. Do you know what that means?"

"A special time just for me and you to talk?" he said meekly.

"That's right. Do you know how to make an appointment?"

Withrow answered, "No," and Booker carefully explained how he needed to "quietly" stop in at the Blind Department office and wait his turn to talk with Miss Simpson and ask for an appointment.

"I'm sorry for shouting at you, Withrow," Booker said calmly. "Shouting isn't normally nice. But I had to get your attention. Do you understand?"

"I do, Mr. Booker," Mulligan murmured.

Booker then introduced Monte to the boy before dismissing him, and he sulked out quietly.

With the boy well out of hearing, Booker lit a cigarette and sighed, "Sorry about that scene, Scott. It's the closest thing to discipline I'm allowed to do now—not like a whap upside the head they used to do to us; more like a verbal slap these days."

Engulfed in a wispy cloud of smoke, his voice took on a subtle shade of pensive lament. "Sometimes . . . sometimes it works. The kid's on medications, and seeing the psychologist, for all the good that does. And on top of it all, his home life's a mess; parents recently split, neither wanting custody. Can you believe it? But he'll be eighteen in two years. And like Anne said, he's basically a good kid." Booker took a last puff from the Camel, then crushed it out. "I'll tell you more about him later. You might find it interesting. And helpful."

Monte's expectations, unexpressed, entailed a great deal more visits from Withrow Mulligan.

Recovering his briefcase upside down in a dusty corner of the room, victim of a turbulent rugby charge, Monte returned to his chair as Booker pulled a file folder and slate and stylus out of a desk drawer, poised to begin their severed discussion. Opening his mouth to speak, he was cut short by a sharp round of rapping on the office doorframe, followed by Charlie Talbert's smiling face poked around the corner, chortling, "Anybody for coffee?"

• • •

Twenty minutes later, reinforced with caffeine, Monte and Booker were back in the little office, christened drolly by Talbert some years before as the *Inner Sanctum*. "Now," Booker began, "what I want to talk about is something you wrote back in April and sent to your supervisor, Danforth. You remember?" Monte's face crinkled in thought, stymied. "School work program?" Booker prodded encouragingly.

The additional clue kindled recall and, enthused, Monte piped, "Oh, yes, you mean 'A Proposal for Part-Time and Summer Work Program for High School Students'?"

"Yes, that's it. I've got a copy right here," Booker noted, opening his folder.

"How did you come by that?" Monte asked, intrigued. "Other than mine, there was only one other copy."

"Friends in low places." Booker grinned conspiratorially. "But that's not important right now. What *is* important is that I want to put your proposal into action, and as soon as possible. The whole concept is something I've dreamed about for years, and you've put all the pieces together. Frankly, it's one of the reasons I wanted you here at the school."

"Danforth didn't reply for weeks," Monte recalled, "then said the agency wasn't interested and rejected the idea as being too complicated and costly."

"Well, I've got it now and want to use it," Booker said excitedly. "There's at least a dozen kids ready to go to work already. What we need are jobs—and to fine-tune the plan for our situation." Animated, Booker poured out ideas, becoming more excited as he rambled. Monte was caught up in the energy as well and listened attentively, though niggled by speculative questions dredged from months before by Danforth's expressly negative attitude and lack of interest.

The proposal was six printed pages in length, and twenty braille pages, opening with a brief synopsis. Following sections dealt with eligibility, logistics of travel, possible funding sources, a brief list of potential jobs, employer contacts, job preparation, and lastly, values and goals of the enterprise. Booker wanted the material read aloud twice, giving opportunity the second time to jot notes.

When completed, he reached in a coat pocket and withdrew a roll of Life Savers in lieu of Camels, popping one in his mouth. Leaning back and locking hands behind his head, he talked around the candy, slurping lustily.

"Danforth's a twit, Monte, no vision or depth. I've known the man for years and think less of him every day. His only goal's promotion, and in that he's succeeded. You gave him something worthwhile and he canned it, or had it canned."

Monte found the comments enlighteningly droll, but said nothing.

"Now, what I propose we do first—" Booker continued, leaning forward only to be halted by his name being spoken courteously and clearly by a huge young man filling the doorway, relating a strange combination of levity and urgency. His pleasant face held the rich hue of ebony wood, voice resonating deeply in the eloquent manner of a buoyant and moving oration.

"Sorry to interrupt, Mr. Booker, but Mr. Gladstone is, uh, trapped . . . in the filing cabinet!"

Visions of injury and mayhem filled Monte's mind as he jumped to his feet, stunned that Booker had oddly melted into an appearance of sullen annoyance.

Rising and sighing extravagantly, Booker muttered, "Thanks a lot, Jellyroll. I guess we'd better . . ."

The lackadaisical response given the circumstance puzzled Monte as the three strolled diagonally across the hallway intersection to Gladstone's classroom to investigate. Finding the room replete with students bantering back and forth, giggling and conversing as if nothing of import were happening, Monte noticed nothing amiss at first glance.

Jellyroll Jackson, doing his best to posture sedate concern but scarcely concealing a burgeoning grin, said stiffly, "He's in the back of the room," then added, "Do you think we should call Maintenance, sir?"

Booker growled something denoting a negative.

Monte saw him then, though only the voluminous rear end of a body bent awkwardly over at the waist, clutching the sides of a filing cabinet as if engaged in dancing or bowing in obeisance for some worship ritual. Moving closer, threading through the desks, Booker spoke up. "What's going on, Clarence?"

Mr. Gladstone was in no position for conversation, yet nonetheless projected surprisingly good humor, chirping, "Oh, er, hi Benjamin. Thanks for coming over."

His frame of mind far from chatty, Booker lowered his head close to Gladstone's ear and whispered flintily, "What the hell have you done this time?"

With flecks of self-effacing laughter, almost choking in the process, Gladstone gurgled, "My . . . my damn tie got caught in the file drawer . . . when I shut it, and something . . . locked up."

"Maybe you should be locked up," Booker seethed under his breath. Turning, he spit out, "See if you can figure out what's going on with this drawer, Scott."

Monte moved around Booker and knelt beside Gladstone. The colorful tie the man was wearing, what little could be seen, was ensnared tightly in a closed file drawer second from the bottom. Peering into a full, fleshy grimace, Monte took in a face colorful and round as a pizza. The poor man, puffing cheerily, managed to say, "Nice to, uh, meet you, Scott. Thanks for helping."

Working an arm under the man's meaty neck, Monte gave the drawer handle several hard pulls with no result. Both ends of the tie were vised tight, he noted, offering no chance of unknotting and slipping it over Gladstone's capacious head. Seeing no lock buttons or push levers anywhere on the drawer, Monte turned to Booker and Jellyroll hovering behind and said calmly, "We need a knife or scissors, I'm afraid."

Not hesitating for instructions, Jellyroll quickly took off, shouting as he went through the classroom door, "Miss Simpson will have some!"

Still kneeling, Monte smiled and said to Gladstone, "We'll have you out soon, but I think we need to cut your tie. There's not room for a pry bar, even if that might work."

"Do what you have to do," Gladstone panted, maintaining a convivial attitude. "It is a shame though. I got this tie . . . on vacation last year . . . in Miami Beach." Monte hoped for Jellyroll's quick return, conscious of quivers in Gladstone's short, thick legs.

A minute later Booker called out, "I hear him!" And in ten seconds, charging through the door like a giant cannonball, Jellyroll gleefully held aloft a pair of large scissors.

With a chagrined Gladstone free, displaying only the short stump of his cherished tie and unable to completely straighten his back, Booker and Scott departed. Reestablished in the inner office,

Monte sensed Booker burned to comment on the rescue operation, several disparaging remarks regarding the English teacher already having been made. Launching into a diatribe of klutzy and inept history, Booker recounted occasions the corpulent gentleman had caused various things to fall over, break, spill, dislodge, crack, burst into flames, unhinge, explode, or disintegrate. Plus, he added, myriad times Gladstone had injured himself with pencils, pencil sharpeners, eating utensils, his own reading glasses, the copy machine, an umbrella, a three-ring binder, fingernail clippers, paper clips, and now, unbelievably, a filing cabinet.

Monte was quickly discovering Booker constituted a man of strongly formed opinions, not obliged to suffer fools—defined by his own criterion—gladly. He understood and accepted hosts of shortcomings in students but leaned heavily against that quality of mercy one was inspirited to employ gently and unstrained toward peers, from whom he expected and demanded a higher standard. Monte supposed one could grow weary over time when subjected to a continual parade of screwups, though presently, he found the subject a delightful source of amusement.

With little time remaining before lunch, they burrowed into how the work program might be structured and implemented within context of the Academy. Booker was anxious to contact employers in the community, while Monte volunteered to explore funding sources. This last item was ticklish, since it would unavoidably involve talking with Marlon Danforth. Checking his watch, Booker said he planned to eat his bag lunch in the office and would set up an afternoon meeting with Mr. Fletcher, seeking approval to proceed with plans. The day being warm and sunny, the inner office claustrophobic, Monte felt naturally drawn to enjoy a quick alfresco break with what little he had brought.

• • •

The spacious green lawn, barely noticed by Monte until today, spread down from the front of Main Hall, flourishing as a paradise of flora: antebellum boxwoods rising twenty feet or more vying with thick rhododendron and holly; dwarf boxwood and azalea bordering walkways and limestone foundations; flower beds once nesting blooms of summer glory, gone now to inceptive traces of autumnal conversion; flowering dogwoods and redbuds stripped to spidery limbs and waning splatters of leaf dully crimson, faded yellow, and subtle plum. The more compellingly awesome, however, were the undisputed royalty of the grounds, monarchs among which he wandered with worshipful deference—*Quercus alba*, ancient and giant white oaks.

Massively broad and tall, enduringly anchored, most were four to five feet or more in diameter, thick, stout limbs reaching and spreading like giant muscular arms, arching in colossal eruptions of tenacious, chartreuse profusion, filling the sky in ascending webs of sylvan glory, turning only now in mid-September days to acknowledge the stealthy, thinning onset of fall. Approaching a particularly mammoth specimen, greyish-white trunk a coarsely textured wall before him, he placed timid palms to the bark, as though avowing a spiritual bond with the life and pulse of this almighty leviathan.

Humbled in serene exhilaration, he felt transfused by a flowing throb of creative beauty—centuries ago birthed as an acorn, aged by nature into a titanic goddess. Without thought, a whispered troth of adoration slipped impetuously from his mouth: "All the years you must have seen, my friend, all the movement of history."

Lost in unfocused reverie, for the slightest, unquestioning moment Monte imagined with little misgiving the sacred monument had spoken clearly and unmistakably in softly feminine response when he heard "Maybe two, three, or four centuries, one ring marking each year of life."

Recovery to the sphere of reality was shockingly quick and embarrassing; someone, he feared, must be hidden on the other side of the tree. Ideas of furtive retreat occurred instantly. Mature impulsion came secondly: painful and candid honesty, presenting oneself abashedly in confession to the phantom voice to face certain mockery.

Slinking around the gigantic circumference, prepared for inevitable embarrassment, he remembered personifications of Joyce Kilmer and felt a measure of justifiable relief. He had not, after all, hugged the tree, sang to or kissed it. Reaching the shielded side, his worries vanished.

She was sitting on the ground, the melodic voice—a young woman, her back resting against the trunk of their sheltering colossus. A brown-bag lunch perched on the grass beside her as she nibbled in pensive concentration at an apple and held an opened book upon her knees. Daring to grovel more fully into view, Monte divined a charmingly amused smile lifted toward him, cobalt-blue eyes luminous in dappled sunlight filtering through a canopy of leaves and limbs above. And in that instant, that magical wondrous instant, he was stabbed to a virginal core with overwhelming veneration and tenderness for this mystical creature, unprecedented in the entirety of his life. So entrancingly and frighteningly implosive was the moment, he stood paralyzed, transfixed and staring, desperate to utter poetic praise and oblation worthy of her eminence.

She spoke first, words poised serenely on the afternoon air, carried not so much to the ear as to the heart. For he knew beyond doubt whatsoever came forth from this woman was to be cherished with reverence. "Do you talk with all trees or just certain ones?" she asked coyly with a ripple of laughter.

Aspects of voice and affectation were immediately and spellbindingly magnetic, toying with his vulnerability, mischievous intimations of mirth curling her mouth and crinkling the smooth sweep of her cheeks. And Monte, utterly beguiled by the saintly figure before him, muttered, "I suppose you think I'm some kind of nut. Maybe an acorn." Too late for amends, still he beseeched the gods to please, please stop him from saying anything else so inane.

Resting her opened book across a leg and holding the apple, she said placidly, "Not at all. In fact, I think dialogue with trees and flowers and birds and squirrels and all sorts of things is quite normal, even therapeutic. Sometimes I even converse with rocks and clouds, and certainly moon and stars."

At first he feared she jested to ease his feelings of foolery, then realized by her authority of manner that she was sincere. About her was an aura of truthful, confessional wholeness and innocence, worn not as a superficial cloak of pride but genuine internal identity. Tilting back her head against the trunk of the tree, she gazed upward as though mystified by the latticed and ordered confusion above, contemplatively murmuring, "Creation inspires us to speak, don't you think?"

No longer feeling quite the buffoon, Monte replied easily, also looking up, reasoning that imaginative metaphors would be impressive, "Or maybe, at times, compel us to silent humility, reveling in ethereal strength and nobility, like these stalwart sentinels standing as if in guardian protection."

She took a disinterested bite of apple, scrutinizing him with circumspect curiosity. Focusing along the top of her head, for her eyes were too constraining, he said with some ruefulness, "I'm, uh, sorry for disturbing your lunch. I didn't know anyone was here. I was . . . just wandering."

She spoke quietly. "It's all right. Why don't you sit down and have *your* lunch?"

"I should go," he protested weakly. "You're trying to read and—"

Suppressing a grin, near to laughter, she said, "Were you planning to jump up and down and sing while you ate?"

Rising flush of uncertain emotion pinkened his neck. "Well . . . no . . ."

"Sorry." She smiled. "I was joking. Please stay." Eying his brown bag—wrinkled, limp, and stained from days of use—she offered, "I have an extra apple and cookies baked this morning in the DLS kitchen. Still warm, almost, if you have an imagination."

The invitation impressed as valid, almost encouraging, and he wanted to stay; Lord above knew he never wanted to leave.

"Okay, thank you, if you're sure." He smiled in return, parking himself on the grass a respectful distance removed, and withdrew a very green banana from his pitiful lunch bag. Titters of muffled laughter coupled with doleful contractions promptly danced from the young woman's face as she spied the unripe object strongly resembling a cucumber. Hastily dropping the pitiable fruit back in the bag and sighing, Monte said, "Maybe I'll, uh, take you up on that extra apple."

She passed him her bag impishly, tinged slightly with commiserating benevolence, saying, "I'm finished. You're welcome to the rest." Peering into the neatly creased little sack, he discovered half an egg salad sandwich, a large red apple, and a few chocolate-chip cookies. She returned to reading, and in a matter of minutes the young man devoured every luscious morsel she had packed.

Satiated and sedate, reclined on his side with head propped on one arm, Monte studied the young woman through surreptitious, sleepy eyes, hoping she would not notice discrete perusal. Desirably and heartily slim, she wore a bright-yellow sweater and dark-brown pleated skirt, yellow socks, and loafers. Her dark hair, the color of rich chocolate, ranged unbound in thick, undulating billows, like fulsome, velvety curtains, across a mantel of narrow shoulders to disappear down her back. Her unblemished skin, a pale-fawn, sandy hue, lustered like memories of summer fading to more muted shades of autumn and winter. A nose well shaped melded gently into a swell of orbicular cheeks, framing full, rubicund lips and a fluidly angular chin.

More striking yet was an undeniable essence of repose and contentment, a salient embodiment and paradigm of wholeness, gracious and tender. Nothing about her spoke need of flattery, for herself or him. She was unembellished in manner and dress, which made her all the more beautiful.

For beauty, defined always in totality, never narrowly focused on façade but radiated from heart and soul of inner strength of being. This was the beauty perceived and sensed in the woman sitting so tranquil before him, at peace with the world. And he hungered, as one starving hungers, to know her depths, to be allied in her emotions and thoughts, her hopes and dreams.

Maintaining appearance of aplomb, he asked lazily, "What are you reading?"

She casually stretched her arms and, not turning eyes from the book, said, "*A Separate Peace*."

Monte sat up. "John Knowles. It's one of my favorites."

"A moving, troubling story, isn't it?" she mused. "Set in a difficult time. But so much of the prose is like poetry, almost metered and so descriptive." And then, leaning her head to one side and closing the book, her eyes fell probingly on his for a fleeting second, and in that peerless moment he felt the press of some transcendent birthing of promise, and knew he would surely die on this patch of grass and live in heavenly bliss forever.

The literary genius of Knowles faded swiftly as Monte fumbled for something, anything, to say, for he yearned to hear her speak. In disparate eagerness, somewhat without sequential logic, he asked, "Are you the Daily Living Skills instructor?" A droll reception betrayed wordless affirmation. "Mr. Talbert says you make the best coffee on campus."

"Oh, yes," she affirmed, "Mr. Talbert's one of my best customers, especially when we're baking." Gazing up once more to the mosaic of limbs and branches and leaves far above, she exhaled lengthily, as though in surrender, and began to gather up her things and stand. Unfolding from the comfort of the grass, Monte painfully wished for more time, mere seconds of prolongation to be in her presence and share her space. Sauntering easily up the slope, she turned after a few steps to see if he would follow, and half-smiled. "Well, we'd . . . I mean, I'd better go. Fifth period starts in ten minutes."

They parted at the top of the hill, she proceeding to Baldwin Hall, her kitchen-classroom being in the basement, Monte on to Cameron to reconnect with Booker. The hallways, in terrifying contrast to Main Hall's lawn, swirled with bodies dashing in all directions, uproarious, ear-splitting chaos flooding his ears, baffling in precision and unity despite contrary appearance and volume. In the thick of the fulmination, deafening shrills of the overhead hall bell signaled countdowns of inviolable schedules.

And then, as though slamming into a wall, Monte froze, realization of simple negligence piercing cognition that in the course of their roving exchange, her name had not been asked, and neither had he given his! Students one after another plowed into, around, and through him, mildly curious when he shouted, "Good grief! What a thickhead!"

CHAPTER FOUR

ONE THIRTY FOUND BOOKER and Scott sitting restlessly on hard wooden chairs in the Blind Department office, listening to incessant clacking of Ramona's typewriter. While Monte bumped the back of his head in steady pulses against the wall, staring at the ceiling, Booker slumped over, tapping both feet on the floor with unsettling, syncopated rhythm, at the same time whacking a roll of wadded notes on alternating knees in a sort of coagulated cadence.

Twenty minutes later Brad Fletcher sprang apologetically through his office door and loftily ushered them into his office. In contrast to the Inner Sanctum, the room was brightly lighted from a large window and several overhead fixtures. His glossy walnut desk was large and uncluttered, behind which reposed an impressive executive-type padded chair with plump headrest. Above, a number of evenly spaced, framed diplomas, certificates, and awards hung on the bright-yellowish-cream wall, adjacent to a centered photograph of a grinning principal standing shoulder to shoulder with the current governor.

"Well, gentlemen, please take a seat," Fletcher oozed, falling back to be swallowed by his chair. "I understand you've been discussing a vocational plan for the, uh, high school students here at the Academy."

Booker answered affirmatively.

Leaning forward and holding out a folder, Monte said, "We have a copy of the proposal here, sir, to help better explain what—"

Cutting in curtly, Fletcher said, "Oh, that won't be necessary. I already have a copy. Marlon sent one during the summer with full details." Reaching into a desk drawer and withdrawing a sheaf of papers, he held them aloft, announcing magisterially, "'Students Entering Training' or SET is what your agency's calling the new program, Mr. Scott. And I must say, the plan he's developed is quite impressive and definitely something I—*we*—could wholeheartedly support . . . if adequate funding's procured, of course."

Stunned, Monte flashed a quick glance to Booker, then turned back to look at Fletcher with a cloudy, quizzical expression. "I don't think . . . I quite know . . . ah, could I take a look at what Mr. Danforth sent you?" Monte asked.

"Of course," Fletcher nodded. "But I'd have thought you'd have received a copy of your own." Monte made no response, only rose and took the proffered sheets and laid them in his lap.

Scanning the pages, cold fingers gripped his core with ever-tightening pressure. What he read was incredible. Clearly, Danforth had essentially incorporated Monte's April proposal into a reworked document labeled "Students Entering Training," penning his own name on the title page and dating the material January of the current year, over three months prior to Monte's memo. Whole sentences and paragraphs appeared word for word what Monte had written in April—sections and headings modified only slightly by merely changing vocabulary or word order. Whether Fletcher knew of or was party to the subterfuge was unknown, and Monte, in the present circumstance, was not going to ask or infer the question. Booker, bemused, knew some wrinkle was amiss upon hearing the "SET" designation, yet quietly accepted Monte's lack of challenge for the moment.

Handing back the principal's copy, Monte impassively said, "Well, that's very interesting. Very thorough and well thought out."

"Yes, I thought so," Fletcher replied with satisfaction. "Something like this could be a real asset to our curricula here at the Academy. I don't know why someone didn't think of it sooner. Our superintendent, Dr. Mullens, was impressed as well, and plans to share the proposal at the next Board of Visitors' meeting."

"May I, er, make a copy of what you have, Mr. Fletcher?" Monte asked evenly. "It varies a bit from what my . . . material reads."

"Sure thing. I'll have Ramona do it right away. But I can't understand why Marlon didn't send you the same thing I have."

"Just a clerical oversight or minor editing changes, I'm sure," Monte replied stoically. "Perhaps we could get a braille copy too?"

Oddly, putting aside plagiarism and dishonesty, the one point Monte found most egregious was the simple epithet "Students Entering Training." The words represented a glaring misnomer and complete misunderstanding of the program's purpose, giving false impressions of what he and Booker were hoping to do. *Training* students was not the goal. Broad introduction to the world of work was the intent and purpose: what working in a job was like, basic requirements and components for successful employment.

As they rose to leave, Fletcher asked, "When do you think we can start the program?"

Monte answered, "I'm meeting with Mr. Danforth next Monday and should know more about funding and procedures afterward."

Booker added, "And we need to follow up on contacts in the community and prepare employment applications for student use, plus parental permission forms."

"Right then!" Fletcher gushed, beaming. "We'll meet again soon. Keep me informed on your progress." Before they could reach the door, the principal called out, "Oh, Benjamin, one other question. What about the, uh, job-readiness class Marlon suggested. Any specific ideas? Sounds like it might be a big help."

Wavering, Booker appeared uncharacteristically off balance for a second, saying only, "Er, Monte—"

Cringing, Monte spoke up quickly, "Yes, we have that covered, Mr. Fletcher. We'll begin classes next Wednesday in the Student Center."

• • •

In the privacy of the inner office, Monte explained the despicable scenario as he could best understand. Booker was livid, offering a barrage of choice words and chain-smoking for the next half hour, arguing and debating what resources they had for retaliation and justice. Imploring him to leave it for now, Monte convinced his companion to wait until after Monday before saying or doing anything. Above all, he emphasized, jeopardizing the work program was the one thing they did not want to let happen, and ultimately, Danforth had control.

During remainder of the afternoon, they visited each location contacted for appointments by Booker earlier in the day. Their first stop, after a long period of tactful wrangling with a rather cantankerous Rutherford Ellington, owner of Talerton Hardware, garnered conditional promise of employment for two suitable students for up to eight hours per week each, hinging on availability of training wages provided by the state or school. Similar conversations, differing only in length and congeniality, were held with Charlotte McKensey at Charlotte's Ice Cream Emporium and, lastly, Geraldine Findley in Findley's Book Shoppe.

Greatly encouraged by initial success, Booker's foul mood—sequestered during their afternoon inquiries—mellowed to more reasonable and tolerable smoldering. Diverting from unpleasant foci of Danforth's mischief, as they prepared to leave for the day Monte delicately raised the question of Daily Living Skills. "DLS?" Booker snorted. "What about it? Every student takes it, in one form or another."

"Well," Monte stumbled, "I, er, happened to meet the, uh, teacher during lunch." He lumbered on, "But didn't exactly . . . uhhh, get her name."

Booker shook his head despairingly and chuckled. "Didn't get her name. Very suave, Scott. Well, let's see. Clare's been here a year; very nice and proper young lady. Kids love her. Makes good coffee . . . and cookies." As if flummoxed, he added, sighing appropriately, "And you didn't think to ask her name." Relaxing back in his chair, his face spread with a sadly mocking smile as he advised, "Well, if I'm reading you right, let me say up front, don't waste your time, son; she's claimed, so I understand—happily hitched."

"You mean . . . ?"

"Like a pony to a wagon. That's the dope, my friend." Booker smiled slyly. "Augsburg, for the record. Clare Augsburg. Best DLS teacher we've ever had. Enjoy the coffee, and hands off everything else. My recommendation would be an art teacher, such as you-know-who."

• • •

The highway to Rivanleigh converged heavily with evening traffic, so much so he detoured on a narrow back road, seeking some measure of transient peace through Jefferson County's bucolic countryside resolutely fending off mounting chills of converging autumn nights with residual warmth of fleeing summer's earth; passing rolling stretches of field corn, erstwhile green, crinkly, crackly dry and pale, hungrily ingested in swirling, dusty combine clouds engulfing row upon lengthy row; golden hay rippling and weaving in the wind, magically sheared and compacted precisely rectangular to bales, disgorged in random solitude across broad fields in wait of stacking hands riding rickety beds of wavering wagons, then cached pyramidally aloft in shielding sheds and barns; all in preparation of coming winter forage when grasses go dormant to sleep soundly beneath ice and snow.

• • •

Clare's Journal:
Wednesday night, September 10, 10:45 PM

School year is off to a roaring start! I have six classes in all ages. For the most part it's a great bunch of kids and already I've compiled a long list of items I need to buy. Some I may have at home. Some might be hidden away in the DLS kitchen.

At lunch today I had a weird encounter. Well, not weird in a bad way, just kind of unusual. I met a man who talks to trees! Ha! Arnold told me later he's the new rehab guy. Very nice, kind of interesting, felt almost like I knew him or we'd met someplace before, yet . . .

He ate my leftovers like he was starving. Hope he doesn't get canned like the others. I forgot to ask his name, or tell him mine. Arnold will know, I'm sure.

I have a lot of good ideas for lesson plans this year, plus ways to . . .

• • •

A trip to Richmond was always undertaken with mixed emotions—city of Monte's birth and childhood, teenage and early adult years. He had played there, gone to school and worked there, had friends residing there still. At junctures, the town had been guardian and tutor, nurturing with careful instructive hands; in other hours, taskmaster wielding tempest force of a demon and brutality of a sadist. Richmond held in trust years of nostalgic souvenirs, some joyful to recall, many sacred and sealed, a few so tenderly implanted as to inflict throbbing aches when remembered.

His home had been the Southside—Manchester in early, independent times, a blue-collar manufacturing town separated from the center city to the north by waters of the mighty James River, incorporated within the fold in 1910. They lived on Thirteenth Street, his parents operating a small grocery store a few blocks away. He had no siblings.

Life as a young boy on the street could be at worst perilous or at best precarious. One learned early to avoid the former and juggle the latter. Most endured, some did not—a roster of mates lost to varying fates writ long and tragic standing as testament to an incalculably capricious sphere. They called their block of asphalt "Lucky Street" as wry misnomer and an insider attempt at ironic wit, though from bitter experience knew the jest was neither funny nor clever. And hardly ever lucky.

Thirteenth Street was in many ways a stratum of hard principles and values, bided by scrupulous men and women who toiled in mills and factories and shops, trekking off with lunch pails at dawn to trudge home in fading twilight, smudged and worn with grime and sweat, wearied by perennial labors, solemnly reciting the rote imperative again and again, year after year until one day discovering a lifetime journey had been expended as passing payment to a master without heart or promise.

And yet, crucial to the human soul to be gleaned from vestige moments, rare islands of comfort, peace, and reward offered blessing, much as a flower or blade of grass pursuing sun and rain through narrow concrete fissures exhorts joy in the miracles of indestructible creative spirit—rest and play, laughter and tears, the binding nuclei of family striving for singular straits of common unity. Long ranks of shabby houses nudged one to another like boxy wooden crates became beloved sanctuaries, safe harbors, and homes. And those within, when at last eroded, crippled, and battered, would move on to that "undiscovered country from whose bourn no traveler returns," whether pauper or king.

Many miles northwest, close upon Richmond's historic Fan District, the Bureau of Services for the Visually Impaired headquarters occupied a squarish two-story brick building. Monte arrived at Danforth's office door at eight Monday morning. The man, chronically aggrieved, huddled behind his large desk, wearing on this crisp, clear day a dark-grey wool suit and expression defining arrogant contempt.

With miserly effort, head lowered and shuffling papers, he snapped, "Scott!" A lazy, distrait drone peevishly followed: "Well, sit down. We don't want to keep you too long from your work, do we?" As directed, Monte sat, attention aimed across the desk much as in July, taking in familiarly vapid features of his superior painstakingly deferring eye contact. "What can you tell me about this business at the, er, Academy for the Blind?" Danforth asked, disinterested and detached.

Monte answered more rigidly than intended, "If you mean the proposed part-time work program, Mr. Booker and I are ready to start at any time."

"Well, of course that's what I mean!" Danforth growled, whipping his head erect and glaring. "The commissioner," he emphasized, "has given me full authority in this matter. He was quite impressed with the proposal I shared with him . . . last January." Danforth's eyes, heretofore averted, now burned into Monte's painfully, as if seeking invitation to challenges of rebuke. Monte merely stared back, feigning a complacent expression.

"The funding question," he continued pedantically, dropping his eyes once more and beginning a nervous drumming of fingers on the desktop, "has been a difficult complexity, which I've satisfactorily solved after much thought and research. As you aren't aware, being a field counselor, there are many—and I'll try to keep this simple—pockets of money within the agency; some we can tap with discretion, some are mandated—earmarked, we say—for particular programs, and some are, well, basically untouchable."

"Yes, sir," Monte said ponderously, as if laboring to grasp some vague, foreign concept.

"As long as there are no disagreements"—he cleared his throat as if in subtle warning—"or complications on your end, I think we're ready to commence. That is to say, if Mr. Booker and the Academy are in agreement. With funding in place, I see no reason why we can't proceed at once." He paused, reclining stiffly as though signaling an end to his comments, blear pinkish disks rouging ugly, spidery webs on otherwise pale cheeks.

During the next half hour, Monte gave a compendium of his and Booker's work on the project: obtaining clearance from Academy administration, employer contacts, eligibility and application forms for students and parents. Danforth listened without comment, head dipping slightly as each point was mentioned—strangely, Monte thought, like one checkmating an opponent, sneering in victory and finding contemptuous satisfaction in the other's loss.

Assuming Monte was done, he offered raised eyebrows and twisted mouth of dismissal, grasping the arms of his chair and leaning forward in faux semblance of standing. Still seated, Monte said mildly, hoping to sound amenable, "There is one thing we wanted to amend, if we could."

"Oh, really? And what would that be?" he asked, warily perturbed.

Monte glanced down at his folder, though he had no need, and spoke as if reading from notes, "The title, 'Students Entering Training,' we think is misleading. We envision the program to be more in the nature of an evaluative and experiential endeavor. We were thinking—"

"You see, Scott!" Danforth burst out, slapping a hand on the desktop as if thoroughly exasperated. "This is the kind of thing I warned you about: disagreements, problems, nitpicking! You don't get the big picture, do you!?"

Respiring as though having run up a long flight of stairs, he regained control and quieted slightly.

"Well, how could you, a field counselor? You haven't experienced all my days of consultation with the commissioner and the Finance Department and all the many other staff people here at headquarters. We've put a lot of time into this project. I can't begin to tell you how many meetings we've had, how much research we've done, and how much thought has gone into this deal. Now you come along with twelve or so brief months on the job and want to change it? No, sir, it can't and won't be done!" Panting, he went on, "The funding, Scott! The funding has to be for training. It's as simple as that!"

He clasped his hands together as though preparing to pray, staring at Monte with agitated displeasure, a bit of spittle clinging to his lower lip. "SET it is and SET it will stay. End of discussion, Scott."

Standing defiantly, Danforth glowered down as Monte slowly closed his folder and rose in silent acquiescence. In the doorway, preparing to leave, he turned and asked, "Will you be sending funding and billing procedures to the Academy?"

"Yes, of course!" the supervisor answered, as though the question were asinine. "Fletcher may already have that information. Ask him."

For a moment, Monte stood motionless, curiously puzzled at what drove a man like Marlon Danforth, a man who could converse without blinking knowing he had stolen and cheated and lied, and knowing Monte knew as well. Some ameliorating rationalization must give a form of solace to his mind, Monte speculated, even perhaps justification to his conscience—something to soothe and mollify whatever fabric of ethic and morality he possessed.

Students lied, cheated, and sometimes stole to gain advantage or impress, to excuse or cover up failure, shirk responsibility, or more often merely to make their lives more bearable. *Or maybe even*—Monte smiled inwardly—*just for the pure hell of it all.* And with these, he could accept and understand and deal. But Danforth was somehow different. Danforth ensconced a grotesque element of chilling evil, slippery and dark, lurking somewhere beneath a surface of presumed normality. A grasping, perfidious lust and cunning. Danforth was nothing like the students. And Monte did not understand him at all.

"Thank you, sir," Monte whispered, and left.

Arriving back at his office in Rivanleigh, Monte called Booker and told him about the meeting. Booker was with a French class, so said, "*Merci beaucoup, mon ami,*" and hung up laughing. His peal of mirth was welcome tonic, easing depression often clinging as a foul odor after a visit to Richmond, unusually draining this day, coupled with melancholy stirrings following like shadows during the whole of his return, and residing still.

• • •

Waning days of September arrived with promised multicolored artistry and fanfare, sedate greens of summer shying from eminence, capitulating to provisional hosts of bursting rainbows awakening beneath. Recurring each fall at the Academy, anxiously anticipated by both performers and audience, was a talent show open to all students and staff. By not keeping judiciously silent in one carelessly unguarded moment, Monte Scott found himself drafted onto the program.

Rosanna Worthington and Eric Rockwell, high school juniors and well-known musical duo, were jamming in the Student Center Wednesday evening, Monte present and listening after conducting his first newly established Job Readiness class. Foolishly, he asked if they knew any Woody Guthrie songs, to which Rosanna replied that they were familiar with a few titles but no words or chords. Borrowing a guitar, Monte played and sang a few verses from several he remembered.

Almost every teenage boy in his Thirteenth Street neighborhood had been part of a folk-rock band at some point—a gaggle of guys collectively knowing three guitar chords and parts of four or five songs. Monte was no exception. That evening in the Student Center, he was "discovered" and innocently thrust into the talent show mix. Complicating matters, Clare Augsburg, who Rosanna knew was gifted with a beautiful voice and sang with her church chorus, had shown interest in participating but had failed to sign up, her piano accompanist from last year having graduated.

Unencumbered by shyness or tact, Rosanna put forward the idea that Monte and Clare should team up, insisting privately to each that their voices would mesh with distinct harmony. Zealously reporting that Clare had not spurned the proposal, Rosanna told Monte Miss Augsburg waited only for some word from him. He considered the scheme ill-advised for several reasons, some he suspected Rosanna and Eric would not comprehend, yet now felt Clare was owed a direct and courteous decline.

Late the following Wednesday afternoon, he crept skittishly to the basement of Baldwin Hall, half hoping the teacher would not be there. Her classroom door stood open, lights on, yet the large room loomed empty. Stepping in and glancing around, he felt awkward, like an interloper trespassing on posted property. In the far rear where a number of tables held sewing machines, he heard movement but saw no one. And then, bundling through a partially opened closet door, she suddenly appeared, wrestling a bulky armload of assorted clothing. Almost hidden behind the heap, her face took on a shade of cautious reserve in confronting an unexpected visitor, long, dark strands of impish hair falling mutinously across forehead and cheeks.

"Hello?" she queried, voice muffled, though pleasant.

Mesmerized to statuary muteness, he drank in as much of her presence as deemed respectful. She dumped the clothes on a table, unveiling a girlish woman in long black skirt and white blouse, sleeves rolled to the elbows, and said breathily, “Oh, it’s you! I couldn’t see at first. Collared by Rosanna, I suspect.”

Rendered dumb and hovering near improperly warm inclinations, he willed her to mere pedestrian objectivity of no amatory interest, managing but a weak, “Yes, I was.”

She brushed her untidy hair back in place, augmenting by a simple motion the young man’s pain. With an unsure smile, hands dropping to her sides, she explained her present chore. “We have a clothes closet down here for kids who might need something.” Turning her eyes to the pile just deposited, she added, “There’s a lot of mending and hemming to do whenever there’s time.”

Feinting seriousness and with immediate regret, Monte blundered, “Have anything that might fit me?”

“No, I doubt it.” She grinned, cocking her head to one side as though calculating. “You’re a bit large . . . well, tall for my inventory.”

Realizing a previous error was about to be repeated, he rushed, “I’m Monte Scott, the, uh, rehab—”

“I know,” she said easily. “Arnold told me. He and Betty talk about you all the time.” Again speechless, he stood in a fog of aimless confusion, intelligent response elusive. Helpfully, she offered, “Oh, and I’m—”

“Clare Augsburg,” Monte whispered, perhaps more keenly than appropriate. “Mr. Booker told me.”

“Well, that’s settled, at least,” she laughed. “Now, what do you think about this talent show idea?”

A kitchen area located at the opposite end of the room held two round tables with chairs. Clare fixed coffee, and as they sat down to talk, a plaintive voice drifted in from the doorway.

“Miss Augsburg? I have a problem.”

Clare raised eyes past Monte’s shoulder and said rather weakly, “Come in, Shaunna.”

A chubby girl of high school age, with stringy brown hair, and pinkish, pimply skin, tottered in, thick-lensed glasses perched low on a round, stubby nose.

Clare rose to meet her and asked, "What is it?"

Near tears, the girl whimpered, her words garbled, "My zipper on this old skirt is . . . is broken."

"Did Mrs. Etheridge look at it?" Clare leaned over to inspect the fastener.

"She told me to come down here," Shaunna answered forcefully, sniveling. Clare seemed mildly displeased.

"I think it's just stuck, Shaunna. Hold on a minute." Clare walked back to the sewing area to open a large wooden cabinet and returned. Fiddling with the zipper for a second, she straightened and said, "There. I think it's fixed for now." Eyeing the young girl with concerned appraisal, Clare said very low, "I think you may have outgrown that skirt, Shaunna. It looks awfully tight."

"Maybe," the girl murmured with a show of pique, sullen and verging on more weepiness.

"Yes, I think it's way too small for you," Clare said gently, placing a reassuring hand on the student's arm. "Why don't you come back tomorrow afternoon and we'll find something that fits better, okay?"

Shaunna gleefully agreed, prospects bolstered, and she shuffled out of the room. Clare watched for a moment before coming back to the table where she sat, expelling a sigh, then chuckled lightly. "The houseparents generally deal with these minor crises, but I think Mrs. Etheridge is mad with me about something and this is her subtle way of showing it."

Monte smiled and said nothing, content with the evolving loveliness and musical intonation of voice before him.

"The school psychologist told Mr. Booker she should be in the MR program, but I didn't agree," Clare went on thoughtfully. "She's slow catching on in some areas, and in others she's quite bright. Lack of confidence is the main issue, I believe." Pondering for a moment, she continued, "To me, there's a vast difference between social retardation and being slow intellectually. I don't even know if they're proper terms, but . . . do you know what I mean?"

Monte nodded.

"So many of the kids are like Shaunna. They've been cared for all their lives with very little or no expectations, no responsibilities, no independence. You must see this all the time."

He did, of course, thankfully admitting there were exceptions; still, though his clients were predominantly adult, many were often treated as invalids. This led into discussions of a rather controversial and ongoing debate pitting residential school education against public school programs, including the often broad choices, nuances, and variables the topic generated—all of which launched opinions on shortcomings of overly protective parents, both readily confessing no valid qualifications.

"I don't know why I get so wrought up about some of these things," Clare said, sipping her coffee. "I've only been here a year, so what do I know?"

Remembering Booker's glowing endorsement of her as the best DLS teacher the school had ever had, Monte questioned her more about the position's varying responsibilities, student goals, and teaching methods, each of which she explained in some detail, then returned the question, asking about his counseling work. Flow of exchange and time moved unerringly and without regard. Or so it seemed, both at last realizing the hour.

Standing beside her at the counter while she washed and he dried their mugs, Monte noticed a queer black box attached high on the wall over the sink. Protruding from the front of the box, facing into the room, was a short tube, giving the odd item passable resemblance to a small movie camera. "What's that?" he asked, staring.

She glanced up and giggled, "That? That was my predecessor's contraption she thought would fool students into thinking the room had a security camera. It's just a cardboard box and toilet-paper tube painted black."

"But . . . why?" Monte continued to stare.

"She had a problem with kids sneaking down here at night and taking food out of the refrigerator and cupboards, so she passed the word around that a security camera had been installed."

"Did the thieving stop?"

Clare laughed, "No. Think about it. Most of our kids don't need lights to do what they want to do, and without light, what good's a security camera?" She paused, then said, "And yes, she told them it worked in the dark, but no one fell for that."

Scarcely aware, Monte gazed at her as though studying a portrait, his attention overpowered and monopolized by her soothingly melodious timbres rather than the words actually spoken—more, he imagined, like acoustical gems floating aloft on soft breezes, distant church bells tolling on a Sunday morning. Far away, his name was called, and called again.

"Monte. Monte!"

Clare stood smiling, observing him strangely.

"Sorry," he said clumsily. "I was, uh, thinking . . ."

"Yes, I know," she said, almost curtly. "In all our gabbing, we haven't talked about the talent show at all, have we?" And then her eyes found his and she laughed.

It was nearly seven when Monte rushed into the Job Readiness classroom in the Student Center basement, finding it full of waiting students. Theorizing without pertinent focus, he wondered if Clare's husband might be concerned about her lateness, or if maybe she normally worked late, or—

No business of mine, he decided, *and why should I care?* Turning attention to twenty eager, waiting faces, he stated firmly, "Okay, class, tonight we want to talk about customer courtesy . . ."

• • •

Journal: Friday, October 3, 11:30 PM

Hectic week, and I hate to say it, but I'm glad it's over. Need a couple days to recoup. During first period Withrow broke a serving dish . . .

Tomorrow I'm helping Mom wash windows, and Sunday there's a mission program at church, and I'm supposed to . . .

Met with rehab man twice this week to practice our songs. Seems we'll be singing together in the talent show. Thank you, Rosanna! Long story. He has a nice baritone and plays guitar well, though says he's never had any formal music training. We blend rather well together. He's also got a great sense of humor and enjoys the kids. I've heard he might be seeing Anne. Not a good match in my estimation, though I don't know why I think that . . . or why I care. It's really none of my business.

Richard and I had dinner with his parents tonight, and they of course made their usual remarks . . .

• • •

Of all Monte's responsibilities, documentation in the form of paperwork was the least desirable. His shabby Rivanleigh office, housed in the Commonwealth Industries for the Blind building, was hardly conducive to concentration, being shared by two other counselors and with a Garnett machine on the floor above daily spitting out miles of cotton wool and consistently vibrating the entire three-story building like a hardware-store paint mixer.

After completing a dozen client-contact reports, placing an equal number of phone calls, and writing several letters, he succumbed to the clarion call of irresistible blue sky and brilliant fall sunlight beckoning outside his office window. Swooping down the stairs and escaping through a side door, he allowed urban figments of nature to swathe him with welcoming arms—dulcet breezes tipping his brow like diaphanous silk veils; drenching golden radiance offering warm and healing embraces, absolving mind and body and spirit in curative touch. The poet Lowell may have preferred the rare, perfect days of June; for Monte, finding joyful amenity with Camus, the second spring of autumn, with every leaf a flower, was the more to be desired, and the loveliest.

He walked along sidewalks, heaved and cracked, through the neighborhood, passing in chilly shade under maples red and gold, elms yellow as ripe lemons, sycamores dull jasmine, blood-purple dogwoods heavily decorated like holiday trees with deep-red, clustered seeds; children busy at games, swirling and whooping on the school playground; slumberous elders reclined on front porches, raising hands in casual greeting; a passing car tooting, the driver waving.

Lastly, he stopped at a corner grocer for soda and peanut butter crackers. The rotund proprietor, attired in grimy, splattered smock, was primed for debate—a full fifteen minutes plowing local gossip, world events, and polity. Hinting no distraction while Monte loitered, the man served a full half dozen customers, continuing with unflagging keenness and energy his partisan discourse, interjecting cheery side comments to each of the other visitors while wrapping and taping their wares in broad sheets of butcher paper with smooth deftness of a surgeon closing a wound.

Admonished by plodding commitment, interludes of freedom drifting behind, Monte returned to the office, thinking of her and wondering why his feelings were so vastly different and apart from anything he had ever known. And why did they linger and penetrate so? Being with her, singing with her only a week before, seemed now like a fairy tale imprinted indelibly in the shelter of his mind, yet had been no more than a single shared tick of life's ever-moving clock.

The evening of the talent show had been pandemonium, the chapel filled to capacity, a raucous assembly laughing and shouting, frisky and effervescent with anticipation, throbbing up and down like a field of pistons. When introduced, Monte and Clare walked confidently to center stage to face an audience in bedlam as Charlie

Talbert, master of ceremonies for the night, gamboled off to one side in throes of a Highland jig, wildly clapping hands above his head.

All performers revel in that first moment of sweeping shock, the initial, dynamic rush of surging electric energy, cheers and screams and applause washing over them like floodwaters, raising tingles of exhilaration. Monte had turned to Clare to see her momentarily stunned, though smiling serenely. When she glanced up and clasped his arm, the crowd exploded in tumultuous appreciation as though sharing an impassioned bond. And the music worked; they meshed and the sound was good. They left the stage with satisfaction performers love to know and feel—affirmation the audience had not been cheated, nor had they disappointed themselves.

When the show was over, the Talberts had hosted a party for participants in their basement recreation room. After some hesitation when invited, Monte and Clare had accepted, riding together in his VW Bug. Food and fellowship were enjoyed, and offered an informal chance for Monte to acquire more knowledge of students and staff. Before anyone realized, the clock struck midnight, and most departed. The night had turned chilly, and Clare had worn only a light sweater. Reaching to the back seat, Monte produced a worn corduroy coat, once part of a treasured suit, and wrapped it round her shoulders.

Few words were spoken during the brief ride back to the Academy, each content to bask in quiet reverie. Her old Ford sedan waited in the lot below Main Hall, outlined in the eerie greenish glow of security lights. Monte told her to keep the coat until the following Wednesday. She expressed worry that he would be cold. He pronounced firmly that he never got cold. She accused him of making that up, and he said he never made things up. And she looked into his eyes as if searching for explanation, fearful of succeeding.

When they reached her car, she smiled pensively and said, "Well, thank you for the music, and the evening . . . and, of course, the coat."

Monte nodded, and for an imperceptible moment, she tokened discomfort, as though captured by some vaguely forbidding debate—the abstraction passing so quickly and without residue as not to have existed at all. And she drove off into the darkness, down the long hill and past the athletic field, taillights dissolving behind a row of thick hedges and shadowed buildings, and on to wherever she called home.

• • •

Journal: Saturday, October 11, 2:05 AM

Can't believe I'm still awake. Tried to sleep as soon as I got home but couldn't. Should be exhausted. Guess I'm too keyed up from the show and all the excitement. Just needed to write some things down while they're fresh.

What an exhilarating experience! And what a wonderful time. Monte was . . . well, I need to write more about that man after I've had time to think for a while, let impressions sort out. His coat is here on the bed with me now. Another story.

Sometimes, like tonight, I wonder why I have a journal if I don't write what I'm really thinking and feeling. Maybe I just don't know, or trust, what I think and feel. Or maybe it's because the feelings are so strange, and different, and new, and scary . . . But anyway, I'll probably not see him again except in passing. There's no reason to now.

Richard had a meeting and wasn't able to come to the show . . .

• • •

The third week of September, Monte had received a call from a friend not seen for over a year nor communicated with for almost six months. In a sense, they had grown up together on Thirteenth Street in Richmond, though his friend did not live there and they attended different schools and church. Circumstances of their initial meeting were due to a combination of fortuitous conditions unscripted and unlikely.

Arthur James Brooks was the first "colored" peer Monte had ever encountered and talked with in a way one does with playmates. Arthur, likewise, had never had a "white" friend. The setting was Richmond, summer of 1949, and both were almost seven. The nearest Black families lived blocks away, south of Hull Street, and, other than Saturday shopping or domestic service, never transgressed north of this unofficial line of demarcation; nor did whites, for any reason imaginable, cross to the south.

Arthur unexpectedly appeared three doors down from Monte's house one hot, humid morning, in front of the home of Lady Matilda Vanderpool-Pierpont, reverently referred to by residents as the "Matriarch of Thirteenth Street." Close to ninety, she claimed to be daughter-in-law of an ex-governor of the state and very wealthy. Her home, slowly deteriorating yet by far still the finest on the block, was nineteen-century Federal with English basement, constructed with oversized brick laid in unusual diamond patterns of weathered reds and salmon pinks, numerous large, multipaned windows fronting the façade.

Arthur was on the sidewalk at the foot of the steps, arms extended outward from his sides, wearing a new pair of roller skates, and appeared to be rooted to the pavement, afraid to move for fear of falling. When Monte asked why he was not gliding around as one would normally expect, Arthur admitted he had never skated before and no one had shown him how. Eyeing the polished and pristine glimmer of the new skates with envy, Monte volunteered, "I can show ya! It's easy as pie." His own pair, worn and damaged from constant use and lack of proper care, had become a teasing embarrassment.

At first reluctant, Arthur finally sat down and released the buckles. And no sooner had he done so than Monte promptly slid them on and sallied down the block and around the corner out of sight.

That his new acquaintance might be upset by his dalliance with the unblemished skates did not enter Monte's mind, for he was far more intent on zipping at high speed by a house on Semmes Avenue where Katie, classmate and current love of his life, resided. Sadly, Katie was unimpressed because Katie, after several swift passes, was not to be seen. "Gone to the playground," her mother said testily when Monte knocked and asked of her whereabouts. "With her boyfriend, Lionel." *Lionel Choo-choo Godwin*, Monte seethed, another classmate he detested and fought with every day before and after school.

Returning humiliated some minutes later, he found Arthur sitting dejectedly on the wide front steps of Lady Vanderpool-Pierpont's front porch, obviously unhappy, but glad to be reunited with his skates. He was a big lad for his age, heavier and taller than Monte, composed and observant. In short order the two fell into friendship neither had interest nor vocabulary to define, often the way of children after the awkward introductory moments are traversed.

Arthur's family had moved from Tennessee the year before, a distant and foreign land to Monte; and Arthur displayed discomfiting sadness when talking of it. But Monte knew nothing in those more halcyon days about moving and homesickness or missing mates and special places gone forever.

The tone of Arthur's skin intrigued and fascinated Monte—a beautiful, golden-brownish hue of strong coffee, tempered slightly in bright sunlight, and black as carbon in dimness of evening; Monte's own complexion never darker than anemic tea or a pale shade of tan on a summer's day, an eerie, chalky luminous at night. And then, amazing to a child mind, came the discovery that their palms, an almost rosy pink, were nearly the same when held together, though Arthur's were larger and stronger. Their hair, too, was curious, Arthur's dark as onyx and neatly woven, Monte's bleached to faded ivory and limp as twine. Week after week they gradually and haphazardly explored these mysteriously dissimilar features with childhood guilelessness perhaps only uncorrupted youth rendered possible, never value judging in their discoveries, merits of one against the other.

With a boy two years older named Vernon Southwood, they formed a trio of sorts and played together throughout their glorious summer holidays, venturing as far south as Hull Street when they had money, to the railroad yards north when brave, and the river beyond to swim when hot. Parents remained ignorant of their travels, saving the one anguish and the other punishment. At the end of summer, when schools reopened and they had to wash and say prayers and retire to bed before dark, the alliance disbanded, Vernon and Monte to one school, Arthur to another.

Arthur's mother, Monte learned incrementally through the years, was an elementary school teacher and graduate of Spelman College, supplementing meager wages during summer months and on Saturdays year-round by providing a multiplicity of services to elderly in need of care in their homes. In constant demand, she came with the highest recommendations and references.

While Lady Vanderpool-Pierpont, initially persnickety and autocratic, fussed and found fault, Mrs. Brooks quietly attended her duties with efficient dignity and aplomb. When not washing and cleaning, shopping and cooking, Mrs. Brooks read to the elderly woman—the Bible, poetry, novels, and biographies. Three months in the summer, from seven in the morning until six in the evening, Mondays through Saturdays, she patiently executed all requests demanded by the churlish dowager. In evenings and on Sundays, a neighbor woman came. Within two weeks, Arthur's mother and her charge became as close as two individuals in their respective positions could, a relationship enduring until Mrs. Vanderpool-Pierpont's death years later.

Arthur's father, a WWII Navy veteran, worked in the circulation department of one of Richmond's largest newspapers. Three children comprised the family: a girl of thirteen, Arthur, and a younger brother, five. During summer months, the girl cared for the youngest while Arthur ostensibly went along with his mother to assist in her work—though generally excused himself to play or pore through the collection of books in her employer's library.

From that first summer and throughout their teenage years, Arthur, Vernon, and Monte forged a rare union. To Monte, they were the siblings he never had. Now, twenty years later, Arthur Brooks had a master's degree in American history with minor in Latin and was searching for another job. For four years he had taught at an elite private boy's school in upper New York State. Unfortunately, the school had suddenly closed, victim of declining enrollment and dearth of wealthy donors.

"So, you've had enough of those Yankees, have you?" Monte joked, knowing the quick wit of Arthur would come back with proper rejoinder.

"Not at all," he snickered. "I'm one of 'em now, a convert, a real Yankee Doodle."

Monte visualized the giant of a man, gentle and jovial as a teddy bear. There was none other in the world with whom Monte felt as close or had as much affection. Their relationship had never wavered or staled, and they could, as real friends always can, take up conversation after months or years as though chatting every day. His snickering was legendary, and hearing it once again after so many months almost brought tears of joyful nostalgia to Monte's eyes. Arthur seldom actually laughed, generally displaying a controlled Southern reserve and expressing his humorous side with more subtle outbursts. He had honed his patented snickering to a fine art, and Monte reveled to hear it once again.

Arthur hoped to begin new employment as soon as possible, he said, and had heard from Vernon that Monte was presently semi-connected with the Academy in Talerton and might arrange a meeting with appropriate staff for an interview.

"No problem," Monte assured him, and asked, "When can you come?"

"Most any time. I'm in Richmond now, visiting my folks. I was wondering about next week or the week after, if that's possible."

"Okay. Leave it with me and I'll make some initial contacts and get back to you in a day or two."

And so, Arthur Brooks came for an appointment with Brad Fletcher and the Personnel Office on the first Wednesday in October, and was given a contract the same day.

CHAPTER FIVE

BY MID-OCTOBER, MONTE and Booker were happily emboldened—in fact, somewhat overwhelmed—by success of the part-time work program: twenty-two students employed in fifteen different stores and businesses in Talerton, with applications from a dozen more enrolled in the Job Readiness class, awaiting additional job openings. Community reception had been amazingly positive, as had enthusiasm from boys and girls participating. Booker, at times inclined to grow disgruntled by the slightest difficulty, was in almost daily high spirits, seeing problems as mere inconveniences to be summarily slain with his sword of rejuvenated optimism, to Monte's relief.

With class schedules and other duties, Booker shouldered most daily maintenance over the enterprise, given that Monte could normally be at the school Wednesdays only. Very soon into the program they realized each student would have to be screened and prepared thoroughly to minimize need for excessive supervision and micromanagement while on the job. Problems had occurred rarely, one case a health issue and two involving tardiness. The former had been replaced and latter reassigned to the Job Readiness class and their employment slots given to two others on the waiting list.

Transportation continued to be a major hurdle, with only a limited number of placements close enough for walking. Others utilized cabs, the ultimate backup, which ate heavily into the allotted budget, even though the program received a small discount from the taxi company. Talerton had no public bus system, and so far only a few volunteer drivers from the community had been enlisted.

• • •

Three new students enrolled in the Blind Department during the first sublime weeks of October: a boy and a girl in the Elementary Department, and a high school senior named Caroline Lehman. Amongst other news, Booker confidentially announced to Monte that he was beginning his annual fall diet, preparing for November and December holidays he referred to as "glutton season"—somewhat, Monte gleaned, in a spirit of gastronomic juxtaposition to the sacrificial weeks of Lent. His stated goal was to lose ten pounds, declaring this ambition at lunch while ingesting a gargantuan chunk of chocolate éclair. The brief part of Booker's proclamation Monte could interpret swelled with resolve of a votary.

• • •

The third week of October, on a chilly Monday morning, Clarence Gladstone went strangely absent from his first-period Classic Literature class, not seen or heard from by anyone. An ad hoc search party quickly organized by Jellyroll Jackson and a few others expected the worst. Less than a half hour later the teacher was discovered sitting in his car in the lower parking lot, snuggly imprisoned by a malfunctioning seat belt—a recent innovation—which could not be coaxed, threatened, or engineered to release.

While one student ran to alert the Maintenance Department, other students gathered around the vehicle, keeping the perpetually jocular teacher entertained. After repeated efforts to coerce the frozen buckle open, one of the maintenance men, having better things to do and growing progressively ill tempered, brazenly pulled out a knife and, before anyone could intervene with less destructive ideas, sliced through the tough nylon belt, and Gladstone was freed, somewhat similar to his recent rescue from a filing cabinet. Word of his entrapment spread rapidly, as news did at the Academy, and was the major topic of conversation and jokes through lunch break.

Wednesday of that same week, Booker had an early dental appointment. Complicating matters, at ten that morning the Academy Board of Visitors had requested—more a command—a full report on and detailed explanation of the new student work program. Rumors, according to Principal Fletcher, were that some members had voiced reservation about the advisability of the project, fearful it might supplant time better spent on academic endeavors, resulting in poorer classroom performance and lower grades. Funding, always a matter of concern to the board, was another issue, even though the bulk of financial support presently came from the state agency.

During the previous week Monte had researched questions of classroom participation and grades of work-program students and drawn up charts to demonstrate his findings. Other graphs showed sources of funding and how monies were being spent. In contrast, Booker felt confidently dispassionate about the ordeal of facing the board, lending a measure of assurance to his younger cohort. They were to meet in Thelma Thompson's office in Main Hall at ten minutes to ten and go with their materials to the large, plush conference room where the board would be assembled.

Earlier that morning, Monte had found his corduroy coat neatly draped over the back of a chair in Booker's inner office, small blue envelope pinned to the lapel. Anxiously tearing it open and holding the note close to his nose in the dimness, he read, *Mr. Scott, Thank you for the loan of your coat. It kept me warm all the way home. My car heater is useless. Coffee (and maybe cookies) will be available whenever you have time. Clare Augsburg.*

Having two hours before the meeting and desiring to take advantage of Inner Sanctum solitude, Monte made calls and wrote up case notes from the previous two days' fieldwork. A little after nine, her invitation before him on the desk with words refusing to leave his mind, he rose and made his way to the Baldwin Hall basement. Peering from the doorway into the classroom, he saw four students working in the kitchen area: one girl at a table mixing a thin batter and another holding a spoon to stir something in a small pan on the stove, while Jellyroll Jackson carefully diced carrots at the counter and Joshua Blandenburg, his long frame bent low, searched inside the refrigerator. Clare moved carefully amongst the students. Enthralled with a tableau of her happily at work, he stood silently and watched, accepting after a moment or two that she was fully occupied and needed no additional interruptions.

Surreptitious withdrawal could easily have been accomplished had it not been for Withrow Mulligan. Surging full throttle down the stairs, the boy dashed across the narrow hallway and plowed a battering-ram head into Monte's unguarded torso, marking the second time the teen had slammed into him. Staggering backward and fighting to maintain balance, Monte reeled drunkenly into the DLS classroom, amazed at the strength of momentum and force Withrow could generate. Though traumatized momentarily, Monte took in a fleeting snapshot of Mulligan falling heavily to his knees in the doorway, blasting out a high-pitched cry of "Son of a bitch! What in hell was that?"

Clare and students spun at the sound of collision, and all might have been less disastrous had not Monte's long legs entangled those of Joshua, in process of delicately balancing a sizeable bowl of tomato sauce across the room, resulting in both men tumbling and spinning out of control in a flurry of extremities, reaching, grabbing, twisting, and buckling, finally sprawling onto a kitchen table, tipping it over sideways and hoisting the poor, shrieking girl's bowl of watery batter in the air where it melded with flying sheets of thick red sauce, forming a pasty, aerial amalgamation and anointing the two young men splayed on the floor with a viscous layer of glutinous pink slime, all in a matter of mere seconds.

Lying in the muck, Monte realized with strange lucidity that no quietly graceful retreat would now be possible.

Clare rushed over, ready to offer sympathy but obviously inclining very much to laughter, and said, "Are you all okay?"

Little dignity can be found prone on a floor after being bowled over by a middle schooler, and even less dignity when covered in tomato sauce and pancake batter. But Monte managed to smile and croaked, "I'm fine. Just a slight accident." To the disorderly figure of Withrow stooped in the doorway, Monte raised his head and barked, "Are you all right, Mulligan?"

The dazed boy gripped the doorframe for support and muttered a dejected, "Yes," expectant that certain doom would soon follow.

Slightly confounded but assuring Clare and Monte he was unhurt, Joshua removed himself from atop Monte and offered a sticky hand up. In the hollow silence which followed, everyone confused as to what to do next, at the counter Jellyroll calmly returned to his carrot dicing, crooning nonchalantly, "That was soooo cool." With tension broken, all smiled, then chuckled, then escalated into roars of laughter. Excepting Withrow, who, fearing the worst, mumbled meekly to Clare, "Does this mean I'm not expelled?"

After the jovial interlude subsided, Joshua said, long arms hanging to drip by his sides, "I'd better go back to the dorm and change clothes, Miss Augsburg." She sent him off at once, a wet, rosy trail marking his wake.

Taking inventory of his own condition, Monte discovered his face, hair, and hands, sport coat, pants, shirt, tie, and even shoes and socks were all stained with a thick substance beginning to congeal into crusty, rust-colored layers. The Board of Visitors, Monte noted, would convene in less than thirty minutes, and once told of the meeting, Clare moved decisively.

"First, you need to get out of those things and into something else. There might be something in the clothes closet you can use temporarily."

In a few minutes she came back holding up a well-worn, washed-out pair of bib overalls and an orange polo shirt. "I'm afraid choices close to your size are limited, but you've got to wear something. We can wipe off your shoes, I think, and you can go without socks."

Down the hallway in the boys' restroom, he cleaned up as best he could and changed, soon returning wearing his new outfit and depositing the soiled clothing with Clare. Staring gloomily, squinting and screwing up her mouth and brow, she considered his slovenly state. The baggy overalls were several sizes too large in the seat and waist and at least six or eight inches too short in length, starkly displaying chalk-white ankles and sinewy lower calves. The shirt, tight as sausage skin, clashed loudly with the pale-blue denim.

Clare put a hand to her mouth, pondering his figure like a piece of not-so-fine art, then shook her head with resolve. "I have an idea. Wait a minute."

She rooted into the clothes closet again and came out with a large, blue, plastic raincoat. "Try putting this on. It'll cover up those clothes, at least partially."

Perhaps sound in principle, in reality the coat was made for a much smaller person, barely covering his thighs, sleeves reaching just beyond his elbows. Not wanting to sound ungrateful, he murmured, "I don't know, Clare. This looks kind of . . . uh . . ."

Options at this juncture were few, and the clock was ticking. Grabbing at any straw, he asked Clare if she knew how many board members were blind. She knew of only three. Given there were twelve on the board, plus Dr. Mullens, Monte opined with phlegmatic capitulation that he was "dead cert" to be noticed. Clare concurred, gathering her face remorsefully.

The sudden flash of horror spreading across Thelma Thompson's expression when Monte came through her office door confirmed his worst fears. Her heretofore positive opinion of him seemed to shatter into a thousand shards of disbelief. For a moment he thought she might scream in terror like a child at the sight of a menacing B-movie alien from space. Thankfully, with years of experience dealing with weird situations and people, she welled up with courageous fortitude. Rising slowly from her chair, she stammered, "What . . . what in the world happened to you, Monte Scott?"

Booker, seated sedately and holding a folder, jumped to his feet, alerted by Thelma's tone that something was amiss. Monte scarcely knew where to begin, so merely said, "I know this looks crazy, but there's a simple explanation. Well, not exactly simple, but . . . I can explain. Well, I can tell you what happened."

Thelma waited behind her desk, wide eyes alert and disconcerted. Unable to contain himself, Booker exclaimed, "What the hell's going on? I hear a crinkling noise when you move, Scott, and you smell like tomato sauce and plastic pancakes!"

With only five minutes before the board meeting, Monte quickly explained his current condition and asked pleadingly, "What do you think we should do?"

Thelma sank down, deep in thought. Ramrod straight as though catatonic, like a wax image, Booker hummed tunelessly. All hope of viable answer was slipping away when all at once Thelma rose back to her feet and said decisively, "Just go in there as you are, Monte! Tell them . . . just apologize and tell them what happened!" Sighing heavily, she added, "In a few minutes, maybe they'll forget what you look like."

Her manner had grown hopefully assertive, though neither Monte nor Booker believed her proposed solution plausible. Sitting back down, Thelma dashed off a few lines on a notepad, tore off the sheet, folded it, and handed the message to Booker, whispering, "Give this to Dr. Mullens as soon as you go in." And with morbidly dubious expression, she wished them luck.

The trek down the long corridor to the conference room was interminable. Halfway, Monte stopped and turned to Booker. "Look, sir, I want you to know how sorry I am. If I've put the work program at risk because of this . . . mess, I'll resign."

"And how do you think that's going to help?" Booker snapped. "Look, Scott! We started this together and we'll finish it together. You must look ridiculous," he scolded mildly, "but you've still got your brains and your vocal chords, so put them to work. Be composed and professional and show some guts. And shut up about that resigning shit."

The thick conference room door was closed, no sound to be heard. Booker tapped, and a stony masculine voice filtered through the ancient pine: "Come in."

And there they sat, ten dignified men and three courtly women rigidly upright along a beautiful dark walnut table perhaps twenty feet in length. Planted at the far end was Dr. Mullens, tensely stoic, while at the near end posed a humorless, professorial man with wispy fringe of grey hair circling ear to ear on the back of his otherwise bald head, gold-framed spectacles with little round lenses firmly affixed on a fiercely hawkish nose. Each man wore a dark-grey, three-piece suit, and white shirt with solid tie, the women all in tailored, long-sleeved tweed outfits, two with contemporary cloche hats and one with a felt bycoket pierced by a large peacock feather. Monte stood back in the doorway, and Booker, quickly locating Dr. Mullens, handed him Thelma's note.

An easel for charts and graphs was set to one side, and as Monte slowly came into view carrying his materials, a reflexive, collective gasp spread throughout the large room, a kind of strangulating death rattle and constricted wheeze, complexions blanching and eyes and mouths agape in stupefied astonishment. With the assemblage paralyzed en masse, austere as tombstones, staring with a kind of personal agnostic repudiation of what was before their eyes, Monte awkwardly peeled off the clinging blue raincoat and, finding no handy place to hang it, folded it onto the floor behind the easel. Moving robotically, self-consciously stiff, orange shirt and bib overalls fully revealed, a renewed and accelerated heave of choking, rumbling squawks emanated from the august body, circling the table like some undertone of fanatical Gregorian chant gone amok.

Booker stood beside him, smiling with natural geniality as Monte cleared his throat, ready to explain his unseemly appearance. However, before any word could be uttered, Dr. Mullens rose from his chair in a mixture of anger and distress, and managed to say with tight hoarseness, "Is this some kind of joke, Mr. Scott? Mr. Booker?"

Board members shook their heads in judgmental wonder, hissing to one another, affirming the unacceptable affront of which the superintendent spoke and to which they were being subjected—the very dignity of the Academy profaned and desecrated by this lewd mockery.

Gathering his wits, Monte tentatively stepped forward to offer explanations when, as a steadfast guardian angel, Booker masterfully interceded and in a voice not unlike Lord Nelson at Trafalgar, firmly unintimidated by the host of steely, challenging guns aimed upon him—or, in the present case, flinty eyes and faces—said not, "*England expects every man will do his duty!*" but perhaps just as bravely, "Gentlemen and ladies, we come in humble apology to each of you and to the excellence and propriety of this board."

He paused, as solemnly commanding as a temple priest, rising to the occasion with a certain theatrical gusto and tantalizing control. Continuing, he propounded as though stirred by the rhapsodic soul of a gifted orator, "We intend no joke, folly, or lampoonery this morning. Mr. Scott, who thankfully was not injured seriously"—Booker lifted an arm to point at Monte, face girding a grim thankfulness—"was involved in a freakish accident just prior to this meeting, resulting in ruination of his clothing and personal possessions, a tragic action not in any way his fault.

"He could easily have absented himself from this gathering with legitimate cause, but instead chose to come humbly, yea, subserviently, in these shabby garments loaned to him from our school's sparse and inadequate clothes closet. He chose to be here and risk ridicule and embarrassment because our student work program is so important and vital, and he, ladies and gentlemen, is the heart and soul behind it. I say without hesitation and unequivocally, there would be no student work program without his dedication and leadership."

The board was now fully in Booker's grasp, dissolving into soft attentiveness. Monte stared at the floor and warded off a sudden bout of shivering brooked by the undeniable reality of being displayed metaphorically naked to strangers who held the power to crush their project. Dr. Mullens reseated himself with disconcerted reluctance and slyly unfolded the note from Thelma, reading it quickly and then slipping the paper surreptitiously into a pocket as Booker went on.

"You graciously invited us to come today to share information about this project and to answer your questions and concerns, and with your kind permission, that is what we are prepared to do now."

Mullens rather urgently stood again, and to the assembly, all of whom turned to hear him, said, "I would, uh, respectfully recommend that we continue with our meeting as planned, if all are agreed, Mister Chairman?" To which the chairman replied, after glancing at each member and receiving consent, "So ordered. Let us proceed. Mr. Booker? Mr. Scott? You may begin when ready. The floor is yours."

For the next two hours Booker and Monte fenced and jousted with their examiners, presenting their case in great detail, with charts, graphs, statistics, and thorough and colorful overviews and vignettes of every component of the program. At times, the board swayed positively, at others yawed unconvinced and skeptical. They asked a host of questions and, when felt merited, made harsh comments and observations. Monte's histrionic vision was of sailing in a small boat on a raging ocean, storms falling upon their craft with merciless fury, the boat tossed and lifted to be cast down in hungry green troughs, leaking and battered, towers of foamy, white-crested waves rising high above, creating devouring mouths of brutal indifference.

Reality was not nearly so barbarous. At length the board gravitated much less threatening and ill-disposed than Booker and Monte expected, even to positions of acceptance and support. One of the women asked if she might accompany Mr. Booker or Mr. Scott to visit a few of their employers and observe a student or students on the job, to which they readily agreed, Booker extending invitation to every board member. Another man, fitted with dark glasses and assumed visually impaired, said, "Wish they'd had a program like this when I was in school here. Would have been good experience for later on. Yes, sir."

As Monte gathered his materials and raincoat after adjournment, another woman, perfect image of Miss Marple, approached and said with grandmotherly concern, "I so hope you can get some decent clothes back soon. I felt so sorry for you during the entire meeting, you poor, poor thing. You must be so uncomfortable. I do believe you're shivering."

Monte thanked her for the sentiment, assuring the elderly lady his clothes were being attended to as they spoke. She went on to confide that he put her in mind of her youngest grandson, now in college, and that personally she thought the idea of boys and girls having job training was wonderful. Moving closer and placing a small, wizened hand on his arm, she related in whispers that the previous three governors had appointed her to the board for three consecutive terms, even though, unbeknownst to them, she had voted in each election for their opponents. And now, being past lunchtime, she professed to being a little tired and hoped a decent luncheon had been prepared at Dr. Mullens' home, unlike the last one, when she had been served pizza and some cheesy things on plastic plates with paper napkins.

Smiling like a Cheshire cat, Booker courteously disengaged Monte from the lady, and they made their way back to the Inner Sanctum.

Exhausted by the governing administration's gauntlet, they flagged into chairs, lazing without words for several minutes, arranging thoughts and impressions of the past hours. Monte stared at the ceiling hovering hazy and distant above, his head uncomfortably crooked on the back of his hard chair. Booker, who looked to be sleeping, stirred at length with a sort of sniggering, chortling sound, and said in poor falsetto, "I felt so sorry for you during the whole meeting, you poor, poor thing."

"Well," Monte retorted, "what about that bit about the 'heart and soul of the program.' Where did that garbage come from?"

"It's true; you are!" Booker exhorted. "And I'd say it helped get us off the hook and win some votes to boot."

Musing, Monte asked, "What do you think was in that note Mrs. Thomson wrote to Dr. Mullens?"

Booker grinned, then said conspiratorially, "Of course, I don't know for sure. But I strongly suspect it may have been a warning that he'd better treat us nice, or there'd be . . . consequences."

"You don't mean . . . ?"

"Oh, yes. No hanky-panky, but twisted round her little pinky." He grinned. "Everybody thinks Mullens is head cheese at the Academy. Truth is, Thelma's the backroom super. He's more of a titular head—the executive image of authority. She runs the school, no question about it. Knows where all the bodies are buried and where all the skeletons are stored. Everything goes through Thelma." Booker laughed, leaning forward, and said seriously, "You, Monte Scott, have a very good and loyal friend in the front office."

That afternoon the Board of Visitors would meet privately to discuss the "Students Entering Training Program," as the project was officially called. In theory, they could jeopardize continuation by recommending against it, though Mullens and Fletcher could, also in theory, appeal such a decision and throw their weight in support.

At the moment, neither Booker nor Monte knew what to expect, but both were inclined to think a positive vote probable. One impressive point both had noted during the meeting, reaping a plethora of positive head nods and encouraging comments from the board, was that students in the work program were showing marked improvement in grades and classroom participation and assignments. Another point, particularly galling to Booker, had also ironically worked in their favor. Marlon Danforth reportedly had allies on the board, and his name was emblazoned on the title page of the so-called original proposal.

• • •

Journal: Wednesday, October 15, 10:20 PM

If I live to be a hundred, the vision of Monte dressed in those awful clothes will still be in my mind's eye. So hilarious and pitiful and helpless. But thankfully his meeting went well. Hope he didn't notice how much I wanted to hug him . . . or maybe I hope he did.

Some guys would have been furious with Withrow, but Monte took it in stride. I've developed an admiration and respect for him as counselor and person . . . and friend. Only wish I could read what's behind those piercing green eyes. Or maybe not.

Richard's been at a conference this week . . .

• • •

Arnold Schnellich had a new wristwatch and was showing it off around the school annoyingly. Heavy and thick, the dial was big as the top of a soda can and imprinted with large black numerals. One had to wonder how the lad's scrawny little arm held up under the weight. Extra holes, he pointed out to Monte, had been punched in the leather band, allowing for thinness of his wrist. Most hoped the novelty would soon wear off, given that Arnold regularly paraded to and from classes with running commentary of elapsed time.

One morning Ramona heard him in the distance, shuffling along from the far end of Perkins Hall, a squeaky, nasal voice announcing, "Eight o'clock and three minutes." Then, as he got closer, "Eight o'clock and four minutes." And so on, as he passed by, head bent, peering at the dial and receding through the doors into Cameron Hall for his math class.

• • •

For Monte Scott, Anne Walden's house party was tedious until the end, and then a little bewildering. The art teacher, met only briefly in Booker's office Monte's second week at the school, had extended a most appealing invitation. Her two-story townhouse in the far northern regions of Talerton was tastefully furnished with a scattering of blond Scandinavian pieces well suited for the open, airy floor plan. To the rear, through sliding glass doors, a large patio area provided perfect space for a charcoal grill manned by three preppy guys nursing bottles of beer and laughing uproariously. A wide and lengthy living and dining area, layered with loud strains of stereo disco, tussled and swayed with an unrestrained agglomeration of young men and women dancing and prattling dementedly, concurrently swilling everything from cocktails to bourbon in flowing abundance.

She welcomed him with a warm kiss on the cheek, smelling of roses and stunning in a short black dress, a sensual work of art cut to excite male libidos and scorch women with envy. Scanning the room for any familiar face, Monte spotted only Elizabeth Blanchard, the music teacher, and Arthur Brooks, his friend and the new history teacher.

Through a maze of bodies, he grabbed a beer from a tub of ice by the patio door, trying to remember why he had agreed to come. He did not want to believe the short black dress culpable, though could not deny that it was a reasonably sufficient place to start. As he watched, she skimmed around the room, floating with graceful flamboyance, rendering equally and individually to all her guests, the perfect hostess in her social element.

Elizabeth stood with a well-fed man in gaudy, lime-green leisure suit and spotless white shoes. She introduced him as her husband, Ted, who over beers soon eagerly revealed himself to be an assistant bank manager. A rather narrowly focused five-minute exchange ensued, centered primarily on current long-term interest rates, home-improvement loans, and no-fee checking accounts. Monte, unreasonably, was never asked about his own endeavors, and soon wandered off as if suddenly distressed and confused.

Arthur had taken up residence with an affable circle of men and women in a sheltered corner of the kitchen and was, by his relaxed pose and expression, very much at ease and enjoying himself. Anne had made a point to invite the new teacher. Catching his eye from a distance, Monte raised his bottle in greeting, and Arthur winked and raised his own.

The three designated chefs staggered in a few minutes later with trays of hamburgers and hot dogs, and everyone began to fill plates, perching helter-skelter on any available surface. Monte joined a more sedate group at a picnic table on the patio, and, after eating and listening to conversation, returned inside to exercise an accustomed party ritual.

Affairs such as Anne's soiree, he had discovered, often decreed an unchanging dynamic and assembled ethos that a segment of attendees would be relegated to the fringes of any action, positioned vaguely on the periphery of a small, unified group, bidding constituency and engagement, edging ever closer yet flippantly disregarded as though invisible. The unwritten rules prescribed that these human ghost ships would optimistically wander from one fellowship to another, grinning and faking merriment in utter ignorance of whatever topic was being discussed or whatever joke was being told, catching only the odd word or fragment of discourse. Inevitably, having been shunned a number of times, these stray, transparent souls would mope off, seeking a quiet seat in some uninhabited corner, evincing impressions of disinterested independence or even aloof superiority, waiting in vain for the party to come to them.

Monte's ritual, properly exercised, required a careful yet subtle survey of the floor, identifying rebuffed sad sacks, then zooming in and forcing company upon them. Most overtures were voraciously welcomed, some not. One could tell within seconds whether to move on or stay and make a new friend.

Numerous solitary specimens exhibited feasibility this evening. Zeroing in on a young man slouched into an incompliant art deco armchair, squinting into the depths of a glass of amber liquid, Monte spoke with lively camaraderie: "Enjoying the party?" The lonely soul raised befuddled, drowsy eyes, as one might after major surgery, and made a hopeless effort to speak, managing only to gurgle a few incomprehensible syllables before withdrawing once again to wallow in never-never land.

Next, Monte approached a statuesque, fleshy woman, her back resting against the wall, one arm folded tightly to her full-figured body funneled liquid-like into a strapless, polka-dot flare dress. Sipping from a cocktail glass held by her free arm, she emoted delightedly over his greeting, launching without prompting into a string of unrelated issues, near as he could follow involving a broad range of negative views on auto repair shops and environmental virtues of organic gardening. Listening raptly for a few minutes, thoughtfully admiring a more-than-adequate cleavage, he then excused himself as she began a complex oration bearing on the daily adventures of her five cats.

About to sidle up to a short man with flattop and heavy, horn-rimmed glasses, Monte felt a hand fall heavily on his shoulder as a voice sniveled, "Well, rehab man, how did you inveigle an invite to the party?"

Tone and tenor reeked with astringent coldness as Monte turned to face the voice. The young man was at least six and a half feet tall, uncomfortably close, topping Monte imperiously by two or three inches. A self-satisfied, icy chuckle followed, giving little quarter for reply. "I've seen you around. Gotta be another of Booker's ninety-day wonders. Where does he find you guys?"

Absent the menacing smirk, he might have fashioned a certain Byronic charm and appeal—swarthy, unblemished complexion, sharp, aquiline features, and deep-brown eyes. Moving back a half step, Monte regarded the face with relaxed amusement, meeting the stare with a muted gaze of his own. Just at that moment, a sturdy, athletic woman holding a glass of red wine joined them and edged close to the man's side, murmuring wispily, "Hello, boys." Tall, mildly ruddy cheeks, hair the color of straw and similarly spiky, her hazel eyes tended to infiltrate and mock as though endowed with primacy, reading one's thoughts for purely teasing pleasure.

The man goggled at the top of her head, slipping a long arm loosely over her shoulders, mouthing with a somewhat ribald inflection, "This lovely creature is my wife, rehab man, Erin Celinski. Isn't she a yummy morsel to behold?"

In turn, she giggled, raising her face to his, "And this handsome hunk is my husband, Thorpe Nowland."

Glibly, in a jittery, robust manner, Celinski carried the conversation, revealing that both taught at the Academy, expounding their job data for the next ten minutes, adding another five on Anne's lovely townhouse. Thorpe grew bored and excused himself to wander the crowded room, dropping a huge hand on other unsuspecting shoulders.

A few minutes later a light punch on the arm revealed Arthur standing beside Monte. "I thought only the elite were being invited to the party," he snickered. "But here you are."

"What's the word meaning a higher status than elite?" Monte asked, wrinkling his face as if in deep contemplation.

"Don't know," Arthur replied glibly. "But I can give you a few for lower status." Sweeping his dark eyes about the room, he dampened a yawn with the back of his hand and moaned very softly, "I'm going to slip out. It's been nice, but . . . you know. Gotta get my beauty sleep. Lord's day tomorrow. You staying for a while?"

Monte nodded. "Yeah, for a while, I think.

By midnight the party had cleared to a few stragglers either too drunk to navigate or simply reluctant to abandon the waning fellowship. Earlier, Anne had asked Monte if he could stay and help with cleanup, so while she collected and shoveled remaining guests out the front door, he gathered plates, cups, and glasses for washing. She changed into jeans and sweatshirt, and they joined forces in a kitchen sink of hot soapy water, hips bumping and rubbing sensuously as they worked.

With implements cleaned and stowed away in cabinets, trash bins emptied and furniture back in place, they strolled out to the patio with coffee. Moist night air was pleasantly chilly, and aside from hums of distant traffic and faint sounds of a barking dog, all was serenely quiet. Comfortably reclined in patio chairs, Anne spoke, her voice rippling softly. "I'm glad you came tonight, Monte. I've been . . . wanting to get to know you better."

Lifting his mug leisurely, he sipped a minute taste of hot brew, illegible eyes fixed speculatively on hers, and said without smiling, "I'm glad too." She waited, expectant of more, and he added, "You have some crazy friends . . . and give nice parties."

Gripping her cup as a warmer in both hands, reflected illumination shimmered across the pale outline of her face. With words light as eiderdown, she whispered, "It's quite late to be driving back to Rivanleigh, don't you think? Perhaps . . . you should stay."

Through thick opacity of the night, the near absoluteness of her welled up and hovered in devilish mystery, intoxicating his mind and rendering a flash of weak, unbidden appeal once given prayerfully by Saint Augustine: "Lord, make me pure, but not yet."

CHAPTER SIX

INSIDE THE GREY ENVELOPE lying on his chair in the Inner Sanctum was a large peanut butter cookie and note reading, *To help sustain you. Coffee available upon request. DLS Dept.* He drifted one finger over the writing as though it were braille, then lifted the cookie to his nose and breathed deeply.

Badly, achingly Monte wanted to go and find her, despite the guilt, the inappropriateness, the sheer wrongness of motive. Yet he—they—had done nothing, would do or say nothing. Her strength of character and foundation of ethic would never entertain even thought of trespass. And whatever sense of morality he might cling to would forbid it, if only for her sake. She was fashioned too pure, too precious, too perfectly created to be sullied by a fallen world and past that drenched his soul in failure and weakness. Yet she would vehemently deny the burden of honor he placed upon her; humility would dismiss and deny it. Nonetheless, angelic visions comforted that such a one as she could walk the earth in guise of flesh and blood, and lay healing hands of peace and joy upon those she daily touched.

The drive from Talerton to Rivanleigh Sunday early morning had been longer and more arduous than usual, immersed with mental wanderings, not of recent realities of Anne Walden but rather constant images of Clare. Childishly he counted the days since he had last seen her, then counted the weeks since they first met. Calculation seemed to tickle some useless curiosity but ultimately told him nothing and served no purpose, other than perhaps to keep him awake in the bleak hours before dawn. The obvious solution taunted him: shun her, deflect contact, employ taciturn rudeness if necessary. Lingering in this swamp of pointlessness would only mount additional distress. No good could come of it.

Meantime, regimens of self-restraint and adherence to blatant facts would condition his attitudes. *She is married* would become his guiding mantra. *She belongs with someone else, loves and shares life with another person—no doubt a fine, devoted man.* Certainly she would welcome the commitment, freed from distraction or any fallacy of temptation. Still, there lingered this undeniable foreboding of loss, possibilities wiped clean. Would he ever look at her without enduring stabs of painful longing? Accept her simply as colleague and friend? Chat, laugh, and joke, then separate to private, personal worlds, discarding remnants of sorrow and regret? And put aside, forget, a soft late-summer day beneath a giant oak tree?

His father's philosophy would have labeled him a ridiculous fool; rational persons did not experience love in mere minutes. In fact, for the old man love was superfluous. The key element in a relationship, he had insisted, was a sort of dispassionate "compatibility." Only in songs and movies and romance novels did one encounter what often is called "love at first sight." Having naught against compatibility or other principles his father had tried to teach him, Monte accepted what he was told.

Until that hour he met Clare Augsburg and, for the first time in his life, discovered an undeniably broader and deeper truth.

• • •

Booker's slamming the phone down jerked Monte back to immediacy. "We have a situation with two students over at Lambert's." In recent weeks there had been but a few minor problems. This one, he said, sounded potentially serious. They left right away, and en route Booker filled in details.

Lambert and Son, fruit and vegetable distributor, was housed in an old three-story brick warehouse a few blocks from downtown. The oldest section of Talerton by decades, the area dated to the early nineteenth century, five or six blocks of mostly red brick structures interspersed with several iron fronts, all laid out along a major rail line, in years past quartering an aggregation of wagon makers, slaughterhouses, tanneries, metal fabricators, and lumber mills.

Aging sepia pictures Monte had seen from those harsh, germinal days resurrected realism to the bustling streets and alleys. Blurred tangles of horses and wagons and men; dapper gentlemen standing aside, daintily observing, donned in proper coats and derby hats; gory, dark-stained smocks wrapped on thickly muscled, sweating torsos; brawny, robust men, black and white, brown and yellow, stripped to the waist and bent, struggling mightily, backs and necks rippling, rolling thundering hogsheads and barrels across loading docks and cobbled streets, arms and necks stout as gnarly tree limbs; air thickly infused by sweet scents of bright leaf and burley; heavy lathers of man and beast, leavened with muck and dung, leather and straw; mayhem of tumultuous bedlam and brawling commerce.

And one could stare at the brittle, grainy photographs and hear a constancy of screams and shouts and neighs and whinnies, thuds and crashes and throbs and pounding of freight and lumber, bales and crates of cotton and tobacco; clatters of iron-banded wagon wheels dancing and recoiling combatively against stone and brick; shrill whistles and clanging bells of massive locomotives coughing black clouds of cinders and smoke, roiling in volcanic eruption, coarse as obsidian sand, layering the sky, unnumbered tons of iron and steel shaking the ground in tremulous, pulsating cadence, tantrums of steaming vapor, chugging and drifting in ponderance to rest in moorings of worn and oily platforms.

Though many of the same buildings remained, the scene a century and a half later was notably dissimilar. Activity and noise persisted, more measured and less chaotic and messy, yet still with an air of urgency. Trucks came and went in sequence from loading docks like restless suckling newborns nestled to a mother's breast, feeding hunger until sated, then moving on. Others, laden with goods, disgorged their cargos box by box, stack by stack, forklifts and hand trucks hurriedly weaving in brash, contorted patterns, scurrying back and forth, extracting wares and goods with robotic, heartbeat precision.

Wilson Lambert met them in a hectic and stuffy third-floor office, a large, undivided space with tall windows overlooking the street, bottom panels swung widely open in hope of freshening air pervaded with leafy, organic aromas, a cornucopian ambience of fruit and vegetable produce, acrid and earthy. Women dominated, a few in unvaried haste along the aisles, others in hunched captivity at a half dozen desks covered in folders, invoices, catalogs, paper trays, and clutter, fingers flying blindly on typewriters and adding machines, heads pivoting in mechanized cadence. Grey and green filing cabinets lined one entire wall, another partially covered with bulletin boards plastered with schedules, regulations, and esoteric notices, alongside dozens of clipboards hanging like unfinished sketches on row upon row of nails.

He was probably sixty, solidly built with greyish hair combed straight back from a broad, furrowed forehead. A harried, nervous manner, stiffly clumsy, conveyed inveterate intolerance of small talk and social graces.

"I hated to call you, Mr. Booker, but we may have a problem and thought best not to put it off." His eyes wandered, unnervingly stealthy, while he rested the tail of his suit coat and broad derriere against a desk, arms folded, his breathing shallow and constricted, seemingly unbothered by incessant staccato noise streaming from behind him.

After introducing Monte, Booker asked with concern about specifics. Two students working two hours on weekdays and six to eight hours on Saturdays were employed in the warehouse, performing mostly manual labor—stacking boxes and crates on docks or in storage areas and coolers, loading and unloading trucks, keeping floors clear of debris. Previous weekly reports had been satisfactory.

"The trouble is—" Lambert cleared his throat loudly, putting a belated fist to his mouth. One of the closer women looked up from her work and smiled at Monte mysteriously. "We've been losing inventory," he fretted. "Maybe a box or two of oranges here, a crate of apples there, not huge amounts, but enough to be noticeable when tallied, and more than can be accounted from shrinkage. That's throwaway stuff, rotten and damaged items."

One of Booker's primary emphases within the work program was honesty. He stressed this point at all stages of student involvement, from application to evaluation to orientation and placement. In a warehouse operation like Lambert's, appropriating a few samples of fruit or vegetables would be easy and common. Larger amounts were another matter, and not at all likely. Monte, smiling inwardly, found it hard to imagine one of their visually impaired students hauling a sixty-pound crate of fruit from downtown Talerton to the Academy campus without being noticed and arousing suspicion.

Lambert continued, "I have no proof your boys are involved. But we began to notice the discrepancies soon after they came and started to wonder. I don't want to let 'em go. They're good kids, but I need guidance from you all as to what I should do. If there's something amiss, we want to solve it."

Booker spoke up forthrightly. "I wish you'd called sooner, Mr. Lambert. If there *is* a problem with our students, we'll definitely deal with it and make it right."

"Have you, or any of your folks, said anything to the boys about this?" Monte queried.

Lambert shook his head as if unsure, answering, "Uh, no. I don't think so. Well, maybe my son, Marcus, has, but I doubt it. I asked our warehouse foreman to keep an eye out as best he could, but so far, nothing."

Booker glanced at Monte, then said to Lambert, "If you're willing, give us a few days to look into it and have a, ah, conversation with the boys and see what we can uncover. Would that be agreeable?"

Lambert nodded eagerly. "Sure, sure."

Monte asked, "Would it be all right if we spoke to the foreman, or anyone else the students work with?" Lambert agreed straightaway without further comment, shaking his head vigorously as though relieved. Responsibility was now out of the man's lap, at least for a while.

Booker's greatest fear, Monte knew, other than a student being injured or injuring someone else, was public embarrassment tainting the program or the school and other students by association. Even rumor of misconduct or malfeasance could jeopardize the integrity of SET in the minds of community business people on whom the project depended. Back in the car, Booker sat pensive, absorbed in reflection of what they had been told and, perhaps more troubling, what they had not been told. Investigation would be needed before any conclusions could be reached.

"Not to contradict anything Mr. Lambert said," Monte offered, "but don't you feel like his concerns might be a bit premature and specious? I mean, think about it. They have, what . . . fifty or more employees, and he's connecting these two boys to possible theft with no real evidence, just speculations? They may be guilty as sin, I admit, but we don't know that. And they may be completely innocent. They deserve a fair hearing."

Booker turned, hands clenched in tight fists, and with categorical assurance muttered, "And they'll get one, Scott. We'll see to that." Pausing for a moment, he turned back to the front, exhaling lengthily, and asked, "How should we handle this?"

Monte had been ready to ask the same question. "What do you think?"

"Let's have 'em in and see what they have to say," Booker suggested. "We could try asking a few direct questions, or we could not say much of anything and see how they react, you know, kind of like silent treatment."

Monte had reservations about silent treatment, believing it dishonest, perhaps leaning too much toward assumption of guilt. Booker, however, pressed the point, and Monte agreed temperately, if used only as an opening ploy. The situation at Lambert's had a curious, cloudy flavor, and he began to think out a plan which might lead to where these puzzling vibes originated. For now, of that part, Booker would be left out. If things went wrong and there were repercussions, only he, Monte, would be culpable.

Roland and Oliver were juniors and solid *C* students with no history of problems. Booker decided to wait until the following day to meet with them, using the intervening time to organize his thoughts and questions. Monte meantime would meet casually with the boys' teachers and houseparents. These contacts took most of the afternoon, after which Monte made calls and rearranged his schedule of fieldwork for the next day.

• • •

Later, Booker having gone to the Business Office in Main Hall, Monte remained in the Inner Sanctum poring through a stack of files. A slight peripheral motion broke his concentration, and he pulled his head up rapidly. A boy of no more than eight stood just inside the doorway, obviously perturbed. Scallops of wispy hair the shade of peach skin swept his head in raging defiance of order, glasses clinging precariously askew a pudgy nose, small, dark-blue eyes attempting fierceness behind the smudged lenses. Erectly at attention, bursting to speak, the lad announced himself pompously as Millard J. Crumbley.

Once, weeks before and with some surety, he had informed Monte that, after discussions with Arnold Schnellich, he believed his parents had named him in honor of a duck. When told the bird he referred to was more likely a *mallard*, the boy had bobbed his head in agreement and said, "Right." As to past president Fillmore, unresearched so far, he expressed no firm opinion. On this current occasion, he seemed vexed to the point of utter exasperation.

"What's up, Millard?" Monte asked prudently. The boy wasted no time with small talk, coming fully into the office.

"Irving Funkworth said I was a metal case, and I don't think that was a very nice thing to say! It made me very mad."

"He probably said *mental* case, Millard," Monte reasoned. "And you're right; it wasn't a very nice thing to say. What do you think caused him to do that?" Monte felt confident his gentle, circumspective approach would make his counseling professors proud.

"Well," Millard said, pursing his lips in the way one would to kiss a grandmother's cheek, "I was sort of pleated out after lunch and wanted to sit down and think and let my stomach go smoothy. And Irving . . ." Millard climbed into the chair in front of the desk and rummaged into a sitting position, leaving only the top half of his face visible. "Irving, he started— May I use this chair, Mr. Scott?"

"Yes, that's fine, Millard."

"Irving started singing some stupid song about frogs just to anoint me, and I told him to shut up and go someplace else if he wanted to sing. Well, then he started singing nasal, and I hate it when he sings nasal, or even talks nasal. It makes my skin go creepy, so I covered my ears and started humming real loud and got up and bounced up and down and that's when he called me a metal case!"

"Mental case."

"Right."

"Well, Millard, I'll have a talk with Irving and see what he has to say. And in the meantime, just try to get along and not irritate each other."

"Right." A long, thoughtful pause ensued and then a look of puzzlement. "Mr. Scott, what's a mean time? I thought we were supposed to have nice time."

"Yes, you are supposed to have a nice time, Millard. Meantime refers to the time between now and when I talk with Irving."

"How long is it I have to be nice?"

"Well, try to be nice all the time, and particularly nice until I talk with Irving."

"Mr. Scott?"

"Yes, Millard."

"Is patricularty better niceness or worser niceness?"

"Better niceness, Millard."

"Okay, Mr. Scott. I have udder compidence in you as a, uh, guide, so I think I'll just go now." Giving Monte one last stare of circumspection, he slipped off the chair and turned for the door, took two steps, stopped, and turned back. "Mr. Scott?"

"Yes, Millard."

"Why do we need not to irrigate each other?"

"Irritate, Millard. Not make each other mad, be nice to each other. Try to be friends."

"Oh," Millard said, lighting up with happy reassurance. "We *are* friends, Mr. Scott. Irving is my very bestest friend in the whole school."

For once, Monte gave thanks for the hall bell crashing through the Inner Sanctum doorway like a Sherman tank.

• • •

Preparing to leave the building, engulfed in worries of Lambert's subtle accusations and feeling anything but gregariously inclined, Monte was hailed brashly by a man speaking louder than needed. "Hey! You there! Scott!"

Spinning around, he confronted a fairly tall individual, perhaps late thirties, well dressed yet harried in overall aspect, lugging a large attaché case, reminiscent of someone running to catch a bus, winded and overwrought. Monte replied neutrally, "Yes, sir?"

With a few quick strides, the man approached, gathered himself, and plopped the briefcase down by his feet, wheezing, "I think we need to talk."

Monte said, "All right. And with whom am I speaking?"

As though he found the question offensive, the man replied snidely, "I'm Dr. Reginald London, the school psychologist."

"Sorry, Dr. London. I guess we haven't met," Monte said evenly.

Plunging on shrilly, London said, "I've been trying to find you for weeks now. Apparently you don't operate on any type of set schedule, do you?"

Rather put off by the doctor's tone, Monte briefly explained that he normally came to the Academy only on Wednesdays. London huffed, "Must be nice to work one day a week."

Almost laughing at the ludicrous display of assumption and attitude, Monte simply responded, "What is it exactly that you want? I was just getting ready to leave."

"I said we need to talk!" London chafed.

"And I said all right. Talk about what, Doctor?" Monte said impatiently.

London twisted his head to one side, looking thoroughly disgusted, seething, "Good God, man! You don't look anencephalic!" Moving closer, snapping off the words, he said sharply, "You may be in breach of school policy, as well as improper and inappropriate conduct with a minor female student!"

Though late in the day, students strolled by from time to time, leaving Monte uncomfortable with what had become a public confrontation, as well as being stunned by the blatant imputations. Stepping closer, eyeing the top of London's nose, he whispered with distinct clarity, "Look, Dr. London, in the first place I don't understand your nonsensical attitude or accusations, and in the second place, a hallway's no place to have a discussion."

London backed away a half step, flustered but only slightly less agitated, and said, "My office is just upstairs."

The room was larger than the Inner Sanctum, brighter and well appointed, replete with filing cabinets, bookshelves, and upholstered chairs. Encouraging posters festooned the walls, promoting platitudinous bromides for self-improvement and mental health, some offering quotes from Skinner, Frankl, Jung, and others. Behind London's walnut desk hung a beautifully framed doctoral diploma awarded in clinical psychology from Duke University, paired with a color photograph of the school's Chapel Tower. Void of papers, the desktop held only a small, spooky ceramic bust of Sigmund Freud.

Legitimately clueless as to why the man was so perturbed, Monte sat and waited impassively for elucidation. London squirmed into his desk chair in the manner of a dog settling in his bed and began to speak in breathily hushed tones, head lowered as if reading from a script in his lap.

"We have, here at the Academy, Mr., uh, Scott . . ." He halted to clear his throat and shift to a more pedantic voice. "Here at the Academy, we, er, have policies and protocols apropos teacher and staff interaction with student populations." Eyes now raised, they oddly rotated side to side as if searching perimeters. "Especially interaction with minors or those of a different gender." Pausing to draw a quick breath, he went on, "Perhaps, giving you, uh, benefit of the doubt, being new to our campus, you were not aware of these, er, codes."

Monte made no response, watching and waiting quietly.

Hesitating, eyebrows arched, London dropped his chin as though peering over spectacles, finding focus on Monte's face, then continued, "These policies, and I might go so far as to call them regulations, were developed to . . . to protect not only the children in our care, but also the caregivers, as I'm sure you can appreciate." With growing impatience and stirrings of apprehension, Monte still said nothing. "Frankly, you've made several missteps, Mr. Scott, which we need to . . . are imperative we discuss."

"I'm listening, Dr. London," Monte said with directness, leaning slightly forward.

With undisguised relish, London grinned eerily and plunged on. "Do you recall an encounter you had with a female student named Betty? I believe it was the first part of September? Betty Davidson?" Threateningly triumphant, he uttered as one announcing checkmate, "I could look up the exact date if need be, sir!"

"Yes, I do, certainly," Monte acknowledged, unlikely to ever forget that memorable afternoon on a stairway in Perkins Hall.

"You," the doctor fumbled, almost hissing, searching for words, "you . . . *insinuated* yourself into a situation quite inappropriately and . . . and could have done irreparable harm to that vulnerable child. You should have immediately referred her to me as school psychologist and not delved into something for which you have not the training nor the expertise. You, sir, are not a trained therapist and . . . and it is not your job to try and pass yourself off as one. To put it bluntly, you were completely out of line and in violation of . . . of several rules!"

London had worked himself into fitful umbrage, appearing to swell in his chair, his last words spit out with vigorous petulance. Somewhat disconcerted, Monte had no ready rebuttal, nor did he feel mandated to produce one, quietly offering instead as a mitigating morsel of explanation, "I strongly encouraged her to see you, Dr. London, and she promised she would. In fact, I later checked to confirm she had."

"All right, all right! I admit, that's good, that's good!"

Falling back in his chair, eyes wandering as if confused, he ran a hand slowly through thinning, disheveled hair, breathing in a series of shallow gulps. However, he was far from pacified. Regaining a fractious air, he carried on censoriously, "But . . . you spent a half hour, or twenty minutes, or nobody knows how long with her, alone, in a crisis situation! Doing what? Saying what? Some *Reader's Digest* mumbo-jumbo gestalt theory off the top of your head?"

Monte waited before responding, finding London's elated facial expression theatrically emotive though poorly performed. Easily, he then said, "No, I didn't, Dr. London. And I'd suggest we might have a more fruitful discussion if you'd get hold of yourself, simmer down, and act like the professional you purport to be."

Whether from embarrassment or anger, the psychologist's face reddened deeply. Dicing his words through clenched teeth with unconcealed vehemence, he said, "I don't need to be lectured by a . . . a bachelor-degreed rehab technician, mister!"

Confirming his status, he pivoted violently in his chair and pointed a finger to the impressively bound doctoral diploma hanging on the wall above his head. For a fleeting, humorous second, Monte thought of typical playground disputes wrangled in elementary school daily between childhood combatants: "My [fill in the blank] is better than yours!"

The room had grown warm, almost oppressive. Monte felt strong inclinations to stand and walk out, instead reclining comfortably, soft pressure of chair cushions soothing. Though said with egregious intent, he knew "rehab technician" was not far off the mark; admittedly, most of his efforts were of necessity more technical than therapeutic in nature. He was called "counselor" but did very little real counseling. Currently his caseload consisted of almost 150 clients spread across eight counties and several towns and colleges, itineraries and time dictated by urgent and immediate need or a list of simple matters to be cleared quickly so a next, more important step could be taken. In truth, the entire system was chaotic and unmanageable and basically out of control. And he saw no hope for change or improvement, or any reasoned defense of the disorganization.

Having vented, London studied Monte with a nod to moderation, realizing perhaps he had been unnecessarily rude and pursuing the issue unproductively. He too settled back in his chair and spoke more judiciously, focusing on hands clasped in front of his face. "What you don't understand yet, Mr. Scott, with your presumptive, *a priori* view of the world, is that students cannot be trusted to tell the truth. This is a cardinal assumption, perhaps even rule, in working with children and young people. They manipulate and they lie, either most of the time or in perpetual streams, simply because . . . because they want sympathy and special treatment, or can't accept the reality of their . . . sad lives—that they're not like other kids, normal kids. That they're *blind*. They live in make-believe dream worlds that don't exist except in frivolous imagination. And many of them, most of them, drag the baggage of dysfunctional personal lives and home environments into their lives here at the school, spreading a disease contagion of misconduct . . . and connivance and dishonesty."

Instantly, icy paralysis gripped Monte's entire being, mind, and body, astounded by London's all-encompassing indictment, given without apology or any ameliorating exclusion or reservation, offered soberly and factually as firmly held belief of daily, universal normality.

Did this man sincerely believe what he had just stated? And if so, how had he reached such negative conclusions? And more importantly, how could he possibly establish any helping, positive relationships with students while carrying these convictions as a dominating premise and foundation?

Monte found breathing difficult, heart pounding in his chest. From behind the desk, cold, black eyes grown angry stared through him like menacing gun barrels, taking careful, felonious aim beyond his figure and all he represented to a target only the psychologist could see and comprehend.

Reaching for some tenable refutation, Monte leaned forward after a few moments and said, "You must have reasons for saying these things, London, though for now, I can't imagine even one. Subjectively, you may have convinced yourself your opinions are valid, but, in doing so, haven't you built a wall between yourself . . . your effectiveness and the students?"

"A wall, Mr. Scott? A wall of intolerance to fawningly accept unacceptable behavior, perhaps? Is that what you're saying?" he demanded, the words minced with blustering hubris. "You think you know better? Some therapy you picked up from a TV show? The rehab man with all the answers. Let's compare credentials, shall we?"

Ignoring the foul comments, feeling his way along carefully, Monte said, "Aside from your opinions—your beliefs—being repulsive for someone in your position, you strike me as harboring hostility toward the very group you're here to serve." He gathered a deep breath. "You mentioned gestalt theory, so surely you know the whole is not only greater than the sum of its parts, but can be *other* than the sum of its parts.

"I'm not naïve, Doctor, or stupid. Yes, kids lie, and they embellish and they dream. Politicians, preachers, doctors, salesmen lie. But think about it and see a bigger picture, not just singular components. These students you're talking about, these boys and girls, are often revealing truth to us, to you and me, with their untruths. What you call lies and manipulation are often protective wrappings covering what they don't know how to share or say any other way. I'm not defending the lies, Doctor, but I am defending the kids. Every lie they might tell is a step, a key toward discovering truth, their truth. And don't you think it's worth our efforts to dig deep enough to uncover that truth, or at least some part? To see through what's said to who they really are? Don't you think they deserve that chance, and the best we can give them?"

The encounter had harvested abject emotional exhaustion, and like two boxers between rounds, the men subsided in retreat to their corners. As Monte waited for his perhaps arrogantly untutored beliefs to be challenged, London remained unmoved, sulkily fixing his eyes upon his lap, as if enervated by insolence and ignorance. After some moments, Monte ventured to ask a troubling question with great reluctance. "Are you saying Betty lied to me?"

Lifting his head, London mumbled, peevish as a spoiled child, "We can't discuss Betty. You know that!"

"Dammit, mister!" Monte countered sharply, surprising himself. "We *have* been discussing Betty! Hell, you started this whole damned confrontation *because* of Betty!"

"All right!" London relented, raising eyes to the ceiling in escape. "No, I don't necessarily mean Betty. She's too . . . she hasn't perfected the art of complicity and deception. Yet. But she will. She has no choice if she wants to survive in this . . . reformatory atmosphere." Again, Monte was stunned, though in some largely important sense placated.

For a full minute they sat, as though regaining a measure of circumspection. London's hard, embedded eyes roiled unfocused, and at length he said bluntly, "There is the matter of physical impropriety, Mr. Scott. Your *embrace* with the child. With Betty."

Expecting "the hug" might eventually be at issue, and surprised London had waited so long to address it, Monte spoke candidly, admitting, "Yes, that was a bit uncomfortable for me. But I wasn't going to rebuke her, not in the circumstance. I believe that would have been cruel. And, just to be clear, Doctor, it wasn't an embrace, only a quick and innocent hug in full view."

Hoping London might show a modicum of empathy for the broader situation, Monte said, looking at him with as much indulgence as he could muster, "She needed that contact, Dr. London, brief and innocuous as it was. Perhaps as a way of showing gratitude. Or maybe confirmation of . . . possibilities of life. Or simply a small therapeutic connection with another human being she believed she could trust."

The meeting ended from entrenchment more than any satisfaction of mutuality, leaving lingering disappointment and intransigence. Churning fear took root inside Monte—not for himself, but for the school and the students. The man potentially wielded great power and influence, yet was probably, by any measure, ill-suited for his position. Still, he was a Duke-educated doctor of clinical psychology, a formidable opponent for a lowly field counselor. Monte wondered what Booker's reaction would be.

• • •

Well after six, Monte lumbered down to the lower parking lot where his little VW Bug waited in twilight. The right front tire greeted him immediately, squished flat to the asphalt.

Mental sequences one begins to tick off in situations of this nature have defined order, beginning with "Do I have a spare tire?" Followed by "In what condition is this tire?" and then "Where might that spare be residing?" One moves on at this point, entertaining vague memories of a certain tire jack that may or may not exist, and where this piece of machinery might conceal itself if in fact it does exist.

Upon extensive exploration, discoveries were rewarding and relieving. Both a spare and jack materialized, the former being short on tread and air pressure, but useable, the latter being greasy and complicated in a German engineering sort of way. The lug wrench, more recalcitrant, was found after a series of choice imprecations, concealed under a blanket of candy wrappers beneath the passenger seat.

An owner's manual with step-by-step instructions miraculously surfaced, tattered, torn, and filthy, hiding deep in a corner of the glove box along with an assortment of items too numerous and embarrassing to mention. Wheel lug nuts had obviously been bolted by Hercules, not in the least budgeable by mere arm strength. Standing on the lug wrench and bouncing, a balancing feat of gymnastic prowess in itself, he was able to apply enough torsion to force a horrible screech from the first nut and stud, a most encouraging sound giving rise to a shouted "Yes!"

Certain words and phrases often help in changing a tire, though he refrained from indulging in anything too audible, keeping muffled threats and encouragements to a sequence of grunts, moans, and snarls. The second nut broke loose with an eerie, satisfying whine, and for a moment Monte imagined himself a gladiator standing victorious over a fallen opponent. Only then, pumping a fist savagely in the air, did he realize with chagrin that a visitor had materialized during the squawking and springing—a curious young man about his age.

Neatly dressed in brown suede jacket and sharply pressed tan slacks, his darkish-brown hair fell nicely trimmed and groomed in neat lineations. Medium tall, his complexion appeared as very pale flaxen in the waning light. Yet what stood apart in definition was a simple pleasantness and ease of manner. A warm, inquisitive smile broadened even more when Monte rather sheepishly peered at him and said, "Oh . . . uh, hello."

Inspecting the predicament with sympathy, the visitor asked, "Flat tire?" His voice was gentle with sincerity and kindness, which immediately quelled Monte's inclination to give a ludicrous answer.

"Afraid so," Monte laughed weakly. "Better it happen here, though, than on the road," he added with a bit of unnecessary optimism.

"Can I help?" Again, sincerity and kindness.

"I think I've about got it. But thanks for asking."

The observer took a step forward and held out his hand. "I'm Richard Weisner."

Quickly wiping dirty hands on a rag, Monte received a soft, firm grip and answered, "Monte Scott." And when next Weisner spoke, Monte's breath momentarily disrupted as though sucker punched in the gut.

"Oh, right," Weisner said brightly. "Clare's mentioned you several times. You sang together in a talent show, I believe."

A chill inched up Monte's spine like a slithering serpent. *So this is the man,* Monte concluded. *This is the husband.* Somehow he managed with mouth crusty as burnt toast, "So you must be . . . um . . ." And no more would come forth.

Weisner revealed no notice of Monte's agitation and said, "Yes. I'm here to meet Clare. We have a dinner function this evening over at her church."

Among the words, Monte understood only, "I'm here to meet Clare," the rest a jumble of vibrating, irrelevant tones. He could think of nothing more to say, so nodded and returned doggedly to the flat tire and rebellious lug nuts.

Weisner continued to stand by, and though warned of the grime, as the nuts were loosened he carefully knelt beside Monte and held them while the tire was pulled off the hub and the spare wrestled on. Chattering affably while they worked, Monte could almost imagine him as comrade, striving shoulder to shoulder, sharing some mutual challenge. Weisner praised what he termed the superiority of foreign automobiles, particularly Monte's 1961 VW Bug, admitting with humorous contrition that his present vehicle was a gas-guzzling 1968 Buick station wagon, large as a yacht.

A minute later, flickering in the corner of Monte's eye, Clare came into view, walking across the parking lot toward them. In the crook of one arm she carried a bundle of books, in the other a large canvas tote bag hanging almost to the ground. When she spied the two men crouched by the wheel, she slowed as if baffled, furrows gathering her brow into a vigilant frown. Weisner noticed her then, standing and smiling to lift an arm in greeting. Clare smiled feebly, coming toward them with unhurried, measured steps while Monte continued tightening lugs, pretending preoccupation in his labors.

When she was close, Weisner piped cheerfully, "Hey there! Need help with those things?" *Such an obliging husband,* Monte thought sarcastically, then admonished himself for being such a boorish ingrate.

Halting beside them, surveying the scene with stilted evaluation and bit by bit piecing together why the pair had been congregated around the VW, she distractedly murmured, "No, thanks. I'm okay."

Weisner chuckled, noticing her uncertainty, and in a tone of apologetic confession pointed at the car and said, "Monte had a flat."

"So, you two have met?" she managed with effort, focusing a tight smile on Weisner.

"Yes! We have!" he answered zealously, clumsily holding out smudged hands for inspection as proof.

Feeling no longer justified in pretending to work on the wheel, Monte stood and said congenially, glancing toward Richard, "He's been a great help, and . . . good company." A brave attempt to smile failed.

Clare took a rather deep breath and sighed, rigidly poised, looking not at Monte but at Richard, as if expecting him to speak. He returned her look blankly, then said, "Well, gosh. I guess we'd better hit the road or we'll be late." To Monte, he said graciously, "Very nice meeting you. Maybe we'll see each other again sometime."

With little fanfare, Monte answered, "Yes, maybe we will. And . . . thanks for your help." Obligatory politeness forced a sidelong squint at Clare, rooted inexplicably obscure and distant, and he could think of nothing apt to say.

She moved toward the giant Buick, and, whether imagined, wished, or true, Monte perceived with no more than a single twitching flexion of involuntary movement that some core essence had been offered, and within one heartbeat their eyes locked, then vanished into wonder.

• • •

Journal: Wednesday, October 22, 10:30 PM

At last I'm alone and in my bedroom where I can write and think without interruption.

As soon as I got home from the church dinner and visiting Mom and Dad, Big Sis corralled me into a discussion about our grocery allowance and monthly apartment expenses.

Never had such an uncomfortable experience like this afternoon in my entire life. Thought my insides would burst as we left school. I wanted and needed to talk with him so badly, even if just a word or two . . . anything. His face said it all, and I was curt to him and to Richard. Why?

After we left, Richard asked if I was feeling ill. Maybe a bug, I told him, and then cried, mostly inside, though I'm sure he noticed and wondered.

Seeing them together was such an unexpected shock. And again I ask why? I must have looked very strange . . . at least that's the way I felt.

All day I assumed he'd ignored my note (and why did I assume that?) but later Arnold, bless his heart, came and told me he and Mr. Booker had had an issue with some work students.

I'm one very confused girl right now, Lord. Out of sync. Or am I? Could I be seeing, but not accepting what I see? What's going on? Need you more than ever.

• • •

Lying in bed that night, staring at the ceiling and replaying events of the day, something Richard said that afternoon nagged Monte's mind, something incongruent, a word or phrase that did not fit neatly into the picture. But it escaped him, even going over the memory several times. Perhaps nothing of significance, he mulled, and maybe would surface later. A last vision before slumber veiled his brooding was the penetrating, haunting mystery he saw in Clare's eyes for that briefest of milliseconds as she walked away.

CHAPTER SEVEN

RONALD AND OLIVER CAME in late in the afternoon the next day, not knowing why they were summoned, ill at ease, crowded together and sitting stiffly in chairs fronting Booker's desk. Monte stood stoically against the wall beside the filing cabinet. Booker began the disputed silent routine, relaxed in his chair, expressionless, tilting his head to one side, then the other, leaning forward as if to speak, only to sigh and fall back as though rethinking. Monte, somewhat amused, drummed fingers lightly on top of the filing cabinet, staring at the boys with a curious half smile, until in frustration Ronald spoke up.

"Why did you want to see us?" His voice was dismally tinny.

Still, Booker did not speak. Monte cleared his throat, and in the quietness of the little room the rasping sound was like a growl, causing the lads to lurch in their seats. Ronald turned his head to Oliver, sitting mute as though afraid to move. According to their teachers, Oliver was the more astute, Ronald the compliant follower. Both were hefty, Ronald heavier and taller. Neatly dressed in blue jeans, untucked plaid flannel shirts, and black high top tennis shoes, both wore light-brown hair trimmed short.

Booker, apparently seeing no further need for silence, gave a prearranged sign and Monte said lightly, "How's your work going down at Lambert's?" Two heads jerked toward him in unison, straining to discern his expression in the dimness.

Ronald again glanced quickly to Oliver, who spoke with tensity. "Good. Very good. We like it there. It's hard work sometimes, but . . . we like it."

Ronald muttered agreement.

"Any problems?" Booker asked, leaning forward, speaking with adroit nonchalance. Both said no, then dropped their eyes.

"Anything you want to tell us? Anything you want to share?" Monte added from his shadowy perch. Again they answered negatively. *Perhaps too quickly,* he thought.

Inhaling deeply, Booker then sighed, droning in a calm, fatherly tone, "Well, we're going to level with you boys. And we want you to level with us." He paused, clasping hands together prayerfully, and said, "Work reports have been good, and as far as we knew, all was going well, until yesterday." His face faded to hints of disappointment, the boys frozen, staring. "Mr. Lambert told us some merchandise has gone missing. Would either of you know anything about that, anything at all?"

Both shook their heads as though astonished.

Booker sat woodenly, not speaking for a long minute, the boys snatching glances at each other and Monte as if confused.

"Okay," Booker said at length, exhaling resignedly and standing, "I've got to go out for a while. Mr. Scott has some things he'll discuss with you, so sit tight." With the boys watching carefully, he moved to the Inner Sanctum door, opened it slowly, and stepped into the classroom, then turned back and said somberly, "Be smart, guys. Be smart. Always better in the long run to be honest." And then he pulled the door shut behind him.

Booker and Monte had outlined a plan for the meeting earlier that morning using an old ruse that often elicited concealed information: convince the questionee that the questioner knew more than he actually did. Monte moved to Booker's desk and perched on the side, two pair of wary eyes following his every move. Taking his time, he finally spoke quietly but firmly.

"Mr. Booker left because he didn't want to hear what we're going to talk about." Ronald snatched an unsettled, sideways peep at Oliver, whose eyes remained fixed on Monte.

Letting his vague statement hang in the air for a moment, Monte then said, "You see, Oliver, Ronald, if Mr. Booker heard certain things, certain facts, being a teacher at the Academy, he'd have to report that information to Mr. Fletcher and Dr. Mullens. And if that information was serious enough, they might have to bring in the police. And then the whole mess would be out of our hands and there'd be nothing we could do to help."

The boys sat immobile as concrete pillars, eyes unblinking. Rising from the edge of the desk and slipping around to Booker's chair, he sat wearily, filling the small room with a mournful sigh. Almost whispering, Monte continued, "But I'm not a teacher at the Academy. I don't work for the Academy. I'm not bound by the same rules and regulations as Mr. Booker." He waited for only a second, then edged forward, staring sternly at the boys, and assured them, "Anything and everything we say in this room can be between you and me, and only between you and me, no one else."

Monte thought Ronald close to tears, Oliver reflective. When neither spoke, Monte gambled his trump card. With an air of blithe tolerance, he smiled and stated, "You see, boys, I know what's been going on. I've talked to Mr. Berkshire, your foreman. All I need from you now are a few facts and we can close out this whole ordeal."

Monte gazed expectantly at each boy and waited, feigning relaxation yet pressed hard against the back of his chair, a trickle of warm sweat beginning to course down his forehead. His mind haunted with misgiving, he prayed above all else that he was not bringing some awful, cruel injustice down upon these young men who sat before him—boys who so vividly mirrored who he had been not many years before.

• • •

Booker slumped at his desk in a cloud of smoke, anxious to hear Monte's saga of Ronald and Oliver. "In the first place," Monte chuckled, "nothing's been stolen, at least nothing of significance. The whole episode boils down to a kind of family tug-of-war between Lambert and his son, Markus. The boys were scared to tell us anything, believing they'd be fired if we found out what was going on. After I bluffed them into thinking I knew everything, they broke down and spilled the complete story."

"And?" Booker said harshly, urging Monte to continue.

"Well, you know I talked with Lambert again, and to Markus and a few of the secretaries, and most importantly to Bertie Berkshire, the foreman; who, by the way, is a really fine fellow and likes Ronald and Oliver very much. Not like Markus, I'm afraid, who I suspect you wouldn't care for. I know I didn't—a whining, spoiled, thirty-five-year-old jerk.

"The company's doing very well, making money and about to expand into frozen foods and organics, as well as leasing a neighboring building for cold storage, at least that's the father's plan. According to office gossip, Markus has zero interest in the business, never has, and wants to sell and retire to Florida to indulge his playboy lifestyle. At every turn he's been undermining his father and the company operation to make it look like they're losing money and having labor problems, including thievery. He was against participation in the work program and clashed with his father over that issue, and so started circulating an idea that the boys were stealing in hopes they'd be terminated. The stupid thing is, in all these efforts, he's only been hurting himself. He's not a potential member of Mensa, believe me." Monte laughed, "He could also do with some improved social skills."

Booker put a cigarette to his lips and demanded, "Well, go on, go on!"

"Berkshire's been asking for more help in the warehouse, seriously needed, but Markus nixed any more hiring or overtime, claiming they couldn't afford it. Bertie was afraid to go over the son's head to Mr. Lambert, knowing Markus would lie and plead ignorance about the whole issue and then make things rough for Bertie, and maybe for Oliver and Ronald. The boys knew about the shortage of workers and asked Berkshire if they could come in for a few extra hours on Sunday mornings to help catch up, a time when the houseparents believed they'd be in Sunday school and church. Of course, the boys told Bertie they had permission from the school to work the additional hours.

"Berkshire paid the boys from his own pocket and petty cash, same as they received per hour from the work program. They profited, Bertie got some extra help, and we and the Lamberts knew nothing about it. Those few hours didn't solve the labor problem, but did help in some small ways. Now the boys are wondering what's going to happen. And that's a decision you and Lambert will have to make. Markus, by the way, according to the father, is out of the picture and will not be part of the process."

Booker fell back, arms dangling at his sides. And then he grinned strangely and exclaimed, "Damn it, Monte! I knew those kids weren't thieves! Hot damn! I knew it! Not my kids!"

With Booker, everything always came back to the kids, his kids, the ones he ultimately cared for the most. And though disguised, Monte easily detected a slight tremor in his voice and bit of dampness in his eyes.

When Ronald and Oliver came back in the next day, Booker put both on probation for a month with stern warnings to work only prescribed hours, also informing the boys no mention of recent happenings at Lambert and Son would be made to anyone, and nothing would be placed in any file or record. For their part, the overjoyed young men issued a flood of thanks. Booker merely stood and told them to get out and count their blessings. When they were gone, he sat staring at the doorway and said with peculiar softness, "And there go I, about twenty-five years ago."

To which Monte replied, perhaps with a tremor of his own, "I know what you mean. I know exactly what you mean."

• • •

Dr. Reginald London did not much care for Mr. Booker, or Booker for him, Monte discovered. They worked together only with uneasy mandatory collaboration, a mutual grain of tenuous professional respect. Booker felt strongly at odds with the psychologist for his dogmas and doctrines. Like much enmity, Monte initially wanted to believe the rancor separating the two largely a matter of personalities, differing styles and roles. Everyone, he reasoned, had the occasional bad day which could be overlooked, aberrant pique or conduct not emblematic of definable norm or practice.

Until Monte met the man, and Booker made him rethink the matter.

The sullen response and abrupt change of subject Monte received after sharing the one contact he'd had with London should have been a red flag. However, it took a memo from the principal's office one chilly Wednesday morning to renew the subject in their minds. Going through mail, nothing of particular interest emerged until Monte read the note from Fletcher:

> *All eleventh and twelfth-grade students will be scheduled for a battery of tests, including achievement, interest, and psychological profiles conducted by Dr. Reginald London, who will be contacting all teachers and staff to set up a schedule. The cooperation and assistance of everyone will be greatly appreciated.*

A cloud of despondency, like psychic depression, descended over Booker in a way almost frightening. Suddenly withdrawn, an air of hopeless surrender seemed to grip him with a power for which he had no defense. Monte laid down the memo, watching the uncharacteristic deterioration with puzzled wonder. Timidly he asked, "What is it, Mr. Booker?"

As though deaf, Booker made no reply, appearing only to shrink in denial as one might when told of personal tragedy. Posturing a breath of abdication, drawn out and deep, in a faraway tone he said at last, "I fear, Monte . . . I fear what this means for our kids." The reaction, so inordinately heavy and forlorn, drove Monte to perplexed silence.

Shifting in his chair, Booker sat more squarely. "You may think I'm overreacting, but I have a . . . a belief that we're making a huge mistake." He paused, placing his hands flat on the desktop. "I should talk to Fletcher, but I know he won't listen. And if he listens, he won't understand. And even if he understands, he still won't do anything about it."

Monte asked fervently, "What is it? What do you mean?"

Booker's fingers gradually curled into clenched fists, knuckles milky as large pearls, face suffocatingly dark. "London's going to write about our kids, Scott, document material for their files, part of a permanent record that'll follow them for years to come. And he doesn't know *shit* about these kids! He projects things that aren't there and misses important things that are. He's incompetent and a damn fool! And quite frankly, I believe the man's sick," he admitted, his breathing labored not so much in anger, Monte sensed, but aggrievement inflamed by burning energy destitute of resolution.

Two truths came sharply into focus: the underestimated danger of London's malevolence to students, and the profound depth of Benjamin Booker's commitment to boys and girls of the Academy. Fearfully approaching sensitive ground, Monte murmured, "If you really believe that to be true, Benjamin, you have to do something."

"I've said Fletcher won't listen, so what can I do?" Booker retorted heatedly. "I have no control!" Though confined behind a desk, he gave appearance of a man pacing the floor and wringing his hands in a funk of pitiable conundrum.

"You can enlist others who feel the same way!" Monte replied sharply. "It's not your battle alone." Pausing for a heartbeat, he then reasoned, "If you go as a body, a group of teachers, not as an individual, Fletcher will have to listen."

For a moment Booker reacted as though slapped or shaken roughly by the shoulders, and then the plaguing grimness of defeat began to fade, and, looking up, he whispered, "Maybe. Maybe you're right, Scott. Enlist some other teachers, form a committee."

• • •

Benjamin Alexander Booker in many respects was a mystery to Monte. Snippets of his life history had been gleaned from extended personal conversation with the man, supplemented by colorful morsels from Charlie Talbert and Dr. Bartlett, slowly forming a partial image of persona—morals, ethics, and mindset. Certain data were not in dispute: born in a clapboard shanty in far Southwest Virginia forty-two years ago; taken in by an aunt in Norfolk when almost five and schooled at the Academy and University of Virginia; public school teacher for several years before returning to the Academy; married almost two decades to Gwen, a nurse; three children—a son, sixteen, and two daughters, thirteen and four.

Had he not been born blind, no doubt he would have lived out his days as a coal miner like his father and grandfather before him. Contrarily, a keen mind, unbounded curiosity, and energy led him to pursue academics: four-year degree in history and geography, fluency in Spanish and French, master's degree in counseling, and partial work toward a doctorate in education.

However, facts, as with any biography, fell woefully short of defining the person. Monte had observed during his brief tenure a man who could swing almost in one breath from childlike naïveté to Solomonic wisdom. He could laugh and curse and weep simultaneously. He was seldom lukewarm toward anything, excepting his Presbyterian church. He avoided those few persons he disliked and cherished the rest with steadfast care and friendship; Monte had yet to discern Booker's criteria for the two categories, expecting perhaps, on further examination, a daily flux. He often thought working with the man was similar to playing a trout while fly fishing, knowing when to tug and when to ease off.

On some plane of insensate consciousness, Monte was aware that Booker was anatomically blind. But he would never be a *blind man*, only a man who happened to be inconvenienced by a lack of sight. His extraordinary sensory and spatial perceptions were such that Monte often forgot this simple fact. Knowing when and when not to be helpful presented learning curves, and Booker was a master trainer and forthright director. He knew when assistance was needed or not, and would say so. And woe to the person who dared treat him as an invalid, for which the penalty was homicide.

• • •

Sunday afternoon, Monte called Anne Walden and was surprised when she did not hang up. He had not talked with her since the house party. The appealing invitation of overnight accommodation that evening had laid before him temptation to enhance a budding friendship; and there was no denying her arousing magnetism. Frankly, Monte had no memory of ever meeting anyone endowed with such glamorous allure and hedonic charm. Talbert simply called her a "head turner," and Booker suggested a wax figure of her likeness be placed in the Smithsonian, representing the epitome of all womanhood.

However, Monte had a problematic obstacle in the form of Clare Augsburg. For reasons known only to the gods, and possibly not even to them, he had shouldered a burden of incomprehensible fidelity to a married woman known only casually. Baffling and enigmatic beyond reason, there existed an allegiance which could not be dismissed. Nor did he want to dismiss it, even when taunted by enticing gratuities. Booker would have called him a fool had he known. Indeed, Monte tried to convince himself it made as much sense as insisting to pay a debt when no debt was required.

Anne agreed to go for a ride in late afternoon on the Blue Ridge Parkway. They watched the sun set from Raven's Roost, wrapped in a wool blanket, sitting on a cold, stone wall. She had brought a thermos of coffee, and they lingered until chilled as twilight faded to evening. After a light supper in Wolvercote, they returned to her townhouse. No invitation to stay was suggested, and before leaving Monte felt compelled to risk clearing the air.

"About the other night, Anne, after the party, I—"

She stopped him with a shake of her head, and said, "Don't worry about that, Monte. I understand perfectly. I think I was feeling so relaxed and relieved the party was over I, well, I hope I didn't offend you."

"Offend me?" Peering into her seductive eyes, he said, "No, not at all. I was . . . flattered."

Despite the earnest declaration, Monte knew she did not understand, and he did not want her to. Truth was too personal, too private—most of all, too sacred. Had she known, she would have thought him an even bigger fool than would Booker. He went on softly, "It just wasn't the right time. I'm sorry. I hope I didn't offend *you*."

"You didn't," she sighed. "After you left, I was glad the way things turned out." She paused and looked up at him with a tender smile. "Perhaps you saved me from myself."

Driving back to Rivanleigh, he suddenly remembered the incongruous statement Richard had made on that flat-tire day in the Academy parking lot, the item that did not fit. It came in a bolt, the way a forgotten fact or word sometimes does. Weisner had said that he and Clare were going to dinner at *her* church; *her* church, not *our* church. Certainly, Monte reasoned, as a married couple they went to church together. Perhaps he meant her parents' church, the church she attended when a child.

Concluding the question did not matter, that he was only trifling in mind games, wordplay, tantalizing himself with made-up mysteries that were no mysteries at all, he laid his musing aside, resurrecting his mantra: *She is married, she is married.*

• • •

Journal: Tuesday, October 28, 11:00 PM

Been frustrated all afternoon over nothing. Why would I let myself feel this way because of a simple remark overheard in the teachers' lounge during lunch (where I seldom ever go! That'll teach me!). Someone asked Anne about her weekend and she mentioned being with Monte Sunday evening. No details or gush of emotion, just a silly suggestive smile. Right now I'm angry (furious!) with myself. Not only is my reaction inappropriate, it's idiotic, stupid and shallow! What's wrong with me?

Richard and I had a lovely dinner this evening in Stonebridge. He is so caring and kind (though tells me more about work than I want or need to know, ha!). Fearful he's working up to ask the big question soon. And everyone, including him, assumes . . .

• • •

Brad Fletcher received a phone call early Monday morning from a man demanding to speak with someone in authority vis-*à*-vis the part-time work program, in which, he said, his son was a participant. T. Allen Bridgemeyer III had the sound of one not to be passed off lightly or placated with banalities. Fletcher's end of the conversation, according to Ramona, was an obsequious series of "Yes, sirs," and "No, sirs," concluding with dewy beads of sweat covering his brow and cheeks flaring rubescent as though having been smacked repeatedly.

Booker was summoned from a Spanish class and ordered to the principal's office where the unhappy phone conversation was related tersely. At attention in front of the principal's desk, Booker listened calmly, projecting mellow cheerfulness, infuriating Fletcher's sensibilities even more than had the irate call. Seething with indignation, the besieged principal barked that *he alone* had been the one forced to take the brunt of Bridgemeyer's acrimonious message, somehow implying to Booker a violation of dignity enjoined to entitlements of his office and from which he should have been insulated.

"This is *your* program, Benjamin, and I'm leaving this . . . this complaint squarely in your lap!" Fletcher ranted imperiously. "The man's coming Wednesday and wants to meet with you and Scott." He emphasized the word *man* as if it might properly be rendered in giant capital letters. “This . . . person,” he growled displeasingly, putting Booker in mind of a disgruntled boar hog, “runs a big investment firm in Northern Virginia and sounds like he’s used to getting his way.”

“Yes, sir,” Booker said more confidently than Fletcher wanted to hear, preferring that those around him share his anxiety. Grinning despite himself, Booker offered, “His son’s Theodore. Theo to most of us.”

“Yes, I know Theodore,” Fletcher gasped impatiently. And then, more evenly, “Nice boy. Good student.”

“He is,” Booker affirmed. “Don’t worry, Brad. We’ll handle whatever concerns Mr. Bridgemeyer has. No problem.” Warm, sympathetic tones did little to placate the principal.

“Well, I hope so,” Fletcher mused. “Bridgemeyer’s connected, you know. Plays golf with the governor, on boards of several large corporations. Wife’s DAR, I’m informed.” He sighed. “God almighty, first damned thing Monday morning!”

Booker bowed with enjoyment and left the room, grinning at Ramona while behind him the principal hollered for the secretary to come into his office immediately and bring her steno pad.

Theodore Allen Bridgemeyer IV was a high school senior, well mannered and well liked by teachers and students, a handsome young man who had lost his vision in a hunting accident four years previous. Adjustment to blindness and the new world of the Academy had not come easily, early weeks and months having been an excruciating struggle of fear, pain, and anguish. One hesitated to say struggle of life and death, yet this, fundamentally, was what it came down to. After his physical wounds healed, Theo’s emotional and mental state had teetered on a knife edge of collapse, spiraling close to withdrawal into the same darkness he now abided visually. Blindness from birth, congenital blindness, is not the same as suddenly being blinded as an active, carefree boy of thirteen. To Theo, the loss was a death sentence from which there would be no reprieve or pardon.

Whence came the strength and will to wrestle with such adversity no one could say. But Theo found them, sought and seized them, held them close like a sacred healing talisman. His family too, devastated by the accident, suffered anguish and pains of adjustment in their own lives while seeking to give what palliation they could to their son. Measuring one slow, halting step at a time, buoyed by unquenchable love from parents, family, and friends, and the daily patient care and guidance of the school, the boy seized life and carried it forward with transcendent courage.

To Booker, Theo once said, "I can't ever totally be my old self, can I? But I can be a new self, and maybe an even better self." Such a mindset, Monte concluded, such audacious bravery, might well be near the core of any successful adjustment in life—finding and grasping a will and desire to never give up. *To strive, to seek, to find, and not to yield.*

Bridgemeyer arrived at ten Wednesday morning, driving a new silver Cadillac Sedan DeVille. Monte, dispatched by Booker, greeted him in the visitor parking lot. Never having had any contact with the man, he knew him only by reputation and conversations with Theo. Two words—*distinguished* and *formidable*—came to mind in the first seconds of their meeting. Bridgemeyer informing Monte officiously that he needed no guide, they nonetheless walked together to Booker's office.

Sandwiched into the Inner Sanctum after perfunctory introductions, Booker sat compacted behind his desk, Monte standing in shadows by the file cabinet and Mr. Bridgemeyer indulgently resolved to the one wooden chair, which bizarrely had sprouted a thick seat pad. The desktop had been cleared, and Monte had turned on the overhead light, simple amenities which did little to improve the stagnant austerity of the tiny room.

Bridgemeyer's discordance with the spartan surroundings was almost comical, an executive accustomed to more opulence. Not a big man, he carried himself impressively as one, affecting dominance even when seated. Habitually tilting his head slightly back when speaking, peering down the slope of his sharp nose as though taking aim, he gave sophisticated pretense of gauging the effect of his words on the listener. This he carried off with a certain detached cordiality, mouth set rigidly between smile and smirk. Finding the trait irksome, Monte rallied with determination to avoid falling prey to bias against their guest, if only for Theo's sake.

After obsequious apologies for the environment, Booker yielded Bridgemeyer the floor without delay, having at the outset been informed with fustian precision that their visitor's time was limited.

"The issue here, Mr. Booker," Bridgemeyer began gruffly, waving an arm in a swooping oratorical arc to draw an opened-handed bead on Booker's forehead, "is my son's future. This conversation could easily have been handled by a simple phone call, but my wife insisted—*insisted*—that I come all the way down here in person and talk with you. And"—glancing at Monte with mechanical courtesy—"Mr. Scott." His "all the way down here" was drawn out with such lugubrious and onerous effort, Monte could not help but picture the poor man trudging hip deep through a muddy swamp all the distance from Northern Virginia.

Booker responded politely, "Yes, I understand, and we appreciate your taking time to come. I know you're a busy man."

"You all," Bridgemeyer went on firmly, yet with a scintilla of entreaty, "have my son in an employment situation for which he is completely ill-suited and far removed from concerting with his career goals. Theodore is college-bound, hopefully to an Ivy League school or one of that caliber. He has no time to waste in a shoe shop, though I realize it's a noble trade." His "noble trade" came with a look of turgid conciliation.

Theo had, for the past three weeks, worked in a downtown business known as Moseley's Shoe and Leather Goods, exposed to shoe and boot repair and helping customers choose a particular backpack, knapsack, belt, or other item from a host of high-quality and varied products.

Booker and Monte had earlier discussed how best to deal with Bridgemeyer's concerns. His opening salvo was milder than expected, given the tenor of his call to Fletcher. Monte wondered if in the interim his wife or Theo had stirred some moderation. Despite the father's anticipated objections, both men felt nascent encouragement for a reasoned conversation and mutually agreeable conclusion.

Bridgemeyer continued, "I never gave permission for Theodore to be in this program in the first place. That was his mother, and she never discussed it with me. Had I been told," he said huffily, "I most assuredly would have said no and we wouldn't be having this conversation now."

Pinched in a corner, listening and watching, Monte had a burgeoning idea that the man's initially haughty assault was perhaps more smokescreen than substance—setting himself up, waiting to be convinced of the value of what Theo was doing, probing for a graceful way to accede to the worth of the program without admitting to such by his own volition. As he had stated, phoning would have been a much quicker and easier way to withdraw permission for his son's involvement. Instead, he had driven almost three hours, attributing the reason to satisfying his wife. Monte found it difficult to accept Bridgemeyer as a man who caved quite that readily, even to his spouse. Rather, Monte believed, he had *wanted* to come.

Booker then took the floor with an attitude of calm solicitude and proceeded to explain the background and organization of the student-employment project, delving meticulously into funding—an area they wagered Bridgemeyer might appreciate—and the application and eligibility process, number and variety of students involved, and diversified work being done. Bridgemeyer listened, stoically polite, asked a few questions, and made several benign comments.

"Sounds like a fine, well-thought-out program, Mr. Booker," Bridgemeyer said agreeably, "and an excellent project. I commend you and Mr. Scott for what you're trying to do. However, I don't see it benefiting Theodore. I mean . . ." Pausing as though stymied, he went on, asking, "A shoe store? For a boy who in a few years will have an MBA?"

Moving from the wall, attempting a façade combining confidence, camaraderie, and humility, Monte said, "If I may, sir, I'd like to share just a few things." Booker smiled silently, pleased for his comrade's involvement. Bridgemeyer sat back with civil, forbearing appraisal, though folding arms across his body protectively.

In a timbre of quiet accommodation, Monte proceeded, "Mr. Booker, I believe, has explained the part-time program clearly and completely, and we all, I think, are in agreement it's a good and worthwhile endeavor." Pausing, his glance passed between both men as if reading their reactions. "But, as I see it, that's not the issue before us. What I'm hearing in our conversation, and what I hear you, Mr. Bridgemeyer, asking with valid concern, is, *How does working in a shoe store advance Theodore's readiness to reach his ultimate career goals?*" Waiting a few seconds, allowing the words to penetrate, Monte ventured, "When you were a kid, sir, did you ever mow lawns, wash cars, paint fences, or do other odd jobs to make a little money?"

Monte feared the answer might well boomerang as "Certainly not!" But the gambit paid off and Bridgemeyer acknowledged with relaxed modesty, "Oh, yes." Then he perked up and leaned forward with convivial animation and pride, almost laughing, "And did quite well too, as I remember. Had the largest paper route of anybody in the area. Helped pay for college and my first car."

"Right now we have twenty-seven students on the job in the work program," Monte continued, "and hope to have more in future, and I dare say, not a single one will end up in the type of work he or she is presently doing. That's not the point, you see, and never was or will be. What you and I learned mowing lawns, and what Mr. Booker learned washing pots and cars, was being reliable, showing up when we were supposed to, doing a good job, getting along with all sorts of people, following directions and being courteous, planning our schedules and taking care of our equipment, all these things and a hundred more. In other words, learning to be responsible."

Bridgemeyer's expression grew thoughtful. More seriously focused, Monte leaned over the edge of Booker's desk for emphasis and said ardently, "Theodore is an exceptional young man, and I know you and Mrs. Bridgemeyer are very proud of him, as we are too. He'll be successful in whatever he chooses to do with his life." Pausing for a deep breath, he then said, "Because he has the inner strength and the ability and courage and sheer will to succeed. Whether he remains in the work program or not, these essential endowments, these innate parts of him, will not change." Again pausing, Bridgemeyer intense and unblinking as though being chastened, Monte then said, "I also believe the program could help him, not with training per se, but with broad employment experience and basic, general maturation."

Bridgemeyer stared past him to the wall behind Booker, then lowered his head, silent. In that moment Monte remembered a chat he and Theo recently shared. His father, Theo told him, had been very successful in business, belonged to a local country club, served on boards of several community organizations, was active in his church, consistently shot in the mid-eighties on the golf course, and had a history of high cholesterol. And one other thing.

"I believe you're a numismatist, Mr. Bridgemeyer?" Monte queried, knowing he was.

The man's face lifted with an expression curious at the swift change in topic, and he said cautiously, "Yes, I am. How did you know?"

"Oh, just something Theodore mentioned one day while we were chatting." Monte backed to the wall again, doing his best to sound amiably indifferent. Booker sat in silence, puzzled. Self-effacingly, as if of little consequence, Monte said, "My uncle left me a small collection some years ago, including some fairly nice pieces: a few rare Indian Head pennies and early Mercury dimes, Liberty silver dollars. Have you ever seen a 1913 Liberty Head nickel?"

Bridgemeyer straightened, staring with wide, probing eyes at Monte's enigmatic smile. "Only twice. Once in the ANA Museum in Colorado and recently in the Smithsonian." His voice had taken on a stunned, strained quality. "Why . . . why do you ask?"

"I saw one, if you can believe it, in a bar in New York City in 1960. My uncle and I happened to be there and actually held the piece in our hands for a minute or two, the one that's now in the ANA Museum."

Bridgemeyer was aghast, speaking slowly and deliberately. "You . . . you held it in your hands? My God! How?"

As if speaking confidentially, Monte explained that this one specimen had been privately circulated, the owner at the time often carrying it with him to show around and boast about its rarity, only five having been minted in mysterious circumstances. Their value back then was estimated in the hundreds of thousands each, much more now.

Shaking his head in disbelief, Bridgemeyer said, "You are very fortunate, and I must say, I envy you that experience."

While Monte told him more about his uncle's collection, Booker sat back grinning, though still somewhat baffled at the twist of conversation. Bridgemeyer, in turn, gave a brief inventory of his own coins, insisting Monte come and see it and bring his own. Overtaken by a childlike euphoria, Bridgemeyer seemed to have forgotten his limited time schedule, at length gazing dreamily, almost lustfully at Monte's hands and murmuring, "A 1913 V Nickel, in your hand. Damn. Wish I could've been there."

Twenty minutes later Booker and Bridgemeyer shook hands warmly as they stood together in the congested confines of the dark inner office, after which Monte walked to the parking lot with Theo's father, asking if he planned to have lunch with his son. Deliberating, the man voiced decision to postpone his afternoon appointments and stay. Monte thanked him for coming and for his honest concerns, urging him to talk with Theo and hear what he had to share about his work.

Then with unanticipated and serendipitous candor, Bridgemeyer appraised him carefully, keenness sparkling in his eyes, and said, "I'll do that, Monte. I surely will. And just so you and Mr. Booker know, I'll encourage him to stay with the program if that's what he wants to do."

Later that day, Booker, still mulling over the whole episode, said jokingly, "Who would think a freaking nickel could make so much difference to a man responsible for millions, maybe billions? Lord almighty!"

CHAPTER EIGHT

MARLON DANFORTH SELDOM VISITED field offices, customarily imposing on counselors to arrange trips to his cushy sinecure in Richmond when meetings necessitated. He arrived in Rivanleigh at 1:30 Friday afternoon as scheduled and to Monte's amazement asked flaccidly after his health.

He made no apology for short notice of his visit, expecting underlings to rearrange their schedules no matter the inconvenience or disruption. The four counselors assigned to the Rivanleigh office gathered for the first hour, after which only Monte was told to remain. Alone in the office, the two conversed randomly for a few minutes, touching on minor questions of reporting dates and other agency esoterica. Then, inclining forward and glancing around conspiratorially, voice low, Danforth stated, though meant as a question, "I understand the, ah, SET Program is going very well."

"Yes, sir. It is." Monte nodded, expressionless.

Smiling with satisfaction, the man leaned back, lifting his shoulders and head as though posing for a portrait. "I'm very glad to hear it, very glad. The commissioner queries me about it almost daily and, uh, I'm going to be, er, working up an official report for him and the agency board for their quarterly meeting. Naturally, I'll need complete, current, updated information from you—detailed data dealing with all aspects of the project."

He paused and stared, dropping his chin as if to gauge Monte's absorption, then clarified, "You know, numbers of participates, grades, ages, gender, and so forth, places of employment, type of work they're doing, transportation issues, pay rates and funding sources, problems or difficulties of any sort." He paused again to breathe deeply and clear his throat. Continuing, he crooned almost pleasantly, "Just anything and everything you can think of that might be pertinent. Be creative, Scott, and comprehensive. I thought some actual quotes and anecdotes from some of the students and employers would be nice too. Maybe even a few photographs. Anything to add a little color and personal touch."

Monte, pretending engagement, silently jotted notes on a legal pad as the man talked. Certainly he was well aware, Monte mulled, that the extensive task outlined would require a lengthy, time-consuming chronicle involving many days of work. Hesitating, Monte verbalized his concerns. "You realize, sir, this much detailed and varied material will take some time to compile."

Danforth's heretofore amiable manner markedly receded with little apparent transition, leaving distorted impatience more typical of his normal persona. "Of course I realize it will!" he burst indignantly. "Is that a problem?"

"My fieldwork—"

"Your fieldwork can wait a few days! This can't."

"Yes, sir. What kind of timetable do you—"

"ASAP! ASAP!" the supervisor seethed irascibly. "When the commissioner asks for something, Scott, he doesn't like to hear excuses and be kept waiting. Get on it right away."

"So, just to be clear, you want me to drop everything else to work on this?" Monte asked, aware his tone bordered on insolence.

Less querulous than expected, more distractedly annoyed, Danforth stared with restraint at the ceiling for a second or two, then said in a low, steady voice, "Just get it done, Scott. Just get it done. I'll be at the Academy next Monday for a meeting with Brad. Have everything finished by then. I'd also like you and Mr. Booker to come prepared to answer any questions we might have, got it?" His face, set to stolid hardness as if daring vacillation, had grown mottled in shades of pink.

Resigned, Monte nodded. "I'll do my best to have a report for you by then, sir."

Not finished, Danforth crossed his arms and cocked his head to one side as if sorrowfully worried. In lamenting tones he fretted, "The Case Review Task Force reported to me last month that you're behind on your new-referral contact-and-update data summaries." And then, as though talking to a recalcitrant kindergartner, he bleated, "You know what we say, Scott: the job's not done 'til the paperwork's done. Get those figures up to date. Gotta keep the CRTF boys and girls happy." The shrill cackle that followed was bloodcurdling.

• • •

Monday morning, Monte arrived at the Academy early. Friday night and all day Saturday and Sunday had been spent working in his Rivanleigh office with what limited work program and student data were to be had—most material unavailable until today, being filed at the school in Talerton. Booker had graciously made the inner office available as a relatively quiet place to research and write Danforth's mandated report. In addition to his derelict briefcase and a few snacks, Monte had brought a small desk lamp to illuminate the dark room. He soon discovered a dearth of wall sockets, of which the Inner Sanctum had none. Searching, he discovered one socket located nearly ten feet away on a strip of baseboard in the classroom, somewhat crusty and without grounding. He called Ramona to ask about extension cords. She had none, she pouted sorrowfully, and did not know where to find any, suggesting he might call Maintenance.

At first, a Mr. Baumgard was stumped as to the definition of *extension cord*, surmising Monte was referring to an item for opening or closing window blinds or shades. Before the question could be clarified, he instructed Monte in vapid non sequiturs to "just use some rope or twine like we've always done in these cases," and hung up. Monte called back and Baumgard answered again, his voice garbled as if eating. Making a crucial error, Monte slowly explained that the windows had no shades or blinds and were in perfect working order, however—

Baumgard cut in and blurted, "Order? New shades and blinds? What size are the windows? And how many are there? Somebody'll have to come over and measure for approval! We don't keep those in stock, you know!"

Monte patiently proceeded to tell him that what was needed at the moment was an electric extension cord, perhaps twelve feet long, or several shorter lengths, for a desk lamp. Unfortunately, in the confusion, the only words Baumgard heard were the last two, "desk lamp." Dropping the phone with a clunk, he retreated for two or three minutes, then came back on the line and said with some perturbation that as far as he knew, they did not have any desk lamps in the Maintenance Department and maybe the caller should check with either Melvin, Ross, or Smedley. Without further elucidation, the line quickly disconnected once more with a sharp click.

Calling for a third time, Monte asked optimistically about Melvin. "Yeah!" Baumgard shouted. "Melvin's been here longer'n anybody, knows all the ins and outs . . . only he ain't here today." Brief silence ensued, then, "Well, what I mean is to say, he ain't exactly physically present on the shop premises. Got another commode stoppage over in Webster dorm. Deaf kids been eatin' too much cheese I'd say." A hearty laugh spilled from the phone. "Then he's got a leak'n radiator in Mullen's office. He knows all there is to know about plumbing. I'll tell him you called when he gets back this afternoon—that is, assuming he gets back today at all. Melvin that is, not Mullens." Baumgard was laughing hysterically when he hung up.

Monte called Booker's house and no one answered. Calling Talbert's gave the same result. Then he called Ramona to get a number for the dormitory supervisor and was told in nasal monotone that the person he needed to speak with was out for the week with the flu. Asking about Smedley brought on a titter of giggles. "No, you don't want Smedley, trust me." And she rang off, chuckling in a series of full, gulping hiccups.

Calling the Vocational Department and holding for twelve rings brought no answer. Gladstone was sitting in his classroom eating a donut, flecks of sugary glaze encircling his mouth and coating his fleshy lips like ice crystals. Between bites, he mumbled with the utmost earnestness and empathy his own troubling experience with just the same problem.

"A shortage of electrical sockets," he bemoaned around bites of pastry. As solution, he had purchased an extension cord with his own money after several abortive attempts to have the school provide one—a nice, blue, heavy-duty twelve-footer—only to have it swiped the first day he used it. An investigation conducted by Ramona and the Security Department met with no success. Gladstone had composed a lengthy memo to Fletcher, with copies to Dr. Mullens and the Business Office, asking that he be reimbursed for the cord, and moreover, that funding be designated for some much-needed electrical improvements and renovations in the classrooms. That, he whined, reaching for another donut, was two years ago.

Monte called the Vocational Department again and a man answered; at least, he thought it was a man. An ear-splitting whirring overpowered the voice, forcing him or her to shout in a manner which defied gender identification or the deciphering of what was being said. The noise shifted into a grinding racket, and then a jackhammer-like clatter, followed by an eruption of screeches, as if someone were strangling a large, uncooperative goose. Through it all, the person on the other end of the line was shouting, perhaps to Monte, or maybe to someone in the shop. At length the voice hollered, "Call back later!" and slammed down the receiver.

Confident that Maintenance was still the best prospect, Monte called again. Baumgard answered. Begging him not to hang up until a careful explanation could be made of what was needed, Monte meticulously enunciated each syllable of every word, saying, "I need a ten or twelve-foot electric extension cord up here in Cameron Hall. Do you have something like that? It's for a desk lamp."

"Ten or twelve foot, you say," Baumgard murmured with a worthy show of profound rumination. "That, I'd reckon, would come under the heading of a commercial cord, not household, certainly *not* household. Commercial is much more heavy duty, you know, the orange or yellow ones, sometimes blue, with ground prongs. We'd have to measure to be sure and check voltage specifications."

"I did the measuring myself, Mr. Baum—"

"A shelf? What kind of shelf?"

"Not a shelf, forget the shelf!" Monte seethed. "An extension cord, twelve feet or so."

"Well, that's commercial grade, like I said. You'd need a requisition."

"A requisition? Where would I get that?"

"Business Office, Ludlow, or maybe Irma. Probably take less than a week if you're in a hurry."

"Thanks a lot, Mr. Baumgard. I'll look into it."

Just as Monte dolefully hung up the phone, a small head peeped in around the doorframe, short, curly, reddish hair spreading in a defiant display of chaos and individuality, huge eyes beaming behind monstrous glass circles in dark frames, a nose too large to be elfin, and a wide smile curling with joy of discovery.

"Mr. S!" Arnold exclaimed. "I didn't expect to see you! I'm on my way to the dining hall for breakfast." The route to the dining hall from the elementary dormitory, Monte knew, came nowhere near Booker's room—in fact, would have required a detour of almost a quarter mile. But he made no comment, knowing Arnold always had his strategies.

"I'm cleaning blackboards today," Arnold announced proudly, "so thought a quick look in Cameron would be a jump start before the old cereal bowl." He made it sound completely logical, even praiseworthy.

"That's nice, Arnold," Monte remarked. "I should add you to my student work program report, except you're too young."

By intentional increments, he came all the way into the room and sat down, leaning over to examine the nonworking desk lamp.

"I have one of these in my room. Does it work?" He put his nose almost on the metal bulb cover and ran tiny fingers down the flexible neck.

"It would if I could plug it in. I need an extension cord; no outlets in here, I found out."

"You could buy one at the hardware, I'm sure of that." Arnold clicked the switch on and off a few times, then added in a reflective, unconcerned drawl, "Or I could just go and get one for you."

"What do you mean, you could get one?" Monte asked doubtfully.

"How long does it need to be?" He was turning the lamp upside down, studying the tiny opening where the cord passed into the base.

"Twelve feet would be plenty, but—"

"No problemo, Mr. S. I'll be back in two or three shakes." He scooted out with no further comments.

In less than ten minutes he was back, a heavy-duty blue extension cord luckily affixed with a grounding adaptor looped on his tiny shoulder. On the basis of situational ethics, no further inquiries were conducted. They plugged it in, and the gloomy Inner Sanctum flamed with a burst of mustard-yellow light revealing cracks and historic blemishes of abuse not seen for decades. The ugly, true nature of the room was startlingly depressing, evocative of a Dumas prison chamber.

To Arnold, enamored with the cheap little lamp, dinginess of the room had no apparent dampening effect upon his assiduous and minutial dissection thereof, as he continued to toy with it gingerly. After a few minutes, Monte said, "Thanks very much for the cord. How did you know where to, uh, put your hands on one?"

The lad made a casual shrugging movement of his thin shoulders, as if to show the deed had involved no effort or inconvenience, at the same time working the gooseneck of the lamp back and forth, spotlighting various points of interest around the office.

"I get around," he mumbled, not looking up. And then, a half minute later, Monte thought Arnold may have winked as, with great reluctance, he separated himself from the lamp and scrambled out the door. The rest of the day, Monte worked in uninterrupted solitude, amassing the report data for Danforth.

• • •

The old square clock high on Booker's classroom wall had read ten after six when last checked. Now, thirty minutes later, Monte was packing up to leave.

As anticipated, the detailed account Danforth had demanded had become involved and bureaucratically lengthy. With eyes bleary and neck corded, Monte's head felt as if clamped by an unmerciful vise. He stood and stretched, back muscles and shoulders resisting and stitched tight, and he noted through the one squalid little window that darkness had crept quietly onto the courtyard, blotting the chapel to a pale silhouette only murkily visible. Unbroken, intimidating silence numbed aurality from pursuing any edifying iota of sound, any reassuring verification of living motion beyond confines of the small, musty room. Claustrophobia, after almost eleven hours, had set with vengeance. He yearned for musical piquancy, a voice, any noise confessing human existence.

As if on command, the hallway door opened and footsteps pattered haltingly into the classroom. He waited behind the desk, gathering the last of his things, expecting one of the cleaning ladies to momentarily burst in through the closed inner office door. More steps, closer, delivered a soft knocking, and then a muffled woman's voice filtering through: "Monte?"

He quickly slipped around the desk and opened the door. In blue knitted coat and black wool beret, she stood motionless, smile timidly brittle. Speech lost, two forms rooted in place as though the reel of time had frozen in a single frame from which movement forward or backward was impossible. In the dim light, shimmering as an apparition of herself, Clare Augsburg took on otherworldly, ethereal aspect. Sure he was being cast into a dream, Monte wavered, succumbing to delusions of fatigue, walls of internment compressing perception into false imagery.

With faltering effort, he spoke at last. "I . . . I didn't expect . . ." And that was all his tongue could manage.

She searched his face uneasily, as though fearing rebuff. A voice braced, strained, verging close on tears, said, "Arnold told me . . .

told me you were working late, so I brought coffee." Hesitatingly, she extended an arm, offering a lidded cup, her bearing now a mélange of fragility and tenderness, as though the few words had tempered qualms of risking a visit uninvited. And as he took the cup carefully from her offering hand, distinct currents of warmth spread from the mittened fingers to his own.

Of the many logjammed utterances to be proffered as they stood confounded, what came forth was but a hoarse whisper of unedited feeling. "I haven't seen you since . . ." He struggled to put words together, dismembered by emotion.

"The afternoon in the parking lot," she finished for him, holding firm with glistening eyes, sparkling diamonds encircled by veils of shadow.

"Yes, the parking lot," he whispered. "The flat tire." He dared explore her more fully now, probing for motive which might betray her shrouded intentions or expectations.

"Did you get it fixed?" she said lightly.

"Had to replace it," he said, tension easing. "And another tire too. What about your car heater?"

"It's better . . . but nothing like a corduroy coat." Her laughter was regretfully hollow, catching somewhere deep in her throat.

Standing in a doorway between two cheerless rooms, Monte's face molded into a constrained grin. He stepped back and with a noble sweep of arm said, "Come into my cave and sit down. I haven't seen a person since early this morning, and that happened to be Arnold."

Clare moved past him and was in the act of settling when Mrs. Swartz, one of the cleaning ladies, bustled into the classroom, clanging with equipment. Poking her head into the inner office, her eyes widened in good-humored surprise.

"Oh, you're still here. Sorry to disturb you."

Monte had found her to be a most amiable woman, a fixture of the school for many years, partially deaf, maybe fifty, with a wealth of trivial gossip gleaned from careful listening and discarded letters and notes in wastebaskets.

"You're not disturbing us, Mrs. Swartz," he said. "We're the ones in your way."

"No, no. You just carry on. I'll work out here in the classroom." She towed a top-heavy, rickety cart affair laden with cleaning supplies, large plastic trash can attached to the side, all of which she maneuvered skillfully up, down, and between desk rows.

Clare whispered, "Maybe we should leave so—"

"We're just leaving, Mrs. Swartz," Monte echoed, walking over and placing a hand on her shoulder. "Do you know Clare Augsburg?"

Mrs. Swartz beamed. "Of course I do. She's the cooking teacher. Hello, dear. You're looking lovely this evening."

Clare dropped her eyes as if embarrassed, muttering, "Thank you."

Out on the bridge, they stood by the railing, air crisp and very still. One timorous fixture above the Cameron Hall double doors cast a feeble circle of flossy light around them, ingested to misty obscurity beyond their small sphere by ravenous night. Monte sipped the coffee, a finger of vapor rising from the cup like an enchanted cobra. Clare tilted her head ever so slightly to one side with a genial, somewhat dutiful expression, and said, "I hope it's not too weak; a little milk, no sugar, right?"

The hot liquid could have been muddy pond water strained through dirty socks and Monte would have raved at the savory richness; but in fact, the brew was delicious. "Just right." He grinned. "And appreciated very much, believe me."

Uneasily, Clare quickly straightened, reached down into a coat pocket, and extracted a little square packet and held it out. "I almost forgot about these. I know you had no breaks and ate no lunch today, Mr. Scott."

"Have you been spying on me?" he teased with mock suspicion. "How do you know these things?"

"Oh, I get around," she said, the corners of her mouth curling. "And I have agents and methods."

"Would one of those agents be about four foot tall with curly red hair?" And then they broke into a titter of giggles.

"Only one; the other is very large with black hair," she admitted.

He smiled. "Ah, the two *A*s, Arnold and Arthur."

Wrapped carefully in the napkins was a small stack of chocolate-chip cookies, sweetness whiffing up and teasing his taste buds.

"What a treat. My compliments to the DLS Department, and to the deliverer . . . the delivery woman," he said, chuckling at his tongue-twisted butchery of *deliverer*. "That's not easy to say, is it? Especially when it's cold."

Fragments of laughter dissolved in profound courtyard blackness, scattering on aged chapel walls, ripples of merriment ringing as one echoing chime in the frigid space, vanishing beyond retrieval in the breath of an utterance. She radiated saintly luminescence, more so than ever before, thoroughly impeccant and vulnerable, a diaphanous, angelic perfection she would disclaim with humble servility, enriching her ambience all the more.

Amidst gaiety, she waned into purposeful somberness, some aura of need, he worried, calling to be consoled by confrontation, a neglected, unfinished burden harbored too long and held too tightly. Strong inclinations to turn away, shun, and bury the breach with banalities braced him in defense, dismayed that encumbrance of what her bearing intimated would be destructive with harsh reality—an aggressive, pervasive enemy intent to destroy their quixotic crux of splendor.

And yet, in fairness to truth, he could not forbid her, isolate himself from her need. He knew well imperatives of the heart, restive and heavy. And cursing his mantra within that capsule of time, he grasped for belief in some indefinable unity, a mysterious depth of caring communion allowing no shuttering of one from the other.

She said gently, "I've needed to talk with you, Monte, since that afternoon . . . in the parking lot."

"Clare, please, you don't have to say—" he implored, steeling himself, despite knowing she must.

"Yes, I do, Monte, I do." She stared into his face with urgent entreaty. *For what?* he wrestled. *Charity, forgiveness, salvation of friendship, healing?* And all, he hoped, were freely offered in his eyes. Even sentence of righteous dismissal, declaration of unchangeable fact.

She went on unwaveringly, "I was rude and curt, and I don't know what came over me. Seeing you and Richard there . . . was a surprise, and confusing. And it makes no sense. Such a simple, insignificant—"

Monte moved closer, cautiously relieved, so as to whisper beside her bowed head. "It's all right, Clare. It was nothing. You were tired and I was in a bad mood. Richard was . . . maybe the only sane one."

She raised her face and murmured, "Thank you, Monte Scott, for understanding." And then, almost laughing, clouds freed and erased from her mind, she said, "Now, maybe I can sleep again."

They sauntered down to the parking lot, Monte sipping coffee and munching cookies, tensity of the previous moments evaporating into an air of almost languid prevailing contentment. She told him of Arnold coming to her classroom that morning to borrow an extension cord, which, he had exclaimed with winded excitement, "Mr. S. needs ASAP for an emergency!"

"At first I was concerned," Clare related, "and then realized it was just Arnold being melodramatic. He was quite puffed up and said, 'Mr. Scott is at his very most wit's end!' and that I couldn't picture."

With interims of near humor, she captivated and calmed some restless place in his soul, a bromide of lightness to knit hours of fatigue and disordered abstraction. Inclined together against the side of her old Ford, troubling, wicked ruminations invaded imagination laboring in vain at deflection. Shunning propriety gave freedom to dream, to enfold her in his arms and bring her close, breathing her freshness and warmth forever, to become as one in mind and soul and body. Some obstructing clarity of fear erased the tempting joy of his vision, adjudicating boundaries of respect and esteem he held for her, and for himself. *Yet knowing a thing is wrong,* he pondered guiltily, *seldom deters wishful human rationality from doubtful license.*

Indefinable divine intervention rather than rational choice had often diverted his dubious paths, God never missing a chance to move in mysterious ways, saving one from a careless, caroming self.

"Richard said he likes you," she said weakly, as though wielding the words as a shield.

Staring into the distance, wondering if musing fantasies had become transparent, his eyes sought a place to rest, mind seeking clarity. Some oblique compliment, he felt, was demanded. Quietly and simply, he said, "He seems a very good man, and I liked him too."

A touch of reverence he could not decipher overcast Clare's face, as she looked not at him when she spoke but to a deeply inculcated oath of obedience. "He is a good man. A very good man."

A thin layer of awkwardness had sprouted and spread unexpectedly, a flimsy, irritating provocation, a splinter calling for tactful recognition. To smooth the discourse, and perhaps only compounding an air of stiffness, Monte asked blandly, "How long have you been together?"

She gave the impression of expecting the question or something similar, mustering her response and saying in straightforward manner, "Actually, since our senior year in high school, about six years ago. We started rather steady dating and, well, later it became . . . comfortable and compatible." Her lack of smile was unreadable, and, not particularly kindly, he thought she might well have described the affair as habitual, carried forward by safe, neutrally rote momentum.

He lifted his chin in specious enthusiasm and murmured, "Wow, since high school." Feeling he should offer more, he added, "It's nice to have that kind of security, someone you know will be there."

She glanced down for just a second, then raised her head and focused somewhere beyond him, saying in the manner of rehearsed recitation, her delivery taking on a childlike tone, "Yes, it is. His parents are good friends with mine, have been for years and years. We grew up together, nearly like siblings, or cousins. I suppose it was . . . we were just a predestined pairing."

"Yes, I see," Monte said, almost embarrassingly sympathetic. Clearing his throat, he wondered if there was any way she could possibly have fashioned the relationship to sound more dull and passionless. "Are you cold?" he asked more urgently. "I didn't mean to keep you standing out here—"

"No, I'm fine. Feels nice to be outside after being in a stuffy, windowless basement all day." She brightened and breathed deeply, raising her face to the sky, as though some difficult and unpredictable passage had been successfully traversed.

After an interval of palpitant silence, neither making any move to leave, Monte ventured with careful hesitancy, "I'm thinking of going over to Valley Pizza, if you'd like to join me—that is, if it would suit."

Vacillation danced across her face. He had already assumed refusal when with confounding spontaneity she said, "That sounds nice, and I'm starving from watching you eat all those cookies."

They rode downtown in the red Bug, the heater being superior to the Ford's. While they ate, she clarified—somewhat as a justifying confessional, Monte thought—that Richard was out of town for several days for business. No further information was offered or requested. Pizza diminished piece by piece as jovial conversation progressed unabated, until Clare at length glanced at her watch and announced, rather astonished, that it was almost 9:30. Splitting the bill, he refusing her forceful offer to pay, they drove slowly back to the Academy. Reclined, relaxed, and sated, Clare closed her eyes and folded her hands on her lap. Monte considered asking tritely, "A penny for your thoughts?" but constrained the urge, reveling in transient seclusion of togetherness.

Unavoidably, an onus of vague guilt blighted the air, and he wondered, as he had before, how Richard would view the evening. Was their marriage so solid, so open and free, as not to be threatened by an innocent night out with someone else? Did the evening carry significance enough to even mention? By the time they reached the parking lot and her solitary Ford bathed in misty light, questions had faded to no particularly meaningful value, filed away for another time and place.

He stood by her window as she started the Ford's engine and jokingly asked if she needed his corduroy coat.

"Tempting, but not tonight, I think," she said softly.

He smiled. "Drive carefully. And don't fall asleep."

Staring through the windshield for a fleeting second, she then turned, almost grim, and said slowly, "That afternoon in the parking lot, the flat-tire day. I wanted so badly to say . . . something, anything. But you knew that."

The remembrance posed not a question but a statement of intimate knowledge and covenant. Gazing into her darkly burnished eyes, searching a face blanched pale by harsh, bluish light, he was somehow momentarily enjoined with her by a hushed summons of mutual supplication. Averse to risk dissolution of an implicit bond, he could only linger in silent obeisance until at last her exigency prevailed and he whispered, for no other voice existed, "Yes, Clare, I knew. I knew."

• • •

Journal: Monday, November 3, 11:20 PM

What a lovely, wonderful, awful, crazy evening! Started with my finally having nerve enough to go and seek out the man who's been churning my mind (heart?) for almost two weeks (and more before that), and then he asked me to go for dinner.

And we laughed and talked for two hours or more that was like ten minutes. Felt so nice to be with him again. Fortunate he's such a gentlemen. At times my insides were melting. Darn! Someday maybe I'll work up courage to ask about his life and history. I bet Arthur Brooks could tell me.

I should feel guilty and ashamed, though I haven't really done anything wrong (have I?), but it's not right and fair to Richard or to Monte, or wise.

Broke my vow. Am I being foolish? I nearly revealed everything to my mother—my questions and fear. But almost immediately I realized that would be a mistake. Thoughts are not just thoughts to her. She would have to do something. Fix the situation.

What's happening to the Clare I thought I knew so well?

We must have a long, long chat soon, God.

• • •

He found Booker sequestered in the Inner Sanctum late Friday afternoon with Talbert, Dr. Bartlett, Elizabeth Blanchard, and Myron Kinsinger, a young teacher Monte had met only recently and did not know well. Booker sat gravely erect behind his desk, Talbert perched on the edge, Bartlett seated in the chair, and Elizabeth and Myron standing behind him, tight to the wall. "Ah! Is this the sardine gang?" Monte joked, opening the door and smiling.

Everyone grinned except Booker, displaying distaste for any form of jocularity for the moment. "Come in if you can fit," he said firmly. "You might have some input on questions and points we've been discussing."

Monte had been told by phone the previous day an ad hoc committee had been formed to address concerns about the school psychologist, Dr. London. An appointment with a reluctant Principal Fletcher had been sought for later in the week. Squeezing through the door enough to close it, he said, "I'll be glad to help if I can. What've you decided so far?"

Booker motioned to Dr. Bartlett, math instructor and staff person holding the longest tenure at the Academy, as well as unanimous choice to be spokesman. Straightening his round, compact body in the hard oak chair and adjusting spectacles higher up the bridge of his nose, he spoke in a strong, implacable voice.

"We want, first of all, to impress upon Mr. Fletcher our concerns about the negative attitudes Dr. London has exhibited toward our pupils. There are ample examples, and we can document all if necessary. Secondly, we want Dr. London recused from administering any and all psychological testing of our students, and a qualified independent replacement to be retained. Thirdly, we want the administration to evaluate the suitability of Dr. London's continuance in his present position." He exhaled and glanced around the room. The others nodded approval and he quietly said, "That's about it in a nutshell . . . for now, I think."

"Any thoughts, Scott?" Booker asked. Having been at the school but a short time, Monte shrank from the question, yet felt somehow responsible, having urged Booker to instigate the steps now being pursued.

"You understand, I guess," Monte said, "that this, uh, course of action may not be well received by the administration?" Again, all assented. "Are any students aware of the plans?"

Booker spoke up. "No, not to our knowledge. None of us has said anything. For now, we want students left out if possible."

Monte asked, "How about Dr. London? Is he aware?"

Dr. Bartlett answered quickly, "Not as yet."

"But you plan to tell him . . . or not?"

Talbert said, "I'm seeing him before we talk to Fletcher. We thought— We supposed it only fair."

Monte inhaled breathily and scanned the room. "I believe, well, from my inexperienced point of view, that it's vital Mr. Fletcher and Dr. London understand your concerns—*our* concerns—are for the welfare of students and not in any sense a personal vendetta or witch hunt. This, I think, must be emphasized and made very clear."

As though piqued, Dr. Bartlett grated, "The facts of our concerns are manifestly obvious, Monte. And, as I've said, can be well documented. We'll present our case with this in mind and can only hope the principal will listen and understand. None of us has any personal animosity for Dr. London as an individual."

Pondering for a moment, Monte then said, "Mr. Fletcher's probably going to ask why this is just now coming forward and hasn't sooner."

Myron answered modestly, "We thought about that. Two things, er, Monte. Dr. London's changed—regressed might be a better word—in the past month or so, showing signs of stress and irritability that he didn't . . . or we didn't see, previously. And we've also had a large number of recent complaints and comments from students about his attitude and some of the things he's said to them."

Elizabeth added forcefully, "Some of the kids are really frightened of him. I don't think that's generally known."

"Well, sounds like you're well prepared. I hope all works for the best, for everyone, especially the kids." Monte's attempted smile of reassurance stagnated almost at once to a full-bodied wince. Frustrated by ill-defined position within the school community, he wished for freedom to be a more integral, helpful participant—realizing, objectively and guiltily, a status of comfortably safe removal from the fray. The body before him risked much; he risked nothing.

Turning to leave, he stopped and said quietly, "I know this is difficult. However, for what it's worth, I believe what you're doing needs to be done, and it's the right thing to do."

Alone later that night, a solemn, almost shamefully surprising penitence washed over him, questioning the wisdom of his reassuring counsel to the teachers. For he remembered and knew well what history taught and so often had been forgotten: the many instances when a course of action had visited pain, suffering, and destruction on humanity, all in the name of a righteous cause.

• • •

Maintaining nominal allegiance to his diet, and showing little resultant evidence thereof, Booker had compounded his penchant for crankiness by additionally swearing off tobacco products in preparation for the holiday season. His safety net, judging by an unsightly proliferation of paper wrappers migrating about his desk, was chewing gum, brand and flavor evidently a nonissue. And then, in dangerous progression from the junk food and smoking ban, he zealously pledged to tackle the vice of his often colorful language.

Glowing with goodwill Wednesday morning, he adjudged the occasion perfect to explain, in rationalizing and well-thought-out manner, his approach to serious cursing, which he defined as not only the familiar four-letter variety, but in particular the *G* word.

"I have two rules I follow unwaveringly," he declared with a sharp edge of sanctimonious piety, Captain Corcoran come to life. Monte half expected a gallant leap onto the desk in lieu of a poop deck to wail forth an operetta. "First," he moralized, "I never cuss in the hearing of students. That is a cardinal rule." Broken, by Monte's unofficial count, almost daily. Temptation to amend the man's remarks with a hardy chorus of "Well, hardly ever" was almost more than any listener should be asked to bear.

Booker pondered for a few seconds, apparently debating whether additional commentary was required, then sniggered casually, "Of course, they're all familiar with the best words anyway, and use 'em all the time when they can get away with it." Distracted by his own digression, he then blurted out, "But! They won't hear them from me. I will not set a bad example."

Monte squelched a groan, though the effort was painful.

Charging on with no lessening of pharisaical nobility, Booker stated, "Rule two is, I never curse at home."

This, Monte knew, was complete balderdash. Only days before, sitting in Booker's kitchen, he had observed the man light into a malfunctioning toaster which with daily regularity not only seared bread to a charcoal consistency but then sprang the smoldering slices in smoky, arching trajectories halfway across the room. Had it been harnessed, the execrating blue streak Monte witnessed would easily have welded steel plates together. Gwen, his wife, had been unmoved, having endured years of constrained patience with her husband, but his three children had scattered like antelopes fleeing a lion.

The better part of wisdom silenced Monte, and Booker continued unrestrained.

"But the main rule, the one inviolable rule is, I never take the Lord's name in vain."

Only hypertensive effort prevented Monte from pointing out that this was a third rule, even greater effort required to refrain from challenging Booker's memory and accuracy for this particular claim. But rationalization to counter objections had been prepared, should anyone exhibit such reckless courage.

"You're probably thinking you've heard me use the *G* word, and in a way, you'd be right. But in actuality, you'd be wrong."

Monte's wish in this moment was for a jury of twelve astute witnesses, or perhaps merely a tape recorder, to preserve for posterity the concoction of fallacious drivel Booker was outlining. He suspected most was being made up as the story went along—Booker conversing with himself and testing ideas for any substantial cogency.

"You see," Booker said, locking fingers behind his head and leaning back in his chair as if casually delineating Bezout's identity theorem of divisional algorithms to a kindergartner, "there's the *large-G* usage, meaning capital *G*, which is a definite no-no. But"—and here he paused for emphasis, rocking forward and placing his hands flat atop the desk—"there's the harmless *small-g* word which can be used without fear of breaking any commandment, since it refers only to pagan gods that don't exist anyway."

He regarded Monte with the satisfaction of one who had just demonstrated a solution to the time–space continuum question, falling confidently back in his chair to relock fingers behind his neck. "See?" he said with simplicity, as if taking Monte's hand and leading him out of demented ignorance.

Of all possible replies, the best Monte could produce was, "Sure, yeah, I, uh, think I get the drift," simultaneously shaking his head in wonder at the endless parade of Booker's phenomenal logic.

• • •

Dr. London's office door was ajar, and Monte saw him sitting behind the desk, hands folded in his lap and chin down to his chest as if dozing. From the doorway he spoke the man's name, noting drooped eyelids not completely closed. He showed no response when Monte spoke a second time. Moving closer, standing curiously in front of the desk, Monte called out London's name louder.

A ripple of wary vigilance welled up as Monte studied the mute, inert figure for any sign of movement or reaction. Very slowly, so slowly as to be almost imaginary, the doctor's head angled to the side, eyes now only partially shuttered, opened enough to reveal wandering beacons searching the floor and desktop, face a plaster mask stripped of sensory association, hollowed and spiritless. Monte spoke a fourth time, softly, apprehensive of startling the stupored figure, possibly in a state of catatonia. London registered slightly, head ratcheting upward in concise, reflexive steps like solitary frames of film in extreme slow motion.

Leaning over toward him, bracing hands on the desk, Monte whispered, "Reginald, it's me, Monte Scott."

With difficulty, grimacing as if in pain, the doctor worked to focus on the voice. Again Monte said, "Reginald, it's Monte," stretching over to place hands firmly on the man's shoulders.

Monte could almost see his mind, imprisoned in conflict, swimming into cognizance, thrashing against entangling webs of deep sleep, dark currents dragging him back to caverns of comatose captivity. Breath by breath he gained miniscule advantage, eyes closely fixed in bewildered examination to the tip of Monte's nose. Perplexed by this strange vision of solidity invading his private phantom world, a distant banshee moan escaped his throat, filling the small room and lifting hair on the nape of Monte's neck.

"Are you awake, Reginald?" Monte asked firmly. "Can you hear me?"

His lips fluttered into what could have been a smile or prelude to a scream or the beginning of tears. And then, hoarsely slurred, he spoke: "Monte? Hello . . . Monte. What . . . are . . .?" As though exhausted, his eyes faded to sightless refuge. Eerily, his words tinny and jagged like whistles of harsh winter wind in old and loose window frames, he whined, "I shouldn't have . . . have done it . . . should I? Such a fool . . . all this time . . . you were right."

Slumping over to his side in the chair, he panted shallowly, face chalky white, pupils floating wide and black like dark, listless pools, remotely distant, focusing on nothing tangible. And then Monte knew what he should have known sooner.

In anger, he grabbed the phone and called an operator for a rescue squad. With a crew on the way, he called the infirmary, praying a nurse was on duty, his hands vibrating, itching with tremors as though coursed with mild electric current. As luck or fate would have it, there were two, and one would come immediately. Searching the trash can, he found an empty prescription container labeled with a drug he did not recognize, and placed it on the desk.

Not knowing what else to do, Monte began to slap London's cheeks. Taking hold of his shoulders, he rocked him back and forth, his body a huge and heavy rag doll. Within two minutes the nurse bounded up the stairs and into the office. Immediately she raised the man's lowered eyelids, felt for a pulse, and listened to his heart. Then, with one arm pushing his head forward, she forced open his mouth and jammed her other hand as far down his throat as she could. He gasped, gagged, fighting her, and retched violently, disgorging a thin stream of yellowish-green vomit down his tie and onto his pants and the floor. Turning her eyes to Monte, she said with calm urgency, "Now help me get him up."

Carefully and with great difficulty, arms wedged under London's arms, they managed to lift him out of the chair with strength neither knew they possessed. The nurse, breathing hard, gasped, "Let's take him in the hall where there's more room to move around."

With London's feet dragging on the old wood floor and the nurse and Monte struggling with his bulk, heads and necks now awkwardly skewed in the doctor's armpits, they coursed in slow, back-and-forth baby steps. In less than ten minutes, two rescue squad men arrived, rushing up the stairs like angels from heaven to seize their burden and commandeer the situation with smooth efficiency. Monte handed over the prescription vial, and in twenty minutes London was lying on a gurney in Talerton Hospital emergency room.

The nurse immediately went to inform Fletcher, who, aghast and speechless, simply twisted his head in disbelief. At her suggestion, they went back to London's office and after a brief search found several more containers of various drugs in his desk. She called the hospital with this new information.

The meeting between the teachers committee and Principal Fletcher had taken place that morning. Dr. Bartlett had laid out their concerns and was heard with polite gravity, afterward given appreciation for the professionalism and empathy they expressed for the psychologist. All that could be promised in conclusion was careful consideration of the facts and sharing of information with Dr. Mullens. And this was where the matter lay until Monte found Dr. London stuporous in his office.

Booker and Monte visited the hospital that evening, to be told London was conscious and resting and had survived a very close call. No visitation, other than family, of whom he had none local, was being allowed for the present. In the car returning to his house, Booker sat stoic yet fidgety, several times beginning to speak, only to retreat to uneasy muteness.

Mind spinning, unable to focus, Monte said nothing. Once they'd arrived and parked in front of Booker's house, the two men bided restive, respective thoughts a vacuum of otherworldliness, marooned to drift in space. Stirring after an incalculable length of moments, Booker whispered in hoarse, clipped syllables, "Did we . . . are we responsible for pushing him into . . . over the edge?"

Inclination to self-reproach and culpability reared an ugly head, inevitable and threateningly valid. The apparent suicide attempt could clearly be tied to a challenge of London's competence, maybe presenting the final straw to a weight of growing depression. History of drug abuse could only be suspected at this point, yet would help explain mood swings and growing belligerence.

An agitated Booker cracked his knuckles annoyingly, breathing deeply. What emerged layer by layer was harsh reckoning, imputation of a rush to judgement, indictment of what they feared may have been fallacious self-righteousness.

"I think," Monte stumbled. "I wonder now, Benjamin, if . . ." Faltering, exhaling lengthily, the effect like a distant, moaning echo seeking coherence, then fading, he forged on. "Perhaps what we're guilty of is—was—blindly passing by on the other side."

Booker needed no tutor for reference, canting vaguely, no more than a transient tic.

Conviction stronger, Monte said, "He blocked us at every turn from giving what he most needed: simple, caring friendship and support. And we . . . fell for it and turned away, angry, assured and secure in our justification of dislike and opinions. We wrote him off as . . . as a churlish jerk, a loathsome bastard. At least, I know I did."

Pausing and turning his head away, he stared out the car window at a yellow porch light on a house across the street, mellow and welcoming, unadorned symbol of home and warmth and safety. "I suppose in some sense he became the evil, intolerable son of a bitch we perceived him to be."

And Monte, before the "court of conscience" of which Gandhi spoke, held himself up in greater judgment. *Physician, heal thyself.* For it was he who with sanctimonious indignation had lectured London on seeing through student distortions and inventions in order to discover truth, their truth.

They sat a while longer, not speaking, and then, venturing into some defensible place of probity and comfort, Monte mused, his words strained, "Maybe there was nothing we could have done. Sometimes even the best we can do isn't enough. Hell, Benjamin, we fail more often than we succeed! Dammit, I don't know. I have no answers. No excuses."

After a few moments Booker asked, as if to himself, "Well, what's to be done now?"

An aching fatigue took hold, as though arms and shoulders were lead and legs pillars of concrete. "Now?" Monte wondered, perplexed and beaten. "We can't undo what's done, can we? There's never any going back. Maybe we can learn, seek forgiveness, make amends."

The banality of his utterance, said in flat, rote recitation, brought forth no inspiring solace or insight to either man.

Verging on apology for his triteness, Monte was interrupted as Booker said thoughtfully, head lowered, "That's the redeeming part, isn't it? A—what would you say—fundamental essence of humanness, that a broken life can be mended. His, and ours. That so often we're given second chances . . . to atone our wrongs."

Wavering for a second, he went on, "I guess the challenge is to see the need, confess, and have courage to take that second chance." A tear of expiation slowly made its way down his cheek as he breathed deeply and murmured, "I doubt he'll ever come back to the school." And then, reflecting, casting about for any fragment of tenable clarity, he added, "And maybe that's for the best. For everyone."

After some moments, he turned to Monte and said almost hungrily, "But we *were* right, weren't we. To go to Fletcher, I mean?" The question was a simple plea, rabidly cleaved together in search of fragile validation.

More contrite than satisfied, Monte reached over and touched Booker's shoulder, whispering, "I believe what was done had to be done, Benjamin. For the kids." They shared pallid smiles, united in dubiety. And perhaps more truthfully, or only for healing appeasement, he ventured, "And a part of him, I think, hoped we would."

CHAPTER NINE

AS THREATENED, MARLON DANFORTH presented himself at the Academy Monday midmorning. Monte felt at once shabby, confronted by Fletcher and his supervisor in their immaculately tailored grey wool suits, starched white shirts, and ruby-red silk ties, hair neatly trimmed and combed in symmetrical and perfectly proportioned contours; even their fingernails exhibited a superior luster of undefiled purity and class.

"Come in," the principal bade him in welcome, seated in padded comfort behind a pristinely shining walnut desk. Danforth reposed smugly beside him, nestled in a red leather tufted wing chair. Tempering snarling hostility and primordial caveman desire, Monte imagined reaching out and hoisting the men up by their stylish ties to twirl them comically round the room like a cowboy's lariat.

The image lightened his mood, and he smiled and said graciously, "Good morning, Mr. Fletcher, Mr. Danforth."

"This won't take long," Danforth announced, uncrossing his legs and leaning forward, leaving Monte to wonder if he should sit or stand. As no one invited him to take one of the two chairs facing the desk, he chose to remain standing. Turning to Fletcher, Danforth asked, "Where's Booker?" The principal apologized, saying he had taken a sick day, suffering from a persistent bad cold. Huffing, the visitor reached down stiffly into a thin black briefcase idling beside his chair and withdrew a few glossy brochures. Renewed, gleaming with the air of a carnival vendor promoting a peep show, Danforth passed one to Fletcher and one to Monte, sermonizing, "Take a look at this and I think you'll be as impressed as I was."

The front leaf read, in bold lettering, *Career Development Consultation Services, Inc.*, under which was a colorful photograph of a smartly dressed man hovering over a mesmerized couple seated at a table and studying a similar brochure. Interspersed within the pages were additional pictures of deliriously happy men and women ostensibly being doused with propaganda by the same imperiously smiling man, much resembling Danforth's expression when next Monte glanced his way.

During the following twenty minutes, Danforth dissected every word in the smartly designed booklet as if meticulously deciphering fragments of an ancient Dead Sea scroll. "See what it says here on the last page?" he bubbled. "*CDCS, Inc. was created for YOU.* That's what sold me. And after you meet their rep, Atkins Turnage, I know you'll feel exactly the same way."

Fletcher had taken on a thoughtful cast, as though laboring to follow what was being presented, perhaps recalling with some queasiness, Monte pondered with silly projection, the runny eggs, burnt bacon, and dry toast the man had been served for breakfast. Still standing, Monte waited, sickening suspicion arising as to where the narration was headed. Without consciously noticing, he held his breath, not blinking, tightly gripping the back of the chair defending him like a partial barrier.

Had Danforth uncovered a thick vein of pure gold in his front yard and a huge oil deposit in the rear garden, he could not have been more frenzied. "Our key to successful job development and placement is *right here*," he blubbered, flapping the brochure around. Fletcher bobbed his head and stole a cunningly expeditious peek at the wall clock hanging high behind Monte's head.

"Atkins will be spending a week with me at headquarters starting next Monday," Danforth continued, speaking into Fletcher's ear. "We—that is, our agency—have obtained a quite generous grant for his services, and I'm assured of big things."

Monte eschewed temptation to mention anything sarcastically obscene.

Danforth went on, "We can put not only *our* agency but the Academy SET Program on the map. Every blind agency and residential school in the country will look to us as innovators and pioneering leaders in the field."

For a few disoriented moments, Monte felt shaky kinship with the qualmish principal, whose goal seemed only to survive until Danforth ran out of oxygen or died of a sudden stroke. However, without preamble, Danforth took a different tack altogether, eliminating Fletcher abruptly from the discourse.

"I need that report you compiled for me, Scott," he growled. "Do you have it?" His brows arched, mouth firmly set, eyes piercingly fiery—the splenetic man with whom Monte was more familiar.

"Here, sir." Monte picked up a thick folder from the chair seat and handed it over. "There're a few more statistical charts and graphs I want to add, and some photographs being developed, but I can have those by later today or by tomorrow, if that's all right."

"No later!" he fumed. "I've gotta get this material to, er . . . never mind. I just hope it's what I asked for."

"I hope so too, sir. May I, uh, go now?"

Danforth arched his neck and glanced at the principal, then back to Monte, Fletcher daring to sprout mild signs of constipated optimism that the meeting might be drawing to a close.

"Atkins is coming to visit you and Booker in the next couple of weeks," the supervisor clipped concisely. "I'll let you know when. Show him the utmost courtesy. And listen to what he has to say. The man's a genius."

No handshakes were proffered as Monte tipped his head and left, having stood staunchly erect during the entirety of the meeting.

• • •

Arthur James Brooks, bosom friend of Monte Scott for twenty years, had begun teaching history and Latin at the Academy the first week of October. At noon, after his meeting with Danforth and Fletcher and conferences with several students in the Inner Sanctum, Monte sought out the new teacher in his classroom in Perkins Hall. Arthur sat at his desk, absorbed in reading a book propped in front of him, at the same time lifting a food-laden fork from a small plastic container.

The young man looked up to twitch a quick smile as Monte came in. With a deep, lilting baritone accent defying identity but tending toward Jamaican that Arthur sometimes playfully adopted, he called out, "How was your morning with the supervisor and principal, mon?"

Monte could not recall telling him about Danforth's visit, so concluded news must have spread through the school grapevine where nothing was secret or sacred. "Wonderful!" Monte babbled, throwing an arm in the air. "Couldn't have been better. Met every expectation."

"Not what I heard," Arthur said matter-of-factly.

"What would you know about it? You have Fletcher's office bugged?"

"I went to see Ramona at break time," he snickered knowingly, "and saw some obsequious rehab counselor standing at attention before the tribunal."

"I could have used your commanding presence," Monte whined. He plopped down in a student desk, and Arthur began without encouragement to share a summary of his weekend. First, with cursory disregard, he sketched a Saturday evening date.

"She's on the third floor of my apartment building, works at a bank, graduated from a small college with no name in Pennsylvania. And that's all I know so far. Well, almost all I know." He snickered again.

Then, much more directly, he outlined his Sunday afternoon in a voice modulating strangely, eyes more intensely focused. "After church I got a call from someone named Clare Augsburg asking if she and *Richard* could stop by, as she had something for me. I said surely, and they came and stayed for a couple of hours."

"Sounds boring. So, what did they bring you? Or should I ask?" Monte yawned disinterestedly, glancing out the window.

"I'm eating some of it now," he said, holding up his little plastic bowl. "A very nice chicken casserole from Clare and a loaf of her homemade bread. And Richard brought me a basic household tool kit." Ingesting a large forkful of his lunch, he then mumbled with an air of cavalier appreciation, "It's so nice when people think us single guys are helpless and need looking after."

Monte leaned back in the desk and pouted, "Nobody ever brings *me* anything."

"You're not a new guy just relocating from distant lands with no furniture." He shoveled the fork into his mouth again, a few moments later asking, "Aren't you curious what we talked about?" Arthur grinned naughtily, whetting Monte's appetite for both food and information.

"No." Monte stared at the ceiling, studying the dusty light globe, which looked much the same as always.

"Good," Arthur said. "So I'll outline every detail." *He's enjoying the conversation far too much,* Monte thought, intrigued. Turning sideways in the desk, Monte concentrated attention outside, craning his neck as though checking the weather.

"Well, first, I showed them around the apartment. That took two minutes. Thankfully, it was mostly tidy. Richard got interested in my books and magazines and sat on the sofa browsing while I showed Clare some of my most precious mementoes." He took another bite of casserole, eyeing Monte with circumspect hesitancy. "She was, um, especially intrigued by the picture of Vernon and you and me, the one taken when we were about sixteen, standing on top of that junked car roof. And then she saw the record album and—"

Monte groaned loudly, "You showed her the record album? Oh, gosh, Arthur! Please don't tell me you—"

"I did. And she loved it." Arthur smiled jubilantly. "I told her you wrote all the songs, words, and music, and she was duly impressed. Asked if I could make a tape for her, which I plan to do if you don't object." He sniggered. "And if you do, I'll do it anyway."

"Thanks a lot, Arthur Brooks, my dear friend. You don't happen to have any naked baby pictures of me, do you?"

"Wish I did, but I don't. She also saw your boxing trophy." He probed the depths of his plastic container and ate another mouthful.

Distracted for a moment, Monte turned to face him squarely. "You have my boxing trophy? I wondered where that got to." More firmly, he gasped, "Good Lord, man, why did you show her that?"

"It was on a shelf in plain sight. What was I to do?" Arthur said, as if blameless. "Do you want it back?"

Monte shook his head grudgingly. "No. You keep it. Where'd you get it anyway?"

As if debating an answer, he said, "Pulled it out of a trash can, along with some other things I can show you sometime, if you're interested."

"Maybe . . . sometime. I don't know, Arthur." Twisting in the desk, Monte stared once again out the window. Clouds scudded across the sky above the chapel, large and grey, shouldering out sunlight—ominous omens of rain or snow. They sat quietly for several minutes while Arthur finished eating, and at length Monte rose to leave.

"Don't go just yet," Arthur said hastily, motioning for Monte to sit back down. "I have, uh, something else to tell you."

Monte sat and waited while Arthur fumbled and stalled, wiping his hands and desk meticulously, groping for what to say or how to say it, finally leaning forward, elbows braced on the desktop. Monte wondered if his friend might be springing a joke of some kind. "Well?" Monte asked restlessly. "What is it?"

"I found out something just yesterday afternoon that might surprise you. For the past couple of months you've been suffering under a rather serious misconception."

"All right, Arthur, just tell me!" Monte blurted.

"I am, I am," Arthur said quickly, drawing his large body more erect in the chair. "Clare and Richard . . . are *not* married." He waited and stared at Monte. "Clare and Richard are *not* engaged. And Clare and Richard do *not* live together. She shares an apartment with an older sister, Vivian, in Wolvercote, and he lives in Stonebridge with his parents. There're good chances they *will* become engaged in the near future, but for now, they're not." He broke off, deep, russet-brown eyes steady and soft, then said more smoothly, "I thought you might like to know."

Motionless as a stone for what stretched like an age, Monte eventually whispered, "But Booker told me—"

"As I understand it, he told you they were 'hitched,' and you took that to mean they were married. You told me that, and I asked Mr. Booker about it. He was trying to warn you, in a kind of joking way, not to waste time on Clare because she was already involved with someone, had been going with this guy for years. He wanted to encourage a matchup with Anne Walden."

A sly, almost eerie chill gradually pervaded Monte's entire body, morphing into an onerous tightness, constricting breath to burdensome effort. With voice grown weak, he murmured in confusion, "How do you know this, Arthur? Are you sure it's . . . it's true? I mean—"

Arthur nodded affirmation, and then flatly said, "I don't think they'd have lied about it, do you? And how I found out was easy. I asked. Something you could have done weeks ago. From the very beginning, I've suspected they weren't married, which is why I talked to Booker about it. Now I have confirmation."

"Well, all this time, I just assumed," Monte stammered. "And . . . and I did kind of ask, once . . . vaguely," he added defensively and with finality, searching for justifiable, firmer ground and staring at the floor. "What's it to me anyway?" he said with a touch of bitterness.

"Geez, Scott!" Arthur's voice rose. "I thought you'd be glad."

"What difference does it make, Arthur?" Monte argued petulantly. "She's with him, has been with him for years, will always be with him." His voice waned, continuing thoughtfully. "They're committed to each other, fit together, made for each other. Their families, their history, their church, their world . . . everything."

"If you say so. I'm not sure I completely agree." Arthur favored him with a smile that was more a smug scowl.

"Does Clare know that, all this time, I've been thinking she . . ." Monte sighed.

"I'm not sure what she knows, but I got the impression she wanted *you* to know the truth," Arthur said lowly.

Arthur, Monte remembered, had a provoking, judicious way of stating propositions that brought further questions to mind. However, students soon would be coming in, so they made plans to meet after school. Later, sitting in the Inner Sanctum with a partially recovered, sniffing and coughing Booker, hearing nothing of what he was discussing, and worse, not caring, irrational profundity flashed upon his befuddled consciousness: *Everything has changed, and nothing has changed at all.*

• • •

Breaking from her concomitant typewriter, Ramona hailed Monte as he passed the Blind Department office door. "You have mail!"

To say she shouted would be misleading; however, the volume projected was far beyond any decibel measure she had ever been heard to reach before. Standing behind the glass counter, she waved aloft a large business envelope addressed to *Scott and Booker.*

"Do you think I should open it?" Monte asked, taking it from her hand.

"Why not? It's addressed to you," she said with a slightly squealing anxiousness.

Inside was a letter in neat cursive and, folded within, a check made out to the Academy for 1,000 dollars. The missive read,

My Dear Mr. Booker and Mr. Scott, Thank you for meeting with me recently, and forgive the delay in writing to you. Enclosed is a small donation I hope you can use for the work program, or in any other way you have need. Theodore says he's doing well, and his mother and I appreciate all you have done and are doing on his behalf, and on behalf of all the students. If I can be of assistance in some way, please contact me at any time. Yours truly, T. Allen Bridgemeyer, III (Allen)

Though Monte said nothing to Ramona, the thought of a single miraculous nickel was much in his mind.

• • •

Richard Weisner, in six years, had never entertained doubts in regard to Clare, neither her faithfulness nor devotion—or availability, for that matter. In high school and college, even when going out with others, a salient understanding remained; the two were an inseparable couple. He had always known that they would surely marry someday. He was doing well now in his father's insurance firm, maturing and learning, earning more money than he had ever dreamed of, and Clare was happily established and teaching at the Academy. There appeared no need to rush into matrimony, despite their parents' and friends' constant encouragements.

And yet, lately, subtle mood changes, a vague, indefinable coolness, the occasional screen of evasion and preoccupation, body language . . . His diagnosis rested on nascent restlessness coaxing her to move on to the next stage of their long relationship, a ticking biological clock, and again, all the mounting pressure from family and friends.

Only there was a troubling alternative diagnosis, a series of elusive images Richard, with contrite abhorrence, found difficult to confront in depth. But still, dwelling in recesses of his mind was one vivid picture, a haunting sensation he could not put asunder. The afternoon he had met *him*, in the parking lot—the flat tire, and the look in her eyes and on her face. And Richard had felt then a nudging to act, to linger no longer, to claim his rightful prize. He would consult with his parents, seek their wisdom, and then, with their approval, propose. And she would say, "Yes," and the bonds would be sealed and safe . . . forever.

• • •

Dillon Grabowski, junior high student known for being overly helpful at times, marched into the classroom pushing one young boy in front of him like a shopping cart and pulling another lad behind him like a wagon. He prided himself on having quite decent visual acuity in his one good eye, and often took it upon himself to guide totally blind students around the school, despite being told almost daily by mobility instructors not to do so. Both Dillon's charges carried long canes, which Monte knew they were capable of using and should have been using, not herded to and fro and class to class, even if the assistance was well meaning.

"Okay, we have fifty minutes together, so let's not waste it," Monte said, smiling. Twenty-four blank faces stared back, but the twenty-fifth also smiled. Seated near the front, Betty Davidson, his little sister from his first day at the school, raised her hand and was preparing to speak when a boy slithered in, tardy and sheepish, and took a seat in the back.

Monte had been asked by Booker to sit with Gladstone's fifth-period English class due to last-minute reports that the teacher was at the infirmary, having sustained a dislocated toe while allegedly trying to kick a pebble off the Main Hall steps.

"We've been studying parts of speech," Betty said helpfully. "You know, nouns and verbs and adjectives and things. We could talk about that if you wanted."

"Yes, thanks, Betty," Monte said. "That sounds like a good—"

An eruption of frenzied sneezing cut him off, simultaneous with a girl bolting up from her desk in the rear of the room, eyes red and watery, then another, both holding handkerchiefs to their noses. And still another broke out in a fit of violent coughing, wiping his eyes, until the whole rear half of the class was milling around in major chaos.

Baffled and moving quickly, Monte demanded, "What's going on?"

Dillon, ever helpful, jumped to his feet and shouted, pointing in distress at the boy who had come in late, "It's Emerson, Mr. Scott. He *stinks*!"

Emerson Broadsteiner sat quietly reposed in his desk, unmoved by and above the turmoil, staring at Dillon with innocent, composed disdain.

And indeed, as Monte came closer, the boy strongly exuded a very unpleasant pungency from the immediate sphere of his clothing and person. In smaller doses, a slight whiff here and there, the scent might have been almost endurable, but in the intimate, closely packed confines of the classroom, the smell was more an encompassing stench, akin to fumes of melting plastic on a rubbish heap, overwhelmingly sickening. Redolent, invisible clouds invaded every nostril with sharp clarity, spreading like a fogbank, creeping between desks with miasmic intensity, engulfing now even the front part of the room.

One hysterical girl, pinching her nose, screamed nasally, “It’s some kind of poison gas!”

Dillon bellowed feverishly, “No it ain’t! It’s some kind of . . . some kind of rotten perfume made to shuffalate all of us!”

“Open the windows!” Monte commanded. “Emerson, go out in the hall. Now! The rest of you go to the windows if you need to, and take deep breaths. You’ll be all right in a minute.”

Emerson evidently had doused himself thoroughly with some brand of cheap, spicy cologne even an airy hallway failed to suppress. “What is that stuff?” Monte demanded, stepping back from the boy lounging guileless as a nun.

“It’s called *Eau de Rapture*. I got it on sale at the drug store.” He grinned impressively.

“Go back to the dorm right now, Emerson, and take a bath or a shower. Or both. That stuff is lethal. And please don’t ever, ever use it again.”

“But . . . I have a whole bottle—”

“Too bad,” Monte barked. “Throw it away!”

Most had recovered and reseated when Monte returned, so he began, “All right, parts of speech. Who’d like to tell me—”

A hand shot up in the front row, a stout boy with pink cheeks and hair so short and light he could have been taken for bald without close inspection.

“Can we ask questions?” he queried. Monte said he could. Squinting as if light sensitive, he went on, “What’s more important, Mr. Scott, a sergeant or a general?”

Glancing down at his shoes and then to the ceiling, Monte patiently considered some fitting reply. “That’s an interesting question, uh, Kevin. But I thought we were discussing parts of speech.”

"Yes, sir," he said, deflated. "Only, well, we never get to ask about things on our minds."

Not sure if he was being manipulated or had stumbled on opportunity, Monte cautiously replied, "Okay. You want to know about sergeants and generals. What made you think of that?"

Kevin was inspired, wriggling happily. "Well, my dad's a sergeant. And he says he'd never in a hundred years want to be a general. But they make more money and don't have to work as hard or get shot at as much."

Looking around the room, Monte noted the class had taken up Kevin's interest. Military ranks were not his specialty, two clumsy, inept years in ROTC during college being the extent of his armed forces career. If only Vernon were here—eighteen months in Viet Nam. Still, Monte forged ahead, primed to offer elemental information about chain of command within an army, ignoring comparative ranks in the Navy, Air Force, and Coast Guard, of which he knew even less.

"All right, now for Kevin's question," Monte said. "Both sergeants and generals are important because they have different responsibilities, training, and experience. Each one functions in a different way and different roles. Think about school staff. Who's more important, Mr. Gladstone or Dr. Mullens?"

Rising up from the back of the room, buried behind two large boys, a thin, shrill voice sniffled, "Who's Dr. Mullens?"—followed by a gracefully handsome girl a few rows from the front with flowing black hair and complexion the shade of dark-amber honey offering sadly, "Mr. Gladstone is injured."

"Yes, I believe he is, Tahirah," Monte said calmly, "But . . . not seriously. Thank you. And about Dr. Mullens—"

Betty, trying to assist, put forth, "It's like clerks and managers, right?"

"Well, sort of," Monte answered, and before he could elaborate, a lad named Alton stood and announced skeptically, "Withrow Mulligan says boogers can be sucked into your lungs. Is that true?" A bevy of moans arose around the room. Someone called out, "Sit down, doofus!"

"No, Alton, I doubt there's any danger of that happening. Still, it's best to keep your nose clean." Monte paused. "With a tissue."

A red-haired girl named Loretta, splattered with freckles, wanted to know if Monte was married. He told her he was not, but to please not ask personal questions. Not discouraged, she went on, "Well, do you have any pets?" He said he did not at present, but once had a turtle when he was seven. She dropped her head as if disappointed.

A tall, Black lad with cherubic smile named Louis asked if Monte knew anything about tuning pianos. After some discussion of the trade, Monte gave him the name of a teacher in the Vocational Department who could provide more information.

And then a frail, pallid boy said softly, "I don't have any idea what light is, Mr. Scott, or what it means to . . . see things, but I've wondered, what if there was no light and nobody could see? Would I still be called blind?"

The room went suddenly soundless, unified curiosity rotating from questioner to teacher. How Monte felt in that moment would have filled volumes and still fallen short of any defining or satisfying conclusion. Had his deficiencies been revealed? The chink in his armor?

Perhaps at that point the counselor should have bailed out, confessed and pleaded ignorance, yet something spurred risk. *O Lord, be merciful to me, a fool!*

"Well, Amos, I . . . I may not be able to answer your question; maybe no one could. But let me just say a few things that come to mind. First," Monte said shakily, "if there were no such thing as what we call 'light,' that is, if light didn't exist, had never existed, therefore no one could see, *visually*, then by definition we'd all be blind. But in that case, the words, the concepts of light and blindness, would be meaningless; they'd have no practical application because there'd be no alternative, no distinction between sighted and blind. Probably humans would not have the organs, the mechanism of sight, of seeing—at least the way we use the terms."

And here, groping for some semblance of clarity, he said, "Try to imagine a world where everyone is exactly the same size, no one tall or short, large or small, the same exact size and shape, perfect duplicates. Words describing those traits wouldn't have any descriptive value, except in comparison to other objects, such as 'He's larger than an ant, or smaller than a horse.' Does that help at all, Amos?" he offered apologetically.

Amos smiled agreeably. "I think it does." He waited, then asked, as if unsure, "So, I'd be the same as everybody else."

"Only so far as that *one* trait," Monte said. "In a world where everyone is the same height, or where no one . . . has vision, people would still be different, what we call *unique*. You are Amos, and Betty is Betty, and no one else in the world is exactly like you or her, or anyone in this room. All of us are unique, one-of-a-kind individual creations." Light laughter rose and then died. "Think of fingerprints, often used to identify a particular person. We hear about it all the time on television, in movies and books, all different whorls and curving lines on our fingertips.

"Remember, Amos, and as you all know, the word *seeing*, and the whole concept of sight, is used in many different ways. Let's say I handed you a ball—a baseball or a basketball. You could probably tell more about it than I could. Sometimes what we call 'vision,' seeing with our eyes, just gets in the way of *really* seeing things. We have at least four other senses, don't we? Smell, touch, hearing, and taste? I might look at a ball and think, *Oh, it's red, or blue*, where you would see it with your hands and fingers, and maybe even your nose." More scattered laughter from around the room. "And those senses would reveal things about the ball I might never notice, maybe important things, like texture, shape, weight, or some small defect."

"Right," Amos said. "I see. I mean . . . I understand." And then the entire class laughed loudly.

More questions came, somewhat like pitch and catch; they tossed at Monte, and he tossed back. And then, a small, pink-fingered hand arose, head and body still hidden in the depths behind the two hulking boys in the back of the room. A diminutive voice, almost an echo, sincere and resolute, squeaked, "But . . . who *is* Dr. Mullens?"

As if on cue, the hall bell detonated, rattling with seismic fury and exploding into the room. Class concluded.

• • •

Arthur and Monte decided on Louie's Diner in downtown Talerton for an early supper. Patrons were few, one man at the counter and two couples in booths. The proprietor was absent, and a young man who could have been his son rushed to wait on them as soon as they took barstools. A chalkboard announced meat loaf or pork chops as evening entrees. Arthur chose the latter, Monte the former.

His desire to take up their lunch conversation regarding Clare and Richard had waned appreciably in the past few hours, so Monte asked about Arthur's classes and how he was assimilating to life at the Academy and the new location. Arthur's response was not surprising.

"You don't want to talk about it, do you?" he said bluntly, eyeing his companion, taking a sip of iced tea. His peremptory perceptiveness, though usually accurate, was always aggravating to Monte.

"Not really," he muttered. And then, stewing for a few moments, he relented and said, "What did you mean when you said you thought Clare wanted me to know she wasn't married?"

Reflectively pausing, Arthur said, "I'm not sure. Just impressions she gave when we talked outside Richard's hearing, asking so many questions about you, trying to make it sound casual and conversational—beating about the bush, my dad would say. Maybe she only wanted to clear up a misconception, knowing she couldn't just come out and suddenly announce she wasn't married. Or maybe . . . I could ask her if you want me to." These last words came with an evil snicker.

"Oh, yes, Arthur. You should do that," Monte hissed. "And while you're at it, why don't you announce I'm madly in love with her!" The man sitting at the counter a few seats down turned and glanced their way with a curious smile, then returned to his dinner.

"Are you?" Arthur said much too seriously, and then, evidently deciding to withhold nothing, went on, "Because I think she may be in love with *you*." Monte stared at him with mild contempt, not speaking, which only entrenched his friend more firmly.

Their dinners arrived and they ate in silence for several minutes, enjoying the home-cooked flavors and complex seasonings for which Louie was famous. Finally, Monte spoke, staring down at his plate and whispering to avoid being overheard by the growing number of diners. "Why do you say that? You know it's ridiculous."

Arthur continued eating as if he had not heard, until at length saying, "Again, just an impression. Subtle changes and clues. The way her voice modulates whenever your name comes up, certain body language. Truthfully, my theory is she may not realize how she feels, or, more likely, won't admit it to herself. She's known you casually for, what, two months? Richard for most of her life. Probably sees these new emotions, or thoughts, as betrayal or . . . forbidden temptation. Probably scares her. I'm very good with vibes, you know."

He paused, took a forkful of green beans, and continued, smothering a snicker, "I mean, think about it, Monte Alonzo. Why would she want a copy of your album? You have to admit the music ain't that good. It has to be some misguided personal admiration."

"So, Arthur James, vibe expert," Monte said caustically. "Are you feeling any vibes from me right now? Have you ever seriously thought about joining the Foreign Legion?" The kind, giant man stared smugly down his nose at his dear friend, then, unable to help himself, burst into rare laughter. Monte joined him, and they finished their dinners and ordered dessert and coffee.

• • •

That evening, Monte visited Reginald London, now in a Rivanleigh rehab facility and reportedly doing well. They talked of his future, still in limbo, though he mentioned the possibility of returning to his native Pennsylvania to teach or resume private practice. He asked about the Academy and staff, and said Betty Davidson had sent a card. When Monte stood to leave, the psychologist became tearful and mewled, "Thanks for saving my life, you and all the others. I'm . . . I'm going to work very hard to make sure it wasn't in vain."

Somewhere, Monte thought he heard an angel sing, maybe very close to his shoulder.

• • •

Jimmy Dunsmore, tenth grader at the Academy, was within a few days of being sixteen. He also, for his entire two years residing at the school, had been a troublemaker—fighting, disruptive behavior in class, dorm, and dining hall, petty thievery, smoking and drinking, flouting rules and requests with disdain. Rarely a day went by without his punching another student over some trivial matter. Demerits and threats of expulsion were met with derisive laughter and profane bravado, daring authorities to do what they wished. Having been sent to the school from a youth-offender facility, being booted from the Academy would mean only a return whence he came. According to Booker, the school had in essence been instructed that unless the young lad committed a felony, he was not to be expelled.

Monte had been asked to meet with the boy primarily because of questionable assumption that he and Jimmy might have some form of token commonality. Jimmy was a Northside Richmond delinquent; Monte, Southside.

"My contacts and experiences in that part of the city," Monte had told Booker, "were infrequent and always unpleasant. Gangs tended to be, as I remember, more loosely organized and less territorial—what we called 'rover boys' or, as they liked to call themselves, 'bushwhackers or marauders.' Allegiance was brittle and leadership rotated constantly, as did various neighborhoods controlled by any one group. Mostly it was a never-ending free-for-all."

Generally, Monte had explained, Northside bandits held no significance for Southside crews, being far removed. The few conflicts he could recall took place on neutral ground: downtown shopping areas, city ballpark and arena, or special events like parades, street parties, carnivals, and fairs.

Jimmy had two older brothers currently confined in the state penitentiary in Richmond, the result of a comically sloppy bank holdup, and he liked to boast that when they gained release, the three would form a new and more successful gang. Roughly calculating, Monte determined Jimmy would be in his mid-thirties when and if this dream ever materialized. The only positive influence in his life, Booker said, was the lad's mother, a widow in a manner of speaking, having never been officially married to the father of her children, three boys and a girl. Booker reported her as a hard worker who had tried to raise the family with care and good example. Perhaps, Monte hoped, her efforts had been more successful with the daughter.

Life on the street, certainly for the sons, had unfortunately won out over whatever influence life in the home had offered. According to Dunmore's file, with additional anecdotes from Booker, before the older children were even in their teens, the father had been killed in a knife fight over a cache of disputed drugs. He was not particularly missed, though on better days had provided occasional discipline when needed. A parish priest encouraged the boys and girl to join youth groups and various church activities, meeting with little progress, his efforts expeditiously abandoned after one of the older boys threatened to "de-ball" the clergyman if ever he showed his "puss" on their doorstep again. One may suppose, on reflection, that even celibates have qualms about losing segments of their ostensibly unnecessary body parts; one could never be too careful.

By the time Jimmy was thirteen, skills had been finely honed as an accomplished housebreaker, the work easy, exciting, and profitable. Gaining entrance while families were at work, he would often crawl through basement windows or, since very thin, through dog flaps. Valuables, mostly jewelry, handguns, silverware, and such, were fenced to neighborhood thugs for a fraction of their worth, yet enough to satisfy a fledgling thief trying to impress mates and brothers. He was, of course, eventually caught and arrested and sent off to the juvenile facility.

During a physical examination he was found to be almost legally blind due to a congenital corneal condition. One of the court-appointed social workers, knowing of the State Academy for the Blind in Talerton, thought placement in the facility presented an excellent opportunity for rehabilitation. Jimmy liked the sound of a school for the blind where restrictions would be few and lucrative avenues of pilferage might be found. The social worker happened to be niece of the state attorney general, which boded well for Jimmy. Arrangements were made for his transfer to the Academy, being placed as an eighth grader, despite tests showing he read on a third-grade level.

His first week at the school, Jimmy formed an inexplicable friendship with Alec Beasley, even-tempered tenth grader of modest academic ability. Whether Jimmy saw this new acquaintance as a kindred spirit or was merely impressed by Alec's contrived anecdotes of his family's Mafia connections, no one could be sure. They became fast companions, likely the closest bonding with a peer Jimmy had ever known, and his behavior actually improved, a mystery Academy staff found difficult to understand but immensely welcome.

Even before sitting down, Jimmy's first words to Monte one November afternoon in the Inner Sanctum were "I've heard about you: South Richmond, tight mouth and tough; got a thing going with the art teacher." A smile, twisted and taunting, sneered across the desk as he dropped into a chair, drooping a thin arm over the back.

His wiry, medium-height frame came clad in tight-fitting black jeans and black T-shirt; light-brown hair skimmed the top of his head thickly, sides almost bare, somewhat resembling a Mohawk. Despite his combative smirk, he possessed an appealing, youthful innocence, an image, Monte guessed, that would in a few years develop a handsome adult visage, useful perhaps for the boy's stated underworld ambitions.

Bright cerulean eyes boldly engaged a battle of wills with Monte's emeralds, a childish game to determine who would blink first. Ceding the contest to smile lazily unimpressed, Monte cocked his head to one side, surveying the boy, and said pleasantly, "Twenty-five percent."

Confused, Jimmy barked, "Twenty-five percent? What the hell does that mean?"

"One right, three wrong, Mr. Dunsmore."

"Maybe." He scowled as though personally offended. "But I know what I heard." He leaned a little forward, mimicking a show of threat, then, as an afterthought, relaxed and said cockily, "Which three?"

Monte held a chuckle in check at Jimmy's show of curiosity, remaining blank and focused, and said, "You figure it out, wise guy."

Dunmore's look came with a mask of sullen contempt, almost a glower of rage, though he said nothing in reply. Monte grinned and said, "Well, Jimmy, I heard you were a smart guy, but I guess that can't be."

"Whatta you mean?" he exclaimed, sitting up straighter. "I am a smart guy! Not with the books maybe, but with things that count. I can—"

"You can what?" Monte goaded, interrupting loudly. "Hustle some poor wino slob down a dark alley? Steal a candy bar from the corner store or a hubcap from a bozo down the street? Pop some stoned punk in the mouth? Bust a vending machine for small change? Grab an old lady's pocket book? Is that what you're calling smart? Don't give me that crap, kid. You're not talking to a bleeding-heart social worker or some gullible teacher. You're talking to somebody who comes from where you come from and maybe even a little lower down the food chain and a little dirtier. And, frankly, you're not knocking me out with your brains."

Monte tilted back, lacing fingers together behind his head to wait, vaunting contentment.

"Yeah? Well, frankly, I'm not impressed with you either!" Jimmy fairly spit the words, settling back and crossing his arms, staring at a point between Monte's eyes.

Waiting briefly, Monte said, "Well, now we've got that understanding out of our way, let's talk about your career goals."

Jimmy ruffled his shoulders, studying the man warily. "What career goals?"

"I was told your great plan was to start a new . . . shall we say, organization. A kind of family enterprise? You know, the kind of setup that withdraws from the rich and transfers to the poor."

The boy turned his head and stared at the wall, saying glibly, "Yeah, well, that's my business, ain't it?"

"Of course it is," Monte chirped. "That's just the point I'm making." Pausing, facing Jimmy placidly with eyebrows raised, Monte asked, "Got it?" Jimmy said nothing, only frowned as if muddled, afraid something vital had been missed. Monte continued, "You see, Jimmy, a business like you want to establish needs three basic components supplied by three types of people, none of which you come close to being."

"I don't have any idea what you're talking about," Jimmy mumbled dismissively, twisting his body sideways in his chair. "Mr. Booker said we was going to talk about the work program. I'll be sixteen Saturday and be eligible."

"Right. According to your records, you will be." Monte picked up a folder from the top of the desk and pretended to study the contents disinterestedly, flipping over a few sheets of paper.

With an air of frustration, Jimmy finally spouted, "Well, what about it?"

"What about what?"

"Damn! About the work program! Jesus!"

"Why are you interested in the work program? I thought you were starting your own business," Monte said as if puzzled.

Jimmy, truly flustered, fairly shouted, "God bless it, mister, since you know everything, you should damn well know that's not going to happen until . . . until later, probably years from now!" He turned away, sulky and indignant. "Anyway, I can't talk about that. You wouldn't understand even if I did."

Monte dipped his head and conversationally said, "Oh, I see. You mean later, when you're older, when you go back to the city."

"Yeah, right. Now you're catching on," Jimmy mouthed sarcastically.

Sitting quietly as if mulling over the situation, Monte then said, "But we still have a problem, don't we? Or you do."

"What problem?" Jimmy said churlishly.

"Well, like I said, the three components to being successful in the taking-and-lifting business. And when I look at you, I don't see squat giving any indication you'll ever make it. And what good will a part-time work program do for you? As far as I can see, it'll only provide another place for you to screw up and cause trouble."

Now the young boy withdrew, as if a vulnerable spot had been touched, brooding and unsure of what to retort. Monte stared silently. At length Jimmy said, almost civilly, "I'm mixed up. What are we talking about?"

Leaning slightly toward him with bombastic insincerity, Monte orated, "Your future, Mr. Dunsmore! Your career! Your great plan! In two or three years you'll most likely be out of this place and on your own, a free man, eighteen or nineteen." Lowering his voice, Monte looked across the desk, adding laconically, "Then what?"

"Okay, you tell me," Jimmy demanded.

"All right, I will!" Monte uttered sharply. Hoisting up straighter, he said in a tone of pedantic aspersion, "To do what you want to do, you've got to be smart, you've got to have brains, which I don't think you have." The boy started to interrupt, but Monte stopped him, quickly holding out an arm, fingers spread with palm forward. "Let me finish. If you don't have brains, then you need muscle. You know, like an enforcer, a guy who convinces people. And that ain't Jimmy Dunsmore. You're just a punk kid, and in three years you'll still be a punk kid."

Allowing Jimmy to think for a moment, Monte then said, as if wanting to chuckle at the absurdity, "But . . . there is something you could have, that third component, if you'd be interested enough to work at it and apply yourself, which I know you aren't, and wouldn't. And I know this because you lack component number one and component number two, brains and strength, which we'll call, in this case, ambition . . . or maybe motivation."

"What?" Jimmy asked with a mocking flavor, though his expression was noncommittal.

No answer was offered right away, Monte settling back in the chair, sighing and lowering his head as though considering a proper answer.

"What, dammit? What third thing . . . component?" the boy demanded more seriously.

"You really want to know?" Monte teased him unkindly.

"Yeah, I really wanna know!"

"Skill, Mr. Dunsmore. A trade. A specialty." The words lay between them like a facedown playing card daring to be turned over.

"Something you could learn to do well. Something no one else, or very few could do."

"Well, okay, and what would that be?" Jimmy asked flippantly.

"Learning about locks, safes, and security systems."

Jimmy stared across the desk, wanting to laugh but seeing no point. Brow furrowed and eyes squinched, fearful of being the butt of some practical joke, he scoffed almost gleefully, "Oh, you've got a great sense of humor, you have, mister counselor." He waited and Monte said nothing, lightly rubbing the tip of his nose and scanning the desktop. And then, in a low, probing voice, Jimmy jeered, "You're not serious?"

Booker had thought Monte foolish at first. However, Monte's reasoning was quite simple. Jimmy would eventually, perhaps even purposely, mess up any job in which he was placed unless there existed a personal investment, a legitimate reason for wanting to succeed, a goal and challenge to do well. The risks were obvious, and possibly the plan would backfire. That was the chance they were taking—Monte was taking.

Yet, he also knew Jimmy had to be provoked, perhaps cruelly and against every rule of positive reinforcement Monte had ever been taught. The boy had to be demeaned and goaded into some passionate, deep-seated need to prove Monte wrong. To succeed was the one way, maybe the only way, Jimmy could triumph and be declared the victor.

"Am I?" Monte asked mildly. "If it was up to me, Dunsmore, you'd never get within a mile of the work program, because you're a screwup. But I'm not the boss, Booker is. There's a job slot over at Andersen Lock and Key, and Booker wants to offer it to you. Eight to ten or twelve hours a week, after school and Saturdays, starting as soon as you finish the Job Readiness Program and turn sixteen." Monte paused to watch the boy's reaction, and then, almost grinning, said quietly with one final jab, "I give you a week at most before you blow it."

Jimmy lifted his head higher, eyes shining as though reveling in the prediction, and said derisively, "We'll see, won't we?" He waited tightly, receiving only a pitying, almost sorrowful headshaking in response from behind the desk. Rising then, he gave out in a clear strong voice, smiling contemptuously, "And by the way, you got two wrong and one right. No, I'm not a muscle man, probably never will be. But I can learn a skill if I want to. And I do have brains, and I'm smarter than you think I am." With a parting sneer, he walked out, head held high, exuding a strong air of at least partial advantage.

CHAPTER TEN

MRS. AUGSBURG, CLARE'S MOTHER, had concocted a rather simple plan: entice her youngest daughter into coming for dinner and ambush her with an engagement party.

Of course, she would never have used quite those terms, being a righteous woman of principle who loved all her children devotedly. "Invite Clare to dinner and surprise her" would have been the preferred wording. Richard's family would help organize the event. Of the entire group of parents and siblings, Mr. Augsburg was the sole voice openly questioning the wisdom of such a scheme. His objections overruled and ignored, he succumbed to a position of neutrality for the sake of peace, trusting his youngest daughter would see the occasion as well meaning, if not altogether conventional.

Clare would come, the ploy dictated, on the first Friday evening in December, expecting a quiet meal with her parents, where they and the others would be lying in wait to shout, "Surprise!" as she came through the door. Richard would drop to one knee and say, "Clare, will you be my wife?"—the answer being a predestined certainty, their steadily solid relationship of the past few years a crowning assurance. Blushing, she would say, "Yes!" and perhaps shed tears of joy. Richard would put arms around her and they would all sing "Bless Be the Tie" and have prayer. After a wonderful dinner,

Richard and Clare would pick a mutually agreeable wedding date, all the troubling, unrealistic, and frivolous thoughts she had lately been harboring put to rest and banished from her head forever.

Richard had been carried along with the plot, acquiescing to his mother's insistence, saying little. Not that he had serious doubts of Clare rejecting his offer, but he thought the whole setup a bit too theatrical and perhaps not something she would enjoy. Maybe, he hoped, the evening would be fun, something to laugh about in years to come.

• • •

"Have you heard from Atkins Turnage yet?" Marlon Danforth's voice crackled over the phone.

Innocently, his mind blank, Monte answered, "Atkins Turnage, sir?"

"Yes, Scott, Atkins! Atkins Turnage!" Danforth's volume increased, connoting the beginnings of exasperation. "Atkins Turnage? From CDCS, Inc. He's supposed to be contacting you."

And then Monte recalled the pamphlet and pictures Danforth had shown him in Brad Fletcher's office the week before. "I believe you said you'd let me know when he was coming, sir."

"Damn it, Scott! I don't remember saying anything like that, and anyway, what difference does it make? Just wait for his call and he'll get you and Booker straightened out on this student-work project. The guy's phenomenal!" And the line went dead.

• • •

Atkins Turnage arrived Wednesday morning, two hours later than expected. Booker, having put aside needful tasks and student-counseling sessions, seethed when Ramona reported at 10:20, "There's a man down here gabbing with Mr. Fletcher who says you're supposed to meet with him today."

In a voice so tight Monte thought Booker might choke, the purple-faced man said, "Tell him to come whenever it's convenient. We're waiting like good little boys." As he slammed down the receiver, the hall bell blasted through the room as if the crash of the phone had detonated a giant echo throughout the building.

Twenty minutes later Turnage breezily arrived, smiling cautiously and hefting a large leather attaché case onto Booker's desktop. His grey wool suit was almost certainly tailor made, Monte observed, fitting with perfect finesse the little man's narrow shoulders perched on a squat torso flaring out to broad hips supported by stubby legs. At once he began gushing apologies for tardiness, due, he gabbled, to making a wrong turn in town and then "getting bogged down with Brad."

Booker remained stubbornly in his chair, leaving Monte to greet their unsolicited guru.

"Very nice to meet you, Mr. Turnage," Monte smiled, offering a hand, which Turnage more held than shook, his palms and fingers softly lubricious.

Booker abruptly stood at this point, announcing in strong superlatives his plan to go for a coffee in the lounge. Brushing past Turnage, who stepped backward to avoid being shouldered aside, Booker stomped determinedly out of the room and down the hall as the two remaining men watched, bewildered. Monte sensed their inaugural introductions were not going well.

Turnage eased down into the one available chair after carefully inspecting and dusting the worn surface with a white handkerchief.

"Don't mind Mr. Booker, Mr. Atkins—I mean, Mr. Turnage," Monte offered placatingly. "He has a headache, but he'll be back in a minute or two I'm sure, and we can get started."

Booker returned soothed ten minutes later and extended a perfunctory hand to the visitor, then took his rightful place behind the desk. As Turnage leaned to open his briefcase, Erskine Nesbitt, a diminutive second grader, poked his closely shorn head around the doorframe, pleading, beady eyes suggesting a docious newborn lamb, fragile and defenseless. His puffy-cheeked countenance, a modest mocha brown, was so angelic every teacher and houseparent doted on and coddled him with smothering, protective affection, much as they might a kitten or puppy. An unprompted visitation to Booker's office was surprising, since he had never been so bold as to come before, being barely seven years old and never, to their knowledge, having been in trouble of any kind.

"Mr. Scott, sir," he stammered by way of announcing his arrival, narrowing his purposes to Monte. "Miss Ramona . . . I mean, Simpson, said I should come and talk to you about a really important question I have to face." In minute degrees, the little lad worked his way entirely into the room, a waggle of profound anxiety, taking up a post in close proximity to Turnage's shoulder. Monte thought the man paled slightly, slanting eyes askance at the boy as if concerned Erskine might suddenly become a potential threat.

Monte had not the heart to turn him away, succumbing as everyone did to his cherubic charm. "What is it, Erskine? We're pretty busy right now." Booker remained aloof, silently smirking, obviously welcoming the intrusion.

"I have to let them know by tomorrow so I can get a uniform like the other boys," Nesbitt said with some breathless urgency, though not pushy. He seemed absolutely assured Monte knew what he was talking about.

"Let who know what, Erskine? Explain."

Standing tall as a three-foot-six frame would allow, he said proudly, "The den mother, Mr. Scott, so I can join the Cub Scouts. I have to decide today."

Turnage dropped his head in a crumbling exhibition of defeat, as if all lifeboats had been lowered from a sinking ship and he alone were left standing on the tilting deck. For aural effect, he made a faint but deep moaning sound.

"Well," Monte said, worming carefully around Turnage and gently attempting to usher Erskine out of his anchored spot and toward the door. "You should definitely join the Cub Scouts. I was a Cub Scout and so was Mr. Brooks, and probably some of the other teachers too. You'll learn many things, and have a lot of fun."

Erskine glowed with elation. "They have refreshments at every meeting, Miss Ramona says, and outings," he giggled, beaming. Then, spinning to confront Monte more directly, he queried seriously, "What's an outing?" The lad held out with stiff resolution against the gradual pressure Monte applied on his spare, bony shoulders, prying him away from Turnage.

"It's when you go somewhere and have an activity or see something interesting, like the zoo or circus or a picnic," Monte explained.

"Going to the zoo and a circus sounds really cool! An outing and picnic and refreshments! Golly! Where could I go wrong?" He bubbled with excitement, then added, "And a uniform!" Monte noted Booker's face now glowed bright crimson, a few muffled, hiccupy giggles escaping. Turnage rather morosely studied the crease in his grey wool pants, running one finger slowly back and forth along its sharp edge and humming what sounded vaguely like an off-key fugue.

Moving the boy through the door as best he could with a series of easy yet persistent shoves, Monte encouraged, "Yep, I think you'll really enjoy the Cub Scouts, Erskine."

"When do you think I'll be an Eagle, Mr. Scott?" he asked, squinching up his face anxiously.

Monte dared a glance to the ceiling and said patiently, "You don't become an Eagle in Cub Scouts, Erskine. That's after you're in Boy Scouts, when you're older."

"Well, what do I become in Cub Scouts?" For someone so small, he was quite difficult to goad forward once he had his little feet set.

"Your den mother will explain everything when you join, okay?" Monte said, continuing to apply pressure in the middle of Erskine's back. He was only partially appeased, and Monte could tell he was loading up for another question. "I'd like to talk more about this, Erskine, but I need to get back to my meeting. Why don't you come back later in the afternoon, before dining hall, and we'll have time to chat then, all right?" In slow, minimal accretion, they had progressed into the classroom.

Sounding very adult, and standing rigidly upright, Erskine said, "Well, I have to go now anyway. And thanks for telling me stuff." When he had gone maybe two paces into the hallway, he turned and waved, smiling widely, and shouted, "The Cub Scouts are definitely for me!"

Again the bell sounded, waves of sonic booms forcing Monte to cower back into the Inner Sanctum.

Who the initiator was or how the subject arose was unknown; Booker and Turnage were now in lively conversation concerning comparative merits of Eastern Carolina, Texas, and Saint Louis–style barbeques. Booker barked with great fanfare and much too loudly, "This guy, Scott, knows his barbeque! Beef or pork! Yes, sir!"

Monte returned to his place beside the filing cabinet, bewildered and exhausted.

Turnage had leaned once again to his briefcase when there ensued a steady knocking on the doorframe, followed by a timid voice inquiring, "Mr. Booker, are you there?"

Eudora Dupriest, studious seventh grader, appeared pearly white as a snowwoman and similarly rounded; in fact, friends affectionately called her "Snowball," an appellation she found gave a unique self-image on which to cultivate her industrious persona and gregarious personality. She wore dark-tinted glasses as those with albinism often do. More notable, however, even than the chalky brilliance of her pudgy face, was a crown of hair resembling the aftermath of a feather pillow explosion, a profusion of white, gyrating plumes. Capping the flocculent chaos was a fiery red ribbon tied in a huge bow, putting one in mind of an animated Christmas gift.

Booker responded with glee, "Come in, Eudora. What can we do for you?"

Having little option, the room so confining, she installed herself excessively in the personal space of a suddenly cowering Atkins Turnage, compressing her starchy, pleated cotton dress, undergirded by several crinolines, against their distinguished visitor's pristine wool suit coat, enveloping his arm and shoulder in gaudily blossoming fashion and bringing on a kind of reflexive, shuddering jolt to surge through his body and lurch him sideways in the chair. With great resolve, Monte smothered a burst of laughter, concealing the guffaws as a brief bout of coughing.

"Dr. Bartlett," Eudora imparted politely, "said I should talk with you about my schedule for next semester. He wants me to take advanced math classes and wondered if I'd have room." Soft spoken for someone so visually dynamic, Monte noted she always communicated clearly and concisely. In the present case, he knew also of her interest and proficiency in math and science.

"I talked with Dr. Bartlett about that yesterday, Eudora," Booker said. "He probably hasn't had a chance to tell you. With your core courses in English, history, PE, DLS, and O&M, you still have room for one math and one science class. But Mr. Brooks said you wanted to continue with Latin, and that may be a problem."

Eudora arched her head back, contemplating, then dipped forward and said, "Well, Latin's optional, I suppose, for now, but I really want to take more before I graduate."

The conversation between Eudora and Booker went on for several minutes, Turnage retreating within himself like a turtle, shriveling into his chair. Whatever vision and hopes the man had of their first meeting was so far not turning out well. Monte feared to think what he might report to Danforth.

After Eudora left, they again turned attention to Turnage, who quickly jerked up a folder from his briefcase. "I have here some basic job-preparation procedures developed by some of the leading CEOs in the country. Men like—"

A persistent, loud whishing sound coming from the classroom and approaching briskly provoked a synchronized swiveling of heads to stare at the doorway. Turnage grew waxen.

The noise, like vigorously applied sandpaper, was Agnew Whitherspoon's baggy corduroy pants Monte estimated to be at least three or four sizes too large. He was a husky tenth grader and avid wrestler, second in the state finals for his weight division the previous year, currently out of breath and obviously anxious to talk. Booker calmed him with a few words and asked why he had burst in unannounced.

"I'm in a heck of a mess, Mr. Booker, and I don't know what to do." His cheeks blotched with perturbation that rendered him unaware of his bulk crowding upon the much slighter and more friable Turnage.

"What kind of mess, Agnew?" Booker inquired good-humoredly.

The boy went on to explain that funding cuts for the Athletic Department, in preference to purchasing more equipment for playgrounds, had resulted in wrestling team members becoming responsible for paying a large portion of expenses to attend tournaments, costs the Academy had in years past largely supplemented.

"I don't have that kind of money, Mr. Booker, and neither does my mother. You know I'm working part time in the dining hall, but that's only a few dollars a week and not nearly enough." His large brown eyes, almost sightless, were the shade of rich Turkish coffee in the shadowy dimness. "Some of the other guys are in the same fix. Is there a way we could borrow money and pay it back later?"

Booker leaned back in his chair, attention fixed on Agnew. "There might be a way. I'm not sure. But I have an idea. It'll take a day or two to look into and then I'll call you, okay?"

Whitherspoon brightened. "Yes, sir. Thank you, sir. Anything you can do will be great." He took a step back, only then becoming aware of proximity to a hunched human body. With mild alarm and apologetic dismay, he said, "Oh, I'm sorry. I didn't see you sitting there. I'm very sorry."

Turnage peered up from his scrunched position and croaked, "It's all right. Don't worry. I'm fine."

As soon as Agnew was gone, Turnage hardened. "Now look, Mr. Booker, Mr. Scott, we're not getting anywhere like this. I made clear we need periods of uninterrupted time, and so far—" The phone rang, and Booker, without hesitation, picked it up and listened. Turnage turned an annoyed appeal to Monte, as if soliciting supportive pity, shaking his head slowly back and forth in a kind of sad, helpless derailment.

"It's for you, Mr. Turnage," Booker giggled, handing the receiver across the desk.

Turnage spoke brusquely, then smiled as though relieved. "All right, thank you." Handing the receiver back, he said, "That was Brad. We're having luncheon with Dr. Mullens at his home. I'll be gone for an hour or so and when I return I hope we can get on with our work."

Executing a shallow bow, he picked up his briefcase and departed.

Booker burst into a round of hearty chuckles while Monte studied him with growing suspicion. "What have you done?"

"Me?" Booker answered, suppressing his mirth to a mere titter.

"You've sabotaged the whole morning, haven't you? Those kids coming in and interrupting, you set it up."

"All I did, honestly, was mention that this morning might be a good time to come in with questions and problems, since we'd both be here and . . ." Booker angled his head, indicating the rest was obvious.

"And it would mess up Turnage's plans," Monte finished.

"Well, let's just say," Booker emphasized more firmly, "I wasn't going to let him come into my office and dictate ground rules." Thinking of Danforth's reaction to what Turnage might report, Monte quaked.

• • •

"What we, Career Development Consultation Services, pride ourselves in providing is simply a more sophisticated approach to determinative and generalized occupational training and employment evolutionary exploration and applicability. Our innovative umbrella of programs opens new and exciting vistas of dynamic opportunism, using both qualitative and quantitative data to establish a rhythm and continuity within the broad spectrum of community ethos. This proliferation of function, multi-faceted and congruently oriented, will . . ."

Somewhere far on a distant horizon, Turnage slogged along, imparting technological wisdom in words and phrases that came to Monte's ears like the rumble of an idling engine. Booker's head cocked over at an awkward angle, supported precariously by a nest of fingers in turn braced by an elbow on the arm of his chair. Breathing heavily, from time to time he teetered forward or sideways, only to jerk himself back to a semi-upright position with a series of unnerving gasps and grunts.

Monte, superficially alert, was far from pondering the wondrous concepts offered by their visitor. Over and over the circumspect voice of Arthur whispered in his ear, "She's not married. She's not married."

A facetiously glib statement by Booker had convinced him. And why not? There was no evidence against it. Yes, he had questions, vague senses; Richard's absence from the talent show, his talk about *her* church, her rare mention of him. She wore no wedding band and did not refer to herself as Mrs. Weisner. All these observations could be explained, yet when added up . . .

After lunch, an invigorated Turnage had given a draconian directive: no interruptions and no smoking, no trips to the lounge, and absolute attention and concentration of the subject at hand, *please*. Proceeding with punctilious intensity, he commenced a series of rote lectures comparable to a linguistic jungle maze. Booker was at once repelled. Though Monte struggled mightily to maintain a receptive mind, when Turnage began a discourse on the topic of "horizontal and vertical labor cognition enhancement," he folded like a cheap drugstore poncho. Forty-five minutes later they were assaulted with "gender and racial assessment ratio management," followed by thirty minutes of "integrated time chart alimentation in reference to dilatory patterning compliance."

After a short interlude, while Booker contemplated the relative merits of murder or suicide, they were given almost an hour of "dress code options in the conurbation venue in opposition to agronomic and suburban milieu." Consciousness became a challenge as the afternoon wore on, and then they were bombarded with "self-identity reporting mechanisms and programmatic review stipulations."

Booker, in the name of détente, had adhered to the sacrifice of tobacco, though by four o'clock had exhausted his supplies of chewing gum, Life Savers, cookies, and assorted snacks and candies. Monte saw a crisis fast approaching, unbeknownst to Turnage, who persisted with his esoterica unperturbed. When Booker began manifesting a rhythmic bouncing of his head in short little jerks, as if keeping time to imaginary music, Monte knew he had to act.

Moving out from the filing cabinet hastily as Turnage explained "employer/employee review coordination in universal attitudinal spectrums," Monte exclaimed, "Oh, good grief, Mr. Turnage, sorry to cut in, but . . . !" Looking somewhat frenetically at Booker, he gushed, "Have you forgotten your afternoon medication?"

Without hesitation Booker seized on the moment and stood, reeling violently, convincingly woozy and disoriented, stumbling around the desk toward the door with his head in his hands, mumbling, "My God! I'd better get my pills! And quickly! Time is running out!"

A startled Turnage blanched, looking up from his notes with huge eyes, and said pathetically, "Right! We'll take a break. I didn't realize—"

Booker blundered through the door, bleating wretchedly and faking an unnecessary slight limp; maneuvered through the classroom, knocking over several desks; and exited into the hallway, scooting out of sight around the intersection corner in the direction of Perkins Hall.

"I'd better go with him, Mr. Turnage!" Monte cried in mock desperation. "No telling where the poor crazed man might end up!"

"Right, right! You'd better . . ." Turnage shrieked, dumbfounded.

"We'll try to get back as soon as possible, but . . . who knows!?" Monte shouted over his shoulder, hustling into the hall, heading, as Booker had, toward Perkins and freedom.

• • •

Journal: Sunday, November 16, 9:15 PM

So nice getting to know Arthur. He has real affection for Monte and last Sunday told me so many stories and showed me pictures and other things—album, trophy, mementos of their lives in Richmond. I know there's much more he didn't tell me. Anxious to visit him again. I'm glad he's at the school and back in Monte's life. He needs a friend.

And I have to confess, I miss him, his smile and wit, the way he looks at me with such tenderness in our rare moments. Two long weeks since that luscious night. And I know that soon I'll never see him again and all will be but memory. When I'm ninety will I still remember? And regret? How could I have let this happen?

Richard is so good and kind. And I love him. We will make our parents happy, our friends happy. And I will do what I must. When all's said and done, there is no choice.

Give me assurance, Lord, and light to my path. And forgive my weakness and doubt.

• • •

Thursday morning, a call came from Danforth.

"Atkins tells me his visit with you yesterday was a disaster. He said Mr. Booker was rude and inattentive, dozed most of the time, and only wanted to talk about barbeque, whatever the hell that means. He also said the room was so dark he couldn't see, and there were interruptions every five minutes. And, to top it off, you were in zombie land all afternoon."

Deciding contriteness the best defense, every accusation being true, Monte confessed, "He's correct, sir. It wasn't a very good day for a number of reasons. First, we got a late start and—"

Danforth interrupted harshly, "And that's another thing! No one gave Atkins proper directions and the poor man got lost."

"That was unfortunate." Monte gritted his teeth, thinking it best not to point out that directions had been left with the man's secretary days before, not to mention Turnage's rude lingering in Fletcher's office while Monte and Booker waited. "We had a few crisis situations come up while he was there, sir, which accounts for the interruptions. And Mr. Booker's taking some new medications which make him drowsy and a little incoherent. And I know it didn't always show, but I was paying very close attention to everything

Mr. Turnage said, and very stimulating it was, sir. Although we did think he might have asked something about our students and their employers and work assignments."

The line went dead silent for a few moments and then Danforth said gruffly, "Well, Atkins is coming back up there, and I hope to hear a better report. I *better* hear a . . . a better report, and see some results." Monte had no idea what was meant by results, and had the good sense not to ask.

• • •

Arnold Schnellich had two new coveted possessions. One had come from his father, the other from his optometrist: a small pocket flashlight and a monocular. The light had a little button switch and used two double-A batteries. Arnold had gone through six so far, shining beams on the ceiling of his dorm room after bedtime and reading books under the covers. The monocular had an adjustable focusing ring allowing Arnold to read clocks and signs and see other objects more sharply from a distance. It also had a looped cord he could put around his neck. The heavy tug of the monocular bouncing against his thin chest gave Arnold a sense of superiority he had never had before.

With these new treasures, Arnold's world expanded as he sought out places heretofore eschewed; and, even more exciting to his adventurous mind, he could now spy on people from afar without their knowledge. He had discovered, for instance, that Mr. Gladstone kept a stash of chewing gum in the upper left-hand drawer of his desk and often surreptitiously slipped a stick of Juicy Fruit into his mouth while some distracting student read aloud, the class unaware of his stingy subterfuge. In chapel, Arnold had been shocked to see Dr. Mullens yawn during the Lord's Prayer, and wondered if it was considered a venial or mortal sin. He made a note to ask his priest.

• • •

Jimmy Dunsmore came to the Inner Sanctum late one afternoon, smirking and convincingly defiant. Monte was alone.

"Just thought I'd let you know I've been on the job for a whole week and Mr. Andersen says I'm doing great."

Indeed, Jimmy had been doing well, with no behavioral problems, no absences or tardiness, always neatly and appropriately dressed. His near vision, they found, was so acute that working with very small items gave him little difficulty with proper lighting and magnification. Andersen also reported that Jimmy possessed an innate aptitude for comprehending mechanical relationships and functioning. *Perhaps,* Monte thought, *it's time to risk giving the young lad a token of positive reinforcement.*

"You're right, Jimmy," Monte said, sounding mildly pleased, yet more surprised. "Let's see how the next few weeks go."

A rather radical idea had been percolating in Monte's head for some time, a notion not discussed with Booker or anyone. Now all he had to do was make a few phone calls, explore possibilities, and make a quick road trip.

CHAPTER ELEVEN

THE FIRST TWO WEEKS of November, comfortably seasonal, had seduced the Academy and town into a stupor of temperate expectations, leaving it unprepared for the frigid polar vortex winging down from the Arctic the following week. Heavy coats rested mothballed, forgotten, and useless in closets, scarves and caps and gloves secreted in drawers or boxed obscurely on high, secluded shelves—conveniently sensible repositories in spring, now adding to the puzzlement of where these suddenly necessary accoutrements might be found.

Booker, aggrieved by a missing trench coat he insistently called a Burberry, additionally disparaged the local meteorologist brutally over her lack of adequate forewarning and contrition for the cold snap. Rugged, leaden clouds draped low in the sky overhead, crawling portentously west to east with dark-grey threats of icy precipitation. As though collectively hunkering down, life at the school ground forward bravely.

And then, thrusting weather to back pages, a shocking scandal blasted the entirety of campus and, to a slightly lesser extent, the town itself, leaving in its wake a disbelieving and shaken community.

Gossip, rumor, blather, and innuendo rolled off every tongue like a vocalized tsunami, passing from one ravenous citizen, student, or teacher to another, gathering momentum and compounding speculation as it spread, unencumbered by any weight of verifiable fact or accuracy. All anyone really knew, initially, was that a horde of police had descended on the grand old school much as an invading Northern army had done little over a hundred years before, followed by a fanatical and hungry wave of television, radio, and newspaper reporters setting up strategic positions in front of Main Hall.

Layer by layer as the day wore on, revelations, relatively straightforward though disturbingly serious, leaked out. Leonard Claremont Abbot, business manager of the State Academy for the Deaf and the Blind, a trusted and respected member of the school administration for over fifteen years, had been discovered to be a sort of in-house, right-under-their-noses bootlegger. Not of whiskey or any alcoholic potation, but plain, everyday cigarettes—coffin nails, smokes, cigs, or baccy sticks. Hundreds of boxes containing thousands of cartons had been surreptitiously stored in a remote area unused since the turn of the century in the broad, recondite reaches of the Main Hall basement, a smallish, forgotten room almost directly under the desk of Dr. Mullens. This latter fact alone gave the Fourth Estate a ready-made headline, written with vociferous relish.

North Carolina and Virginia taxed cigarettes at the lowest rate in the country, while New York and other states and cities to the north were among the highest. Therefore, the simple economic rule of buy low, sell high offered potential to make a person very rich with reasonably little effort. The fly in the ointment, stinking up the whole plan, was that bootlegging cigarettes is a federal crime. One could go to prison for a lengthy leave of absence if caught and convicted, not to mention stiff fines.

Entrusted with all financial transactions of the Academy, Abbot had never during the whole of his tenure taken even one thin dime of the school's money. His ethic prevented the very thought. Married, with grandchildren, a pillar of the township of Talerton, an elder in his church, and leading member of several civic organizations, his standing was beyond question. Misconduct began almost innocently—somewhat as a lark, Charlie Talbert joked—in a minor way, as many investments in crime often do: buying a few cartons of smokes for friends and relatives in New York, pocketing a few extra, unreported dollars. A friendly gesture with no harm done. But Abbot could multiply, and if a few cartons could make a few bucks, many cartons could make a lot of bucks. Though hard for someone outside a situation to understand, before one realizes what is happening, a full-scale illegal business can be operating.

Less understandable, over time bootlegging escalated into hijacking and thievery of truckloads of tobacco products. Accomplices, locally and in New York, were not difficult to find. A most embarrassing situation for Booker and Monte was revelation that two of their part-time work students had on occasion helped load and unload contraband into the secret room and other undisclosed locations, being told the boxes contained office supplies. Thankfully, this tidbit of inadvertent sleaze was not picked up by the media.

Booker had never liked Abbot, finding him obstructive, particularly and ironically on matters concerning the student work program. As Booker said on one occasion, "The man's a stickler for procedure and detail, and can always find a dozen reasons why we can't do something, but never one why we can. He's just a negative son of a bitch who likes control." Apparently, outside his duties at the school, he was also avariciously ambitious and creative.

The picture initially painted by the media, and supported by Dr. Mullens when interviewed, was quite at odds with Booker's view. Abbot was portrayed as a saint who stumbled, influenced by the wrong kind of people, who used him for personal gain. As more facts became known, however, this humble portrait grew fainter and fainter, until even Abbot's staunchest supporters had to admit the man was nothing more than an ordinary—though intelligent and somewhat selective—crook. The perpetual struggle between good and evil, T. S. Eliot once said, was the one thing that never changed. The problem and dilemma for so many was determining which was which, and how many shades of grey one was willing to tolerate.

Even so, being a crook does not negate need for sympathy and twinges of pity—and much more than a twinge for the family and all those who knew him well and looked up to him. Perhaps many were reminded how personal choices can have broad consequences and repercussions in the lives of others. It saddened Monte to think of the man's faultless wife and children and grandchildren stigmatized by felonious actions of someone they loved very much. Many lives were injured and changed; one might say, as Booker did, they'd gone up in smoke.

Still, the Academy suffered no death from the scandal. In fact, there was no discernible evidence that even a minor wound had been inflicted. The school had endured worse "Sturm und Drang" during its long history, including a bloody war engaged on the hills and fields surrounding the old buildings. Dark, blackish stains on upper floors of Main Hall bore witness to lost lives of wounded and dying soldiers treated there. And the chapel, could the structure speak, would tell stories of hundreds, if not thousands of young men, mortally injured and traumatized, who breathed their last within its walls. Illegal cigarettes were as nothing, a mere superficial scratch, almost laughable; as the Bard said, "*Come what come may, Time and the hour runs through the roughest day.*" The Academy breathed deeply, brushed itself off, stared steadfastly ahead, and moved on.

• • •

Caroline Lehman had been at the Academy less than two months and now was ill—ill enough to be taken to the infirmary and from there to the emergency room at the local hospital. For over a week she had suffered fatigue, loss of appetite, and dull-aching joints, as well as inability to sleep for more than a few hours each night. The critical incident resulting in hospitalization occurred one evening in her dorm. With great difficulty and pain, she had made her way back to Baldwin Hall after dinner, only to collapse on the vestibule floor. To this point, no one had realized the seriousness of her condition, she being reserved, never complaining or signaling personal discomfort.

Frailness and sallowness had lain fairly hidden due to mode of dress prescribed by her faith: dark, long-sleeved, ankle-to-neck dresses, black stockings and shoes, and gauzy white head covering. Unbeknownst to the houseparents and teachers, she had gradually lost strength and shed weight at an alarming rate. Still, Caroline had indicated nothing, sought no accommodation, and no one noticed until she fell to the dorm tiles, a pitiable heap of dark-blue muslin.

Initially, doctors diagnosed anemia and flu or possibly pneumonia, compounded by her general rundown condition. Given fluids and medication for sleep, temperature returning to normal, she was sent back to school after three days, feeling somewhat better with strict instructions to rest. That night, her houseparent found Caroline sitting on the side of her bed, head buried in her hands, gasping for breath and crying. Mrs. Baxter had raised five children of her own and was no stranger to sickness. She immediately called the nurse on duty in the infirmary, and Caroline was taken there for the remainder of the night.

In the morning she ate a few bites of breakfast, took pain medication, and maintained she was feeling well enough to attend classes. The nurse made an appointment for Caroline to see a doctor, and was given a date two weeks hence. The crisis having abated, nothing else was done for the moment.

• • •

Saturday and Sunday evening before Thanksgiving, Rosanna Worthington and Eric Rockwell, junior high students responsible for Monte and Clare's talent show appearance, played folk music at Valley Pizza in downtown Talerton, earning not only wages and food, but generous tips from appreciative customers. Monte attended both nights, first with Booker and his family, then with Talbert and his wife, Nancy. Eric insisted Monte sit in on two songs each night, to which he agreed reluctantly, being a bit rusty but having a fun time with enthusiastic crowds.

Wednesday a service was held in the chapel, various choral groups sharing pieces practiced for weeks. Elizabeth Blanchard, music instructor, a harrowed wreck offstage, ably projected controlled calm to the audience as if strolling at a seaside spa. How she organized dozens of blind and visually impaired students, many mere children, into cohesive groups was a feat beyond comprehension. Not only succeeding, she triumphed. And the music was moving and beautiful.

Dr. Mullens submitted a fitting homily, interspersed by congregational hymns. Between choral-group offerings, as Elizabeth and mobility instructors shuffled one group off and another on—a not-so-simple task to execute gracefully, given four-tier risers and ever-present danger of someone possibly wandering off the edge of the stage—Monte found a snug seat in the most rearward row.

Without warning he was immediately pounced upon by an encroaching disruption, shrill and squeaky, mindful of a gyrating chipmunk. Arnold's version of whispering was to keep volume to a level audible only in six or seven adjacent rows. Hissing in Monte's ear, he shared, "Hey, Mr. S. I'm a little late. Overslept and got sidetracked. They say turkey makes you sleepy, and I haven't even eaten any yet." He giggled.

"Keep your voice down, Arnold," Monte whispered. "They're getting ready to sing."

Arnold bobbed his head up and down as if planning to comply, only to move closer and fizzle, "I just wanted to let you know what I'm doing over the holidays." His enthused broadcast gained magnitude, attempting to overcome the music.

"What, Arnold? Make it quick," Monte mumbled.

"I'm taking yodeling lessons!" the boy blurted. "From a man my dad knows from Louisiana!"

Several annoyed heads turned their way as Monte very softly groaned, "That's nice, Arnold. We'll talk about it when you get back. Now go and find your class."

"Blasting off now, Mr. S!" he screeched. "Happy turkey day!"

Mouthing goodbye and slouching down to avoid a host of hostile, disgruntled stares, Monte grinned tightly in atonement, stripes of warm crimson creeping up his neck to blush his cheeks.

• • •

Late that afternoon, Monte sat in a dusky Inner Sanctum, Booker having dismissed a French class minutes before to leave hurriedly for a few-days' holiday with Gwen's family in West Virginia. The classroom, in marked contrast to recent cacophony, donned a hushed blanket of loneliness. Moving to one of the large windows, Monte raised the heavy sash a foot or so and received a gush of densely cold air. By midafternoon during freezing weather, rooms in Cameron and Perkins Halls baked oven-like from scorching-hot air emanating in endless waves from the waist-high cast iron radiators lined along outside walls. Beginning in coal-fired boilers, super-heated steam traveled through large steel tubes perhaps a quarter mile from Valley Hospital, an ancient state mental facility often referred to with anachronistic insensitivity as the "Lunatic Asylum."

Huge pyramids of black Pocahontas bituminous coal rose like a string of giant saw teeth beneath a long railroad viaduct paralleling the main highway descending a steep hill into Talerton from the east, tons devoured by furnaces week after week to warm the many aging structures of hospital and Academy.

With additional effort, the window gave another foot, allowing space to prop elbows on the wide sill, chin in hands. Before him spread an unhampered view of chapel and courtyard. Eddies of raw air circulated about his head and neck and arms, frigid runnels biting and tingling yet soothingly invigorating. As though competing, the tireless immediacy of heat at his waist wrapped torso and legs in near-scalding embrace like hot blankets grafted to flesh. He filled his lungs, glacial air penetrating and numbing, at once a stinging fire and syrupy algidity.

An empty courtyard dimmed in gathering shadows, the late-November afternoon withdrawing in final displays of ambrosial light, gentle curtains of evening settling leisurely. There augured no colloquy of voice, no evidence of common verve to contest unyielding silence or hulking primacy of the old buildings. Students not home for the holiday rallied in the dining hall now, afterward marching off to study hall and tutorials, then repairing laggardly to dormitories to douse in soapy showers, scrambling hence for spartan rooms and retirement to bed. There would be no official classes until Monday, a classic turkey dinner being prepared in the dining hall Thursday for those remaining on campus. Parents were always invited, though few would come.

Twilight, Monte often found, imposed a ponderosity of suffusing sadness—melancholia heedless of discernible reason or invitation or even consciousness of existence, tiptoeing stealthily to violate and plant fingers upon one's soul, encircling arms about shoulders and chest like a vaporous interloper indelibly imbued to dwell as integrant part of mind and being, befouling, weakening the very marrow of self, challenging every labored breath and constraining every beat of the heart.

He strived to think of Anne and succeeded for a few restless minutes—waiting at her apartment, waiting to share dinner. And yet the dead abyss of chapel windows reverted his gaze to search his own pith of fallible ideal and worth, courtyard swallowed now in cold grey darkness. Wishing for the impossible dream, he dredged forth words estranged and foreign, treasured talisman once precious, now lost and discarded upon the journey. *Forgive me for weakness, Lord. And help me find courage to accept the things I cannot change . . .*

• • •

A certain amount of red tape had to be unstuck to visit a state prison. Without exception, one had to be placed on an approved list. Being a rehabilitation counselor with a state agency, Monte found, impressed no one and in fact erected the greater disadvantage of being labeled a well-meaning, quixotic do-gooder at odds with a punitive criminal justice system.

At least, that was his jaundiced view in working through the required procedures. His good friend Vernon Southwood, lieutenant with the Richmond Police Department, expedited matters by making a few calls to key people in the Corrections Department. This, along with help from Jimmy Dunsmore's mother, gained agreement from the brothers to see him.

Saturday afternoon, hazy grey and chilly, Monte parked his car on a side road off Spring Street in Richmond, just east of Oregon Hill.

Entrance to the prison was impressively unwelcoming, reminiscent of an eighteenth-century workhouse. Inside, an abundance of uniformed guards went about their duties with impersonal proficiency, neither friendly nor hostile, though with a definite air of wary menace.

Everything not glass was concrete, tile, or steel, stark and exceptionally clean. Visitors spoke in murmurs and subdued whispers, whereas officers spoke in their normal tones, barking discourse reverberating down long hallway caverns leading into the heart of the facility. Caustic disinfectants, nauseous perfumes, stale tobacco, and body odor and sweat permeated every breath. Surfaces other than yellowish wall tile were covered in thick layers of sickly, institutional-green paint, much like many walls and stair rails of the Academy.

After checking in, Monte was told to wait. Mrs. Dunsmore had suggested bringing cigarettes and cookies or other treats, which he carried in a paper bag. Waiting rooms were packed for Thanksgiving weekend: tight, clandestine knots of men and women circled like covered wagons in familial security and closeted invisibility; women alone, solitary islands of fragile gravitas, eyes clouded with hollow fear and anger; mothers fatigued and worn, endlessly coping with restless children, constrained to be there for reasons no longer felt but honored still with habitual devotion and fidelity; older couples, hearts broken, frozen, haggard faces despondent, aged shoulders bending burdensome, yet staunch in hope of something better on which to cling in waning years, though they knew not what. Like a thick pall, layers of fable covered the congregants, reality wearily ignored for futile dreams of some surrogate, redeeming history resolving all.

Occasions of routine, daily normalcy had passed them by, their lives like shattered china strewn across wasted years. His eyes were drawn as to a car wreck or some nameless catastrophe—guiltily, pathetically, thankfully. And not one person gave even the least hint, the smallest reflection, of finding any recompense in that place of suffocating misery.

Monte soon learned there was an order of preference to whom was called. Death-row inmates were given priority, he was told by a man sitting next to him who came every weekend from West Virginia to visit a brother. *Greater love hath no man,* Monte thought, the words not quite fitting. Women with children were called next, and then more elderly individuals and couples, and soon the waiting rooms were thinned to younger couples and single men.

Fifteen minutes later Monte was called, package examined, coat taken, and body whisked rapidly with a metal detecting wand. A guard as huge and black as Arthur led him down a long, well-lighted hallway, passing through two electronic gates of steel bars and then into a large, bright room where inmates and visitors were already gathered on benches and tables bolted to the floor. He was told to sit, and in ten minutes the Dunsmore brothers were ushered in, watched with vigilant nonchalance by blank stares on every flank, both comforting and disquieting.

The brothers' grey prison issue hung baggily. Monte's first impression was stunned amusement, for they imaged the scrawniest, frowsiest, most innocent and docile-looking men one was ever likely to encounter. Pictures of emaciated concentration camp prisoners of war came to mind. Almost laughing to himself, he had to wonder how this pitiful duo ever coerced any bank employee into handing over bundles of cash. They took seats across the table, hands folded dutifully, staring. Some would have defined their eyes as beady. To Monte they resembled small, round, black buttons, heedful and curious, darting to and fro, naïvely anticipatory, like children walking overwhelmed into a circus tent for the first time.

He introduced himself and gave the older brother, George, ostensibly the dominant sibling, the package he had brought, younger Ralph anxiously glancing to his brother as if for cues and guidance. After a few brief desultory pleasantries, Monte produced a picture of Jimmy taken on the job at Andersen Lock and Key. They inspected it closely, smiling broadly, almost tenderly, commenting by word and gesture between themselves. Monte answered their questions and related how well Jimmy was doing, not only at work, but also with improved academic studies.

Whether projected or real, Monte felt distinctly that the two men's interest and care for their little brother was deeply sincere. George, holding the picture and beaming with satisfaction, said simply, "He looks good, and we're glad he's doing okay. I know Mom's happy."

Ralph, more reserved, impressed Monte by his mute observation, more contemplative. After a time he leaned back, eyes warily on Monte's face, and said, "You know, all this is nice, Mr. Scott—cigarettes, candy, and pictures. But why the hell are you really here? You coulda sent this stuff in the mail anytime."

Though he spoke earnestly and without rancor, George turned quickly toward him as to censoriously object. However, before he could speak, Ralph continued, not with insolence or cynicism, but with simple, tactful bluntness. "You come all the way down here on a Saturday, a holiday weekend to boot, to visit a couple of losers you don't even know. You smile, tell us and show us wonderful things about Jimmy, just like we're all old pals." He paused, as if searching for clues. "I don't get it, man. What's your angle anyway?"

Ralph had opened a door with skeptical, salient queries on points Monte had been unsure how to broach. No reason now existed to tread with disingenuous ambiguity. "You're right, Ralph," he answered, staring back soberly. "I do have an angle, as you say, for being here."

In some form of familial cohesion, Monte sensed the brothers gathering ranks, tensed for manipulation. With one ill-advised word, he feared they might withdraw into intractable shells and the game would be over, eyes and ears closed, any risk of trust dissolved.

As semblance to solemn confession, laced with humility, he admitted, "You figured it out, Ralph. Both of you probably saw right through me from the beginning." He paused, then went on, "I need your help; not for me, but for Jimmy."

George spoke guardedly. "What kind of help?" And then with a sneering grin he said, glancing at Ralph, "As you can see, we're not exactly free right now."

Monte was reminded of what he knew of these men: barely an elementary education, histories of delinquency and crime from their teens, dysfunctional family background, lack of respect for law and proper civil conduct, mistrust of authority, potential for violence; a basic, one-dimensional view of life as nothing more than materialistic hedonism, little insight into cause and effect, actions and consequences; two young men who had walked into a bank wearing stocking masks, holding paper bags and water pistols and a note on the back of their mother's rent receipt scrawled with the words, *Give us the munney.*

And now perhaps one moment existed to weave a path through twenty-five years of feckless, inutile history and penetrate a complex *Weltanschauung* rooted in the very fiber of their being. He hoped, literally prayed, that the one absolute, incorruptible vehicle at his disposal—their feelings for Jimmy—would dislodge a modicum of comprehending affirmation for what he was about to ask.

Gazing from one to the other, he said pointedly, "I want to ask you, George, Ralph, to help save Jimmy's life."

George reacted as though slapped in the face, mouth open, speechless. Ralph glared and made to stand, caught himself, then seemed to fiercely inflate, gushing, "What the hell are you talking about?"

Gazing steadily, allowing space for calm, Monte waited, wondering if some divine hand might nudge an opening of ears and minds, for he felt drained in that moment of any capability of his own. Then, like a rudderless ship, he plunged ahead.

"Your younger brother, Jimmy, has ability and potential to . . ." And here he was stymied, a thousand possibilities rising at once, so he simply said, ". . . make a good life for himself, a future. He's not only intelligent, he's smart. He sees things and understands things. He takes locks apart, some with dozens of small pieces, complicated mechanisms, and puts them back together. His grades improve every day, and he has friends, real friends. Jimmy could probably go on to college if he wants it."

An agitated George sputtered, "We know that, mister! We know what he can do! What does that have to do with saving his life?"

Monte dropped his eyes to the table for a few moments before raising his head once more.

"Because, George, in the next year or so Jimmy'll have to make some very important decisions, decisions about what he's going to do with his life, with the years ahead of him. And you and Ralph, whether you realize or not, can help him make those decisions." Minute by minute Monte felt a growing conviction that Ralph was an older version of Jimmy rather than a younger version of George. Ralph's eyes hard upon Monte's confirmed he understood what was meant.

"Jimmy loves you guys very much," Monte said. "And because of loyalty to you, he's convinced himself he wants to be like you." Searching with pleading eyes from George to Ralph, Monte whispered, "All I'm asking for you to consider is to please try and help him see there's a better way. I believe he'll listen to you."

They watched him restlessly, perhaps giving thought to what was said, perhaps puzzled, unsure, devoid of any reasoned digestion of the words and meaning. Ralph spoke first, speech bitter and troubled, eyes smoldering. "I don't know what we can do, Mr. Scott. We're certainly not good examples." Tilting his face closer to Monte and lowering his voice to a mere whisper, he went on, "But one thing I damn well know for sure. We don't want Jimmy to end up like us any more than you do. You . . . you tell us what to do, and what to say, and we'll do it. We'd do anything for Jimmy."

George, ceding leadership to his younger brother, looked at him with a certain curiosity, and then to Monte, and slowly nodded.

Monte drove out of Richmond with an anxiety rooted in helplessness, dependence on unknowns, faith bearing on faith. There were no assurances. There seldom are. But Monte well remembered how at critical times in life he, as so many others, had needed guidance—an emancipating light, benevolent redemption, deliverance. And though most would reason sources of such benefaction must come from lofty and saintly hands, he questioned now, as he had in the prison, if God in his mercy and wisdom might ordain convicts as well.

• • •

Journal: Sunday, November 30, 10:30 PM

Thursday we had our Thanksgiving prayer breakfast at church, then later a family dinner at home, all five siblings present plus Grandmother Augsburg.

Back to school tomorrow. Friday we cleaned and visited, ate leftovers and napped, and I reread A Separate Peace, thinking only of him and our oak tree with every page. To be truthful, I thought of him during all the other times too, wondering what he did for Thanksgiving, where he was, who he was with, if anyone. Another conversation with Arthur should be scheduled. There's so much I want to ask, to know. But how?

I glimpsed him from a distance at the school program Wednesday, talking with Arnold. But he disappeared by the time it was over. We haven't talked in almost a month (28 days actually). Leaving a note or taking coffee on a Wednesday is beyond my capacity for boldness. Why doesn't he visit me? And yet I know why. Or think I do. And soon it won't matter. Doesn't matter now.

Cleaned my room and washed clothes Sat. morn, then baked bread. Saturday night had dinner at Weisner's. Richard and his dad went to visit a friend in hospital and I stayed to visit with his mom. She makes me feel nervous, as if she sees into my head and reads my thoughts. And why does her sweetness often seem to have a pinch of bitterness?

Writing down my deepest thoughts and feelings

has become difficult. Maybe putting something personal to paper is a kind of confirmation, or confession, or wish and prayer . . .

• • •

Arriving the following Wednesday morning at the Academy, Monte found Talmadge Grobanheimer, a studious boy of fourteen whose heroes were David Hume and Albert Einstein, balanced atop a chair, pontificating to a cluster of peers in Booker's classroom, arms spread in a manner of oration and, in his own tumble of words, exuding "metaphysical superiority." His self-promoting speech, however, was short lived, to relief of all, when one of his listeners knocked him off his perch with a heavy copy of Nietzsche's *Beyond Good and Evil*, a judgment of human nature difficult to deny.

On the sidewalk in front of Baldwin Hall that afternoon, Monte encountered Gerald Sampson, known now by almost everyone on campus as "the judge" because of his role in Mr. Talbert's class during the cherry pie trial. An enfeebled amber sun squatted low in the west, skewered atop a fringe of trees on the far southern border of the athletic field, frigid air stalking and dulling senses until one discerned not chill or frostiness but only biting numbness. His Afro had grown to full bloom, and Gerald was without hat, gloves, or coat, his only concessions to the cold being a heavy wool sweater and corduroy pants.

"Hello, Mr. Scott," he greeted after Monte had spoken. "Have you heard anything about Caroline Lehman? How she's doing?" he asked with concern.

Monte noted again the quick recognition and graciousness of manner proceeding so naturally and sincerely. One could easily see why the young man enjoyed popularity and respect from teachers and students. And too, no detriment accrued that he was strikingly handsome and prodigiously intelligent yet displayed no arrogance or egotism. In Monte's rehab mind, the young man was marked for great achievement.

"Only that she's in hospital and having tests done," Monte said, wishing he knew more. "I'm planning to go over later. If I find out anything, I'll let Mr. Fletcher and Ramona know."

"Tim Sommers is really worried," Gerald said, disquieted, resting hands atop his long cane. "He and Caroline have kind of a thing, you know."

"No, I didn't know." Keeping abreast of student romances and alliances was a task requiring daily, even hourly attention. "Maybe she'll be back at school soon, or, if not, can at least have visitors."

"Well, we're having a prayer vigil tonight, and sending a card," he said encouragingly.

"That's good, Gerald. I know she'll appreciate it. I'm sure a lot of people are praying."

• • •

Visiting hours were nearly over by the time Monte arrived. Hospitalized on Monday, Caroline was in a ward with three other patients, privacy curtains drawn in minor poses of seclusion, each bed with visitors emanating whispered conversations inaudible as words—a kind of ongoing, vibrating drone punctured by occasional laughter. Caroline was alone and appeared to be asleep, complexion sallow and drawn, serene as a napping infant. Monte found a chair and carefully placed it beside the bed and sat down. Her breathing came in shallow wisps, measured in slow, almost soundless inhalations and expirations, raising and lowering the white sheet across the plane of her meager chest negligibly. Thin white arms lay inert along her sides outside the covers.

Her lamp was off, and on the bedside table rested a large-print Bible next to a small glass vase containing a simple arrangement of spring flowers. He saw no card. A nurse looked in and asked if everything was all right. Monte nodded. As he scanned the room, always returning to the reposed, untroubled face of Caroline, Gerald's words came potently to mind—a promise of prayers and mention of Tim's worry.

Sitting alongside this girl he scarcely knew on the threshold of womanhood, searingly sad convictions of need for God's grace arose, weighted by his undeniable separation and alienation. Neglected wounds festered for healing; deep hungers cried to be fed. Sacred evidence of meaning beyond the fallible sphere of himself craved communion, some truth above the breadth of simple knowledge and transient mortality. Somewhere along the way, his faith had been bruised in a pique of nihilistic rebellion against littered chaos of events, perhaps a sense of righteous anger at misfortune. He had claimed entitlement as defense of disbelief, deeming his soul cursed and abandoned.

Caroline sighed, the sound floating to his ears with the weight of a down feather. And then, gentle as the breath of a baby, he perceived an insentient touch, like the negligible mark of a pencil on the sheer granite wall of a mountain. The words were faint as mist, weak, yet clear, filled with power and radiance, covering him with a cloak of inscrutable loving kindness: "*Remember, Monte, the light of God will always overcome our darkness.*"

Rising later from the chair, his eyes infolded in wonder the slumbering body. Delicately, he stroked one finger along the back of a blanched ivory hand, desirous to offer some prayer, knowing with perfect assurance God needed no supplication to render care upon this one. She was held securely, and would be all through the night.

• • •

Monte's Rivanleigh trailer park neighbor pounded on the side of his mobile abode early Sunday morning, calling his name obstreperously with volume anyone else would have considered shouting—normal decibels for her. "Hey! Wake up in there, sleepyhead!"

Thankfully, he was semi-dressed and nearly coherent. She stood squinting up in the narrow space between the two trailers, full, round face nested in a jumble of newly minted orange curls she stylishly referenced as "henna," her expression contorted into crevices and bulges rendering what could have been called a smirk and, to a stranger, imminent threat worthy of retreat. He cranked open a window and said drowsily, "Good morning, Dolores."

She was never invited in, and he dared not go into her home unless the husband, Stanley, was present. Untrustworthy, Dolores Hartman often failed to conduct her person as a properly monogamous lady. Natural inclinations for warm friendship too often turned to warmer passions without preliminary warnings. And her bountiful gift for sharing apparently knew no observable limits. This morning, however, he knew Stanley was home, so felt relatively safe speaking with her through a window some four feet above her flaming head.

"Hey, neighbor!" she said, maybe a half decibel below the revving brattle of a chain saw. "Wanna come over for breakfast? Stan's cookin'." The smoky aroma of sizzling bacon and strong perked coffee drifted through the window, wrapping a delicious lariat of hunger around Monte's neck. Stan was a great and tempting cook, but he declined, citing fictitious preparations for church.

"Suit yourself. We oughta go ourselves, but we're too lazy. The roof might fall in if we did anyhow," she cackled loudly. "Anyway, I got some'em important to tell you." Her manner turned deliberately eager, eyes brighter and excited.

Through a window on a Lord's Day morning, Dolores related news about a cabin for sale across the mountains, in the valley, not far from Wolvercote. Her sister and husband had only just placed the property on the market, she said, and she thought Monte might have interest since he worked that area much of the time. Asking location and selling price, he received approximations and suggestion he call for more information. He wrote down the number, thanked her, and said he would contact them that afternoon to set up an appointment to visit.

• • •

Since being at the Academy, Monte had experienced one harrowing episode with the Orientation and Mobility Department, O&M for short. Three instructors taught at the school, one with the Elementary Department and two with junior and senior high. Of the basic and necessary skills needed by visually impaired persons which sighted individuals often take for granted, mobility, i.e., the ability to move efficiently, effectively, and safely within one's environment, is one of the most important.

Well known to the general public is the use of dog guides, often seen in films and on television. This particular choice of travel assistance, while appropriate and viable for some—more often in urban areas, Monte had been told—is not always fitting for others. Dog-guide travel requires lengthy investments of training time at a certified school, being matched with a suitable animal, and the subsequent responsibility of daily care and maintenance of the canine.

The long cane, sometimes called a Hoover cane, is the conventional and generally preferred instrument of choice for most blind and visually impaired individuals. Usually made of lightweight aluminum with golf-club grip and variety of tips, the canes are designed to fit the individual's height, most often measured from floor to sternum, or midpoint of the upper arm. Canes can be fixed or folding, the latter more convenient for stowing away when not in use, especially when traveling on planes, trains, or buses. The choice of dog or cane is often dictated by circumstance, level of skill, age, or personal preference. No working dogs were at the Academy, only a plethora of canes in all sizes.

The O&M Department was also responsible for evaluation and prescription of low-vision aids. Many students, like Arnold, benefited from some type of visual aid, whether a magnifier for close work and reading, or monocular for distance. In some additional cases, a specialized device affixed to glasses could be adapted. Development of electronic devices and appliances, such as closed-circuit televisions for reading, was a fairly recent innovation in the field and one predicted to be of great benefit, though presently very expensive and not always readily available.

One afternoon, Monte spent several hours observing low-vision examinations thoroughly and competently performed by O&M staff and a specially trained local optometrist.

During his second week at the Academy, Monte had spent a very shaky and humbling morning with Brent Greenburg, senior O&M instructor at the school, who, after a thorough briefing on technique, put him under the blindfold to make their way downtown. The experience was not an assimilation of what it meant to be blind, but merely temporary exposure of what it was like to be without sight. For Monte, as with many, he felt constantly in danger of colliding with a telephone pole or street sign, falling into a pit, or tripping over a curb or tree root. Swinging the long cane in an arc across the front of his body, feeling his way along the sidewalk and visualizing what he recalled about the terrain, he listened for sound cues, one of the most important and vital techniques of safe travel.

Brent was patient and proficient and kind, and did not laugh or become upset when his pupil made the same mistakes over and over, though Monte did strongly perceive the instructor was even more relieved than he when they returned safely back to the school and the blindfold came off. A brief traveling adventure and observation of instructors at work with students, plus a bonus of watching low-vision exams, gave Monte a new and challenging perspective on the whole learning curve of working in the field of blindness and visual impairments.

CHAPTER TWELVE

NOVEMBER PASSED EFFORTLESSLY INTO December, and on the first Tuesday of the month Talerton was gifted by overnight snow with temperatures well below freezing. Wednesday morning, Clarence Gladstone, singing merrily, seized this irresistible opportunity to crash his car into one of the Academy's main entrance pillars. No visible damage was done to the brick-and-stone column, and only minor scrapes to the car, though Clarence bumped his face rather hard on the steering wheel and bled all over the front of his white shirt and treasured necktie emblazoned with images of tiny puppies, a birthday gift from a maiden aunt. No police report was filed, and Gladstone was treated in the infirmary, working the remainder of the day with his nose encased by a large white bandage and shirt stained with a dark-reddish blotch, reported by some to resemble an inverted South America—festive and jolly nature not in the least constrained.

Booker was testy, Monte discovered when asking after his Thanksgiving holiday with Gwen's family in West Virginia.

"One of her aunts called me a chauvinist pig! A chauvinist pig, mind you! I had a few names for her, but was too polite . . . too much a gentleman to degrade myself and get into a crap-slinging contest with the bitch!"

Monte smothered laughter and smiled. "Otherwise, how was the turkey and dressing?"

"Oh, shut up! These women libbers, or whatever they are . . . ! Do you think I'm chauvinistic? I always treat women with respect and courtesy, don't I?"

Monte did not answer right away, giving consideration for a suitably neutral response.

"Well!" Booker demanded after a few seconds.

"I think so," Monte said without enthusiasm. Then stupidly added, "If anything, you sometimes can be a little boorish, but—"

"Boorish!? Boorish, my ass!" Booker exploded. "When have I ever been boorish? That's bullshit! Show me one time I've ever been boorish!"

• • •

Mrs. Augsburg's grand plan, in her and the Weisner family's estimation, worked to perfection. Clare came on Friday evening for what she thought was dinner with her parents, only to find herself besieged by a feverish gathering of eagerly beaming faces filling the living room, Richard awkwardly on one knee, gazing up and smiling at her grotesquely, his words unintelligible as a foreign tongue.

The concussion felt in that horrific, swirling moment was like both being crushed in a large vise and thrown into a giant mixing bowl, all sense of time and space and mental functioning spinning out of control and lost. She became in one blindsided moment as a pawn or marionette, manipulated to and fro at the behest of staged dynamism. There existed within the outlined parameters no options, no choices, no bargaining, and above all, no retreat.

She was not surprised by the fact of Richard's proposal, expected for over a year—though certainly not within this circumstance. *Only,* she pondered guiltily, *these happy, well-meaning people staring at me have no idea the Clare of a year ago, or even a few months ago, is not the person standing before them now.* And how could they? She had said nothing, confided in no one but her mother, and only then in vague, exploratory terms, testing reactions, probing her own sense of direction. Perhaps, she now feared, that confidential sharing had brought the present confrontation to fruition.

His question demanded an answer, and Richard waited—dear, kindly, expectant Richard. A fragment of scripture came suddenly to her mind, words having no application to the present dilemma, yet burning with some new, poignant meaning: *You are not your own. You have been bought with a price.* Her eyes sought out her father, standing apart, silent and wise, his face filled with sadness and pride only a parent can know. And he smiled the most caring and gentle smile she had ever seen, then slowly closed his eyes and lowered his head. The decision was hers alone to make. He had raised her and loved her, and now . . . he must let her go.

Looking down on Richard through distorting rivulets of warm tears, she drew in one last breath of freedom, then murmured, "Yes."

• • •

Journal: Saturday, December 6, after midnight

And so the long-awaited commitment is made and my fate is sealed. Everyone is happy and I'm glad for them and find some solace in that. Richard is a saint and will be a wonderful husband and father. What more could any woman want?

His parents will provide space in their home for us after we're married, until we're able to buy a place of our own in Stonebridge. And his father has offered a job in their insurance office.

Why was Mother so thrilled, when Dad looked so sad? Does he think he's losing me? Maybe I need to reassure him all is well and I am content, even if . . . even if I'm not. But now I've put away childish things, quixotic dreams of . . . what?

How could I have ever thought, believed, even for a second, that he could change the tide of destiny.

• • •

"Hey!" The voice was more piercing than frantic, temper and tone unusually strange. "Where've you been? I've been calling all evening." In four months at the school, Booker had never once phoned Monte at home. Much less late on a Sunday night.

Monte's body tightened, casting the pitch of his reply to an unexpected higher range in explanation. "At the hospital with Caroline, then the grocery store and— What's going on?"

"Sorry to bother you with this," Booker said crisply. "But I knew you'd want to know, and maybe change your plans for tomorrow. One of our work students, Sara Bleasdale, has gone missing. Mrs. Hindgardner said she left the dorm after lunch to go downtown and hasn't come back."

Reflexively, Monte glanced at the wall clock hanging in the kitchen nook: 10:30. Obvious, trite questions crowded his mind. Was she with anyone, where downtown, had police or anyone else been notified, her parents, any noticeable issues or problems? Booker answered each with concise brevity.

"She was supposed to meet a few other girls at the movie theater, but didn't show. Houseparents aren't aware of any abnormal problems. Fletcher's hesitant to call police or parents yet, but said he would if she hasn't appeared by midnight. Oh, and Hindgardner said she had one of those small backpack things the kids often use around school."

"Well, what's being done?" Monte asked forcefully. "Anybody out looking for her?" Anger entwined with bafflement shook his words, immediately regretted.

"Don't jump on me! I'm asking the same questions. Fletcher says kids have gone missing before and they always show up as soon as an alarm goes out, to quote the man. I mean, no one wants to overreact, but this is a young girl. And you know Sara. She's a responsible student and worker. Never any trouble—"

"But is anyone out looking!" Monte emphasized strongly once more.

"There's only the one security man on duty, and Fletcher says he's checked all the obvious places on campus."

Remaining silent for a few moments, Monte sensed a gentle ripple of soothing clarity taking control. "Fletcher might be correct . . . and then, he might not. In any account, I'm coming over now. I'll call from Arthur's for an update when I get there. And if she's not back in an hour, call the police, please."

The night air was moist and cold, the dark, moonless sky splattered whimsically with pinpricks of unfocused luminance. Mist scurried across the highway atop the mountain, ghostly brilliant in the headlights, shunting aside in obeyance like the Red Sea for Moses.

Arthur was initially irritable, placated when given explanation—enough to make coffee while Monte called Booker.

"She's not back yet," Monte said, hanging up the phone and taking a mug from Arthur's hand. "Fletcher called Talerton police, finally, for what good it did. They're sending someone over to question Mrs. Hindgardner. Nothing much they can do for twenty-four hours, someone said. Though they did seem more concerned when told she was only sixteen and visually impaired. Said they'd interview her friends in the morning, check the movie theater and bus station, talk with the parents."

"So what are you going to do?" Arthur asked blearily.

"Just about the same thing, only I'm going to start now."

Few places are more depressing than an empty bus depot at two in the morning. Harsh fluorescent lighting magnified the large room, somehow sharpening wafting odors of diesel fuel from the damp street outside, overcooked steamed hot dogs rotating in a glass box, stale coffee, and tattered, sweaty leather seats from within. Only now did Monte remember his few Richmond experiences with disappearance. Most had been mere petulant tirades, runaway friends in conflict with parents or siblings, returning defiantly within the same day or the next, hungry for supper and home; some, not so fortunate, lost forever on train tracks, waters of the James, or some tragic entanglement in alley or street. And he would never forget one group of four small children locked in an old icebox, found too late.

Still, he assured himself, there was no need to think the worst yet.

A boy standing behind the counter who looked scarcely sixteen told him Mr. Ranney, the station manager, had gone off at eleven and would be in at seven in the morning. Since noon, four buses had departed, one each south to Fordhurst, north to Washington, west to Charleston, and the last to Richmond. All but this last made numerous stops along the way. No other buses would be arriving or leaving for three hours. Ticket information, the lad said, was locked in the safe, and no, he had not seen anyone answering Sara's description. Monte mentally noted to check school files and make a copy of the girl's picture.

Cruising downtown streets, he saw not a single person on foot and only two occupied vehicles. The movie theater had an emergency number posted inside the ticket booth window, which, when called, connected Monte to the fire department. At five he sacked out on Arthur's sofa with plans to be back at the bus station by seven, despite lack of any evidence the girl might have left town. At six, Booker reported a cursory search of campus had been done, with a more thorough exploration scheduled for later that morning by security staff and local police. Bulletins were placed on local radio stations, the one television outlet, and the daily Talerton newspaper.

Fletcher's conversation with the Bleasdale mother did not go well, as expected. She and her husband had recently separated, adding another layer of anxiety to the mix. An infirmary nurse came forward with information that Sara had been frequently nauseous in recent weeks, coming in every few days for medication, accompanied by mild anxiety attacks, both unusual for a girl normally exhibiting excellent health and pleasant demeanor.

Circumstances resulted in Monte not being able to talk with Claude Ranney until almost eight o'clock. The station manager had been initially interviewed by a patrolman at three that morning, roused from sleep at his apartment to howl obscenities, denying knowledge of any young girl from the Academy. Two detectives came at seven to interview him again, huddled at the counter and keeping everyone else out of hearing. As soon as they left, a queue formed to purchase tickets for the daily 7:20 commuter bus to Rivanleigh. Monte joined impatiently at the end of the line, ill-tempered with fatigue. Combined with Ranney's normally foul mood, the interchange was not productive.

"You ain't a cop or official from the school or a family member, or as far as I can tell, you ain't nobody with any authority to ask nothing." He leaned over the counter, bare arms braced on the top, his raspy breath thick with volatile aromas of aged cheese compounded by pungent, neglected, unwashed laundry, cheap cologne failing to fully mask odors reminiscent of sweaty locker rooms. Watery red eyes focused sharply on Monte's face, the thin, wiry body tensed. Oily dark hair fell across his forehead and ears, chin and jowls shadowed with day-old whiskers like smudges of charcoal.

Monte's inclination to grasp the front of the man's T-shirt and hoist him over the counter was enticing, yet likely an unwise and unhelpful move. Calmly, he said, "You're right, Mr. Ranney, I'm not. Sara's a student in our work program—"

"Look, whoever you are or whatever you are is of no interest to me," Ranney muttered, easing his stance and scooping up a stack of ticket stubs. "I've got work to do and I'm sure you do too. So . . ."

Surprisingly, Booker, seated erect at his desk with a Camel in the Inner Sanctum, had more current information, freshly gleaned from Fletcher after a conference with police.

"She's almost certainly in Richmond, they say, based on what Ranney and the mother told them. She has relatives there and probably took a bus yesterday evening. That's the foci of the search right now."

Monte listened, afraid to sit too long for fear of nodding asleep. Already he felt his mind drifting into fog. Still, there were avenues he wanted to scout, three in particular.

Booker wondered legitimately why Monte bothered to get further involved, with so many others already diligently working to locate the young girl and Monte having so much else he should be doing. After all, as Ranney pointed out, he had no authority to question anyone, and no one was obliged to speak with him.

Though no military tactician, Monte did know the value of flanking attacks, hoping perhaps his insignificance and lack of official connection with the school or police might open a few doors and mouths. Perhaps after a nap at Arthur's.

• • •

Withrow Mulligan, who had the habit of turning any environment upside down and almost always doing the exact opposite of whatever was expected or requested, came charging—his only speed—into Booker's classroom at noon, obviously agitated. An altercation at lunch, not an unusual occurrence, had precipitated his appearance. Sent by Mrs. Fitzgerald, manager of the dining hall, to Mr. Fletcher's office, the boy was then directed by Ramona, in the principal's absence, to see Mr. Booker.

"I was in the right!" Withrow testified convincingly, standing at attention, rumpled and flustered in front of Booker's desk. "Norton doesn't know what he's talking about."

Booker sank despairingly into his chair, a tyrannized man shrinking before Monte's eyes, knowing from pragmatic experience an entangled and tortuous story was about to unfold. "What was he talking about?" Booker muttered, trying not to let his disinterest show.

"He said Jesus wasn't born on Christmas!"

Booker sighed with a drone of misery. A damned theological problem. Monte was certain he could see the man's lips moving, raising dismayed appeals to the ceiling. "Norton said that, did he? Norton Zimmerman? What else did he say, Withrow? What got you so riled up?"

"He claimed Jesus was born in the spring, in a cave! And any fool knows Jesus was born in a stable and killed in the spring. That's Easter holidays!"

Booker exhaled audibly, more an extended groan, scrabbling to remember what course he might have taken in college dealing with issues of this nature. Recalling none, he mumbled aside to Monte leaning against the file cabinet, "Good grief, Scott! Don't kids fight over girls or comic books or dirty looks anymore?"

Pausing as if fatigued, he waved an arm at Mulligan, and sighed again. "Sit down, Withrow, and listen." Withrow sat, smug in righteousness, confident of having his doctrines vindicated. Plaintively, Booker said, "Whether Jesus was born on Christmas or in spring is not the question. Save those questions for Sunday school, or college or seminary, or any place other than here. Fighting in the dining hall is the question, Withrow. Fighting with Norton in the dining hall. Ramona said Mrs. Fitzgerald told her you hit him in the mouth with a stale cinnamon bun. You can't—"

"It wasn't, I swear!" Withrow interjected, partially standing. "It was a . . . a leftover English muffin with apple butter. And I didn't exactly hit him with it, just kind of shoved it in his direction and part of it went into his mouth, which just happened to be open. Like it usually is!" The last bit he added colorfully for emphasis.

Booker glanced over toward Monte again and exhaled sorrowfully. "Okay, Withrow, I've heard enough. That's ten demerits and no Student Center for a week. One more fight and you'll be suspended. And I don't think your mother would like that. Now go." *Booker,* Monte thought admiringly, *always the wise judge and jury.*

Mulligan rose dissatisfied from his chair and shuffled halfway through the doorway, sulking, then turned and said in an even voice, "Well, Jesus was born on Christmas. That much I know for real, no matter what stupid Norton says."

"Go, Withrow, now!" Booker shouted.

When the young boy was out of hearing, he turned to Monte and smiled wistfully, suppressing a chuckle, and mused, "You know, one has to wonder how the Son of God, savior of mankind, views having his natal history defended by Withrow Mulligan. Lord in heaven! If I were ever to write a book, no one would believe this stuff."

• • •

By midafternoon, Fletcher had received updates from police. Richmond authorities reported no one at the bus station remembered seeing anyone like Sara getting off any bus from Talerton on Sunday or Monday. Stops had also been made in Rivanleigh, and station personnel there were questioned with the same negative results. Sara's parents in Fordhurst had heard nothing from either their daughter or their relatives, and claimed they knew of no reason why Sara would want to disappear. The couple, though recently separated, said they remained on friendly terms. Police and security interviews with roommates and other friends were redundantly unrewarding. Monte was dissatisfied and decided to call Vernon Southwood.

"Is this the great detective, Lieutenant Clouseau, with whom I'm speaking?" Monte chuckled.

"Wrong number, pal. And it's a little early in the day for you to be boozed, isn't it?" Vernon retorted, then laughed. "If you're calling to borrow money again, you've come to the wrong place."

Monte smiled, visualizing his friend of over twenty years, now with the Richmond police and heading Major Crimes Division. In broad strokes he outlined the story of Sara Bleasdale, Vernon remaining attentively quiet.

"So, how can I help?" he asked when Monte was finished. "I've heard nothing from Missing Persons or anybody else, but I can check it out." The voice was concerned and reassuring; Southwood was married with two young children. Monte felt guilty bothering the man with something that was probably trivial.

"Well, that would be appreciated," Monte said, hesitatingly, "but really, I just wanted advice on what we—I—could do. So far it's pretty much a blank."

A moment of silence ensued, only a pondering sigh seeping through the phone. "First off," Vernon then began suddenly, "I'm sure everyone's doing the best they can. Leave it to them, which I know you won't. I could call the Talerton chief if you like. But I'd rather not. The best thing you can do is talk with her friends, especially her closest friend, boy or girl. Teens seldom do something like this independently. Somebody will know something. But you might have to push . . . or go easy. You know the routine. Use your good sense of judgment."

Ranney, in the meantime, had been interviewed by Talerton police a third time, maintaining his original story and coming in for some rather harsh criticism for not being a bit more suspicious of a girl Sara's age purchasing a bus ticket that time of night. He was adamant in denial of any culpability or dereliction of duty, defending himself with whining conviction by saying it was not unusual for young people to come in and buy bus tickets; kids from the Academy and other schools did so all the time. And in fact, he asserted in justification, changing his original testimony somewhat, it had not been at night, but just before noon, the 11:55 terminating in Norfolk with local stops the entire distance—meaning every station on the route had to be checked.

With renewed memory, further flummoxing police, Ranney added he now recalled she had been with a group of seven girls from a local private college, buying one-way tickets and paying cash, each carrying small backpacks. The driver of the bus, tracked down at his home, could say only that he remembered collecting tickets, but seldom recalled faces.

"All girls that age look pretty much the same to me," he claimed innocently. Being re-interviewed, Mrs. Hindgardner admitted misspeaking when originally questioned, clarifying that Sara had left after a late breakfast, not lunch, implying she was going to church downtown.

• • •

Later Monday afternoon, Monte sought out Clare Augsburg. He had not seen her since the first week of November. She seemed pleased to see him, offering coffee in subdued fashion when he appeared at her classroom door, despite having five students engaged in various culinary pursuits around the kitchen with two more in the sewing area. She, of course, knew of Sara's disappearance, readily agreeing to help with inquiries when told what information he needed from the girls' dormitory.

Smiling discreetly and placing a steaming mug in his hand, she murmured, "Good idea you asked me to do the snooping around in

Baldwin. You might have encountered some embarrassing difficulties if, in fact, you'd been brave or foolish enough to try."

As he drank his coffee, he watched her patiently and competently endow each student with a sense of independence and confidence. When he walked into the hallway to leave, she walked with him. Almost laughing, she said, "I must say, Monte, when you're around, life is never dull, just one surprise after another. Now you're turning into a regular Inspector Javert, and in a very good way, or is it Sherlock Holmes?"

"How about Hercule Poirot?" He grinned.

Shaking her head, face radiant with amusement, she gazed into his eyes with a potency that forced upon him every ounce of self-control he could muster to keep from wrapping arms around her. With the slightest of giggles, she whispered, "No, not Poirot. You're not much like a Poirot. For one thing, your accent's all wrong."

By evening, Clare had found and questioned Sara's best friend, a girl named Lana. At first, as expected, she denied knowing anything, just as she had with security and the police. When probed further, she admitted Sara had been very depressed lately because of her parents' separation and ongoing fight over custody of the three children. And all at Christmas. At one point Lana broke down and cried, swearing she did not know where her friend might be but believed she was safe and being cared for.

The boyfriend, Alex, was a student in the Deaf Department. Questioning him would have to wait until morning.

• • •

Journal: Monday, December 8, 9:30 PM

He came today, so easily and naturally. Thirty-six days passing like a decade of vacuum, or perhaps only ten seconds. Time seems to have little meaning anymore. His mission was legitimately worthy and I was able to help. What can I say except to admit how much I've missed him? Lord, how I've missed him. And I could see in his eyes he wanted me. He wanted me. The one thing, maybe the only thing, I cannot give.

God, if my love is wrong, a sin, then I must accept it and ask forgiveness. Only you know my heart. Please give me strength and light.

• • •

Monte's sign language was not proficient. Fortunately, Alex Ramos was an excellent lip-reader, his speech passably understandable. Meeting early in the dining hall, they wrangled deftly and politely for less than ten minutes while the boy ate breakfast. The most Monte could pry out of him was the adamant fact that Sara was fine and would show up when ready, perhaps in a few days or at most a week. With great reservation, Monte promised him cover and anonymity for one more day, assuring him the only concern was for Sara's well-being. Ramos, respectfully firm in telling him nothing more, had in their brief conversation unwittingly confirmed a suspicion Monte had held from the beginning of Sara's disappearance. Now he needed one more piece of testimony for proof.

Monte had no liking or trust for Claude Ranney, believing the man was hiding valuable information for reasons as yet undisclosed. The dark shadows of Monday's whiskers had advanced to a short bristle of black stubble by midmorning Tuesday, general aroma and appearance unimproved. The lethal glare he fixed on Monte might have been amusing in a movie or a poster; in the present moment, it was chilling. Not shrinking, Monte moved to the counter, thankful the room was occupied by only one other person, a teenage boy grappling with a pinball machine in a far corner, uttering low strings of expletives.

"Good morning, Mr. Ranney. You remember me, Monte Scott? We chatted for a bit yesterday about Sara Bleasdale?"

Since that time, Monte had cumulated a fairly broad dossier on the man from a variety of sources. Divorced twice, with no known children, he had worked as the station manager for twenty years; Korean War Army veteran and native of Talerton, well known, liked, and trusted by the police department with whom he had frequent contact due to his often unruly and unpredictable clientele. Based on this familiarity with law enforcement, Monte believed authorities had not confronted Ranney with the vigor they might have done with someone lesser known.

His gaze and body language, sullen and antagonistic, moved him as before to lean forward and brace thin, bare arms stiffly on the countertop. Monte pictured him as a snarling guard dog held at bay only by a thick leash of uncertainty. "If you ain't here to buy a ticket, bud, you might as well turn around and walk out."

Monte sighed and lowered his head as if in defeat. Slowly, softly, he said, "I've got no beef with you, Mr. Ranney, and no interest in causing trouble for anybody. My one and only concern is Sara Bleasdale, that's all. If you can help in any way, we'd be most grateful." Difficult to discern, Monte thought the staunch body before him eased slightly, face softening a degree.

"What's your connection?" the gnarly man asked, warily strident, moving back a half step from the counter and rising to full height. "I've told the police every damned thing I know. My God, man, they've fucking questioned me three or four times already."

Monte nodded sympathetically and replied, "Sara's a friend, a client actually, student in our work program at the Academy." And then, deeply serious, bending forward and placing hands flat on the counter as if talking to an old and dear acquaintance, he said quietly, "What you may not know is . . . she's not well, Mr. Ranney. Not many people know, and I'm sharing this with you in confidence. The police probably didn't tell you. I'm what you'd call her counselor, and she could be in need of medical attention, and that's the truth, so help me."

Ranney smirked, his tone mocking. "And why wouldn't they have told me something like that, something that important?" The man was no gullible fool, Monte concluded. Everything said to him had to be convincingly true, or at least sound that way.

"Because of school policy, Mr. Ranney, legalities," Monte said tightly. "Personal, private medical information prohibited by law from being disclosed." As if debating with himself, Monte added, "It's not necessarily life threatening, but she could get very sick if she doesn't receive—"

Shaking his head side to side, eyes turning to a far wall, Ranney said, "You have your rules, mister. I understand that, and I have mine." His lean frame inflated with a laboriously deep breath as he spoke almost reverently. "I made a promise, so how can I break that? She trusts me."

Exhaling, he forced an awkwardly ill-fitting smile. "I love those kids. They come in here all the time and hang around. Down here they can cuss and smoke, play pinball and carry on—you know, have a good time. I guess I feel sorry for 'em in a way. I try to help 'em if I can. I'm not gonna rat 'em out over some joke and make trouble for 'em . . . and myself at the same time."

Moved by the confession, Monte said gently, "Anything you tell me, Mr. Ranney, I promise will be just between the two of us. No witnesses, no wires. Our conversation never happened. I have no interest in anything other than knowing Sara's safe."

Gaze pensively contemplating, Ranney reached down to shuffle some papers on the countertop, finally tilting his head to the side, speaking to a distant entity: "She might have met up with someone. A boy. A deaf kid. I don't know his name." He took another deep breath and in so doing reverted to his more normal persona, voice stronger. "If you quote me, I'll say you're lying, and I'll . . . I'll tell the police you came in here and tried to sell me dope and then tried to rob me."

Monte almost laughed at the feeble threats, deciding to merely ignore them. "Why didn't you tell the police that when you were questioned, Mr. Ranney? I mean—"

"Because," he interjected forcefully, "she begged me to keep it secret and I promised I would, at least for a few days, or a week. Said it was a harmless stunt her and her friend was pulling. I didn't know she was sick. Goddammit! She looked fine to me!" He dropped his eyes to the counter and continued more mildly, "She never got on no bus. I . . . I faked her ticket." Raising his face to Monte's, he said, "But I don't know where they went, and that's the God's honest truth."

Now Monte had proof. Sara Bleasdale was somewhere close, somewhere in the area. A house or apartment of a friend, some connection to Ramos perhaps? Or even someplace at the school? Farfetched but possible. Visceral instinct told him she was safe. He would withhold what he knew until tomorrow. The next step would be done this evening.

• • •

White Cane, name adopted by Rosanna and Eric for their musical duo, had added a bassist and mandolin player with promise of a drummer. Rosanna was a commotion of jiggles and giggles when she caught Monte in the hallway outside Booker's classroom to share the news. Labeled by many adults a "little doll," she gave definition to descriptive words like *cute*, *pert*, and *contagious merriment*, a petite bundle of tittering joy everyone loved because she spread her vibrancy in every corner. Totally blind since birth, straight-A student, she could play piano, guitar, and banjo as well as anyone he knew.

In Monte, she ignited an unwelcome tendency of familial duty to exercise vigilant protection, a calling perhaps, similar to his relationship with Betty—for him to act as patriarchal or brotherly advocate and shield from a cruel and dangerous society and world, to keep her always safely untouched by sorrow, disappointment, and evil.

He realized, of course, the patent weakness and absurdity these attitudes and feelings presented, yet still acknowledged their lingering existence, no matter how naïve and detrimental in the long term. Intellectually, objectively, he knew Rosanna had to be freed to grow and scope out uncertainties of life, to stand and walk and survive. Booker and others offered reminders from time to time how good intentions often went awry and damaged those one longed to help, sometimes almost as much as blatant malevolence. Ultimately, though hard to abide when witnessing guileless innocence, the pages of these young lives had to unfold with whatever preparation could be offered and provided. And then, protectors standing aside with fearful hope, they would be sent forth, ready to challenge an uncharted future and murky universe.

"That's great news, Rosanna," Monte said excitedly. "When will they start?"

"Probably Friday night's gig at Valley Pizza, if we can find time to practice," she wheezed breathlessly.

Daily schedules at the Academy were fairly rigid from early morning until bedtime, the philosophy being that consistent and orderly regimens benefited children who often lacked these at home, aiding in future behavioral and vocational demands as adults. Free or elective time was a premium, precious gift, and days before Christmas vacation were especially full.

"Well, I hope you can work it out. I'll try to come." Tentative plans had been made with Anne Walden to hear the group play on Friday evening.

"I hope so," she spouted gleefully. "We want you to do a few of those songs you wrote."

"Don't count on that," he laughed as she turned and struggled rapidly down the hall, burdened with her normal load of books, brailler, and cane.

• • •

With the knowledge Ramos and Ranney had provided, Monte suddenly realized his unofficial involvement had now become a kind of potentially questionable complicity in Sara's disappearance. Not only was he risking her well-being in assuming she was safe, he was also risking his job and career. And why? To avoid making her actions a police matter? Police were already involved, and would be again in any case. Still, he reasoned, if she voluntarily came forward, unhounded like an escaped criminal, and on her own terms, dignity intact . . . Would he live to regret his decision?

Following someone at night is not as easy as often appears on television or in movies, Monte found—especially a quick and agile young boy who knew the campus layout much better than he. Carrying a large paper sack, Ramos left the Deaf Department boys' dormitory at about eight o'clock, slithered between two classroom buildings, and made his way to the Student Activity Center where he was met by none other than Lana, Sara's best friend, also carrying a sack.

Thoughts of Arnold's monocular came to Monte's mind, how useful it might be in a situation like this, especially if equipped with night-vision capabilities. Keeping in the shadows, Alex and Lana skirted the chapel and entered a rear door off the courtyard into the basement of Main Hall.

Waiting about thirty seconds, Monte slipped through the same door quietly. The space before him was pitch black, and he had brought no flashlight, a fundamental oversight. Standing perfectly still, he listened for any clue of sound, detecting nothing other than a soft hum of security lights from the courtyard. Alex and Lana had to be close by, but where? Ironically, he felt quite blind in spite of a minute sliver of ambient glow flowing under the door and spreading across his feet on the gritty concrete floor. His only choices seemed to be fumbling around in the darkness, or to stand and wait until either seeing or hearing something helpful. He wisely chose the latter.

For what might have been half an hour, he remained anchored to the same spot, feeling much like a failure and fool, outsmarted by two sixteen-year-old kids many would have labeled "impaired." *Not an altogether negative circumstance*, he concluded with risible humility; after all, was not his calling and aim to promote independence, ingenuity, and resourcefulness?

Next morning very early, beginning of the fourth day since Sara had gone missing, Monte ventured back to the basement of Main Hall, this time with a flashlight. A certain weariness close to boredom yet nerve-rackingly impulsive drove him with desire to bring this mystery to a satisfactory conclusion. Using vacation leave for the past two days, his field duties had been neglected, threatening negative attention from his supervisor, Marlon Danforth—encounters always to be avoided.

On the phone rather late the previous night, he had spoken with Charlie Talbert, who knew the school labyrinths probably better than anyone. Recollections from his student years of Main Hall basement, which he called "the catacombs," were of a series of rooms, enclosures, passageways, and generally divided spaces which, over the years, had been utilized for shops, classrooms, storage, offices, and even cafeteria. Rumors abounded of Civil War soldiers entombed there.

An hour after they talked, Talbert called back, having remembered details he thought might be worthwhile. On the chapel side, against a back wall, he described a large walk-in refrigeration unit once used for perishables, which might now have been appropriated for a varmint-proof storage closet. In addition, tucked away in a small front corner room, was a smaller, soundproof enclosure divided within by a thickly insulated partition fitted with a double glass panel, employed in earlier years for hearing tests, amounting to a sort of room within a room, or "box within a box," Charlie chuckled. A more modern version was now located in one of the newer buildings on the Deaf Department campus.

Monte decided to investigate these two locations first, both sounding like excellent refuges for hiding in semi-comfort and security. The cooling unit, no longer cold, was obvious—a huge, stainless steel cube with wood-paneled interior situated only a few steps from the courtyard entrance. The massive original door had been replaced in recent years by a framed screen affair, and crammed inside from floor to ceiling were cleaning and custodial supplies. No evidence of a stowaway, past or present, was anywhere apparent.

Finding the soundproof enclosure took some time. From the cooler, he was confronted by a mind-boggling maze of choices, every direction appearing worthy of exploration. Before him was a vision of desolation, scenes of rushed abandonment, as if the past had been hurriedly cast aside to decay, eager for a brighter, more modern future. Here, within the quiet, dilapidated space, a weight of historical significance rose suddenly to a prominence of foreboding excitement. Secrets, dormant and precious, floated like the stale aroma of old clothes packed for decades in ancient steamer trunks. Trysts and treasures stowed as undying echoes and remembrance, restless temperament embedded in the walls, permeating the air with dignity, bequeathing a sense of honor and holy permanence. *They are in this place still,* Monte knew: the beloved children, frightened and eager; staid, dedicated instructors; and for a time, blooded soldiers, grey and blue, longing only for home; all dead a century or more, lost to grassy graveyards, eroded tombstones unreadable, nameless and forgotten.

His flashlight scanned crumbling plaster—once troweled expertly smooth and thick, coat upon coat—transformed to ugly stained and decaying patches, heavy chunks and slabs fallen askew to the floor, like bergs birthed from a giant mother cliff of ice and glacier; naked, stout pine framing, solid still as a permanence of bones, affixed by peeling strips of lathe, complacent, duty fulfilled, each sawed and hammered, precisely configured. Pulsating shouts and laughter abided, raucous curses and confrontation; carpenters, plasterers, painters, stone carriers, and masons toiling day upon day, season to season, on this, a school for deaf and blind children; nascent ideals of courageous aspiration, a blueprint conceived from thoughtful dream to severe solidity so long ago. He felt as an unwelcome intruder, much like his first day on campus—surrounded by mystery, an unworthy observer in an alien domain.

Two front corner locations were possible, according to Talbert, complicated by crisscrossing hallways, subdivided spaces, general disorientation, and darkness. One could quickly see the value of such a setting for hidden contraband—cartons of stolen cigarettes for instance. Corners he had assumed the night before would be easy to find were not. A snarl of similar rooms and passageways presented a roadmap of confusion. Clutter was an additional irritation: old desks, crates, and boxes, chairs, and tables jumbled and stacked in every available space, some almost fully blocking doors and corridors. These, at least, seemed unlikely hiding spots. Monte at length deemed patient, time-consuming search the only viable plan.

An hour later, he found a used tissue balled up on the floor, seemingly fresh. A short distance away, a plastic straw hid flat against a grimy baseboard. Two paces farther along was an unimpeded closed door, and inside, a small room filled with stacks of old wooden folding chairs, nearly obscuring a smaller chamber paneled with a black fibrous material. The retired unit for hearing tests, Monte wagered. Maneuvering around a jumble of boxes, Monte stood for a moment listening—then, with some chagrin, remembered the unit was soundproof.

The chamber door camouflaged by use of the same black material as the walls was substantial, requiring a fairly hard tug before giving way. A warm light glowed within. Sitting serenely in a chair beside a cot, reading a large-print book, was a young girl. She looked up with tempered disappointment, not surprised by the intrusion, and forced a crookedly penitent grin.

"Hello, Sara," he said, releasing a sigh and smiling with reassurance. "It's Monte Scott. We've been a little worried about you."

After a rather sullen trek to Brad Fletcher's office and leaving her in the capable hands of Ramona, he left the Academy to return to Rivanleigh, fearing what he might find after an absence of several days.

Reality was worse than imagination. His shared secretary, Joan, announced as he came through the door that a team from Richmond headquarters was coming on Monday to review all his currently active case files. Danforth had reported—with glee, she added—that every field counselor was undergoing this modern form of torture, though he euphemistically referred to the exercise as "an inspection to help us all be more efficient in our jobs and develop better work habits." Unlucky enough to be chosen first on their list, Monte laughed hysterically. Plans to visit clients in his eight counties were squashed. The remainder of the day and days to come, including the weekend, would be spent on neglected paperwork, endeavoring to put 150 case folders in tolerable order.

• • •

Journal: Thursday, December 11, 11:15 PM

One part of me, the agitated, scary part, was afraid he would come, and the other, that part I find so . . . what? Warm, exciting, curious . . . wanted him to come, if only for a minute, just to assure me all was well, just to see his smile and hear his voice, look into his eyes.

Arnold says he's back in Rivanleigh, and I dare not bother Arthur, though it's tempting.

So afraid I have hurt him without intention. If he only knew how much I was hurting too. Our friendship was never supposed to be like this. How did it happen? How did I let it happen? And yet from that first day . . .

When I look at Richard, my heart breaks because I know he cares so much, and now I've made a promise, a vow, not only to him, but everyone.

Please Lord, give us peace, and show me the way.

CHAPTER THIRTEEN

A VISIT TO THE cabin Monte's neighbor Dolores had told him about two weeks before had finally been scheduled, coming as a brief, welcome Sunday-afternoon break from case file reviews. The property was being sold by Dolores's sister, and directions given were somewhat confusing. Several miles south of Wolvercote, hidden on a network of country byways, Monte found the anonymous lane, a rutted, potholed track showing slight evidence of maintenance other than large river rocks dumped into the deeper depressions, demanding travel no faster than a leisurely walk. Severity of the rugged path extended over a quarter mile across dormant cornfields bordering on either side, then burrowed into a thick stand of hardwoods and pines, opening a few hundred yards farther on to a small clearing in which nestled a one-story, neatly kept board-and-batten cabin.

Dolores had told him the structure was not large, and indeed, Monte found the description accurate. A cursory tour by the sister revealed a living–dining area with fireplace, tiny adjacent kitchen, two small bedrooms, and bath. She was anxious to sell and move back to town, inconvenience of living so remotely at her stage of life troubling. Monte thought the asking price reasonable and, subject to approval of a suitable bank loan and home inspection, verbal agreement was reached.

• • •

Elizabeth Blanchard, barely recovered from the Thanksgiving program, was now saddled with organizing music for the Christmas concert: kindergarten ensemble, two elementary choirs, a junior high chorale, and two high school choruses. She also, in consort with Anne Walden and Erin Celinski, was planning and directing a Christmas pageant.

In one of his moments of questionable creativity, Mr. Fletcher put forth the idea of Christmas caroling in neighboring streets one evening before the Academy closed for holidays as an effort in community building. In an even more creative moment, causing many to suspect he must have lost all sense of prudent proportion and any remaining figment of rational intellect, the principal appointed Gladstone to head up the excursion.

Gladstone could not sing and readily admitted to tone deafness, and had never been involved on any level with any type of singing group. Once, when ten years of age, he had taken a single aborted piano lesson, mysteriously spraining a thumb and index finger. Even so, in the spirit of Christmas, the school staff looked on with hopeful, though cautious, optimism that community relations would not be irreparably damaged. After all, as Arnold Schnellich nonchalantly said to Monte one afternoon, "What could go wrong?" Cackling laughter as the lad traipsed away sent chills down Monte's spine, burdening him with dismay the remainder of the week.

After Thanksgiving holidays, Dr. Mullens always had a large evergreen erected and decorated in the vestibule of Main Hall, necessary work being done by the Maintenance Department, never to be touched by students, deaf or blind. Hearing rumors the Deaf Department was putting up a tree of their own, Mr. Fletcher, in another burst of seasonally competitive spontaneity, felt a Blind Department tree would heighten the holiday spirit even more. Spearheading this task fell to a sulking, unjolly Ramona, who brooded behind her typewriter for days, though no one seemed to notice.

Always ready to foment a bit of mischievous confusion—more like lighthearted sabotage, Monte thought—Booker suggested that a small group of elementary kids, chosen by lot, be picked to decorate the tree as a kind of integrating reward. The artistic wisdom of this proposal was challenged strongly by Mr. Fletcher, who approached Christmas-tree decking with solemn exactness of a Michelangelo, daring to state in the hearing of several teachers that he did not want a "Jackson Pollack job done in my department by a bunch of little blind neophytes."

This foolishly insensitive and blasphemous declaration infuriated everyone in the Elementary Department, and Fletcher, swearing over and over that he had never used the word *blind*, was forced to recant and apologize, doing his best to downplay the incident and claim he was quoted out of context. Booker was ecstatic.

• • •

In what he later acknowledged to be a foolish and regrettable act, Monte impulsively made his way to the basement of Baldwin Hall late on a Wednesday afternoon, concentrating his mind with each step to the purpose of merely offering felicitous seasonal greetings and nothing more. Clare was mopping the DLS kitchen floor, softly humming the Lightfoot song they had sung in the talent show in October. He stood in the doorway and watched, charmed by the lithe, efficient way she moved, wishing to join her and transform the chore into some mawkish imagery from an old motion picture musical. Transfixed by the scene and lost in idyllic thoughts, he did not notice the approach of a body behind him until a wee small voice with more authority than volume questioned, "Whatcha think yer doin'?"

Flipping around, he found himself contested by a tiny girl of no more than six or seven bearing a rich, dark-caramel frown, piercing, deep-brown eyes behind heavy, horn-rimmed spectacles, and hair tight in cornrows across the top of her head and braided down her back. A bright, flowery dress under a much-too-large quilted cotton coat clashed appealingly with purple knee socks and pink tennis shoes. Standing with hands locked behind her back, she inspected

Monte as if making a curious and possibly problematic discovery, giving no sense of shyness or lack of confidence.

He knelt down to be more on her level, and smiled. "I'm here to visit Miss Augsburg. My name's Mr. Scott. What's yours?"

Gathering herself as though coming to attention, she intoned with practiced eloquence, "My name is Annabelle Sharada LilyMae Johnson. My family call me Annabelle, except for my daddy who calls me his Little Lily because I'm so sweet and pretty. You can call me Annabelle if you want to." Her mildly brazen focus and broad twinkling smile were as disarming as any femme fatale Hollywood ever produced; Monte's heart had been delightfully conquered. And then Annabelle, pausing to ponder, staring at him invasively, said, "Do I know you?"

By now Clare was behind him, smothering a smile, on the verge of laughter. She said to Annabelle, "Mr. Scott helps out here at the school sometimes. He's a counselor."

Annabelle flashed Clare a noncommittal glance, apparently ingesting the new information with judicious measures of contemplation, deciding whether more questions were merited. Rather quickly, focusing another look in Monte's direction, she seemed to conclude the matter could be summarily dismissed without further investigation and given a dispensational burial, saying blithely, "Okay, that's all right then." Reflecting a moment more, she veered into more ticklish territory and asked, leaning closer, "Are you married?"

Clare said sharply, "I think that's enough questions for now, Annabelle. Did you bring the assignment I asked you to work on?"

Dissuaded for the moment, angling her head up, Annabelle gushed politely, "Yes, ma'am, I did." After some digging, she produced a small, rumpled sheet of paper from a coat pocket and presented it to Clare, who studied it with curious reservation.

"Annabelle, this paper has peanut butter and jelly stains all over it. And it's sticky."

"Yes, ma'am, I believe it does. Rhonda Lou Fabinski—do you know Rhonda Lou Fabinski? Well, she was having a snack . . . [*giggles*] Don't you think that's a funny word? Snack. Well, she was having a snack . . . [*more giggles*] I can't hardly say it without laughing my head off. She was having a *treat,* and some of it got on my paper. Lord knows how it happened. She was mostly way across the room, except when she helped me spell *broccoli*."

"All right, Annabelle," Clare said patiently, almost giggling herself. "Other than the . . . stickiness, and the stains, you did a good job. Take the paper with you and make a clean copy for when we meet on Friday, okay?"

Annabelle took the paper and held it carefully between thumb and index finger, apparently pleased with herself. Monte contributed a broad smile. "Bye, Annabelle. It was nice to meet you."

She peered up with ambivalent scrutiny, her little body still firmly in place, and said with a hint of innocent guile, "Well, if you're not married, maybe you could consider marrying Miss Augsburg. She hasn't got—"

With mild urgency, Clare interjected, "Goodbye, Annabelle. You'd better get back to the dorm. It's almost dinnertime."

Executing a uniquely modified pirouette, knowing full well a prompt exit was expedient, Annabelle Sharada LilyMae Johnson sashayed down the hall and up the stairs, gaily singing, flapping her arms like wings, and tossing her head side to side, long braids following behind, swinging and fluttering.

Smiling weakly at Clare, Monte lowered his eyes as she said, "Uh, come in. I could make some coffee if you'd like." While she busied herself at the counter, speaking over her shoulder, he sat uneasily at a table. "Sorry about the interruption. I'd asked Annabelle to make a list of foods she liked and disliked as a homework assignment, and that's what she brought. She was supposed to bring it to class today. I didn't expect it to be covered in peanut butter and jelly," Clare chuckled mildly.

She turned and placed two steaming mugs on the table and sat down across from him, somewhat sober but smiling thoughtfully. "She's a precocious kid," Clare continued. "Says anything that pops into her head, anywhere, anytime. I think she'll be president someday." After a titter of mirth, she looked at Monte guardedly. "I hope you weren't embarrassed."

"No, not at all," he lied. "And I hope you weren't," he offered, peeking cautiously over the rim of his mug.

"Goodness, no. She's just a child. And, well, anyway, kids get the craziest ideas, say the craziest things."

An uneasy silence descended until both leaned slightly forward and spoke at once, "We haven't—" Halting quickly together, they laughed.

Monte said, "Sorry. You go ahead."

"No. You, please." Clare smiled politely, perhaps too anxiously.

"Well, I was just going to say that . . . we haven't talked, uh, really talked for a while." Monte feared the words implied an accusation, and added quickly, "I mean, uh, last week was a rush, and I never adequately thanked you for finding Sara's friend Lana, and talking with her and—"

"There was no need to thank me, though I think you did," she said graciously. "The main thing is you found her safe. And, no, we haven't had a good talk in quite a while," she agreed reflectively. "Well over a month, I think." Her eyes scanned his face vigilantly, then dropped to study reflections of light shimmering atop the round russet mirror within her cup, knowing the span had been exactly forty-three days, and thinking it seemed so much longer, and with so much transformation. And then straightening, she went on uneasily, "I haven't told anyone yet, except Mr. Fletcher, but I . . . I may be leaving soon. Possibly after the first of the year."

He had known, since hearing rumors from both Ramona and Arnold, that their paths would cross sooner or later, though until today's impulsive decision he had postponed confrontation. Still, during the past few days he had practiced what might be said by way of congratulatory sentiment if and when they did meet—something suitably disingenuous, scripted childishly, pretending the implicit engagement was of little or no consequence, his attention burdened by myriad interests and duties of much weightier import. The idea had momentarily pleased him, relishing and refining the image of a man above the fray, oblivious to foggy wedding speculations which, given the circumstances, were nothing more to him than tautological grandstanding, the parties having spent the past four years or more preparing for the epiphanic celebration.

In fact, Monte had decided only the night before, after a brief but impassioned Jungian conflict, that today, if matters so required, would be his aloof day. His debonair, urbane-persona day—dignified, poised, and distantly charming day. Arriving at the Academy early, he stowed away in the Inner Sanctum to pantomime a suitably bored and jaded countenance, not only facial but full-bodied external physiognomy. Having no mirror, he could only guess what blasé air he projected, if any. Sanguine guises of a confluent Leo Bloom and Holden Caulfield came to mind.

By ten o'clock, best efforts had sadly eroded into a sort of Thirteenth Street redux day. Gloria Pepperdine, studious ninth grader, thought Monte had lost his hearing and began to shout questions when he malingered nonresponsive; Wooten Brachovich opined confidentially to Cecilia Norheim that Valium or some other tranquilizing drug might be at play; and a second grader named Dwight Lesterholt, tasked with delivering Booker's cache of morning mail, marched dutifully back to Ramona and reported, "Mr. Scott's been taken over by an evil trance." No choice remained but to give up the charade, greatly relieving everyone.

A host of questions rushed into his mind when she ceased to speak, bemused by her oblique method of validating engagement to Weisner without announcing the event plainly. Intending to say nothing, reflexive civility murmured, "I . . . see."

"I'll be giving final notice to Mr. Fletcher as soon as I know more, so they can find another . . . a replacement," she continued calmly, focus wandering, questioning with disgruntlement why she had opened herself to this sensitive topic with *him*. "I'll be, it seems I'll be, eventually, moving to Stonebridge," she compounded, patently unable to silence the confessional flow of her mind. Wincing, she imagined the figure of a woman in a play reciting lines with dedicated realism, assuming a supportive role, knowing every word to be nothing but fantasy, a fiction of some fanciful mind, yet demanding truthful adherence to action and dialogue, fidelity to theme and plot. One became the given character, more surely and confidently scene to scene, beginning to end, programmed and compelled to utter at proper junctures whatever might be required.

Monte waited for her to say more. When she did not, he said, more blandly than meant, "I, well, I wish you all the best in whatever you do, and I know you'll be missed . . . here at the Academy."

"Thank you, Monte." And then she quickly offered explanations, brightly edgy, though hollow with melancholy. "I'll be working in Richard's insurance office, but I hope to find a teaching job or maybe . . . There're no definite plans right now." Earnest attempt at lightness was stymied by a flagrant thickness of projection, enunciation swallowed by suppressed whimperings embedded deep in her throat. "There're so many things we, Richard and I, haven't talked about."

To pronounce the words *engagement* or *marriage* was a bridge too far, a mountain too precipitous, a concept overladen with ambiguity, perhaps fearing mere mention would blemish an ideal dearly revered, personal and private. *But to whom or for whom?* he questioned, unsure if she would know.

Monte smiled tightly, gauging her unusually moody demeanor.

"Moving to a new place can be a little scary, along with adjusting to a new . . . situation and . . . other things." She looked away as though in denial when he added, "Yet, I believe it's much easier when you're going to something you want, rather than running away from something you fear."

"Yes," she murmured dryly—almost, he thought, stolidly withdrawn, displaced to a different plane. Queasy silence entombed them then like heavy fog, until her eyes came cautiously probing back to his, daring to question, gently, fearfully, "Which was it for you?"

Yawed by her candid percipience, he contemplated a few moments before saying, "Both, I suppose. Mine is a long and complicated story, Clare. All I can truthfully say is I'm thankful for where I am now. It's much more, so much more than I deserve."

Curiosity, no. Concern, maybe. Investment, perhaps. Care . . . likely. All burned within her as motivation to know more, yet she could not ask, had no right to ask, did not know how to ask. For what purpose could now be served? Some moral judgment, mere factual satisfaction, more ground of legitimacy for allegiance to Richard? An inner voice spoke then, reminding with strenuous sharpness that nothing about the man sitting before her mattered anymore, had never mattered. Her burdens and future were rooted in another life, with potent seeds sown from birth—another dimension, mindset, and philosophy. Monte was, had been, but a passing—

Without forewarning, blinding tears burst forth, flooding her reddened cheeks in hot streams of uncontrolled misery. Embarrassed and shocked, she buried her wet face in a shielding refuge of cupped hands and wept more intensely and bitterly than she thought the well of her emotional reservoir capable.

Taken aback, Monte hesitantly rose and went to stand beside her chair, mutely surveying the tremors racking her body. Delicately, he placed a palm on one hunched shoulder, feeling a constancy of shivers as from one overcome by severe and icy chills. And then, unexpectedly, arising slowly, weakly, she stood and leaned against him, forehead hard upon his chest, face enveloped by a thick richness of dark flowing hair.

After a few moments she muttered with sniffling sobs, "I'm sorry, Monte. I'm so very sorry." Sighing into the softness of his shirt, she inhaled a wildly bucolic scent of leaves and grass, hands clinging to the solidity of his presence. Faintly, she whispered, "Nothing I've said, or could ever say, would be enough . . . could begin to define . . ."

He held her then without shame, closer than they had ever been. Awakened for the first time to the nectarous savor of her essence, he breathed in the slightest whisper of honeysuckle, as one might the sweet fragrance permeating the air along fringes of pine forest on a warm and sun-drenched day in spring. Substance of her nearness became surreal: gentle heaves of her chest, fingers spread on his back, nose nestled into his shirt. Enmeshed in depths between them, he felt a fragile, pattering tempo of heartbeat, unsure if his own or hers—perhaps, he dared to believe, some teasing, transient duet.

Muffled, she said again, "I'm sorry for so much."

"Never be sorry for tears," he said lowly, close to her ear. "Tears are like raindrops of purity from the heart and mind of heaven."

She thought him oblivious of why she cried, why she was sorry. And she could not tell him. Instead, she found succor in honest deception.

"I sometimes think," she rasped, finding speech suddenly onerous, "neither my heart nor mind are anything akin to pure." Moving apart from him, hands weakly imprinted upon his chest, cheeks crimson and streaked with dampness, she gazed up into his eyes and pleaded, "Go away, Monte Scott. Please, go away, and leave me as I was . . . the day you found me. The way I'll always be."

• • •

Regardless of holiday season, Monte's fieldwork demands ground on unendingly. In three days he drove two hundred miles and visited two dozen clients up and down the valley. A collage of decorated homes greeted him: evergreens festooned with fancy ornaments and multicolored bulbs, tops soaring to ceilings; diminutive afterthoughts thinned from woodlots bedecked on tabletops; white pine boughs, sprigs of holly, and cedar greenery draped like stoles across fireplace mantles, windowsills, and doorframes; rainbows of lights winding and arching, steadily glowing as distant multicolored stars, or blinking and pulsating like luminous heartbeats, softening dark and drab affectations of otherwise bromidic dwelling places.

December chills penetrating his bones were warmed again and again by grateful hands offering coffee, cocoa, or eggnog; sugar cookies topped with crystalline sprinkles; rum-soaked fruitcake; or rich brownies pervaded by pecans or walnuts. Often he feared his appearance at a front door would be taken as akin to a visit from the Grim Reaper, stark reminder and evidence of misfortune and trauma; and at times he found this to be true. However, almost always, the welcomes he received belied this fear and laid qualms to rest. Some shred of hope, perhaps, clung to his presence, what he represented: symbolic, empathic conjoining with others in similar circumstance, suggestion and affirmation of a larger community sharing holiday celebration with precarious joy.

Not until the last visit of the day was past did fatigue of body or weariness of mind and emotion prevail, having retreated in abeyance through every hour of his journey. Indeed, he felt lifted, remarkably inspired, and rejuvenated by each person, each conversation, no matter how difficult or tragic or painful. Tears of anger, fear, and sorrow, he observed, often became strengthening and cathartic, evidence of incipient movement to acceptance, resolution, and adjustment.

Still, personal, arduous, and frightening, no path could ever be diminished or denied, each strewn with obstacles and Augean conflicts and confusion so overwhelming as to smother a soul into temptations of depressing surrender. Never, he knew, could one truly fathom the struggles, or perceive the depth, of grievous loss; he could only in humility look on with meager offerings and awed reverence that any person could possess such mettle to rise and move forward with his or her life.

Blindness, a seminal book written by Father Thomas Carroll many years ago, listed twenty losses a person experiences when vision is taken away: self-esteem, confidence, security, mobility, communication, and so on, each a dispossession to be overcome, adjusted to, and remade. Always the physical losses throw open doors to a challenging new world—a world of myriad secondary losses no less frightening and disruptive. Common, mundane tasks, simple acts done a thousand times reflexively and without thought, become formidable puzzles of impossibility or, at best, difficulty.

No person, Monte soon discovered, was ever like another, none to be neatly categorized in singularly prescriptive slots. One young man, not yet thirty, lost all his vision, indeed a portion of his face, in a horrifying explosion, sun upon his brow erased to eerie blackness in a split second. To his wife and children, and more so himself, he became a stranger, an alien intruder, unknown and apart, transformed in one turn of fate from the man who left home in the morning smiling, cheery, strong, and affectionate, to a sodden heap of bandaged flesh, tubed and wired together in a hospital bed. On a grey December day, Monte talked with him in his living room, six months hence—six months into new existence, his four-year-old daughter snug upon his lap.

Another, a woman, older, vigorous with broad intellect and spontaneity, found herself becoming clumsier, hindered by unexplainable, irritating shadows, stealthy encroachments upon her universe of radiance, creeping daily with unrelenting invasion, like an evil force pulling ever so slowly on cords of a curtain, extinguishing light, until only a sliver remained, a tiny slice of vision. And that, too, she knew, would one day be gone: one morning when she woke, one evening when she turned to look at her husband for reassurance, or the day she tried with more will than thought possible to scan pictures of her children and grandchildren. Monte sat one afternoon hour with her, sipping coffee at a kitchen table, awed and blessed by an unfathomably courageous spirit.

And young people, children, blind or visually impaired from birth, like portraits of helpless, precious nativity, compressed upon his mind; infants and toddlers—eye sockets anophthalmically deserted, retinas scored by retrolental fibroplasia, lenses clouded opaque by congenital cataracts, or a hundred more mysterious causes, rare and baffling—resting upon piteous laps of loving kindness, mothers and fathers confusingly guilty, drained and tormented by absence of joy once so anticipated and promising. Parents besieged by choices and decisions foreign and bewildering.

Booker had asked if Monte might take time to stop and see a few of these families. Weighing merits of the Academy as alternative to public schools in their home area, or some other special placement, the parents questioned him, hope clinging to their faces. He was told by professionals in the field of blind education that many of the children were abstrusely labeled normal, vision being their only disability. Others, multi-handicapped, had special needs requiring more individualized and focused programs which might involve not only teachers, but physical, occupational, and speech therapists, as well as other disciplines. Complications and diversity of need could be endless. Vocabulary once unknown and unpronounceable, words utilized regularly with impersonal candor, became routine in his life and work—language, he feared, often prone to cool detachment from any crux of intimate humanity.

One day, Monte visited a few of these homes, sharing what he knew and what he had observed of the state residential facility in Talerton. They listened closely with guarded uncertainty, in polite desperation asking endless questions, critical decisions hanging above like a sword of Damocles potentially affecting the life of their precious loved one for years to come. Time and again wavering voices asked counsel of him, wisdom from which he could draw no eloquent contribution, shamefully and inadequately impoverished for the task. Faces reached out in staring appeal, frightened eyes seeking guidance, some measure of strength to walk the long, mysterious road upon which they had been placed, with no maps or signs of absolute correctness. And what could he say but only confirm their onerous burden?

And yet, often not shared for fear of being unfair or directive, he maintained an unerringly constant beacon of confidence in his visions of those hundreds of beautiful children who blessed him each week at the school, full with life and courage, dreams and ambitions.

"Come and see" was all he dared say. "Come and see."

• • •

Journal: Wednesday, December 17, 10:45 PM

What a fool I made of myself, crying like an adolescent schoolgirl! And I blame that man, that awful man who by innocently doing nothing and saying nothing these past months has stolen my heart and turned a comfortably patterned, perfectly planned world upside down. That man who dared hold me in his arms, comforting and wise, made me laugh these four months a thousand times and opened my eyes to truly see the earth and all around me with wonder, who talked to trees, stooped down and conversed with brash little girls who thought he should marry me. The man who's dedicated his life for something good. The man I've always wanted and needed, the man I've dreamed about and fell in love with when I was five. The man to share a lifetime with.

And now he's here and real. And I told him, begged him, to go away because, without even knowing, he called me to leave, to abandon the hopes and wishes of so many people I love, family and friends who've been part of my life forever, my foundation and roots. My mind screams that to be with him is selfish, placing my own questionable desires above all else. Where is righteousness and peace to be found in that?

For what do I really know about him? In so many ways he's a mystery. He needs someone like an Anne who can make him happy. And why am I writing all this? It's like sorting through garbage. There's no point. He can be nothing to me now but a distant fantasy. I'll be married in a few months—or . . . the date isn't important—and never think of him again. Never, ever again.

Dear God, when have I ever hurt so much, so deeply? Please give me strength and light to do what I know I should do. What I must do.

CHAPTER FOURTEEN

SOMEONE ONCE SAID, DOUBTLESS an obscure Pisces sage, that the gods do not deduct from a man's allotted span of life the time spent fishing. *If that postulation be true,* Monte contended, *time spent in a laundromat, particularly at two in the morning, will be tallied as additional double bonus for a lifespan.* Under a blinding fluorescent glare, he had to wonder if Thoreau ever envisioned any person, studious or otherwise, sitting on a damp and grimy concrete floor, hunched against an unsteady, vibrating clothes dryer, reading with wavering concentration the naturalist's thoughts on the topic of civil disobedience.

Monte's second load juggled within the monstrous washer, chugging like a baked-enamel steam engine, the first toppling and tumbling in continuous, flopping cartwheel clumps in the groaning dryer.

Only one other person was in evidence in the all-white room, she being the sole contribution of coloration to the sterile, gleaming décor. For that he was thankful, not only for pigmented vitality but more for a certain feisty companionship. She served as a bastion of inspiration, an adroit comrade in arms, no wasted motion or obvious boredom, leaning into her work with practiced and inexorable acceptance, knowing the obligatory tedium would soon pass and she would exit the premises once again fulfilled.

As it happened, she had insights into Thoreau seldom heard in any classroom or read in any book.

"Why would a reasonably intelligent white man," she asked, folding pillowcases with nimble exactness, "with so many pithy thoughts and incisive observations, go out and live in a woods for two years in something the size of a doghouse writing doggerel—excuse me—when he could just as well have been putting himself to good use as an abolitionist or, at the very least, making a better pencil?"

For that, Monte had no rejoinder, suitable or otherwise, fearing exposure as dully witless and without imagination. With practiced patience, she showed him how to manipulate the coin machine: insert a legal-tender dollar bill, and four quarters appear in return. Simple; even someone with a master's degree could do it, with proper guidance.

Another thought struck in his leisurely pensiveness, brain spinning much as the cascading underwear he felt compelled to watch swirling like the loop reel of an avalanche in the round, sudsy window, as to whether the long-range effects of acrid soap and bleach fumes would be deleterious to intelligence in his declining years, if he happened to reach that stage of dying.

Presenting the issue to Mrs. Gilliam, laundromat cohort extraordinaire, she offered that cleansing effects far outweighed any detriment and actually—proved by studies and lab tests performed harmlessly on hamsters by soap manufacturers—showed increases in one's kinetic energy, a coveted advantage if one were inclined to spend exorbitant amounts of time running on a little wheel in a cage. A condition, she observed, a large percentage of the population engaged in daily with detached, spellbound capitulation.

Setting Thoreau aside for the moment, digging deeper, he concentrated thoughts on the recurring mystery and broader aspects of air, the all-enveloping ocean in which humanity lives and breathes. Laundromat air, logic dictated, should be amongst the saintliest on earth, saturated as it is with the bite of chlorine and the scouring of detergent, abiding no obtrusive impurities or pernicious elements to convene. And yet, nothing in or of the building bore an aroma of cleanliness, condoned no freshness or lightness, but a heaviness of scrubbing efficiency, stinging the eyes and burning the nose and tongue, enjoining one never to inhale too deeply. *Even worse than the tentacles of sterile fetor in hospital environs,* he thought with grimacing recall.

Nothing at all like the atmosphere of a high mountain peak or freshly mowed, grassy slope below Main Hall, where open atmospheres were almost comestibly sweet with unblemished richness. And something within him surged, surrounded and trapped as he was by raucous machines, offensively reeking of nauseous ozone—aching and hungering for un-impinged, Edenic spaces.

Reflective and humorous wanderings had often brought salvation to his soul in the past. In the laundromat on this cold December morning, Monte now used them as a counterattack on grievous assaults of sadness and loss for one he had hardly known and on whom he had no claim. She had edged innocently into his life and would soon be gone. Had he believed more fully in a purposeful God manipulating his creatures toward blessings of happiness and fulfillment, instead of one who operated unfathomably with a hand of capricious fate, scattering rains of good and bad luck—karma?—on the heads of both just and unjust without distinction, perhaps he would have found more solid ground on which to stake at least a small claim of optimism.

Why could he not have the faith of a Caroline Lehman, or an Arthur Brooks, or a Clare Augsburg? Why at times did he believe so strongly in the loving presence of God, and at others endure a dark and miserable feeling of abandonment? Were these latter moments when he found some strange solace in fatuous, distracting humor? Something perhaps of a psychological, spiritual crutch? At its very core, unraveled in austere moments, he premised life as a tight, prosaic entwining of tragedy and comedy, one complementing the other with maddening absurdity, daring him to choose, yet in essentia leaving no choice, concealing by sleight of hand and mind that both were much the same.

And then, as so often happened, he was transported back to an epiphany; two, actually. First was a saying by a poet whose name he could not recall, who said, fundamentally, "Sometimes you have to believe before you can see." The second, a sermon he had heard years before in a chapel service. From the Old Testament book of Habakkuk, he was reminded that faith in God included faith in his timing. One was often asked to be still and wait. Caroline and Clare, he knew, would understand. And thus, in searing light and unrelenting babel of a laundromat, Monte whispered, "Help me be more like them, Lord, and so doing, more like you."

• • •

The detention room, known by students as "Alcatraz" and located in a dismal section of Main Hall's antiquated second story, was more fully occupied than usual; in fact, Ramona had reported the old, windowless classroom overflowing. Cold-weather confinement and holiday anticipation apparently had unleashed a surfeit of infractions, most minor in nature, in the form of ill-advised practical jokes, scuffles, smoking, and cursing, books and debris tossed from dorm windows, joyrides down spiral fire-escape tubes, and general uncharacteristically belligerent and spirited conduct. Much the same seemed to infect teachers and staff as well, evidenced by shortened tolerance for any form of misbehavior, leading to more immediate and severe punishment.

A story was circulating—Monte heard it from both Arnold and Withrow—that two days previous Dr. Mullens had been mercilessly pelted by snowballs while crossing the bridge from Perkins Hall to his office in Main Hall. Hat and glasses were knocked from the man's head by a well-aimed barrage rendering him partially deaf until compacted snow melted and could be drained from one ear. Usually a calm, forbearing man, on this occasion he felt a line had been crossed and examples needed to be made. A few evenings embowered in the gloom of detention overseen by a matronly Miss Houchmann, a stern, humorless lady of a certain age, was punishment not soon forgotten.

• • •

Rosanna came by the Inner Sanctum Wednesday lunchtime to tell Monte their band, White Cane, now had a drummer. "Leon Blackwell!" she said excitedly. "And he plays accordion and trumpet too!" She paused and then confessed, "Well, actually, he only plays trumpet and accordion. But he *wants* to play drums, *and he's learning*."

Monte had met Leon on a few occasions, a likable junior high student with wry sense of humor—compact, focused, studious, and energetic. One morning over coffee Talbert had related a bit of interesting Academy history which, in a way, directly involved Leon. His cousin, a lad named Mercer, had been the first Black student at the school, an entry not without negative comments from a few students but which in relatively short time, because of the new pupil's courage and personality, slipped into wary curiosity and, within a few months, full acceptance by most. As one might have expected, the more serious and troubling objections came from parents. Threats were made to withdraw sons or daughters from the school, and a few families considered frivolous lawsuits. None of these fulminations, Talbert said with a certain satisfaction, ever came to fruition.

In subsequent years, additional Black students arrived, along with children of Asian, Latino, European, and Middle Eastern heritage, until, over time, with parents serving their various countries in embassies in Washington less than three hours away, the Academy had boys and girls enrolled from all over the world. As Talbert said in his whimsical way, yet with deep feeling, "We welcome all, any which way they come—color, shape, size, religion, country, or gender. The more the merrier." And every day Monte spent at the school observing and learning, the more he wondered if there existed any other institution like it on earth.

• • •

Hanging in the hallway outside the Blind Department office was a large cork bulletin board known to be the sole purview of Ramona, who proudly and meticulously saw to all updates and tidiness. The Department of Education and other agencies sent posters almost daily touting particular programs that promoted the latest trends and fads in educational thinking—the goal, one supposed, being to stimulate critical thinking in the minds of teachers and students, even though a good portion of the Academy population could not see them or never bothered to look.

As many others did, Monte often used it as a relatively soft cushion to lean his head and shoulders against while waiting for the office door to be unlocked.

One large and colorful announcement Ramona had thumbtacked early one Monday morning covered over half the board space. Stirringly, though somewhat cloudily, the erudite message screamed in a towering column of block lettering, each word stacked slightly askew atop another as if ready to topple, *Observation, Investigation, Evaluation, Clarification,* and in even larger lettering at the bottom, as a shocking and catchy apotheosis, *EDUCATION.*

Booker had projected to Monte with some admitted cynicism that the whole idea was likely a culmination of weeks or even months of arduous committee meetings, subcommittee meetings, consultant interviews, and study groups, editing and reediting, arguing and debating as though the academic kingdom of the state and entire nation would disintegrate to chaos had not each word been chosen with the utmost care and precision—costs he adjudged to run into hundreds of thousands, if not more.

Passing by the board a day after the message was posted, Ramona noticed someone had neatly printed in a lower corner, using a bright-red, felt-tip pen, the word *Masturbation,* under which someone else had written in black ink, underlined and in flowery cursive, *Fornication,* and beneath that, scribbled in dull pencil, *Frustration.* Later she admitted satisfaction that at least a few of the students, or staff, had taken time to read the poster.

• • •

News came from Arthur that a group of students had asked him to sponsor a proposed high school Bible Club, and he had agreed, suggesting a broader title of Faith and Religion Club. Their first meeting, he told Monte, was to be one evening that week in the Student Center. To date, sixteen students had signed on, leaders initially being Gerald, Rosanna, and Jellyroll. Time permitting, Monte said he would be glad to help.

Arthur drolly related between snickers, "So far we have two Presbyterians, three Baptists, two Catholics, two Methodists, an Episcopalian, a Jew, a Mennonite, a Hindu, a Muslim, and two undecided, though one claims to be a Druid. Should be a ball."

Uncommonly and inclusively ecumenical, Monte thought.

• • •

Caroline Lehman, still a patient in the UVA hospital, was found to have a number of small tumors on her lungs. Surgery had been postponed until she gained strength and further tests were conducted. Entering her ward one afternoon, Monte thought she looked much improved from his last visit several days before. She asked anxiously about school and friends, and then, blushing, about Timothy Sommers. He had sent flowers and a card, she said, and hoped to make a trip to Rivanleigh if a way could be found. Monte mentally noted to make certain this was arranged.

As she talked on about Tim, Monte perched on a chair beside the bed, picturing the young man in whom she was so interested. Husky and fair skinned with hair like fine threads the color of carrots, he maintained annual honor roll status and had not, in twelve years at the school, received even one demerit. Though he was quiet to the point of exasperation most of the time, Caroline had brought him to blossom. Monte had often observed them walking or sitting together quietly contented at the Academy, and wondered if they ever verbally conversed, both so unassumingly shy.

Stirred from reverie, Monte became aware she had used the name of Clare Augsburg.

"She's come a few times and helped me with school assignments," Caroline said. "And she always reads to me from the Bible, some of my favorite passages. When I first came to the Academy she was so nice, helping me feel welcome and introducing me to other girls. She understands, you know, because she's like me. Well, something like me. Not Amish, but Mennonite. She appreciates the way . . . the reasons I have to dress the way I do, and all about my beliefs and faith. Some of her cousins, she said, are like me, and her boyfriend's relatives too."

Had Monte been a dog, both ears would be lifted alertly. He sat forward and stared at the young girl, smiling weirdly as though suddenly numbed. "I didn't know," he murmured. "She never said."

In some undefined way, significance hovered in the knowing, explaining the secure ethic and confidence of direction and allegiance to her path. The wall between them now loomed higher, the moat wider and deeper. From that first day, the first words, he had been but an alien, ignorant of her customs and mores, strength of inherent loyalties, the preordaining of her future—of the whole of her life.

And yet . . . and yet . . . there had to be some undisclosed element beyond a narrow intrinsic definition, some buried, secret haunt rarely sojourned. For he had seen renegade hunger in her eyes and heard bemused vibrations of anarchy in her voice, breaches perhaps constrained unaware. Still, he was reminded, this mattered little now, had never mattered, aside from the momentary light of knowing, the passing joy of sharing, or pretending to.

All are branded in some way, he supposed, *imprints placed upon us from birth, instilled in youth to be cemented in maturity, captives everyone. Free will only within the confined boundary of our cages.* He thought of Jimmy Dunsmore and his brothers, then the prophet Jeremiah: "Can the Ethiopian change his skin, or the leopard his spots?" Monte's father had often simply said dismissively, "You are what you are." *Fools repeat their folly, swine return to the mud, dogs to their vomit,* Monte remembered. *There is no lasting hope of escape, no salvation, unless . . . from without.*

He stayed by Caroline's bed until the meager square of visible sky gathered beyond the window faded from late-afternoon pinkish blue to coal-black night. She spurned her dinner, aimlessly rearranging portions in hope the nurse would be appeased. Reluctantly swallowing pills from miniature paper cups, she almost choked on one large, oblong capsule. Conversation waned to a few desultory remarks when at length Monte realized she had fallen asleep, quietly reposed, pure as a sheen of morning dew and innocent as a helpless fawn. Shallow breaths rose and fell in slow cadence from her thin body, secure in the arms of peace beyond all understanding.

• • •

Rolf Andersen, owner of Andersen Lock and Key, left a phone message with Ramona asking Monte to contact him as soon as possible about a concern involving Jimmy Dunsmore. When she handed over the little slip of pink paper, Monte's heart sank. Now, he feared, they had trouble. The long-shot gamble had not paid off.

According to reports, Jimmy had been doing so well, hopes growing daily for his success. Working at Andersen's had by all accounts inspired positive development in other areas of his life, personal, social, and academic. Teachers and staff raved on his change in attitude, and improved conduct and performance in the classroom. Deflated, Monte cursed silently with a strong touch of anger, perhaps partly in retaliation for feeling he had been foolishly duped by a sixteen-year-old punk.

Booker was teaching a French class, so Monte went immediately to town, dreading the trip. An uneasy embarrassment at what the lad might have done gnawed his insides—fought with a coworker, disobeyed directions, made obscene remarks to staff or a customer, slacked off in his work, even stolen some item from the business? And Monte blamed himself. He, above all, should have known a boy like Jimmy could never function for long in decent and ordered society. He held the bad blood of a North Richmond hood, and that was never going to change. Given a fair shot and opportunity, he had flunked. No alternative existed now but to apologize to Mr. Andersen and remove Jimmy from the program. Beyond this, Monte's mind was blank to any recourse.

Andersen Lock and Key was not a large business, occupying a one-story, nondescript brick building two blocks north of Main Street.

Well known throughout the area for selling quality products and providing dependable service, they had been in business for almost fifty years. Two brothers owned the company, inherited from their father, currently with twelve employees. A middle-aged woman with frenetic bleached hair greeted Monte heartily in the reception area, knowing him well from previous visits. She said Mr. Andersen was waiting and ushered Monte into a small office as if an honored guest.

Rolf Andersen, casually dressed in open-collared sport shirt and cotton chinos, rose from his chair behind a large desk amassed with catalogues, folders, and various scattered stacks of papers, bills, and receipts. A sturdy man of perhaps forty, he offered a firm hand and broad smile, gushing as an old friend, "Monte! Thanks for coming over so quickly. I hope it's not an inconvenience."

"Not at all, sir," Monte said rather gravely as Andersen pumped his hand. "I'm just so very sorry—"

"Have a seat!" the man boomed. "How about coffee? Or a Coke?"

His bubbly cheerfulness was unexpected considering the reason for their meeting. Maybe the man was trying to politely soften a bad situation. Monte said no to coffee or soft drink.

"Okay!" Andersen piped, rubbing his hands briskly together as one might in freezing weather. "Let me tell you why I asked you to come over. Something of this nature I felt, uh, better done in person than over the phone. You don't mind if I call you Monte?" He grinned, leaning a little forward over the desk before sitting down heavily, his chair swiveling, squeaks emanating in protest.

"Of course. That's fine, Mr. Andersen." Monte tensed, shamed by such irrational cordiality.

He beamed. "Call me Rolf, Monte. We don't stand on ceremony around here. Now! Jimmy Dunsmore!" Andersen announced loudly, a more serious expression gradually commanding his face as he snatched up a folder from atop the debris on his desk and gently cleared his throat. "He's been with us, ahhhh, here it is." Slipping on reading glasses, he stared down at a page, moving the sheet away and then bringing it closer. "Almost four weeks, I think." He raised his eyes and frowned. "Lord, has it been that long already?"

"And Mr. Booker and I so much appreciate your working with him, Mr. Andersen. We're only sorry that—"

"Ah! Here's what I'm looking for," Rolf said with satisfaction, nose back in the folder. "Ten hours a week, plus the time he's put in on Saturdays without your sponsorship. All total about sixty hours, I believe." He closed the folder and smiled with satisfaction, then immediately opened it again, face scrunched with mild uncertainty. "This may not be completely up to date. I think he has more hours than that. Florence has the latest figures. I believe it's more like seventy."

He stared down at his desk, scratching the back of his head and shaking it slowly to and fro as if struggling with some baffling dilemma and, before Monte could speak, went on, saying ruefully, "We've done what we could with him, Monte, under the circumstances and within our capabilities, but . . ." Rolf screwed up his mouth, searching for just the right ameliorating words.

"Like I was saying, Mr. Andersen," Monte interjected, his heart numbed, "we really appreciate what you've tried to do, and I'm sure Mr. Booker feels the same way. He—"

"You know, Monte, this kid is . . . is absolutely one of kind! Never known anybody like him!" Andersen cut in, continuing to shake his head as though disbelieving some great event or good fortune. "*Exceptional* is all I can say! Never seen anything like it! What we used to call a real whiz kid! I don't know there's much else we can teach him," he gushed with delight. "The boy picks up even the most complicated instructions right away, only has to be shown something once and he's got it. Bingo! I think he must have the sharpest mind I've ever seen for someone so young." Rolf's head persisted in rotating side to side with pleasant incredulity. "I hope he's planning on college, because that's where this kid belongs. Some school with a strong mechanical or electrical engineering program, or maybe architecture or something similar."

Glued to his chair in a swoon of shock, Monte sat dumfounded, emitting a series of guttural "uhs," face and eyes fixedly squinted in utter amazement. What was this man telling him? Was he serious?

Were they talking about Jimmy Dunsmore from the Academy? The Northside petty criminal?

"We'll be more than happy to keep him on for as long as he wants to stay, but I'd advise you and Booker to look into getting him in with some outfit that could better help develop his talents, maybe a design engineering company or an architectural firm." Andersen's evangelical zeal emerged with the pride of a parent. "Lord, Monte, I wish we had ten more like him."

Monte's mind clearing, awareness grew of a lightness of heart, joy close to jubilation, very near to tears, and at the same time rueful chagrin at assuming the worst—he, who had harbored such secret high hopes for the boy, belief strong enough to attempt enlisting help from incarcerated brothers.

For the moment all Monte could intelligently mutter was, "Thank you, Mr. Andersen. *Thank you* for all you've done for Jimmy. You don't know how happy this makes me . . . and Mr. Booker." Uttering to himself a small prayer of gratitude for unexpected blessings, he silently added a humble apology to a vision of Jimmy, in his mind's eye, smirking with smug satisfaction.

• • •

Anne Walden, Erin Celinski, and Elizabeth Blanchard had written a simple script for what began as a contemporary Christmas pageant. After additions, deletions, and editing, the enterprise morphed into a more traditional story, though changes continued daily. Characters written in were written out, animals added were deleted, the setting relocated from a stable in Bethlehem to a farmhouse in Maine and then to a mountain resort in Virginia, finally returning to the Holy Land. When auditions were held, Withrow Mulligan tested for the part of King Herod, later being assigned a nonspeaking part as the rear body and legs of a camel, Talmadge Grobanheimer the front half. Alec Beasley was miscast as a Wise Man, along with two other boys, Irving Jones and Gilmore Rathman, a dispute arising immediately as to which Magus would carry the gold, none having the slightest idea to what use a mother and baby would put frankincense and myrrh, even if they happened to know of what the strange stuff consisted. The whole production was turning into something reminiscent of vaudeville or a yuletide farce.

After plans began to gel, Mr. Fletcher decreed not to include anything too heavy or religious. More lighthearted fare, he directed, with an emphasis on parts for younger kids—perhaps, the committee thought, attempting amends for his earlier faux pas related to tree decorating. He suggested a series of vignettes, interspersed with carols and songs by various choral groups. The idea sounded workable, and the committee regrouped for more planning and discussion.

At this point, Cathy Henson, librarian, came forward and volunteered to help, everyone wondering why she had not been asked in the first place. The committee soon discovered she had firsthand theatrical experience, onstage and off, having directed several local productions and authored a number of plays. Pieces fell into place, and the pageant moved forward.

• • •

Returning from the canteen on Wednesday morning, carrying a coffee for himself and one for Booker, Monte met Arnold slogging across the bridge, weighted down with three thick, well-worn tomes, bemoaning the fact he was required to write a one-page paper of no less than two hundred words for his history class. He referred to the assignment rather pompously as a "thesis."

"Two hundred words is almost as much as a whole book," he whined. "Geez!"

Monte asked what he had chosen as a topic.

"The Louisiana Purpose," he said proudly. "You know, about a hundred years ago when Abraham Lincoln bought New Orleans from the Russians." Patiently, somewhat skeptical of getting involved, Monte mentioned the negotiation was generally referred to as the Louisiana Purchase, the 1803 event in question a transaction between Thomas Jefferson's administration and the French. Offhandedly, balancing on one leg and leaning ninety degrees sideways, Arnold quipped, "Well, one of those countries in Asia or possibly Europe. Millard Crumbly said it was someone named Herbert Hooper, but I know that's not right."

When Monte inquired why he had chosen this particular subject, Arnold gushed, "Because I've always wanted to go down there and walk in a big parade all dressed up in a fancy costume and play a trombone!" Monte opined that such an experience would be exciting. "Yeah, it would be," Arnold sighed, obviously deflated, "but my dad's always saying to my mom that the only place we're going is the poorhouse."

• • •

Booker and Monte seldom had direct contact with kindergarten and lower elementary students, though on odd occasions one might unaccountably wander into the classroom or even the Inner Sanctum. Whether these occurrences were by choice or disorientation or furtive attempts to momentarily escape perceived tyranny of a strict instructor, the two mystified men could only guess.

Annabelle Sharada LilyMae Johnson presented herself Wednesday morning when the rest of her class, she reported, had gone to the library. Apparently she had come with a significant mission, one she felt needed—plainly stated while standing confidently in front of Booker's desk—"very much expert guidance and advice." Monte recalled his first encounter with Miss Johnson in the DLS classroom and shuddered at the prospect of attempting to match wits with her a second time.

"Sidney Grover Gillespie—do you know Sidney Grover Gillespie?—well, he asked me to marry him," she said bluntly, absent the slightest hint of humor or amusement. This, both men gawped, from a little girl scarcely three and a half feet tall and six years old.

Approaching the challenge in a professional and straightforward manner, Booker asked, "And how old is Sidney Grover Gillespie, Annabelle?"

"He's almost seven," she said, as if they might have thought him much younger and dismissed his intentions based on immaturity. And then she added encouragingly, "He comes from a very good family. His daddy's in real estate."

Unable to remain prudently silent, Monte asked with seriousness, "Well, Annabelle, what did you say when he asked you to marry him?"

By now she had firmly seated herself, glancing around the room in a perfunctory manner as if harboring distaste at the shabbiness. Focusing on the ceiling for the moment, she said in her patented drawl, "Well, I gave it a lot of thought and made up my mind that at this time in my life I didn't not want to either accept or reject his offer or refuse agreeing to do the opposite of marrying him or not. Do you think that sounds like a wise decision?"

Neither Booker nor Monte responded, staring at her stunned and blank while their petite client remained patiently at ease. Thankfully, her teacher burst in, exasperated and apologetic, to escort Annabelle Sharada LilyMae Johnson back to class, leaving behind a pair of confused and well-educated men cowering in humility.

• • •

That evening at six, Monte drove to Andersen Lock and parked in front to wait for Jimmy Dunsmore. He came out at 6:15 and began to walk his normal route back to school. Monte called out, and Jimmy came over to the car, watchfully defensive.

"Hop in," Monte said leisurely. "I'll give you a ride over to the Academy."

Jimmy stood rooted for a moment, then said in a neutral tone, "That's okay. I'll walk. Thanks anyway." And he started to move off.

"Wait, Jimmy!" Monte spoke more insistently. "We need to talk about something. About your part-time work plans."

Jimmy walked slowly back to the car. "What work plans?"

"I'll explain on the way to school. Okay?"

Debating choices for a few seconds, Jimmy hesitantly opened the passenger door and slid in. Rather than driving to the Academy, Monte directed their route to a diner just south of downtown called Kirby's Drive-In—good food and reasonable prices, and waitresses on roller skates serving patrons in cars after orders were placed via a speaker system.

Pulling into a parking slot, Monte said casually, "I thought we might get something to eat while we talked. All right with you?"

Unsure and uneasy, Jimmy stumbled, "I don't have a pass to miss dinner . . . and—"

"It's okay," Monte assured him, "I took care of it. You won't be in any trouble."

The microphone-speaker device on the driver's side was easily reachable, affixed on a moveable arm. "Burgers and fries all right with you?" Monte asked. "Or would you rather have something else?"

Obviously edgy, Jimmy replied, "Yeah, ah, that's fine, yeah." After a brief pause, he said with some firmness, "I can pay for mine, Mr. Scott. I've got money."

"No, you can't," Monte replied sharply, smiling. "My treat tonight. You pay next time." Jimmy did not argue as Monte thought he might, and instead eased back against the car seat and gazed out his window at waitresses gliding gracefully across the parking lot. Monte asked, "You ever eat here before?"

Without turning, the boy murmured, "No, never." Then, after an interval he added, "I've always heard it was good though. And interesting." His head slowly pivoted toward Monte with a grin. "Kind of unusual, waitresses rolling around on skates. Wonder if they ever fall."

Monte chuckled and shook his head, adding, "I would for sure, especially trying to carry a tray loaded with food." Jimmy laughed lightly and looked away.

After placing their order, Monte turned more serious, speaking with deliberation. "About the plan I mentioned, Mr. Dunsmore. How would you like to work with an engineering company?"

"An engineering company?" He sounded skeptical, though hinting pleasant astonishment.

"Yes," Monte nodded. "Moyer's Engineering, north end of Talerton. Well-known company, does work all over the state, but still not a large firm." Charlie Talbert attended church with Vincent Moyer, owner and founder, and had confirmed the business was interested in providing placement for a capable student. In light of Rolf Andersen's report, Jimmy had come to mind at once.

"What would I do there?" He twisted his body around to face Monte, guardedly inquisitive.

"Everything from designing buildings and other structures, figuring stress loads, beam sizes, types of materials required, and a million other things I don't understand." Monte spoke with an air of nonchalance, noting a dreamy wisp of smile capture Jimmy lips, then quickly fade to doubt.

He could see the young man sorting through a host of questions, ever leery there might be some slippery subterfuge at work. Jimmy said, "What about my job with Mr. Andersen?"

"You could stay on there if you chose, but I wanted you to know about this other, particular opportunity," Monte answered.

Jimmy pondered what had been said, then asked dubiously, "Do you think . . . I'd be qualified to do a job like that? With an engineering company like Moyers?"

Remembering Rolf Andersen and what several teachers at the Academy had reported, Monte replied, "Maybe not right away, but you've got an engineering, mechanical mind, aptitude and interest, and you've shown yourself to be a quick and determined learner."

In previous dealings, Jimmy had never looked at Monte the way he did in this moment. Some distasteful restraint, if not overcome, at least was rendered less formidable and more palatable. Perhaps distrust and dislike on a certain level remained, yet Jimmy's inclination appeared tilting toward willingness to negotiate, maybe join forces for a common good. Monte went on to suggest, envisaging higher education after the Academy, that Jimmy take as many math and science classes as could be scheduled. Booker, Dr. Bartlett, and other teachers, Monte said, had already offered to help make this a realistic possibility for his junior year.

During the following forty-five minutes, they ate and talked. Monte told Jimmy everything he had learned about Moyer's Engineering, mentioning various types of engineering in general, Jimmy countering with a continuous string of pithy questions and comments. Back at school, Monte pulled into the driveway closest to the boys' dorm, leaving the engine running.

Jimmy gripped the door handle as if to get out, then stopped, staring restively out the windshield. Waiting, Monte watched him. After several moments the boy sighed and said quietly, "You went down to, uh, visit Ralph and George, didn't you?"

Monte regarded him coolly without answering, thinking he had never seen the boy dare to look so openly frail. His speech was almost tender, conciliatory, eyes softly fearful. "I . . . I hope you won't take this the wrong way, Mr. Scott," he muddled, "but maybe I was, at first, a bit wrong about you." And then, directing a hard gaze to Monte's eyes, he muttered, "I mean, maybe— I don't know, maybe, back in the beginning, we just got off on the wrong foot, you know?"

Smiling wistfully at the young man, who now seemed transformed to a mere needful child, he replied, "Yeah, maybe so. But think about it, Jimmy. Northside, Southside. We're just natural enemies, aren't we?" Searching Monte's face for clues, not knowing what to say, somewhat ruffled, Jimmy reacted as though disheartened. And then Monte broke into ripples of laughter, sorry for his coarse attempt at lightness. Jimmy, releasing a burst of breath, shyly joined in the mirth.

As Jimmy bounded up the steps of Pennington Hall and through the front doors, ancient words of wisdom from the Talmud rested upon Monte's mind: *If you can help save but one life, given time you can save the world.* He nurtured no illusions of saving the world. That was a calling for much larger hands than his. But one life, one life . . .

Perhaps in this he could play a small part.

CHAPTER FIFTEEN

SATURDAY EVENING'S CHRISTMAS PAGEANT convulsed with an abundance of joyous holiday pageantry, the equal of which none could remember: a menagerie of heterogeneous performers and emoting troupers in flashy, dazzling costumes, cavorting and spinning and tumbling as if the chapel platform were a giant mixing bowl, twisting and twirling little bodies in cyclonic confusion of holiday excitement and celebration.

Fascination radiated to every watchful seat, resplendence to every eye, brilliance to every ear, an enchanted audience becoming as one with hosts of dancers and singers, drawn to flurries of motion, every person magically absorbed by melodious harmony and oneness of spirit. And as bonus, Elizabeth again presented a fantastic musical program, choral ensembles rendering joyfully dulcet weavings of carols, hymns, and songs, new and old, secular and religious.

No clear plot could be discerned from the outlandish thespian slant, colorful characters sustaining a convoluted nexus of steadily unfolding scenes, leaving one to rummage among possibilities of meaning in quests for lucidity and comprehension. Entertaining, all unanimously confessed, purely comic in spurts, and at times almost moving. The scenes, brightly lighted; dozens of munchkins and elves mingling in tight, satiny green suits enclosing all but hands and faces; snow fairies tiptoeing in white crinoline tutus and pink stockings; fuzzy, dun-hued reindeer, heads adorned by drooping antlers and short, perky tails of dark felt; Rudolph prancing in front, smaller than the rest—Arnold—with requisite bright-red nose prominent and glowing.

And then came the enormous sleigh, gift of the Maintenance Department, carrying Mr. and Mrs. Claus: red-suited with furry white trim, monstrous stocking caps topped by snowy, puff-ball blossoms, their streamlined North Pole vehicle piled high with gifts of all shapes and sizes, ablaze in reds, greens, blues, and golds. Gladstone was euphoric as Santa, laughing and waving, ample circumference heaving and jiggling with authenticity not often seen in make-believe Saint Nicks. And for a moment, perhaps in fleeting remembrance of some mystical, long-ago childhood, a spellbound assemblage could almost believe and wish him to be real.

Mrs. Claus, Cathy Henson, organizing force behind the entire production, shone with radiance. Standing far in the back, Monte considered for the millionth time how fortunately the Academy was blessed to have persons like her and Elizabeth and Gladstone and so many others—talented, dedicated, caring persons who loved the children, gave of themselves tirelessly, and approached their work as a hallowed commission. Mr. Fletcher and Dr. Mullens, he noted, sat on the front row, usual sedate reserve creased with laughter, applauding and cheering. *There,* Monte thought, smiling to himself, *is even more evidence of hope for the world.*

Closeted for a few moments within himself, Monte was ironically constrained by an acute consciousness of stirring wonderment, a brightness and sharpness of childlike focus one rarely feels in the slough of daily tides. Clear absorption and captivation of surroundings enthralled a core beyond mind and body, and suddenly he could visualize and encompass beyond temporal sense a world unsullied, lifted and united by some grander and greater propulsion, the whole of mankind enchanted by joy imbuing every breath and step and word.

And he had almost forgotten, shunned, and tamped the simple gift of salvation beneath conceits of self-interest and narrow perception, allowing the light of incarnation to pass dissembled. And at once he knew, and remembered.

For something magical happens during the days between Thanksgiving and Christmas, a kindling and stirring touch of anticipation, a freer and freeing spirit. And for a fleeting, mesmerizing while during these halcyon weeks, one can lay aside and provisionally enshroud missteps and stumbles of past months to niches of forgiveness, ignore the inescapable terror of Janus, two-faced doorman poised to usher in another year. Moments of yuletide call one to dwell in dreams of unfettered wishes, no matter the distance from reach or reality. Bestowed like a glimpse of Eden laid before the feet of mortals, something marvelously ethereal and of unearthly perfection momentarily to be known and touched resides amongst the world of flesh and blood.

For he liked to believe Christmas touched all with something good, whether visions and hopes carried by Santa Claus and elves, decorated trees and presents and turkey dinners, or the story of a newborn infant humbly birthed long ago in a distant land. He believed then, when needed most, Christmas heartened all with the promise of something pure and true, quietly blessed and healing.

He left the chapel that evening with heart buoyed by expectancy yet conflicted with a hard edge of lingering emptiness. Holidays also bring with them the most depressing times, some say—for these hours are given for communion, without which there is little purpose and joy. Friday he had given Booker his gift, and Talbert his, then gone fearfully in search of Clare, intent only to wish her a happy Christmas with Richard and their families. She was not to be found, having departed early, one of the cleaning ladies told him as he stood at the DLS classroom door.

"Did you need to see her?" she asked. "No, I guess not," he said. "Thank you. And Merry Christmas."

Sunday he went to church. There were carols and hymns and prayers and a homily. Talbert and his wife, Nancy, had invited him there, and afterward for lunch at their house. They talked and drank coffee in the afternoon, lazing in sheltered coziness of a little wood-paneled den, holiday music wafting melodias pleasantly familiar. Their two boys, living in other states and grown and married with families of their own, were not expected until Thursday, Christmas Eve.

The Talberts asked him to stay for supper, Monte politely declining, needful to be back in Rivanleigh, he said—marking shamefully that prevaricating was still possible when defensible need arose. *Loneliness is a contagion,* he often thought, *ironically leading one away from fraternity to further depths of isolation.* Being alone for this night was his only craving.

Where would she be, he wondered, *on a Sunday evening? With family, her own or Weisner's,* he presumed with a mental shrug. *Gathered in warm, joyful fellowship, the way families do.* Her gift rested on the passenger seat, carefully wrapped, small and square. He would stop and leave it with Ramona on Monday or Tuesday, the last days before holiday. Would they be Clare's last days at the Academy too?

The mountains were cold and darkly formidable, a golden moon rising silently over the silhouette of high ridges to the east. Sputtering and straining, the Bug climbed defiantly through the night, eager for home. Eager for time and fate to move the earth from one place to another, and then back again.

Music and laughter streamed punishingly strident from the trailer next door, deep bass pulsating in rhythmic tremors amplified through thin metal walls. Stanley and Dolores were hosting a party. If normal patterns held, the soiree would go on until three or four in the morning or until some word or act was adjudged to be of a nature sufficiently insulting or offensive for rebuttal, at which time a fight would break out, spilling over into the parking lot and possibly the street. A responsible citizen in the trailer park would call police, who would, with a kind of drolly bored dedication, come dutifully and restore acceptable calm, revelers banished to home or, if incapacitated, simply left to sleep in cars or on sofas, chairs, and floors in the Hartmans'.

• • •

Monday morning, a grinning Joan, Monte's secretary, brought an envelope to his desk. "It's marked *Personal,* so I didn't open it. The return address is 'Virginia State Penitentiary' in Richmond. Some family member, maybe?"

He took the letter from her hand and said sourly, "Probably."

On a lined sheet of notebook paper, written in cursive with a blunt pencil, was a brief note with several smudged erasures and words obviously marked out. Glancing down to the bottom of the page, he saw the missive came from the Dunsmore brothers, George and Ralph. It read,

Dear Mr. Scott,

Thank you for all the help you have been giving to Jimmy. He likes you very much now. He did not like you at first. He thought you did not like him. He told us you were from Southside and could not be trusted. But changed his mind. Now he thinks you are a good friend. We are happy for him and for what he is doing.

We are doing good here. We could get parole in a few years. And if we do we have plans to start a business painting houses. There is a big need for that.

We hope you will come to visit us again, and also visit Mother. She said to thank you too.

Well, we have to go to the kitchen now and wash dishes and pots and clean up. Tonight is movie night. Someone said Cool Hand Luke was showing. That will be funny.

Thank you again.

George Dunsmore
Ralph Dunsmore

PS We have no hard feelings any more about you being from Southside.

• • •

Booker left early Tuesday, resigned to an afternoon of last-minute Christmas shopping with his wife, Gwen. Monte remained in the Inner Sanctum, making phone calls and writing case notes, which never seemed to end. For the past weeks Marlon Danforth had been shrouded by a mysterious, conspicuous absence of phone calls or memos, a condition eliciting unease and suspicion. A rumor circulated, Monte's secretary said, that the man had taken extended personal leave. No more was known. The voluminous report Monte had compiled on the SET Program for his supervisor had gleaned no comments, favorable or otherwise. *Buried in some filing cabinet,* he projected, days of work wasted.

Many students had departed campus after the pageant Saturday night, those remaining now in process of going, with parents fussily roaming dorms, gathering clothing and personal items, packing car trunks and station wagons with suitcases and boxes. A fair number without transport dawdled at Talerton bus depot or rail station, feeding coins into pinball machines, sitting atop stacks of luggage, or simply leaning restlessly on canes—hardy veterans of claustrophobic and stuffy Trailways and tired, dusty day coaches they called Pullmans. *An empty school,* Monte observed, *is a sad contradiction.*

Winter solstice arrived unnoticed on Sunday evening, and by four o'clock Tuesday afternoon daylight was fast acceding to dusk. The small, grimy Inner Sanctum window was no more than a colorless square framed on the wall, giving little hint of benign, icy slivers converging on the courtyard, shadowing the chapel behind crystalline curtains.

Arthur appeared abruptly, stomping through the classroom and bursting into the inner office. "You're still here, and working?" he snickered.

A sleepy Monte looked up, leaning back in his chair. "I thought you were going to Richmond."

"I am, but not until tomorrow; shopping to do, and a date tonight." He sat down twinkling, surveying the scatter of folders on the desktop. "You're welcome to come for Christmas, my folks say.

The whole family'll be there."

"Did your mother say so? Be truthful." Monte eyed him.

"Yes, she did. She even said she misses you," Arthur emphasized convincingly.

"Uh-huh." Monte offered a doubtful smile. "Like a migraine or bunion. She always blamed me for your failures."

Arthur snickered. "Not true. No, she really wants you to come. We all want you to come. And I can see what you're thinking—"

"Well, why wouldn't I think . . . ?"

"Because we don't do pity, Monte. You know better than that. We've grieved with you, shared sorrow with you, but we'll never do pity." Arthur's voice mellowed, soft yet forceful.

Monte dropped his head for a moment, then raised chastened eyes to his friend. "I'm sorry, Arthur. That was rude and unfair, and I do know better. It's just a mood projecting negativity on everything I see and touch."

"Well, I hope you'll come," Arthur said warmly. "Mom and Ellie're baking pies—pecan just for you." Monte pictured mother and daughter with encompassing affection, Eleanor, now grown with family of her own, laboring busily in the kitchen.

Shamed, he said earnestly, "I'll try, really. And thank you. I'll call, in any event."

"You'd better! And thanks for the gift. Solzhenitsyn'll keep me busy for a while," he snickered. "Your present hasn't arrived, so you may end up getting it for New Year's."

"Hope you hadn't already read it," Monte commented. "It was just published last year."

"Nope, but I'll get into it over the holidays, all seven hundred and some pages." He sighed, inhaled deeply, and stood. "Well, I'd better go and get spruced up. Movie and dinner, and then, who knows."

Monte laughed, "I could guess. Two hours watching late shows and holding hands, hoping you'll get snowed in." Arthur offered an offended stare. "Oh, wait a second! Would you do me a favor, please?" Monte reached to the top of the filing cabinet and brought down a gift. "I forgot to give this to Ramona. It's for Clare. Would you . . .

could you see that she gets it?"

"What is it?" Arthur queried, examining the little package minutely.

"A book of poems. Emily Dickinson," Monte stated, not mentioning the sonnet he had written on the inside back cover.

Arthur was dubious. "She may still be here. Why don't you—"

"Because I can't. Don't ask questions or make any comments, please," Monte entreated.

"I understand. And I'm sorry the way—"

"Let's just drop it for now, Arthur. We'll have a long sit-down sometime soon. Very soon."

"There's always Anne," Arthur quipped, proposing a wisp of consolation.

Monte chuckled wearily. "She's got a new steady—UVA football player who'd kick my ass."

"I doubt it," Arthur said quietly.

A guise of restive ill slinking in blurred steps cloistered the aspect of Monte's demeanor as though each feature were but putty in the hands of a strange, malignant power.

When he looked toward the giant man towering now beside the desk, he saw once again a little boy with new skates, guilelessly trusting and waiting. Monte's next words sounded as a distant echo, hollowed of all but the faintest vitality. "Arthur," he managed, then struggled on, "I'm glad you came back, that you're here at the school. I didn't realize how much . . . how much I draw strength from you." Smiling wanly, he sighed, "Men, I suppose, don't often say to another man how they feel. But I think you know."

Arthur's smile was a welcome beacon leading him from darkness to some semblance of home and security and care. And then, noting a helplessness subdued within his friend's face, Arthur grasped realization that during their twenty years, he had never seen Monte cry—even when his wife died and, two years afterward, his parents. *Perhaps,* he thought, *our greatest sorrows and most significant losses lie too deep for tears.*

The little box in Arthur's coat pocket had become a thorn piercing his side. How ironic that she had entrusted the gift to him only an hour ago, requesting with quaking resolution that he please deliver it to Monte. He now felt a passing urge to joke, lightly referencing his role as intermediary and envoy of both their gifts, but refrained. The air was too delicately stalemated by clutches of emotion, too precariously balanced and pacified. Holding out the small square, Arthur said in a low, condolent timbre, "Clare asked if I'd give this to you."

Monte did not take it, rather studied the shape, thin wrapping of blue tissue and red ribbon held daintily in a strong brown hand—impressions of her captured in its precious simplicity, reaching beyond the walls and chasm between them. When Arthur was gone, he opened it.

A large green acorn lay nestled on a bed of dried grass. She had written a note.

Monte,

At first I was afraid you might find this gift silly. But then I remembered, and knew you wouldn't. You know where it came from, of course. In October I collected two from the ground where we sat, one for you and one for me. Mine, I will plant at my parents' house. Maybe you can plant yours at your cabin. They will grow separately, but always with a bond of communion, a unity of where they were born.

Perhaps sometime in a far distant future their trunks and limbs will provide shelter for another boy and girl on a beautiful late-summer day.

Please don't worry about me, my dear friend. You have much to give, and there is abundance of life to be lived.

May God bless and keep you always, Monte Scott,

Clare

EPILOGUE

AN UNBROKEN SHEET OF new snow veiled the lower parking lot but for a pale rectangle imprinted where her car had stood beside his. Faint tire tracks curved away and passed out of sight down the long slope and past the broad athletic field unblemished, flat, and white as a new satin sheet. Main Hall rose ghostly on the crest above and behind him, a delusion of brick and stone, tall columns woven in a mockery of vaporous grey. There was no sky, no horizon, only a dense quilt of raw cotton encapsulating the world in a dome of silence.

He could make out the giant oak because he knew it was there—leafless, bare, and massively skeletal, upper limbs reaching and disappearing into an arching, heavenly vault. *Gestures of memory to soothe "the troubled midnight and the noon's repose."*

Tomorrow was Christmas Eve, with reports to write, calls to make, people to visit . . . and so many miles, so many roads to travel . . .

www.ingramcontent.com/pod-product-compliance
Lightning Source LLC
Chambersburg PA
CBHW020459310726
48979CB00016B/2726/J

* 9 7 8 1 6 4 6 6 3 4 1 0 1 *